Not
WITHOUT
Courage

T. Elizabeth Renich

Emerald
Books

P.O. Box 635
Lynnwood, Washington 98046

Scripture references are taken from the King James Version of the Bible

The Horse Soldier's Bride (poem)—original work by the author dated March 8, 1994

The Aftermath of a Murderous Cavalry Charge (poem)—original work by the author dated August 3, 1995

Not Without Courage

Copyright © 1996 T. Elizabeth Renich
Published by Emerald Books
P.O. Box 635
Lynnwood, Washington 98046

Library of Congress Cataloging-in-Publication Data

Renich, T. Elizabeth (Tammy Elizabeth), 1964-
    Not without courage / T. Elizabeth Renich.
        p.   cm. — (shadowcreek chronicles : bk. 3)
    ISBN 1-883002-32-X (pbk.)
    1.   United States—History—Civil War, 1861-1865—Fiction.
    2. Women—United States—History—19th century—Fiction.   I. Title.
    II. Series: Renich, T. Elizabeth (Tammy Elizabeth). 1964-
    Shadowcreek chronicles : bk. 3.
    PS3568.E593N68   1996
    813' .54—dc20

Printed in the United States of America.

Dedication

*T*his book is dedicated to all the men in my life for being sources of inspiration, bestowers of encouragement, and sometimes for their insight, but especially to my brother—because I do have one.

Acknowledgments

It was in the wee hours of the morning on September 17th when I finished my *third manuscript* to be included in *The Shadowcreek Chronicles*. I was a kind daughter, though, and waited a few hours until after the sun came up to call Momma and tell her: "It's done!" Then I went to the store before the game started and brought home a bouquet of baby's breath, miniature white carnations, and three blood-red roses—a tribute in celebration to the completion of *Book Three*. My neck and shoulders were feeling much relieved with the absence of the extra tension of a deadline pressing while the regular season was just starting. By God's good grace, I am proud to say, "Here is *Not Without Courage*." The only thing that could make my weekend any sweeter was for the guys, on the road in Philadelphia, to bring home the win—and they did.

Being part of putting a football game together for a Sunday afternoon is certainly not a one-person job—and neither is writing a book. My name gets to be in big letters on the front cover, listed in the sales brochures, included in *Books in Print*, and advertised for book signings, but there are many friends, relatives, co-workers, and other associates who all contribute by their willingness to share information, by pointing me in the right direction, providing advice, encouragement, and inspiration, and mostly by their continued prayers and support. Listed here are some of those individuals who I'd like to specially thank and mention as a token of my heartfelt gratitude. Without them, this story could not have been completed.

The people who buy and read my books, anxiously awaiting more to come, are to be thanked heartily. To know that readers across the country and even in Canada like what I've written does my heart good. I sincerely hope that you will also like this next part of Salina's story.

I am most appreciative to the pleasant, helpful people at Ambler Travel, the Carlsbad Library, the Carnton House and the Carter House in Franklin (TN), Gettysburg National Battlefield Park (PA), Harpers Ferry National Historical Park (WV), Petersburg National Battlefield Park (VA), the Sam Colt Museum (PA), and the Virginia Historical Society (VA) for their assistance in helping me find materials, make travel plans, and answer questions.

Thanks belong to these special people who *always* stand by me, letting me ramble on about my fictitious characters in my made-up stories. Their support, encouragement, and prayers are vital, as they keep me going. For this, I am indebted to: Dick and Joanie Bridgman, Danny Brisco, Joan Chandon, Steve Crumbächer, Daddy, Pat Hediger, Janet Hoffman, Linda Shimamoto, Auntie Jan (Tornell), Lenora (Martha) Varela, and the Wisners. And certainly thanks to my darling Momma, who saves her vacation time to go traipsing across the country with me on my research trips. She, among others, knows how important it is to me to make sure the history is accurate, and doesn't mind waiting in the car for me while I go off on my informational scavenger hunts.

To the following, thanks is given for various and assorted reasons: Pastor Ray Bentley and his secretary, Lois, at Maranatha Chapel, for helping me find the traditionally-worded wedding vows • Bruce Carney, for playing tour guide in and around Richmond, and for taking us to Shoneys for dinner • Chargers, past and present, including Rosemary Bennett, The Brock Girls, Eric Castle, John Friesz, Trent and Julie Green, Burt Grossman, Kelli Hay, Judy Horacek, Stan and Connie Humphries, Jen Jonassen, John and Heidi Kidd, Stan Kwan, Éva Lindsey, Carl, Vicki, Chrissy, Teresa, and Cathy Mauck, Kathy and Joe Milinichik, John and Leigh Parrella, Gary Plummer, "The Specialists" (alias Darren Bennett, David Binn, and my hero, John Carney) for their support, encouragement, and ideas for storylines over the years. In addition, I want to thank Carol and Frank Falks, Karen Hudson, Kevin O'Dea, and Georgette Rogers for always thinking of me and sharing newspaper clippings, magazine articles, books, and other items of interest pertaining to the Civil War time period; and to Ted Sprink, for letting me look through some of his prized collectibles, pictures, and books • Jackie Dawson, for her instant friendship and her reviews • The Ellersons, for taking me in out of the rain at the Herr's Ridge re-enactment and for letting me interrogate them about their cavalry unit • Patricia Epstein for her fact-filled guided tour of the Adams County Historical Society • Cal and Betty Fairbourn, Inn at Antietam, for their hospitality and friendship • Carol Drake Friedman, for her historical knowledge, her insights, and advice • Dr. Susan Heumann for telling me to come to Virginia in time to attend the 1995 Stuart-Mosby Historical Society Annual Meetings, and for waiting so patiently with her mom for me and mine to get un-lost and meet up with them at Mosby's grave • Dr. Phillip Holmes and Trainer Keoki Kamau for helping me with medical details • Michelle Hughes, for being my local reseach assistant during our adventures at the Mission San Diego de Alcalá, Old Town San Diego, and the Presidio—we found that General Jeb Stuart's father-in-law was really here! • Joe Jacoby, for the use of his cars to drive around the countryside in and the umbrellas to keep us dry, and his wife, Irene, for her horse knowledge, for the history articles and profound phone calls, and to Lauren and Jenna for sharing their rooms with us • Dave and Beth-Anne Jahnsen for the accommodations and plantation house and battlefield tours in Franklin, Nashville, Murfreesboro, and Smyrna, TN, where it *wasn't* supposed to snow that week in March. Made any strawberry jam lately? • Dawn and Wes Johnson, for continually suggesting that this series should be made into "Books on Tape" • Bill Keyser and Susan Keyser, for taking Irene and me on the tour of Mosby's Confederacy—it helps tremendously to see places I'm trying to write about, some of them haven't changed in 130 years! • Doug Knapp, Museum of the Confederacy, for his assistance • Jo Marzolino, for her patience with me and all my receipts come tax-time • Ben McVeety, for being my long-distance research assistant, and Andy Boisseau, for stepping in after Ben and Debbie moved to Canada • Patty Melton, for letting us stay with her in Gettysburg, going with us on the train raid, driving through the battlefields after dark, and showing me where the back alleyways are—anything to avoid the traffic circle in town! (She was my guest at that Philadelphia game, presumably having a good time watching our victory) • Jan Palmer for her belief in me and my ability as a writer, and for still teaching me lessons • Tom Perry at the J.E.B. Stuart Birthplace, Inc., for making me feel welcome at the symposium in Mt. Airy, NC, and for helping me get answers to my questions • Nancy Proclivo, for our Tuesday night dinners and history lectures • Teresa Roane, for rescheduling our appointment and for locating the old pictures of places in Richmond from the collection at the Valentine • Ken Ruettgers, for his pep talks and ability to relate as a rookie author • Jeb Stuart IV, for taking the time to meet us, for sharing his knowledge of his famous ancestor, and for sending the words to General Stuart's favorite songs to me • Bob Trout, author, for professional advice, letting me run ideas by him concerning Flora and the Grand Review, checking the feasibility of a midnight July 2nd wedding for the Horse Soldier and his Bride, and for providing articles to aid in my homework • Warren Walsh at Emerald (and Fred and Sue Renich at Pine Hill Graphics) for helping me be the author I am.

Sincere thanks to those who have let me use their names in vain, so to speak—you know who you are. Some of you might even recognize a scene or two along the way...

The glory for this work of historical fiction, however, belongs to the Lord, for I am more than convinced that it is He who continues to guide and inspire the words that fill the pages. It's truly a blessing to be used by

Him according to His purpose, to reach people, and I thank Him for His faithfulness. I strive to remember that He never stops loving me or looking after my best interests. Like Salina, I have learned that He supplies the strength to press on and go forward—but not without courage.

T. Elizabeth Renich
September 17, 1995

Prologue

Late March, 1863
St. Joseph, Missouri

*W*ith a scream of protest, the rusty hinges on the jail cell door swung wide open. Drake didn't budge. He remained where he was, laid out on a lower bunk, his black hat concealing his face.

"Yer free to go, Drake." The deputy sheriff impatiently jangled the ring of keys in his hand. "Come on, yer takin' up space in here." The jail was empty save for this single inmate, though the deputy implied there were more.

"I thought bail had been set at five hundred dollars," Drake murmured in his low, gravelly voice.

"It was—but somebody wants ya out. The man's in the front office. He's expectin' ya."

"Who is he?" Drake still made no move to get up.

"Says his name's Southerland—Lije Southerland. He's a rancher from Kansas, owns the South Union spread. That's all I know of him," the deputy answered. "But he must know you."

"I don't know anyone named Southerland," Drake retorted. "Tell him thanks just the same."

"But you've not heard me out, Mr. Drake." An elderly, gray-haired man sauntered into the cell. "It might be worth your while not to make up your mind dead set 'til you hear the offer."

"I'm in no position to be accepting any offers. I'm waiting to stand trial, in case you'd forgotten," Drake mentioned, a bit sarcastically.

Southerland crossed his arms over his chest. "There's not going to be a trial, Mr. Drake."

"How's that? I'm here because I'm accused of murder. Just because my ma was an Indian doesn't mean I don't have the right to a fair trial."

"There's no need for a trial," Mr. Southerland said patiently. "Two of my ranch hands were at the stables last night when the gunfight took place. Early this morning they were sworn in for a deposition and told the marshal the truth about what happened. Then I took the liberty of having breakfast with the judge, who happens to be an old friend of mine, and I decided to collect on an old, overdue favor. The bottom line is, all charges against you will be dropped—but only as long as you're willing to come with me. You're to leave Missouri, and stay out of his jurisdiction."

Curiosity got the better of Drake, and he peeked out from under the brim of his hat. He'd never seen this man before in his life. "All right, Mr. Southerland." Drake swung his long legs over the edge of the bunk and got to his feet. He was taller than most men, being possessed of a rangy, sinewy build, but to his surprise he found that the rancher's piercing eyes came level with his own. Drake's raven hair hung to his waist. He jammed the black hat down on his head, hiding the jagged white scar that marred his copper-colored forehead. Scrutinizing turquoise eyes, a gift inherited from his white father, bored into those of the old man. "I'm ready to listen to whatever else it is you've got to say, but I'm not making any guarantees. If I don't like the conditions of your proposition, I'll come right back here and get the good deputy to refund the bail money. My case will go to court, and you can be on your way."

"Fair enough," Mr. Southerland nodded. "I'll buy you a drink at the saloon across the street. We can talk there."

A half-smile lifted the corners of Drake's mouth towards his high cheekbones. "Lead on." He noticed the two-gun rig the old man sported. Drake's gun and his hunting knife had been confiscated upon his arrest, and he breathed easier to see that the deputy stood waiting at the door with both weapons in hand.

"Take care, Drake." The deputy handed over both revolver and knife. "See ya soon."

"Not if I can help it," Drake grinned, his white teeth flashing brightly against his bronzed face. "Of course, it still depends on Mr. Southerland and what he has to say."

"If ya don't go with him, no matter *what* he says, yer gonna get yerself hanged, Drake. Ya know it, and I know it, and Lacy Whittaker'd never fergive ya fer it. The judge could convict ya, maybe jist because he thinks yer a no-good half-breed." The deputy knew full well there were some folks who might've taken offense at such statements concerning one's parentage, but he knew such comments to Drake were like water off a duck's back.

Drake had heard similar remarks all his life. Growing up, he'd never quite fit into either the white man's world of his father, or that of his mother's Kiowa-Apache people. It mattered not to him. "Judge just might hang me because I'm part Indian," Drake acknowledged. "But then, he just might be a fair man and plainly see that I only shot that low-down mongrel in self-defense."

"I still think ya'd do well to lay low for a spell," the deputy insisted. "Josiah kin handle the stagecoach run without ya for a time. Give Southerland a chance—he's doin' ya a favor and might be savin' yer hide."

Drake nodded curtly, then turned to leave the lawman. Lije Southerland was already down the boardwalk and halfway across the street to the Lucky Lady Saloon. Drake's long strides caused the fringe edging the sleeves of his buckskin jacket to flutter and sway. His boots struck the boardwalk on the opposite side of the street at the same moment Mr. Southerland arrived at the double swinging doors of the saloon.

"Whiskey?" Southerland asked, spotting an unoccupied table to the left of the bar.

"Sarsaparilla." Drake still had a hangover from the night before, and he knew he needed to keep a clear head today. He was still trying to determine if Lije Southerland was a man he might trust.

A barmaid approached the table. "What kin I git fer you fellas?" she asked, then smiled, "Mornin', Drake."

"Iris," Drake acknowledged brusquely, his demeanor holding no encouragement for her to linger.

Southerland placed their order and, pouting, the hostess scurried away.

"Mr. Drake," Southerland began.

"Look, like the girl said—it's Drake. Not *Mr.*, just plain Drake."

"Fine, then, Drake." Mr. Southerland restated the name, uncertain but knowing better than to ask whether the moniker was his surname or given name. It really didn't make any difference one way or the other, he supposed, nor did the gold hoop earring or the obvious fact that the man was of mixed blood. The steady turquoise eyes were intriguing; they reflected unmistakable veracity. Southerland judged this Drake character to be a man of his word, a man not afraid of hard work or any degree of danger.

"You claim you have a proposition for me," Drake said as Iris served a mug of strong coffee for Mr. Southerland and a bottle of sarsaparilla for himself. "I'm waiting."

Mr. Southerland was waiting, too, and when Iris was gone he wasted no time. "You won't have to rustle or rope or ride the herd; all I need is a trustworthy guide who knows the land and the trail. It has to be someone who's capable of leading a bunch of cowboys with twenty-five hundred head of cattle safely up from Texas," the shrewd eyes of the rancher again sized up the younger man sitting across the table from him. "The pay is a handsome sum," Southerland added, as if dangling a carrot in front of a hungry draft horse.

"Gold?" Drake queried.

"Of course," the gray-haired man answered instantly. "But I'll deduct the first five hundred dollars in compensation for the bail I had to put out to set you free."

"That act was your own choice, but I'm obliged. I'm surprised you don't already have a trail boss," Drake tipped his head to one side.

"I did—he was the man you shot last night," Southerland remarked dryly.

"Then why are you hiring me instead of hanging me?" Drake arched a black eyebrow in question.

"Because I know Wynn Newton, and I know he probably picked the fight. But since Wynn is dead, I need you. You know the country—probably even better than Wynn did—and I suspect you might have a better working relationship with the Indians through the territory."

"Some, perhaps, but there are others who don't care for me at all and would just as soon have my scalp hanging from their belts as any other. There's no love lost," Drake said without emotion. He took another swig from the brown glass bottle, falling into silent observation.

A look of determination burned in the sapphire eyes of the elderly rancher. Those intense blue eyes were the single feature of the man's craggy face that belied his true age. The rancher was the kind of man who wasn't about to let anything stand in the way of getting what he wanted, least of all his advanced years.

Lije Southerland's snapping eyes haunted Drake. They seemed uncannily familiar to him. Somewhere he'd seen the same hue and that very same look of intensity salted with integrity.

Drake squinted, carefully sizing up the man. He wondered if this rancher really meant to follow through with his profitable proposition. Most white men Drake dealt with didn't trust Indians, and they generally made no attempt to hide their distaste or distrust of his mixed parentage. But Drake's heritage didn't seem to bother the rancher. "What kind of operation are you contemplating?" Drake finally asked.

"Fairly simple: move the cattle north from Texas to my ranch in Kansas. The animals will be butchered there, then salted and packed for shipment east."

"Simple? Maybe…" Drake shook his head. "Depends on a lot of factors."

Mr. Southerland agreed. "But that's why I'm hiring you: to keep those factors at a minimum. You'll have to come up through Oklahoma Territory, which can be a hostile place."

"I can handle my own," Drake said firmly. Lifting an eyebrow, which made the jagged white scar on his forehead more pronounced than usual, Drake asked, "When did you expect to move the herd?"

"The sooner the better. I've got a contract from a trader in Memphis, Tennessee. The Rebels need beef for their soldiers—which, in due time, I can deliver—providing someone like yourself is willing to act as guide and scout the trail so we can move the herd."

"Memphis, last time I checked, was occupied by the Federals, not the Rebs," Drake pointed out. "How do you think you're going to sashay into Memphis with barrels of beef for the Confederate army?"

"This trader will do business," Southerland said confidently.

"I've got enough cotton stashed away as an incentive. He'll do what it takes to get the meat through. This is war. People do lots of things for the sake of profit. There's many a trader who's been able to bribe local military authorities into looking the other way. But your job would end when the cattle have safely arrived at South Union. There's no need for you to go to Memphis, unless you've a hankering to do so."

"We'll see." Drake contemplated the original offer again. It was a goodly wage that could be earned in a relatively short amount of time. Time was something Drake could afford. As the deputy had recommended, Drake needed to lay low after the shooting in St. Joseph. A cattle drive would provide not only a much needed change of scenery, but a good place to hide and disappear. The truth of the matter was that he'd never intended to shoot Wynn Newton. The circumstances, however, had been unavoidable. Mr. Southerland might be willing to overlook the fact that Drake had killed the man, but would the other cowboys? Drake was willing to take the chance. He knew how to cover his back. Aside from that, Lacy Whittaker knew how to get a message through to him when it was safe to return to his job with the express company's stage line.

"South Union," Drake murmured the name of the ranch aloud. "How'd you come to call your spread by a name like that? Contradictory terms, wouldn't you say?"

"Indeed," Lije Southerland concurred. "But *South Union* is what my missus settled on and the name stuck. We have—or should I say *had*—six sons. Four of 'em are grown, two are still at home with their mama."

"Had?" Drake asked for conversation's sake.

Southerland nodded. "Those two young'uns at home are alive and well, but of the four older ones, I got two who wear the blue and two who wear the gray. One of the Yankees is in a Southern prison camp, the other was killed at Shiloh. I haven't heard from either of the Rebels in near a year's time, so I don't rightly know whether they're dead or still fighting somewhere. Time will tell, I suppose." He went on with the explanation: "Southerland sometimes gets abbreviated to *South* just because it's quicker to write than spelling it out. My wife added the *Union* part to make it fair, since our family is as divided as the land. The name of the ranch is a tribute to each side equally. God Almighty alone knows the right and might of it."

"Equal—but you're supplying meat to the Confederates?" Drake wondered aloud.

"This time," Lije Southerland conceded. "The last shipment went to the Federals, and will again the time after this. I rotate the recipient in turns, you see. No favoritism, no taking sides. Both equal."

"That's a difficult position these days," Drake muttered. "But if it works for you, then so be it."

"I'll see you tomorrow, then." Southerland extended his hand to seal the business agreement.

Drake shook the old rancher's hand. "Tomorrow. Where?"

Southerland tossed a pair of double eagle gold coins onto the table. "Get yourself a room at the Riverbend Hotel for the night. I'll send Jody to fetch you for breakfast. We'll move out right after that. Anything you need?"

"A good horse and some supplies," Drake suggested, pocketing the forty dollars worth of coinage. "I drove a stagecoach into town and expected to drive it out again."

"I'll have Jody bring you an outfitted rig in the morning," Lije Southerland assured him, tossing another coin down. "Get yourself some ammunition and another set of clothes. Don't worry about the rest: you'll be well taken care of."

The old man was on his feet and had taken two steps away from the table when Drake turned and said, "Thank you, Mr. Southerland, for the chance." He meant it.

"We'll see if you're worth the investment." The rancher tipped his hat, then departed.

Drake nursed his sarsaparilla for awhile longer, thinking about everything and nothing all at the same time. Eventually he left the saloon and headed toward the Riverbend.

Chapter One

June 1863
Culpeper Court House, Virginia

*I*n the dark hour before dawn, a low moan escaped Salina's dry lips. *"Mmmmm..."* Her flushed cheek lay tentatively against the down-filled pillow, an unconscious tear trickling from between her closed, damp lashes. The wet drop, when it fell, was immediately absorbed into the muslin pillowcase.

Shifting restlessly, she turned until her opposite cheek was buried in the pillow. She kicked at the sheet covering her, and her breathing became labored. *"Arghhhhhh..."* A strangled groan escaped from deep in her throat; she tossed and rolled back to her original position. Her hands, seemingly of their own accord, balled themselves into tight fists. Additional tears wet her eyelashes and a cold sweat beaded along her brow. It was the touch of another's hand on her shoulder that startled her into sudden wakefulness with a blood-curdling yell, *"Eeeee-ahhhhhhhh!"*

Delia Carpenter retracted her hand and screamed back, just as loudly, just as unexpectedly. The two cousins stared at each other

16

with wide, fright-filled eyes. "I'm sorry, Salina," Delia apologized in a rush. "I meant to comfort you, not throw you into a panic. You've been thrashing about so. You must've been dreaming something quite awful...But it's all right. You're fine."

The cousins heard a shuffling of footsteps in the hall.

Salina Rose Hastings, her back ramrod straight, every muscle taut, exhaled a long, shuddering sigh. She covered her face with her hands, shaking her head. Her shoulders slumped then, shaking with silent sobs.

"Bless your heart." Delia offered her shoulder for support, stroking Salina's long ebony tresses as they flowed unbound down her back. "Everything's going to be all right."

The aunts, Ruby and Tessa, arrived at the bedroom door in the same instant, followed by a groggy Clarice. "What's the matter?" Delia's younger sister asked, rubbing the sleep from her eyes.

"Salina was dreaming," Delia explained to the others. "She's fine now."

"Then let's all get back to our beds," Tessa Carpenter suggested with a yawn. "Sunrise is not far off and we've a busy day ahead of us."

Ruby patted Salina's hand. "Come, let's you and I go down and fetch a glass of water, hmmm?"

Salina nodded. She looked at her cousin. "Forgive me, Delia. I didn't mean to startle you so."

"We both jumped." Delia's smile was one of understanding.

Ruby put an arm around Salina's shoulders and accompanied her down the broad staircase. In the kitchen, she had Salina sit at the table while she filled a glass of water from the pump and pressed it into Salina's trembling hands. Ruby smoothed Salina's curls back away her tear-streaked face. "What is it that's got you so worked up, child? Will you feel better if you talk to me about it?"

Salina's chest rose and fell in a heavy sigh. "It was awful," she confided. Her breath still came in short, choppy gusts. "I was so terrified, so very, very, scared..."

Ruby Tanner squeezed her niece's hand. "I'm listening."

Salina took another sip of water, then in a shaky voice told her aunt of the nightmare. "I dreamed I was back at Shadowcreek, that I had been captured again at gunpoint, just like before. Major Barnes was using me as bait again to lure Jeremy into a trap—only this time when Jeremy came to my rescue, the Major caught him.

He tied us both up, and then…" Salina's voice faltered. She swallowed hard. "And then he killed Jeremy. Shot him down in cold blood right before my very eyes! Then the Major came towards me and vowed he would kill me too—gloating that my death would mean one less Hastings in the world…"

Ruby took Salina into her arms, rocking her to and fro. "There, there, child, it was just a bad, bad dream. It's not real."

"But it was *so* vivid," Salina argued. "I could *see* the blood oozing from the wound in Jeremy's back…I could *feel* the hatred that burned in Major Barnes' eyes simply because I'm the daughter of Garrett Hastings…"

"Don't torture yourself that way, Salina," Ruby admonished firmly. "Put it out of your mind. You're safe here in Culpeper. The Yankees won't venture behind our lines, and remember how Jeremy and his men were able to save you when you were being held prisoner by Major Barnes? But all that's over now, done with, and you both lived through it." She patted Salina's hand. "Think on how you left Shadowcreek to come here with me—how you hoped to see your young lieutenant because we'd heard the cavalry headquarters were nearby. And sure enough, you've seen Jeremy—last night at General Stuart's ball. And of course you can't possibly forget about this…" Ruby's thumb caressed the diamond-and-garnet engagement ring Jeremy had bestowed upon Salina with a promise of an upcoming wedding. Ruby squeezed Salina's cold fingers comfortingly. "Jeremy's alive and well, and I reckon you'll be his bride very soon, if he has his way about it."

A hint of a smile lifted the corners of Salina's mouth. "He hasn't told me when yet, but he assured me that he'll see to it. I trust him."

"He's a man of his word," Ruby noted with a firm nod. "More water?"

"No, but thank you." Salina set aside the empty glass. "I do feel better, Aunt Ruby. I appreciate you listening to me."

Ruby smiled fondly at her niece. "Go back upstairs and get some sleep if you can. We can't have you appearing with dark circles under your eyes at the Review in the morning, now, can we?"

"No, that would never do," Salina agreed, shaking her dark head. "I'll go up now and think of Jeremy, out there with the cavalry. Perhaps he's dreaming of me…"

Ruby laughed outright. "Oh, I reckon he is! All it takes is a good look into those deep blue eyes of his to see how much he loves you, child. I'm more than convinced that the two of you belong together. In my opinion, the match was inevitable—you're good for each other and your strengths and weaknesses balance each other out. Aside from wanting each other, I honestly believe you need each other."

A blush pinkened Salina's cheeks. "I do love him very much."

"Yes, I know." Ruby winked knowingly. "Get on up to bed now, child, and you dream those good things about your Horse Soldier."

"I will." Salina quickly kissed her aunt's cheek. "Goodnight, Aunt Ruby."

"Goodnight, child," Ruby Tanner replied. "What's left of it, anyway. In an hour it'll be dawn."

☆ ☆ ☆ ☆ ☆ ☆ ☆

Pale pink and golden light tinted the otherwise white page of Salina's gilt-edged journal. Holding an ink bottle in one hand, she balanced the leather-bound book across her knees and gingerly dipped the point of her pen into the black fluid. In her clear, copperplate hand she wrote a heading across the top line: *Dawn, June the 5th, 1863*.

Pausing, Salina absently bit the end of the pen. She rested her dark head against the window sash and closed her emerald green eyes. She was still somewhat shaken by the nightmare, but as the light of day brightened the room lingering shadows were all but chased away. Salina shook off the memory of the bad dream, deciding to concentrate on recollections of the ball at Culpeper Court House, where Jeremy had asked her to marry him *in person*.

Jeremy had made his original proposal to Salina in the form of a poem, which had been delivered to her by the very capable hand of Boone Hunter. Jeremy's writing was precious to her for the love it expressed. The fact that the words existed meant that Jeremy had managed to locate her brother, Ethan, and obtain his consent to their union. Still, no matter how much Salina cherished the lines Jeremy had composed on her behalf, she much preferred his presence to his long distance declarations of love.

She dipped her pen into the ink bottle again and continued writing. When she was through and the ink was dry, she absently flipped through some of the preceding entries.

The pages of her journal told a remarkable tale, for recorded within the front and back covers were the events in the life of one rather independent and intrepid young lady possessed of a keen sense of adventure. Salina had endured quite a bit since her sixteenth birthday last August, when Jubilee had given her the journal. Now, ten months later, the book was nearly full of the accounts of one daring escapade after another. The latter pages held details of events most recently transpired: her frightful abduction at gunpoint by the Yankee Major John Barnes and her and Jeremy's harrowing escape afterwards; her own version of the Battle of Chancellorsville—where General Stuart had taken over command of the Confederate Second Corps for the injured Stonewall Jackson; and the long-awaited births of Cousin Mary Edith's twin daughters, Annie Laurie and Bonnie Lee.

Just a few days ago, Salina had pasted in a newspaper article reporting the train raid near Catlett's Station on the Orange & Alexandria Railroad. Salina and Ruby had been among the passengers on that train when John Singleton Mosby gave the order for his band of Partisan Rangers to fire a cannon ball into the engine's boiler. Unbidden, the scene flashed through Salina's mind. All too vividly she recalled the horrendous crash, the awful wreckage, the shouts and screams of horses and humans, the squeal and grind of metal. Quickly she flipped the page.

There, on the page following the article, was a poem entitled *The Horse Soldier's Bride*—the latest authored by her own Lieutenant Jeremy Barnes. Salina had long since committed the lines to memory and could have easily quoted the words with her eyes shut, but she leisurely read each stanza anew:

> *Stars which glitter in deep, inky skies*
> *Cannot truly compare with the sparkle in her eyes;*
> *Her curls are as dark as the raven's glossy wing,*
> *Raising her soft, sweet voice she oft will sing.*
>
> *Longing to hear the joyous lilt of her laughter,*
> *Yearning for war to be over, then, in the days after*
> *We'll share many long hours, perhaps days on end;*
> *Yet for now by post and letter all my love I must send.*
>
> *She alone is the cause that quickens this heart.*
> *Of my thoughts she occupies more than a small part.*
> *Her endearing smile and winning ways earned my pride.*
> *If she will but say Yes,*
> *I would make her this Horse Soldier's Bride.*

Salina's gaze strayed from the poem to the gold, garnet, and diamond engagement ring adorning her left hand. The daylight made the gemstones sparkle and the gold band shine brightly. Jeremy and Salina had known each other for most of their lives, and he and Ethan had always been close friends. They'd all grown up together, and Salina had to admit that she had loved Jeremy for almost as long as she could remember.

She had missed Jeremy terribly when he'd gone to California in 1860, but now Salina missed him even more every time the war put unwanted distance between them. She had never stopped loving him, even when lack of communication and lies concocted by her cousin Lottie had threatened to ruin their relationship. Granted, Jeremy was not always easy to love, but Salina vowed she would make him understand that her love for him was like none he'd ever known before; she meant to keep her word.

Jeremy Barnes had little experience with genuine affection or the loving bonds of family. His background was by no means sterling, but Salina did not care. She cared only for him—not the circumstances of his birth, his shadowy past, or the fact that he might have killed the man long believed to be his uncle. Salina knew all about Jeremy, and she accepted him without trying to change him. It had taken time for him to believe in her as completely as she did in him. They each knew the road ahead would be neither smooth nor easy, and that it would take nothing less than unwavering commitment and hard work to strengthen their newly-restored bond. Salina, however, considered herself the type who loved a good challenge, and to her, Jeremy was indeed that.

She had his ring, she had his heart, and she was willing to take his name—regardless of the fact that it wasn't truly his. Jeremy's mother had merely given him the name of Barnes because it was the name of her husband at the time. At present, the identity of Jeremy's real father remained as much a mystery as the unknown date when Jeremy and Salina could be wed.

Jeremy voluntarily served with the staff of James Ewell Brown Stuart, also known as Jeb. The nickname resulted from Stuart's habit of simply signing orders with his initials and his surname. Stuart, a Major General and commander in chief of the Confederate Cavalry forces, had first made Jeremy's acquaintance just prior to the battle at Sharpsburg in September of 1862, when Jeremy was captured by the Federals. General Stuart had played a decisive role in arranging for Jeremy to be included in a prisoner exchange that returned him to Virginia and kept him out of a Yankee prison.

On several occasions Jeremy had tried to explain to Salina what his title was, but *volunteer aide-de-camp* was a broad term that tended to encompass responsibilities from "everything" to "a little of this and a little of that." More often than not, Jeremy served as a courier and scout whenever General Stuart needed him, and those duties alone kept him well occupied. Often Salina didn't see Jeremy for weeks at a stretch, but then there were precious times when he was near enough to be seen for a number of days in succession. She knew she was blessed in that respect. Her sister-in-law Taylor Sue, and cousin Mary Edith were not so fortunate as to see their men on any regular basis at all. Salina knew life was uncertain, with no guarantees—that was true even in peacetime, let alone in the midst of battles that tore a nation in two.

After breakfast, Salina hurried to get ready for the Grand Cavalry Review. Ruby lent her a lovely rose-patterned frock to wear and took great care in dressing Salina's long, curly hair. Salina felt a slight twinge of remorse, staring at her bright reflection in the mirror. Customarily, a child mourned the death of a parent for a year's time. Daddy had been dead for nine months, and while Salina was beyond her six-month period of deep mourning, she was three months shy of completing her light mourning. Only recently had she laid aside her dark dresses altogether and put on more colorful frocks. Both her brother and Jeremy had assured her that Daddy wouldn't have wanted her to waste away in grief. Garrett Hastings would prefer a smile to tears any day, they said. Besides, so many had perished in the war, it seemed that practically everyone mourned the death of a loved one. Life, whether one was ready for it or not, went on—day after day after day.

Ruby and Salina heard the blast of trumpets and bugles coming from some distance away. Delia and Clarice burst into the upstairs bedroom in a flutter of lace and brightly hued flounces.

"They're coming!" Delia exclaimed, hurrying to the window. "Our brave Southern cavaliers are parading in the streets!"

"I thought the Review was to start at ten." Tessa, too, entered Delia's room, and the women all stepped out onto the second story veranda to witness the picturesque scene below.

"It does. This is probably just a taste of what General Stuart's got planned," Salina speculated.

General Stuart and his staff rode proudly amid the blaring bugles and waving banners. The cavalry officers were impeccably dressed in their newly purchased uniforms of gray with gold braid

trim. Salina was reminded of a picture she'd seen in a book depict-
ing gallant knights of medieval times. The only thing these Rebel
cavaliers lacked were suits of shining armor to make the scene
complete.

Jubilant spectators leaned out of upper-story windows and
gathered on every veranda and porch to watch the ensemble ride
past. Here and there perfumed hankies fluttered in salute; others
displayed the Confederate Stars and Bars or the battle flag of the
Army of Northern Virginia in tribute. Local ladies tossed June
blooms and fragrant flowers down on the horsemen, showering
them with coquettish smiles and flirtatious waves.

Leaning against the veranda railing of the Carpenter house,
Salina held two freshly-picked roses, the first of which she cast
down as General Stuart passed by. The heavily-bearded commander of the cavalry glanced her way. Upon recognition, he doffed his
plumed hat, covered his heart, and bowed from the saddle in courteous acknowledgment. Salina smiled and waved in return. The
General, at only thirty years of age, enjoyed quite a reputation as
one of the South's most daring heroes, and Salina could understand
why. He had established this cavalry of his, drilling and training it
so that supreme confidence, breathtaking valor, and a tenacious
fighting spirit had become second nature throughout the ranks.
Confederates, both military and civilian, took great pride in Stuart
and the accomplishments of his troopers, cheering heartily whenever they managed to ride circles around the enemy forces—a feat
they had achieved not once, but *twice* during the year of 1862—and
both times while the Army of the Potomac was under the command
of General George B. McClellan.

Salina had learned that after Jeb Stuart's audacious Chambersburg Raid, President Abraham Lincoln reportedly made reference
to a game he'd played as a boy called "Twice Around, and You're
Out." Stuart's second successful ride had been the last straw as far
as Lincoln was concerned, and McClellan had been replaced as
commander. Joseph Hooker, the latest leader of the Federal forces,
had bragged vociferously that he would "bag the Confederate
army." That, however, had certainly *not* been the case at
Chancellorsville, where the Rebels earned a costly, hard-fought
victory.

Salina's second rose was for none other than her intended, and
she waited for just the right moment to take aim and toss the
blood-red bud. Lieutenant Jeremy Barnes snatched the flower in

mid-air, briefly touching the dark velvet petals to his lips. Placing the stem between his teeth, he winked up at Salina, then blew her a jaunty kiss.

"He *is* a dashing one, isn't he?" Clarice remarked saucily, watching a warm smile appear on her cousin's pretty face. "He carries himself with a rather rakish air."

Delia added her own flattering comments. "He's tall, handsome, and I daresay more than a bit dangerous!"

Salina could not dispute either of her cousins' observations, so she didn't bother to try. Her eyes remained fixed on the broad-shouldered, sandy-blond lieutenant until he rode out of her line of vision.

"I didn't see Boone Hunter anywhere," Clarice complained, then blushed profusely over so completely revealing her interest in the young man she'd met only a few days before. "Did you?"

"Boone'll be at the Review," Salina assured her. "He's not a staff officer; that's why he didn't accompany General Stuart."

"Oh." Clarice nodded her comprehension.

Salina stated mischievously, "When I saw the two of you dancing last night…well…I must tell you, I was pleased. Boone's usually quite bashful."

"Perhaps one just has to get to know him," Clarice shrugged, again feeling her cheeks grow warm. "He's got a wonderful sense of humor, really. He kept me in stitches, we laughed so much together."

"Come on," Delia urged, tired of talking about the Rebel riders and wishing to see them instead. "If we don't make haste we'll be late getting over to Auburn. I want to get a good seat, if there are any left to be had!"

☆ ☆ ☆ ☆ ☆ ☆ ☆

Parallel to the railroad tracks of the Orange & Alexandria line, a mile-long furrow had been plowed at the Auburn plantation in preparation for the Review. The wide swath cut through fields of corn, wheat, and oats belonging to one Mr. John Minor Botts, a rather vocal sympathizer of the North. Botts ranted and raved at the perceived destruction of his crops and other property. In light of his political leanings, however, Botts received no sympathy from General Stuart. The Review proceeded just as planned, on schedule, at the site already determined—with no compunction over the fact that it was in the middle of the Botts's fields.

Hundreds of people had flocked to witness the grand spectacle of Stuart's Cavalry Review. Invitations had been issued far and wide—to the local citizens as well as to dignitaries from as far away as Richmond and Charlottesville. Initially, the Review had been the suggestion of General Robert E. Lee, but at the last minute another matter of military significance had prevented him from attending.

To accommodate the vast audience, railroad cars were drawn up on the tracks alongside the reviewing area to provide additional seating. The girls and the aunts had arrived in time to claim seats with a good view for the event. Salina sat demurely on the edge of one of the flatcars, flanked on either side by Delia and Clarice. She angled her parasol to shade herself from the warm, mid-morning sun, content to watch the grandeur of the scene spread out across the plain.

General Stuart and his staff were poised on horseback atop the knoll a few yards to Salina's right, and from that vantage point they monitored the equestrian exercises. Approval shone in the General's bright blue eyes as he intently watched the display put on by his heralded Southern cavalry. If he was disappointed that General Lee had not been able to attend, it was not evident. The Review was staged with all the pomp and circumstance the troops could muster.

Using her field glasses, Salina observed the thousands of drawn sabres glinting and winking in the sun. She watched the horsemen for the majority of the time, but her glance often wandered from the columns of troops passing by to the bewhiskered face of her dashing Horse Soldier. She smiled to herself as she noticed that he'd tucked the rose she'd given him through a buttonhole in the lapel of his shell jacket.

General Stuart had five brigades under his command, close to ten thousand men in number. He certainly seemed to be in his element, and he was obviously proud of his cavalrymen. Each line of troops rode past the reviewing area first at a walk, then at a trot, and finally at a gallop before the charges were made.

A mock battle followed on the heels of the Review. Artillery thunder boomed, at times completely drowning out the martial music performed by the regimental bands. Some of the spectators remained in their buggies and carriages, but as the famed Horse Artillery opened fire, skittish horses had to be held to keep them from bolting. The girls found it amusing to watch people repeatedly scramble out of their conveyances when the horses spooked, then climb back in once the animals were calmed. Some, though, had had the sense to unhitch the horses and so prevent unwarranted mishaps.

The deafening explosions from the cannons thudded deep within Salina, shaking her to the core. Reverberations of the horses' hooves rivaled the pounding of her heart, but the single most chilling instance was when the combined voices of the troopers screeched out an eerie wail known as the *Rebel Yell*. Peculiar corkscrew sensations chased along Salina's straight spine; the horrific sound produced layer upon layer of goose bumps despite the heat of the June day. A sense of patriotism filled Salina as she viewed firsthand these men who fought so diligently for their country's independence. She relished the notion that Jeremy was part of it all, and she found herself caught up in the almost tangible glory and excitement in the air.

When the squadrons were dismissed, Lieutenant Jeremy Barnes determinedly made his way to where Salina and her cousins waited for assistance down from the flatcar. He wanted to spend as much time with Salina as he possibly could before the demands of the war reclaimed his time and concentration.

Jeremy timed his approach to the tracks with deliberation. He waited just until it was Salina's turn for descent from the flatcar, then muttered his excuses and purposefully stepped in front of the gentleman who had already offered his aid. Without Salina's immediate knowledge of the switch, Jeremy smoothly slipped in to take the other man's place.

Effortlessly, he lifted Salina down from the railroad car, his hands lingering around her waist. "Good afternoon, Sallie Rose." He called her by the nickname he'd given her, grinning lopsidedly.

Salina smiled up at him, her hands remaining on his wide shoulders even after her feet were firmly planted on the ground. "Why, good afternoon, Lieutenant Barnes. Such a pleasure to see you again."

"What's all this formality, Sallie?" Jeremy wanted to know. His sapphire blue eyes explored her face, rememorizing each and every lovely detail—her dark curls, creamy complexion, long-lashed emerald eyes, flushed cheeks, and that spirited smile he loved so well. He'd danced with, kissed, and proposed marriage to her just last night, but it seemed like an age ago. "You look stunning."

"So do you," Salina returned the compliment. She would have liked to have had a long talk with him, to keep him all to herself for a time, but her aunts and cousins were waiting to congratulate him on their engagement. "My family is anxious to see you. They're all wanting to know when the wedding will be."

"I'm working on it," Jeremy nodded. "You said you'd let me see to it; don't you trust me?"

"I do—but the aunts were wondering if there was a more substantial answer than *soon*. There are preparations to be looked after. I already told them I'd let them know just as soon I heard from you." Salina slipped her beringed hand into the crook of his arm. "Come, they're waiting for us."

Jeremy kissed the lace-gloved hands of each of Salina's aunts and cousins in turn. He allowed himself to be led into polite conversation, answering all their questions to the best of his ability. Yes, he did intend to marry Salina just as soon as possible, but no, he didn't quite know when that was to be. Yes, the cavalry did indeed look fine, but no, he hadn't heard anything on the status of the Union cavalry... Keeping a possessive arm around Salina's waist, he chatted amiably with her kinfolk in regard to the pageantry and showmanship displayed by the gray cavalrymen.

Boone Hunter appeared at Clarice's side, and C.J., as Carter Jameson preferred to be called, was with Weston Bentley, Curlie Hawkins, and Kidd Carney on the fringe of the gathering. Each of the hovering men wore an amused smirk and a knowing look, but they were wise enough to keep their mouths shut—for the moment, at least. These men who'd volunteered to ride with Jeremy derived great pleasure in harassing him about a certain Miss Salina Rose Hastings. They'd discovered that she was nigh unto being his only weakness, and it proved such a joy to tease him about her that they did so, often and well. Their lighthearted jibes concerning their lieutenant's romantic affair helped break up the monotony of sometimes dull marches and tedious picket duties. Jeremy rarely failed to react, though he knew full well they merely jested with him.

A rider approached the circle. Jeremy and his men saluted the major on horseback. "Pardon the interruption, Lieutenant Barnes, but General Stuart requests to see you. You're to bring along your lady friend. There's someone the General wishes to introduce the two of you to."

"Certainly, Major McClellan. Please tell General Stuart we'll be over directly," Jeremy replied. "Thank you, sir."

Major McClellan nodded and rode back in the direction he had come.

"If you'll excuse us, we'll be back shortly," Jeremy took Salina's hand and led her away from her relatives.

"McClellan? I thought he was a Yankee general," Salina remarked, accompanying Jeremy across the field.

"This is *our* McClellan—Major Henry B.—nephew of the Yankee George B. McClellan. You know as well as anyone the divisions this war has inflicted on families, Sallie."

"I know," Salina nodded, thinking of her Yankee stepfather. "And soon I'm going to have a little brother or sister who will be half-Rebel and half-Yankee."

Jeremy hadn't intended to diminish the brightness of the day by reminding Salina that her Mamma had married Major Duncan Grant, U.S. Army. Jeremy let the matter alone. He was still adjusting to that particular situation. Instead of words, Jeremy squeezed Salina's hand lovingly and began whistling a lively rendition of *Jine the Cavalry*.

Salina hummed the tune as Jeremy sang the musical tribute to Stuart and his Southern horsemen:

> *If you want to have a good time*
> *Jine the Cavalry*
> *Jine the Cavalry*
> *Jine the Cavalry*
> *If you want to catch the Devil*
> *If you want to have fun*
> *If you want to smell hell*
> *Jine the Cavalry*
> *We are the boys who rode around McClell-ian*
> *Rode around McClell-ian*
> *Rode around McClell-ian*
> *We are the boys who rode around McClell-ian*
> *Bully Boy Hey! Bully Boy Ho!*

"Ah, there you are!" General Stuart greeted Salina and Jeremy warmly when they approached. "I appreciate your coming over; there's someone I want you to meet." He brought forward a petite, pretty, brown-haired woman. "My dear, may I present Lieutenant Jeremy Barnes and Miss Salina Hastings. Barnes, Miss Salina, this is my wife—Mrs. General Stuart."

Salina bowed and curtsied as Jeremy politely raised Mrs. Stuart's fingers to his lips. Looking at the Stuarts, anyone could see the lively sparkle of pride and their love for each other whenever their glances touched. Salina wondered if the looks she and Jeremy exchanged were equally as plain; she didn't mind if they were. "It's a pleasure to meet you, Mrs. Stuart."

"And I you," the General's wife smiled, fanning herself with a sandalwood fan. "But please, call me Flora."

While the two couples stood together under the shade of a tree, General Stuart explained to Flora how he had met Jeremy by inadvertently, though providentially, making him part of the prisoner exchange following the Battle of Sharpsburg, near Antietam Creek in Maryland. "Barnes was sick and injured. We got him and three other privates in exchange for one Yankee lieutenant we'd captured. I am pleased to report it was a good trade. Since then, Barnes has proved his worth and been promoted to the rank of lieutenant for the work he did for me."

"I owe my life and my position to the General," Jeremy acknowledged. "It's a privilege and honor to serve with him."

General Stuart brushed Jeremy's praise aside. "Enough, Lieutenant; you're starting to echo Miss Salina's father, the late Garrett Hastings." He turned to Flora. "Miss Salina worked with Captain Hastings and Lieutenant Barnes as a translator of secretly-coded messages, and eventually as a courier to San Francisco. After Captain Hastings' untimely death, Miss Salina gave her best effort to fill in for her father. Captain Hastings not only scouted for me on occasion here in Virginia, but he was part of a scheme to seize the Western territories and California in the name of the Confederacy."

"Really?" Flora asked, her interest piqued. "What happened to the plans?"

"The Yankees captured the documents in San Francisco," Salina confessed, "just before they captured me."

"Goodness!" Flora exclaimed. "You poor dear. What happened to you?"

"I was imprisoned—first at the Presidio, then at Fortress Alcatraz. Afterwards, I was brought back to Washington and taken to the Old Capitol Prison, where I awaited my interview with Abraham Lincoln." Salina told Flora about being pardoned because she had destroyed an assassination plot against the Union president. "Somewhere along the line, to me there was a distinct difference in planning for a Western invasion and murder. I just couldn't bring myself to pass along the assassination plot, so I destroyed it. For that act alone Mr. Lincoln gave me my freedom, in exchange for my promise to *behave*. Behavior—as he defined it—meant not having one of his best scouts traipsing across the country chasing after me. So far, I have been well-behaved in that respect.

"Mr. Lincoln was kind enough—he didn't make me sign an Oath of Allegiance, which I would not have done—and he gave me my traveling papers so that I could return to Virginia. None of that could have come about if it hadn't been for the connections of my Yankee stepfather. Without his intervention, I don't know what might have happened to me—but I certainly would have missed the Review, and I wouldn't have wanted that for anything!"

Flora Cooke Stuart studied the young lady intently, discerning the shadow of sorrow lurking in her clear green eyes as she spoke of the unpleasant ordeal. *A Yankee stepfather?* Flora's heart went out to Salina. If the girl had any affection for this stepfather of hers, Flora could understand her dilemma. She could identify with the pain and difficulty caused by such attachments because Brigadier General Philip St. George Cooke, her own father, had elected to remain loyal to the Union. His choice inflicted a deep, hurtful rift in Flora's family. Stuart had been incensed. He, her brother, and her cousin—as well as many other friends and relatives—each held a place in the Southern army, and they had all counted on General Cooke to come in on the side of the Confederacy. But he did not. No one could believe it. Furious, Stuart went so far as to have the name of their little son changed from Philip St. George Cooke Stuart to James Ewell Brown Stuart, Jr. so that the tribute to the boy's maternal grandfather was erased. Even so, Flora couldn't help but miss her father, regardless of the fact that he wore the uniform of the *other* army. Flora recalled Stuart's chilling vow: her father would regret going against Virginia but once—and that would be continually. During the Seven Days' Battles just outside of Richmond a year ago, as Stuart's selected troopers made their first famed circle of McClellan's army, it was General Cooke whom Stuart mercilessly pursued and would have thrilled to capture. The newspapers had printed such stories...Stuart had written to her, warning her to keep her name out of the press...

Stuart's clear voice drew Flora sharply back to the present. He mentioned that he'd last seen Salina in Richmond. "That was at a time when you and the good lieutenant weren't quite seeing eye to eye on things like loyalty and trust. But judging by the fact that the two of you are here, together, and obviously in good spirits, the misunderstandings have been laid to rest?" He made it a question.

"Yes, sir," Jeremy replied sheepishly. "Salina showed me the letter of endorsement you wrote on her behalf. She's given up her secret service work, I'm glad to say, and last night she agreed to become my wife."

"Then I'd say you patched things up quite nicely," Flora smiled kindly. "Congratulations to you both."

"Yes, congratulations," Stuart echoed. "But tell us, Miss Salina, how is it that you ended up in Culpeper? Did you come out specifically to be near your intended?"

"Yes, sir, that's exactly the reason," Salina replied with an impish grin. "We're hoping to marry soon."

General Stuart's expression transformed from merriment to strict military composure. "It's a pity there's no time to grant him a furlough. The best I can tell you at this point is that there's soon to be a campaign, and I can't afford to spare any of my men once it gets underway."

Flora knew all about the military, having been born in army post barracks, living from fort to fort wherever her father's orders had sent the Cooke family over the years. Salina, too, had somewhat of a military background—she'd been born while Garrett Hastings served during the Mexican War in 1846-47. She was not quite two years old the first time Daddy ever held her.

Salina didn't pretend to understand the fierce conviction or unwritten law which dictated that duty and honor were placed above all else, but she was aware of it nonetheless, and respected it. She stiffened her spine and raised her chin a fraction when she answered slowly and deliberately, "I know duty and honor come first, General Stuart. If there is a fight at hand, then of course Jeremy will be with you. I have told him that I will wait until he can be spared from his responsibilities just long enough to take his vows and change my name to his. I can expect little more than that, but I will continue to hope that it is a day not far off."

General Stuart's reply was a broad smile, one that split his cinnamon-colored whiskers with a showing of teeth and a hearty laugh. "Amen!" he chuckled. "Barnes, I wish you all the best; Miss Salina's got enough determination for the both of you."

Jeremy, too, grinned. "Aye, sir, she does have her share."

Salina colored, but she felt Jeremy's arm tighten slightly

around her waist, wordlessly conveying his pride in her. "I meant no disrespect, General."

"None taken, Miss Salina." General Stuart winked at her. "There are times when duty and honor are cold comfort to the women soldiers leave behind. Ofttimes it's difficult for ladies to accept such circumstances. It sounds to me as though you are going into this marriage with a clear knowledge of your lieutenant's obligations, if not an understanding of what drives him. That knowledge should help down the road, if you remember it."

Salina shivered, and might have been mistaken, but she thought she saw Flora do the same. The General's words seemed to have a taste of foreboding—or were they intended as a strong admonition? Were his words directed solely at her, or possibly at Flora as well? Salina honestly couldn't say, but she knew of an instance last November when General Stuart could not take leave from the front—his young daughter, Little Flora, had died in his absence. *Had Flora balked at the idea that honor and duty had kept her husband from matters of home and family?* Salina wondered. Men seemed to expect their women to bear up under circumstances without question, regardless of the outcome.

The conversation drifted to the Review, and Stuart and Jeremy talked of military matters while the ladies chatted together of more genteel topics. Salina learned that Flora was expecting a child in the fall. "Jimmie has been lonely for his sister," Flora confided. "A new sibling will give him some company."

Salina queried, "Did your little son come with you?"

"Not this time," Flora answered, shaking her head. "He's staying at the home of my sister in Richmond. I don't like leaving him behind—I miss him so—but with all this going on, Stuart wouldn't have had much time to spend with Jimmie anyway. It was easier for me to travel up from Richmond alone. I'm going back tonight."

"But you'll miss the ball," Salina lamented.

"I trust it will be a smashing success, with or without me," Flora smiled softly. "I really don't like being away from Jimmie for long…" The fact of the matter was that Stuart's wife was still in mourning over the loss of Little Flora. It was acceptable for her to reenter society now, and she wouldn't have wanted to miss the Review for anything, but her heart was still heavy. Flora knew her husband grieved as well, but privately. His rank required him to be focused on strategy and his men while the war demanded his full attention. It was only when Stuart was alone in camp, or sometimes in his letters home to her, that he allowed himself to dwell on the memory of the dear little girl who had been such a joy in his life.

Salina overheard the name Mosby mentioned, and her attention was drawn to what the General and Jeremy were saying. The topic of discussion was the recent raid on the Orange & Alexandria Railroad and the skirmishing near Catlett's Station.

"That little mountain Howitzer certainly came in useful," Jeremy recalled, having been a participant that day under Mosby's command. "It only took one shot to blow up the boiler and derail the train." He looked down at Salina. "Of course, then there were the spoils, and the prisoners—mostly Union soldiers, but there were a handful of civilians on board that train, too."

Flora caught the knowing glance between Jeremy and Salina. "Don't tell me you were an unfortunate passenger on that train, Miss Salina. Were you?"

"Yes, I was," Salina admitted. "The train wreck was awful. I was fortunate to come away with a few scratches and a bruised rib or two."

"Mercy!" Flora declared incredulously. "You certainly do seem to have a flair for adventure."

"I suppose I do," Salina had to agree. "I used the letter of endorsement General Stuart wrote for me to secure my release from Major Mosby. Upon reading it, Mosby sent me and my aunt on to Culpeper with fresh horses from the capture. I was instructed to pass along his regards to you, sir, when I next saw you."

Stuart shook his head. "I must echo Flora's sentiment—you certainly have had your share of excitement to date. Barnes, you may have your hands full with this little lady. You never can tell where she's going to turn up or in what circumstance!"

"Yes, I know," Jeremy chuckled ruefully, adding, "but then, that's part of the reason I love her. I know it's no good to try to send her behind our lines and expect her to demurely wait out the war. She's got too much of the fight in her—just like her father before her."

Salina shrugged, "I'm a Hastings." Somehow, it was the only logical explanation she could think of.

Chapter Two

*T*he ball that night was held at the Bradfords, on the green beneath the spreading trees at Afton. Flames from the enormous bonfires lit up the area where dancers were serenaded with merry band music. General Stuart had his own musicians in his camp: Sam Sweeney, a very talented banjoist, was accompanied by violin, guitar and harmonica, and General Stuart's servant, Bob, kept time with the bones. There was much singing and clapping as gaiety and laughter prevailed over thoughts of the war.

Salina rarely stood idle. She was swept along by one dance partner after another until she had danced with Jeremy and each of his men two and three turns apiece. She danced, too, with General Stuart, Major McClellan, and Stuart's Prussian inspector, Johann August Heinrich Heros von Borcke. At length, Salina begged for a reprieve and some refreshment. She was quietly sitting, sipping a cup of punch, when she heard the strains of *The Girl I Left Behind Me*.

General Stuart singled her out, requesting that she join him in the singing. "We've already rehearsed this one—at the White

House in Richmond for one of the Davis's levees. Will you do me the honor of singing with me again, Miss Salina?"

"I'd be delighted, General," Salina accepted his invitation, setting aside her cup and taking his proffered hand. That first song was followed by *Riding a Raid*, and then Flora, who—with Stuart's persuasion—had opted to catch a later train to Richmond and stay for the ball, joined in with them for a lively chorus of *Annie Laurie*. The trio's efforts were applauded by all those who'd gathered round.

Jeremy watched Salina with fond admiration, proud that others enjoyed her melodious voice as much as he did.

At the first opportunity after the singing, Jeremy purposefully led Salina away from the firelit stage and off to a place where they could talk, just the two of them. "I'm tired of sharing you with everyone else here," he complained teasingly. "I'd have you all to myself for awhile."

Salina smiled up at him coyly. "I've been waiting all night for you to do something about it."

"Me? You're the one dancing the night away with my men, singing with the General, and mingling with Mrs. Stuart and the staff officers..." Jeremy touched her cheek in a gentle caress. "I enjoy watching you."

"I enjoy being watched," Salina grinned coquettishly, feeling his arms steal around her waist. "Jeremy, I'm so glad I came here. If it hadn't been for Aunt Ruby's suggestion, and Taylor Sue's insistence, I might not have come to Culpeper. But I hoped you might be here, and I wouldn't have wanted to miss this for anything."

"So it was worth a couple of bruised ribs?" he gibed tenderly.

"I reckon so." Salina sighed contentedly. "Look at the stars, aren't they beautiful tonight?"

"Stars that glitter in deep, inky skies, Cannot truly compare with the sparkle in her eyes," Jeremy quoted.

Salina's laughter floated lightly along the night breeze, but then she turned somber. "Would you really rather I go behind the lines and wait?"

"No," Jeremy said without hesitation. "That wouldn't be like you. I love you, Sallie Rose, and all your adventure and independence. I love your strength and determination. I wouldn't have it any other way."

"I love your stubbornness, too," Salina goaded playfully. "You claim *I'm* independent..."

"And proud, and loyal, and willing to give of yourself," Jeremy tapped the end of her nose with his finger. "I love it all."

Salina leaned her dark head against the wall of his chest. "And I love you, Jeremy Barnes," she whispered blithely.

Jeremy rested his cheek on top of her head. He was content to hold her securely in the circle of his arms. "My own Sallie Rose."

She wasn't sure how long they stood there, mutely listening to the music from round the bonfires, but some time passed before Jeremy hooked his finger under her chin and lifted her face toward him.

"What's the matter, Sallie?" he questioned deliberately, having seen shadows lurking in her eyes. "The way you look at me tonight—it's like you're afraid to let me out of your sight."

Salina averted her eyes, a bit disquieted by his knack for reading her thoughts so clearly, even in the starlit darkness. "I can't hide anything from you—you know me too well," Salina affirmed with a wistful smile, one that faded just as quickly as it had appeared. "I dreamed last night that John Barnes kidnapped me again, only this time he was successful in capturing you, too. In the dream, he killed you, Jeremy. He shot you down right in front of me. Then he turned on me, vowing that I would be the next to die..." Impulsively, she stood on tiptoe to kiss him. "Jeremy," she breathed hoarsely, "I don't think John Barnes is dead. I know you shot back at him the night you rescued me, and we both know he fell. There's just *something* that tells me he didn't die."

"What? What tells you that? Sallie, there's little chance that he could have survived..." Jeremy squeezed her shoulders and saw her wince. He loosened his grip, unaware that he had held her so tight as to hurt her, but then he belatedly remembered her shoulder injury. The night of their escape, Salina had taken a bullet John Barnes had intended for Jeremy. "Hasn't the wound healed?"

"For the most part. The stitches you put in were quite a piece of handiwork." Salina tried to laugh, but her eyes were somber. "Jeremy, when General Stuart sends you out on reconnaissance, promise me you'll be on your guard. Promise me you'll watch your back—that's where your uncle would strike, if he could."

"He's *not* my uncle!" Jeremy snapped angrily. "You told me so yourself."

"My mistake," Salina said penitently. "Habit."

Agitated, Jeremy roughly sighed, "I know." His voice softened, "It's hard for me to think of him as anything else too, but he's not my uncle. It will just take some getting used to."

Jeremy looked at Salina. "Together we've survived John Barnes."

"For now," Salina agreed. "But I can't seem to shake the gnawing feeling that it's not over with him yet. The dream last night was too real…"

"He's dead, Sallie. I killed him." Jeremy's tone was bitter. It was not something he was proud of, but something he'd been forced to do in order to save Salina and himself. "He can't hurt us anymore."

Salina whispered sadly, "Unless he's not really dead."

Jeremy wished he could argue away Salina's doubts, but since he couldn't, he said nothing.

"Taylor Sue is in this bizarre feud now that she's married to my brother," Salina continued. "And although I didn't want to admit it at first, I've come to believe that Duncan was probably right in marrying Mamma and taking her away from Shadowcreek, because if he hadn't, John Barnes might have gotten to her already. If John Barnes is still alive, all of us are still in danger, Jeremy—but especially you."

Jeremy nodded reluctantly, a nerve jumping along his taut jaw. *"If* John Barnes is still alive—which hardly seems likely—then there is cause for caution. The man was eaten up with a cankerous hatred, and he was wicked enough to follow through with his mad vendettas. At this point, however, there's no way to prove for certain if he's alive or if he's dead."

"When your men went back to the mill at Carillon after the fight and explosion, they didn't find his body," Salina pointed out. "What more proof do we need?"

"There must be a way to determine if he *isn't* truly dead. John Barnes was a Yankee major. Surely someone should have missed him by now—on a muster sheet, reporting for duty, orders, assignments…I'm surprised that Duncan Grant hasn't been able to figure out for sure. Duncan works in the Union's War Department. You'd think he could find some indication, some record—*something.*"

"You'd think," Salina nodded, but her intuition didn't require tangible proof. "It may be just a feeling I have, Jeremy, but my instincts have been right before. Please, just take care whenever you're out on patrol."

"I'll be careful," he assured her. He lowered his head to kiss her, a vain effort to allay her fears, to comfort her. Yet in the back of his mind, she had managed to plant the doubt securely. *What if she was right?* He'd be careful; that went without saying. Duncan Grant had told Jeremy once that it would probably kill Salina if anything happened to him. Well, Jeremy certainly didn't intend to let anything happen that would keep them apart—any more than the war already did.

☆ ☆ ☆ ☆ ☆ ☆ ☆

Several hours later, Salina lay in fitful slumber in the cherry wood bed she shared with Delia. In her fisted hand, she clutched a heart-shaped locket that hung from the gold chain around her neck. The locket was a gift from Jeremy, given when she'd visited him in a prison hospital in Washington prior to his exchange…

A small pebble hit the windowpane, rattling the glass. Salina woke up instantly.

A second stone struck the glass pane, and then a third.

Salina pushed aside the sheet and donned her lace-trimmed wrapper. Cautiously, she padded toward the French doors of the veranda. She slipped her hand in the pocket of her robe and securely grasped the pearl-handled pistol concealed there. In the street below, she saw Jeremy dismount and stand with his horse, Orion. The huge black Yankee horse was one Jeremy had captured in Mosby's raid at Miskel's Farm some weeks ago. Salina opened the door and stepped out. "What on earth are you doing here?"

"I've got some news," he whispered loudly. "I couldn't wait until morning to come share it with you." He flashed a disarming grin. "Can you come down? I need to talk to you."

"Are you out of your head?" Her voice held a trace of laughter. Salina put the safety lock back on the gun. "If Aunt Tessa or Aunt Ruby find us together, there'll be trouble. It's not proper," she reminded him.

Disregarding the warning, Jeremy agilely climbed the corner post of the veranda on the first floor, then used the trellis to advance the remainder of the way to the veranda that wrapped around the second floor of the Carpenter house. He walked carefully, softly, so his boots and spurs wouldn't strike or jingle loudly. "This will just take a minute, if you'll let me explain."

"Explain what?" Salina queried, unable to conceal her smile over the pleasure of seeing him.

"Explain that I've found out when we can be married." Jeremy's grin was decidedly lopsided.

In her excitement, Salina gripped his arm. "You have? When?"

Jeremy casually pulled his out his watch, angling the face in the moonlight so he could tell the time. "According to this, it's long past midnight, which makes this the sixth day of June. What do you say we get married the day after tomorrow?"

"Day after tomorrow?!" Salina's emerald eyes grew round in delight. "You mean it? You're not just teasing me?"

"No, I mean it," Jeremy's smile flashed white in the moonlight. "There's going to be another review: strictly business this time, not like the show of today—or should I say yesterday? At any rate, it's on account of General Lee coming over from Fredericksburg. I've found out it's going to be held the morning of June eighth. We can get married when it's over, in the late afternoon, providing that will suit you."

Salina nodded emphatically. "It will suit me just fine! Of course, there are arrangements to be made, but we'll manage!"

Jeremy framed her pretty face with his hands, kissing her soundly. "All right, then. You'll be this Horse Soldier's bride—day after tomorrow."

"Day after tomorrow," Salina repeated, smiling broadly. "I've a hundred things to do between now and then! I shouldn't stay here another minute. I should go downstairs and begin planning! Aunt Tessa and Aunt Ruby will know what's to be done, and Delia and Clarice will help with the details too. I think I have an appropriate dress...We'll fix the food, issue a handful of invitations, gather some flowers, and..." Abruptly Salina stopped; a sudden welling of hot tears blurred her vision. "Oh, Jeremy!" She covered her face and hung her head.

"Tears?" Jeremy lifted her chin, forcing her to meet his eyes. He wouldn't have minded if they were tears of happiness, but these were obviously caused by an unexpected wash of pain. "Talk to me, Sallie. Tell me what's wrong."

Salina bit her bottom lip. "I just remembered..."

Jeremy watched as a teardrop escaped the fringe of her sooty lashes, rolling slowly toward her chin. He wiped her cheek with a gentle stroke of his thumb.

"We're getting married..." Salina began, but her voice faltered again.

Jeremy waited patiently, and listened quietly when she was calm enough to explain.

"I've dreamed of my wedding day for a long time—as most girls do, I suppose," Salina whispered. "I always imagined that my family, all the people I love, would be with me to celebrate my joy." She let out a helpless sigh. "My cousins and my aunts are here, but, Jeremy, *none* of my immediate family can be with us. Duncan will *never* allow Mamma to come from Gettysburg to see us wed."

"Your Mamma probably isn't in any condition to travel right now, even if there was time enough to get her here, and you're right—Duncan wouldn't allow it anyway," Jeremy surmised.

"I know," Salina nodded. "Her baby is due next month. But I know how disappointed she was to miss Ethan and Taylor Sue's wedding in Richmond. It's sad to think that she won't be at ours either. And as for Ethan—even if I knew where he was—he's probably too busy. They say the Medical Corps is overwhelmed with wounded...and..." Another tear trickled down her cheek.

"And what, Sallie?" Jeremy leaned toward her, kissing the salty tear away.

"I wanted Reverend Yates to marry us; I wanted Taylor Sue to stand up for me as my maid—*matron*, rather—of honor, as I stood up for her. I always thought my daddy would give me away...I never thought that Daddy wouldn't be here for me...There are times, Jeremy, when I just *can't* believe he's gone. It almost seems like he's just away on another scouting mission, or maybe working on a new project for the War Department...But then I remember he's dead, and he's *never* coming back to us," Salina cried.

"Ssshhhh." Jeremy collected her into his arms, shifting his weight gently from one foot to the other and back, just holding her.

Inside, Salina heard Delia move in her sleep. She quickly wiped away her tears, once more in control of her volatile emotions. "If Delia finds that you've shinnied the corner post and the trellis to get up here, she'll say it's romantic, but I hardly think the aunts will approve of such behavior. It could too easily be misconstrued as impropriety, even though we haven't done anything wrong. Jeremy, you should go," Salina urged him to make a quick departure. "What if General Stuart misses you out at the encampment?"

"I reckon you're right, Sallie," Jeremy reluctantly admitted, and turned to leave.

But Salina put a staying hand on his arm. "My apologies, Jeremy, for the tears. I didn't mean to sound like I don't want to marry you day after tomorrow, because I most certainly do! In fact, day after tomorrow can't get here soon enough for my liking, and

I'd marry you right this minute if we could arrange it. It's silly of me to complain so."

"Not silly, just honest. I do understand, Sallie Rose." His sapphire-blue eyes bored into her green ones, speaking silent volumes. He hugged her tightly to him again, then kissed her good-bye.

Salina's response might not have been as timid or tentative as it should have been for a proper young maiden, and she kissed him fully in return.

Jeremy's crooked grin revealed itself. "Good night, Sallie," he murmured, running an unsteady hand through his sandy blond hair. He donned his plumed hat calmly, in spite of the erratic pounding of his heart. "I'd best be on my way before someone misses me."

"I'll miss you," Salina retorted saucily, acutely aware of the undercurrents encircling them. In a more serious tone she asked, "Will I see you before the wedding?"

"I'll send word to you. I'm sure General Stuart would have no objection to your visiting camp," Jeremy answered. "There are usually visitors aplenty."

"No doubt he'll order me to sing again," Salina giggled softly. "You watch and see."

"I wouldn't put such an order past the General," Jeremy, too, chuckled. He took a minute to study the glittering gemstones of her engagement ring in the soft moonlight. "Day after tomorrow, Sallie. Not long. You just do the best you can to get things ready— it doesn't have to be anything elaborate, but just so it's how you want it to be. My guess is that we should be able to be wed sometime after half-past four. All right?"

"All right," she nodded eagerly.

"Good," he winked. "You leave the rest to me—I'll handle it."

Salina's brow furrowed with the question: "The rest?"

"Never you mind," Jeremy replied mysteriously. He chastely kissed her forehead, then lowered himself back down to street level. In an effortless, fluid motion he mounted Orion and saluted smartly. Then he rode off toward the cavalry encampment at breakneck speed.

Salina hugged her elbows, quietly retracing her steps and climbing back into bed. She failed to notice that Delia's eyes were wide open until she heard her cousin murmur, "So, you're to be his bride day after tomorrow. We have a lot of work ahead of us, now, don't we?"

"Delia!" Salina sat straight up in bed. "How much did you hear?"

A wicked smile lifted the corners of Delia's mouth. "Most of it, but don't worry. Your secret tryst is safe with me. Get some sleep, Salina, while you have the time."

"As if that's possible!" Salina exclaimed. "Now, I'm too keyed up to sleep!"

Chapter Three

*T*essa and Ruby stared at each other in utter disbelief, then looked at Salina. "Day after *tomorrow*?!" the aunts cried in unison.

Salina nodded, her emerald eyes betraying both her delight and expectation over the prospect. "There's no call for a big fuss, nor time for it. It will be a small celebration, something simple. There won't be many people there—hardly more than a dozen, I reckon. Maybe a few more, if Jeremy's men can attend. There are nine who ride with him, but some of them may be out on duty. Most likely they won't all be able to come."

Clarice was enviously pleased for her cousin. "This is so exciting—but then, it seems that everything exciting always happens to you, Salina."

Ruby and Salina fairly laughed. Salina said, "Some excitement is fine, but there's much I could live without, believe me!"

Delia was making a list of things that had to be done. "I'll bake the cake, Mother can decide on the flowers and decorations, and Aunt Ruby can play the piano. I'm sure the rector won't mind letting us use the church on Monday afternoon. I'll speak to him myself following Sunday service."

Ruby smiled at Salina, affectionately pulling one of her long, dark curls. "Well, child, here's what you've been wishing for. How did this come about so quickly?"

"After the Review, Jeremy told me there's reason to believe the armies will be launching another campaign soon. There's talk that General Lee might be wanting to move north," Salina confided. "Jeremy wants us to be married before that."

"Another invasion?" Tessa reacted with vehemence. "I say more power to General Lee and his Army of Northern Virginia! I should like to see the faces of those *Yankees* when the war roars in their own backyards—they didn't much like the fight at Antietam, did they? Thought it was quite horrible—well, I say let *them* taste the blood and death and tears firsthand!"

"Mother," Clarice tried to calm Tessa, offering her a chair and a glass of lemonade. "Nothing will bring back Brett, and there's no help for the fact that Bryce was wounded," she said, referring to two of her three brothers. Brock, her third brother, was out there too somewhere, probably still fighting alongside her father, Braden Carpenter, under the command of General Nathan Bedford Forrest in what was considered the war's western theatre.

"Live and let live," Tessa quoted the adage. She hated the Yankees for trying to force the Confederate States to stay in the Union. She held to the Rebel Cause, wanting to preserve the lifestyle she'd been accustomed to. If she had been a man, she would have joined in the fight as well.

Salina shared most of her aunt's views, but she did not condone what some referred to as the South's *"peculiar institution."* In Salina's mind slavery was wrong. People should not be bought and sold based on the color of their skin. It was not slavery that she risked her life for—it was her devotion to Virginia. She felt bound to do what she could in the aid of her native state just as Daddy, Ethan, and Jeremy did. Certainly a part of her longed for the old days that Aunt Tessa and Mamma often lamented the passing of, but Salina was painfully learning to accept that the War Between the States was changing everything. Their lives would never again be the same. They had to go on from here, even knowing that there was no end in sight to the conflict.

Planning for the wedding took up most of the morning, but that afternoon Salina had Uncle Saul, the Carpenters' driver, take her to the telegraph office. She had one telegram sent to Mamma, and another to Taylor Sue in care of Tabitha Wheeler at Fairfax Court

House. Tabitha, one of Salina's contacts from Daddy's old Network of civilian spies, was a reliable friend. She would certainly see that Taylor Sue got the message out at Shadowcreek, near Chantilly. It was a slim chance, but Salina needed to just ask if Taylor Sue could possibly travel to Culpeper Court House in time for the wedding.

Taylor Sue and Salina had been the best of friends long before they had become sisters-in-law. Salina had grown to depend on Taylor Sue's quiet strength and unquestioning moral support through their many adventures.

"Please," Salina concluded writing her message for the telegraph operator, *"Come with all haste if you possibly can to this place. Reply requested only if you cannot make the trip."* She signed her name and paid the requisite fee. She watched as the operator tapped out her second message, and then she left.

"Where ta now, Missy? Back ta Miz Tessa's?" the black man asked.

"Yes, I suppose so." Salina toyed with the temptation of asking Uncle Saul to drive her to the cavalry encampment, but Jeremy had told her he would send word, so she disregarded the impetuous notion. "Could we find a place to get a current newspaper?" asked Salina.

"Ah'll fetch one fer ya, Missy," Uncle Saul nodded. "Dey's usually sold up at da store. Ah'll swing by dere an' git one fer ya. Ere ya anxious fer sum news?"

"I'm just curious to find out what's going on," Salina replied. Things were currently at a deceptive lull, and she didn't expect that it could last much longer before something was bound to happen. A chill stole down the length of her spine. Sometimes Salina just seemed to *know* things, instinctively, uncannily. Here again was such a time, for she had the unsettling feeling that there was a very crucial battle not far distant—one with potential to change the course of all their lives, for better or for worse.

☆☆☆☆☆☆☆

"I had intended it to be a surprise," Jeremy began, watching as Ethan methodically, assiduously cleaned each instrument before carefully packing it into his medical kit. Captain Ethan Hastings, Jeremy mused silently, was a good doctor; he knew that from personal experience. Ethan had patched him up before, and Jeremy was pleased to say he was no worse for the wear. *If Garrett*

Hastings had lived to see his son as an assistant surgeon, he would have been proud!

"Meaning?" Ethan arched a thick eyebrow in question. "What's supposed to be a surprise?"

"Last night, after the ball at Stuart's headquarters, I took the liberty of wiring Reverend Yates. I've asked him to come to Culpeper so he can marry your sister and me."

Ethan set a sharp silver scalpel down next to a shiny-clean bone saw. "This is welcome news. You finally got around to proposing for yourself! Not that your poem wasn't eloquent enough, but proposing in person, well, that makes all the difference. You gave Salina the ring?"

Jeremy nodded affirmatively. "I told her to be ready; I think we can be married on Monday afternoon around half-past four."

"Stuart granted you the time off?" Ethan asked.

"Well, not exactly," Jeremy hedged. "He knows we're planning to be married, but the other day he informed us quite bluntly that he cannot spare me for leave. By all appearances, Lee and Stuart have been holding a council of war. Stuart's mind is solely focused on whatever plans are in the works. The adjutants and other aides are keeping to themselves. Bentley heard some mention of another review, which only confirms what I already told you."

"*Another* review? That's three in as many weeks, isn't it? Everyone says General Stuart has a fondness for the flamboyant, but isn't that a little much?" Ethan questioned.

"The Grand Review yesterday was staged at General Lee's request," Jeremy explained. "But he got called away and wasn't able to attend. If we have to get out there and do the whole thing again, with General Lee watching, I'm sure it'll be business only, not another showy pageant. This is the biggest command Stuart's ever had."

"Reports say near ten thousand men," Ethan commented. "Quite a force to be reckoned with. The Yankee cavalry hasn't the leadership to hold a candle to our Rebel cavaliers...not yet anyway."

"Those people are nothing to sneeze at," Jeremy quipped, employing a polite sobriquet oft applied to the Yankees. General Lee rarely called the Northerners "the enemy"; he called them "those people," and his subordinates and other Southerners followed suit. "They shoot real bullets and have sabres just as sharp as ours," Jeremy contined, then grinned, "but fortunately they're just not quick enough to catch us."

"I've heard that Stuart's own father-in-law is on their side. I reckon that'd be enough to make his blood boil. I should know— I've got a Yankee stepfather!"

"Speaking of your Yankee stepfather, Salina's convinced that Duncan Grant will forbid your Mamma to travel here for the wedding." Jeremy crossed his arms on his chest.

"Duncan's very protective of Mamma, especially with the baby coming and all. No, I reckon he'll not let her leave Gettysburg for any reason," Ethan affirmed. "Salina, I'm sure, would like to have her here. I remember how important it was to Taylor Sue to have her family with her on the day we wed, though I don't think she'd have let their absence stop her from marrying me."

"And speaking of Taylor Sue—in my wire to Reverend Yates, I asked if he would bring your wife with him. That's the other part of the surprise—for you and for Salina." Jeremy flashed his crooked grin.

"You sent for Taylor Sue?" Ethan's eyes reflected his heartfelt gratitude. "And have you heard if she's really coming?"

Jeremy pulled a telegram from his breast pocket and tossed it on the empty operating table between them. "She'll be here tonight with the good Reverend. He's arranged for an itinerant preacher to take over his church service tomorrow morning. Said he wouldn't miss this for the world."

Ethan scanned the brief telegram. "I'll speak to Major Shields directly and see if he can spare me for a few hours on Monday afternoon. I don't know if Salina knows where I am."

"She doesn't, and I didn't enlighten her," Jeremy confessed. "I'm not going to be able to spend as much time with her as I'd like, so I guess I'm trying to make up for it by getting all the people around her that she needs the most. Your Mamma's circumstance I can't do anything about, nor the absence of your Daddy."

"Hmmm…That's probably affected Salina the most," Ethan nodded. "Mamma took Daddy's death hard, and knowing her, she continues to grieve privately for him even though she's married to Duncan. My sister, though, will probably never get over Daddy's death. From what Taylor Sue has written in her letters, Salina has just barely put off her mourning clothes. There was such a deep bond of love between Daddy and Salina, it sometimes made me jealous," Ethan conceded. "I loved that man too, Barnes, yet even *you* seemed closer to him than I felt sometimes."

"Garrett Hastings was more of a father to me than Campbell

Barnes ever was—and that could be because Campbell Barnes wasn't really my father," Jeremy said caustically.

Ethan tipped his dark head to one side, his midnight-blue eyes searching the face of his friend. "Tell me once more how you discovered all that."

"Salina stumbled on the truth when she did some translating for Duncan Grant. I wasn't overly pleased that she was assisting your Yankee stepfather, but Duncan enlisted her because he figured there might be something in the journal that he could use to better protect all you Hastings, and maybe even me. Garrett had *confiscated* the journal during one of his reconnaissance missions, and he had the foresight to hold onto it because he thought it might be useful, but he never broke the code. Duncan couldn't make any headway with it either, so he got Salina to crack the code for him and do the transcription work. She's good, your sister, but I'm just as glad to see her out of the Network."

"Does it still exist?" Ethan asked. "I thought that after Salina's capture it had dissolved."

Jeremy shook his head. "It's not as grand as it was, but it's still functioning. At one time Garrett had that Network of his running from Richmond through the lines to Washington, north to Canada, and west to Santa Fe in New Mexico Territory, Virginia City in Nevada Territory, and as far as California—to San Francisco and San Diego. It's my understanding that all that's left is a handful of locals who manage to keep up the flow of information. They call themselves the Remnant."

"And you're quite sure Salina doesn't have a part in it?" Ethan knew his younger sister well, and she was unlikely to passively watch the action happen around her if there was anything she could do to help out.

"Your sister is a trooper, but she's tired, Ethan. That bout of pneumonia took a toll on her; she's not nearly as strong physically as she was before," Jeremy told his brother-in-law-to-be. "Her latest adventure, of course, was the train wreck…" He shook his head in wonder. "There are times when I'd like nothing better than to send Salina to a place where she could get some good, nourishing food, lots of rest, and time to get healthy again. Shadowcreek isn't the place for that, nor is Richmond."

"Don't worry so much, my friend." Ethan clapped his hand on Jeremy's shoulder. "As you said, my sister's a trooper. She'll find a way to manage. She always does."

"Amen. Besides, I'd rather have her close, not so far removed that I can't steal away and see her from time to time," Jeremy smiled wryly. "She's an amazing young lady, better than I deserve."

Ethan's grin was mischievous. "In truth, the two of you probably deserve each other."

The lieutenant chuckled, "I'm going to take that as your blessing, you know."

"You may do so." Ethan granted it as a privilege. "But just remember that if you do anything to cause her aught but happiness, you'll answer to me."

"I love her, Ethan; her well-being and her happiness will be attended to," Jeremy vowed.

"I still say you deserve each other." Ethan couldn't help but laugh.

☆ ☆ ☆ ☆ ☆ ☆ ☆

Uncle Saul took his own time answering the knock at the front door, and Clarice was right on his heels. She stepped around the black man, momentarily usurping his duties as greeter of guests. "Private Hunter, what a delightful surprise! Won't you come in?" Her bright eyes betrayed her feelings.

"Thank you, Miss Clarice." Boone Hunter tipped his forage cap respectfully but did not relinquish it into Uncle Saul's outstretched hand. "I've a message from Lieutenant Barnes for Miss Salina. Is she here?"

"No, she's not at present. She went along with Delia and Aunt Ruby to gather flowers and greenery for decorating the church. Salina wanted roses for her bouquet, so they went to visit a neighbor who grows some of the loveliest ones I've ever seen." Clarice smiled, "Would you care to wait for Salina? I've lemonade, or spiced tea, if you'd prefer."

"Much as I'd like to stay, Miss Clarice, I'm afraid I'll have to leave this with you and head back to camp. Will you see she gets this as soon as she returns? It's rather important," Boone confided.

He was a very tall young man, equally as tall as Jeremy, measuring six feet and two inches, but Boone had a pair of the largest feet anyone in Jeremy's command had ever seen. While Boone was accustomed to the routine joshing from his comrades, he felt awkward standing next to petite Clarice Carpenter, whose honey-colored head didn't even reach his shoulder. Clarice was so slight that she had stood on top of Boone's big boots to keep her toes from being crushed when they danced together at General Stuart's ball. How they had laughed together over that! Boone liked the way Clarice laughed *with* him, not *at* him, like some girls had done. He didn't have the nerve to admit that he'd expressly asked Jeremy for permission to deliver his note to Salina in hopes of seeing Clarice again, even if only for a few fleeting minutes.

"I'll be sure to give the message to Salina," Clarice nodded. "Thank you for stopping by."

Boone tipped his cap again and grinned. "It was my pleasure, Miss."

"Boone?" Clarice impulsively called after him.

"Yes, Miss Clarice?" he asked.

"You'll be at the wedding tomorrow, won't you?" Clarice wanted to know.

"Indeed, I will," Boone nodded. "Promise you'll save a dance for me?"

Clarice smiled brightly, "Of course!"

Returning with armloads of cream, pink, yellow, and red roses, Salina dumped them all on the table the instant Clarice handed her the envelope from Jeremy. Impatiently she tore the seal, then read the lines aloud:

> *Miss Salina Hastings*
> *In the Care of Mrs. Braden Carpenter*
> *Culpeper Court House, Virginia*
>
> *You are cordially invited to partake of late supper at the camp quarters of Lieutenant Jeremy Barnes and detailed comrades, at nine o'clock this evening. Please bring Miss Delia and Miss Clarice to accompany you.*
>
> > *Respectfully,*
> > *your own Horse Soldier*
> > *Lieutenant Jeremy Barnes*
> > *Stuart's Cavalry, C.S.A.*

Delia and Clarice, reading over Salina's shoulder, squealed with delight. "We can go, can't we, Mother?"

"Well, I don't see why not," Tessa granted permission, "Providing you all behave like the proper young ladies you are."

There were hours yet before they were expected for late supper at the cavalry camp. Salina used the time to finalize the wedding preparations.

Delia found her upstairs. "I was wondering if you might need a larger hoopskirt for your dress. A friend of mine has a crinoline that she's offered to let you borrow; it will make your skirt swing like a bell. I'm going over to St. Stephen's Church to start decorating, and Angelica lives near there on East Street. I could stop by and see her about it on my way home," Delia offered. "It would fulfill the requisite *something borrowed*."

"All right," Salina nodded. "If Angelica doesn't mind parting with the hoops for a day, I'll be delighted to wear them." Actually, Salina detested hoops almost as much as she did corsets and stays, but the dress that Taylor Sue had insisted Salina bring along with her in the event of a "special occasion" would look much better with hoops wider than any Salina owned. She smiled. Taylor Sue's dress was the very one she'd worn on the day she married Ethan. Aunt Tessa said it was supposed to bring happiness for a bride to wear something previously worn by another happy bride. The dress was a beautiful shade of sky blue moiré—*something blue*—with an emerald green pattern woven in. Salina's engagement ring was *something new*, and her gold heart-shaped locket was *something old*. Thus the rhyme was complete:

> *Something Old, Something New*
> *Something Borrowed, Something Blue.*

Salina glanced at the ticking clock on the mantle. In less than twenty-four hours, she would be her Horse Soldier's Bride.

Chapter Four

Ssshhhh! Here she comes now!"

Salina snapped her dark head up, hesitating for a moment. She *knew* that voice, and it sounded like—*Reverend Yates*.

A stifled giggle followed, rippling melodiously in the June evening air. It sounded remarkably like her *sister-in-law*...The next voice Salina heard through the canvas tent wall was *positively* her brother's. Curiosity piqued, Salina gathered her hoops to lift them slightly off the ground, and quickened her stride toward Jeremy's quarters. Delia and Clarice followed in her wake.

Jeremy appeared at the tent fly just as Salina was about to enter. He bowed gallantly, greeting her formally: "Miss Hastings, it's an honor and privilege to have you and your lovely cousins as my guests." He suppressed a rakish grin, and Salina could tell he was up to no good. Jeremy made a deliberate show of kissing her gloved hand. "One small concession, however, before you are allowed to enter."

Salina smiled up at him. "What's going on? Who's in there with you?"

"Some of my men," Jeremy replied, reciting the roll call:

"Bentley, Boone, C.J., Curlie, Jake, Kidd Carney..."

"None of them giggle like Taylor Sue! She's in there, isn't she?" Salina stood on tiptoe and tried to look beyond Jeremy into the lantern-lit tent, but his shoulders were too broad. "Ethan's in this with you, isn't he?" she demanded, a twinkle in her eye.

"Here now," Jeremy stilled her, placing his large hands on her shoulders. He pulled a bandanna from his pocket. "Put this on for a minute, and don't ruin my surprise." Jeremy tied the blindfold over her eyes, then took her by the hand and led her inside. When he undid the knot, he had the keen pleasure of witnessing the shock on Salina's pretty face.

"Taylor Sue! *And* Ethan, *and* Reverend Yates! Oh, Jeremy!" She thanked her lieutenant, hugging him gratefully. "They're here! You brought them here for my sake." She flashed a smile at each of them, hugging each one in turn. "You're all *here*!"

"How could we stay away?" Ethan kissed his little sister's flushed cheek. "We had to see this impending wedding for ourselves."

"Aye, witness it firsthand," Reverend Yates put in. The elderly, balding preacher adjusted his wire-rimmed spectacles on the bridge of his nose. "Tabitha wished she could have come as well, but the boarding house is full up, and she couldn't afford to leave at present, if you know what I mean."

Salina did know. Tabitha Wheeler was an active operative in what was now known as the Remnant. From the standpoint of appearance, Tabitha looked merely to be a small, withered, slump-shouldered, white-haired, mostly-toothless old woman who walked with a limp and a cane. Few saw beyond the outer trappings to her propensity for getting people to tell her things they didn't even realize they were sharing. A good many of her boarders were Yankees—soldiers or their relations—and Tabitha gleaned much useful information without raising suspicions in the least. With her connections, Tabitha secretly forwarded any little tidbit she thought might be helpful to the Cause.

Taylor Sue beamed at her sister-in-law. "Good thing I packed that dress of mine for you," she whispered in Salina's ear. "I should say it will come in quite handy tomorrow afternoon, long about half-past four?"

Salina laughed and laughed. "Oh, I can't believe this!" Her eyes sought Jeremy's, and she saw understanding there. He'd taken to heart the words of their moonlight conversation; he knew how much it meant to have her dear ones close, and he'd done all he could to make it right for her. "Thank you," she mouthed her gratitude.

Jeremy winked at her.

Unaware of the wordless communication shared, Taylor Sue stepped between Jeremy and Salina, saying, "Mary Edith wanted to be here too, but Randle's only got a little time left before he has to go back to his ship. It's been refitted, and they'll be running the blockade again before the end of the month."

"How are the twins?" Salina asked. "And Charlie Graham?"

"Little Annie Laurie and little Bonnie Lee are both doing well. It's amazing how fast they grow," Taylor Sue replied. "Charlie is still living in his tent, pitched in the yard in front of the cabin. Both he and Randle send their regards and wish the two of you all the best."

Aromatic smells permeated the tent's interior. When Bentley announced that supper was ready to be served, Salina sat at the head of the table, while Jeremy sat opposite her at the foot. Boone and Clarice contrived to sit next to one another, and C.J. conveniently seated himself on Delia's left, adeptly monopolizing her attention.

C.J. was the newest rider to join Jeremy's little band. He filled the hole left by the death of Browne Williams. When C.J. had first come east from San Antonio, Texas, he'd traveled with specific instructions to find Jeremy, and he carried a letter of introduction from a mutual friend—a half-breed stagecoach driver and former Pony Express rider named Drake.

The sight of C.J. there at the table brought the face of the turquoise-eyed Indian to Salina's mind, and out of curiosity she suddenly asked, "Jeremy, have you gotten word to Drake about all this?"

"I did," Jeremy's lopsided grin appeared. "I took a chance by sending him a wire at Lacy Whittaker's way station. I figured she would know where to forward a message to him if he's on a stagecoach run between San Fransisco and St. Joseph. I can only surmise that Lacy was successful in tracking Drake down because a reply came from him not more than an hour ago. He's in Memphis, Tennessee—how or why is beyond me; he didn't say. What he did say, however, is typical of Drake: *Tell Little One she'll have her hands full trying to keep you in line, Barnes,*" Jeremy read the telegram aloud. *"Many congratulations—the two of you deserve each other."*

Ethan tossed his dark head back and chuckled heartily. "This

Drake fellow must know what he's talking about—even *I* told you that. The two of you *do* deserve each other."

Salina's smile was a replica of Jeremy's.

As the platters of food were circulated around the table, each guest took servings of roasted chicken, fresh creamed vegetables, and hot, buttered biscuits.

Conversation ranged from news of the front lines and tales of glory swapped by men at one end of the table, to dress patterns, recipes, and wedding plans shared by the ladies at the other end. The convivial supper was abruptly interrupted by the unexpected appearance of General Stuart.

The men scrambled to their feet immediately to salute their commanding officer, one accidentally toppling a portable camp stool in the rush.

"Well." General Stuart took inventory of the situation with his keen, piercing blue eyes. He stroked his long whiskers and then clasped his hands behind his back. "You might have informed me, Barnes, that a party was in progress," he said sternly, and then a wide grin split his beard. "I'd have sent Sweeney over to serenade you all with his banjo."

Jeremy heaved a sigh of relief. "Thank you, General. We'd be much obliged."

"Is it someone's birthday? Some event of special significance that I should know about?" Jeb Stuart queried. "Miss Salina?"

"We're getting married, sir. Tomorrow afternoon, with your permission, of course." She swallowed, a knot of trepidation tightening in her stomach.

"Married? Oh, yes, now I remember—I believe you did mention something about a proper proposal just the other day...but I also remember telling you, Barnes, that I could not afford to spare you for leave at this point in time." General Stuart's tone was somber.

"I'm not asking for a furlough," Jeremy replied. "After the review tomorrow, I thought I could be spared for just a few hours, long enough to partake in a marriage ceremony. Salina understands that all I can offer her right now is my name—the rest will come later, when there is time for us to be together."

General Stuart nodded. He took the liberty of snatching a plump, red strawberry and popped it in his mouth. "How much notice did you give her, eh, Barnes?"

"We've talked of marriage for a while, sir, but as for the wedding itself, just about a day and a half," answered Jeremy, shifting uncomfortably.

Stuart chuckled good-naturedly, "That's the style! I admire a man who sees what he wants and goes after it with all his heart. I was engaged to my Flora hardly a fortnight after we met. We were married within a few months, and that was during peacetime. War, however, breeds the necessity of haste in some instances," the General murmured absently. "Well then," he smiled again, "I'll send Sweeney over directly—much happiness to you both, and to all who have a part in sharing your good fortune."

Jeremy followed Stuart out of the tent and privately asked, "Did you need me for something in particular, General? I don't want you to think I'm not available to carry out your orders."

Stuart waved Jeremy's suggestion away. "I don't necessarily need you right now; I can find another courier. But I'll send for you later if need be. Until then, enjoy. Good night, Barnes. Extend my farewell to your guests."

"Good night, General Stuart," Jeremy saluted. "And thank you, sir."

Jeb Stuart touched the brim of his plumed hat in salute.

Jeremy returned to the party. Without words he conveyed to Salina that there was no need to be alarmed; everything was fine. In a matter of minutes Sam Sweeney arrived with his banjo, and music penetrated the canvas walls of the tent. Laughter, which had dissipated upon Stuart's arrival, resumed its merry flow. Ethan raised a flecked enamel mug of tart lemonade, and the others followed his lead. "A toast to the happy couple," he offered.

"Here, here!" came the reply, accompanied by metal spoons clattering noisily against tin plates.

"Just remember, Barnes," Ethan warned mischievously. "She's my little sister!"

"I know, I know," Jeremy grinned sheepishly, a slight flush reddening his cheeks. "Get on with your speech, man!"

Ethan proclaimed, "To my sweet little sister, and to my good friend, who takes her as his bride: May you love each other for now and for all time! God bless your union with the best this life has to give!"

Another rousing "Here, here!" was punctuated by the clanking of raised mugs.

The evening waxed late. Jeremy adjusted the wick of the kerosene lantern on the table to make it burn higher and brighter, banishing shadows to the far corners of the tent. Regretfully, he'd spent no time alone with his bride-to-be, not with all their friends present, so he had to content himself with silent surveillance. Salina returned his scrutiny in kind, letting glances and smiles speak for themselves. Tomorrow was close at hand.

It seemed to Salina that the party had barely started before Uncle Saul came to collect the girls and drive them back to the Carpenter house. "Miz Tessa, she done send me ta cum fetch ya'll; she done say it be way past da time proper young missies should be out a-visitin'. Ya'll cum along home where ya belong. Ah'll take care o'ya, an' git ya home quick-like."

Delia and Clarice bade each of the men their fond farewells, and Salina did too. She collected her handbag and said to Taylor Sue, "There's plenty of room at the Carpenters, if you need a place to stay for the night."

"Thank you, Salina, but Ethan's made accommodations for me. I'll be over in the morning, bright and early," Taylor Sue promised with a nod of her russet head. "Good night."

"Good night to you," Salina nodded back, and Taylor Sue smiled coquettishly as she tucked her hand into the crook of Ethan's arm.

"Good night, little sister." Ethan brushed her cheek with a brotherly kiss. "I've whole-heartedly agreed to stand up with Jeremy tomorrow, and Bentley's volunteered to give you away. Will that be acceptable?"

Salina smiled at Weston Bentley. He was the oldest of Jeremy's companions—nearer to fifty than he ever would be to forty again—and he held the role of father-figure to each of the men. Some of them were more than twenty years younger than Bentley, and even though Jeremy held the superior rank, Bentley served as father, mentor, horse doctor and cook all rolled into one. "I'd be honored if you'd give me away, Bentley."

"Nay, Miss, the honor surely is mine," he bowed to her. "Every eye'll be on me, 'cause I'm the one who'll be marchin' the prettiest little bride they ever saw down the aisle to this scoundrel of a groom. Yer sure ya want ta go through with this, Missie? Ya can still change yer mind—it ain't too late," Bentley teased. He felt a certain fondness for his young lieutenant, and he'd grown fond of the lieutenant's lady as well.

Another round of laughter and a few guffaws encircled the engaged pair. "You're not having second thoughts about marrying me, are you, Sallie?" Jeremy asked.

"No," she assured him quickly. She took note of each detail of his appearance, for she would ever remember how he looked on this night, standing so tall and dashing in his gray uniform: his sandy-blond hair, his black eyebrows and beard, his high cheekbones, the determined set of his jaw, his full lips forming that contagious grin. This was the picture she would carry in her heart, to recall whenever they were separated. "I love you."

"I love you, too." A tender kiss followed his husky declaration.

"Ease up, Lieutenant," Jake Landon ribbed. "Save some of that for the ceremony tomorrow!"

In the midst of his men's laughter, Jeremy lifted Salina into the waiting carriage, yet he did not give up her hand.

"Ere ya ready, missies?" Uncle Saul inquired, making sure his charges were settled in their respective seats.

Clarice waved good-bye to Boone. Delia looked back at C.J. once more prior to casting a questioning look at Salina, who reluctantly nodded.

"We're ready, Uncle Saul," Delia confirmed. The black man clucked to the horses, setting them in motion.

Jeremy held Salina's fingers until the carriage rolled forward, breaking the contact and putting distance between them. By the time he returned to his all but abandoned tent, only the remains of supper, dirty dishes, and Reverend Yates were left.

"I believe she was genuinely surprised," Reverend Yates smiled, recalling the expression on Salina's face when she first arrived. "That was a good thing you did for her, son. Right thoughtful and considerate of you."

"Yes, it worked out quite well, thanks to you. I appreciate you taking the risk to travel out this way. It means a great deal to both of us to have you here, Reverend," Jeremy nodded, clearing the table.

Reverend Yates assisted the young lieutenant. "Is there something on your mind, son?"

Jeremy's initial response was a shaky smile. He sat down on the edge of his cot and remarked, "I don't know *why* she loves me, but Salina does. No one has ever cared about me the way she does."

He took a deep breath and continued, "When she came back to Virginia, free and pardoned, I stupidly accused her of signing an Oath of Allegiance to the Union, and even believed that she might have feelings for that Yankee Lieutenant Lance Colby. I couldn't trust her, I wouldn't believe her, and I didn't give her a fair chance. It took the people all around me to make me see what a fool I was. Taylor Sue upbraided me something fierce one afternoon when I came calling in Richmond," Jeremy smiled, remembering the scene in the front parlour of the Careys' rented house in Linden Row. "Salina loves me so much that even when I'd hurt her badly, she *still* believed in me. By rights, she could have made me work harder to win her back—and she probably should have. But she didn't. She forgave me quicker than I could forgive her. We made an agreement that we would patch the trust and strive to restore our relationship to the way it was before she'd gone away. She knows all about my past—the whippings I endured, my rowdy days in California, the fact that my name isn't really Barnes…Salina loves me enough to marry me *anyway*, in spite of it all."

"Son, that kind of unconditional love hopes all things, bears all things, believes all things. Consider it a rare blessing," Reverend Yates encouraged. "Salina is very giving, very trusting, and loyal to a fault. Even her many adventures haven't changed those qualities. You are four years her senior and have seen much more of the world; she'll look to you for care and guidance as husband, friend, and spiritual leader. Not an easy task, let me tell you, yet one that can be accomplished though prayer and reliance on God's strength, not your own.

"Marriage is no light commitment, son. I don't have to remind you that it is a monumental step in your lives. It requires equal parts of devotion, faithfulness, compromise, understanding, and sharing—plus a myriad of other sacrifices to make it successful. I have no doubt that the two of you can do this—but certainly not without courage. There will be rough times; that's a given since you each have your own ideas on certain things. But you're both ready to make a lasting commitment to one another, whereas a few months ago it seemed nigh unto impossible. You've each learned lessons and will bring experiences with you to enhance the relationship you will build together—starting tomorrow afternoon."

Jeremy pondered the Reverend's words. "I want to be a good husband to her," he said at last, "but the truth is I'll not be around much to be any kind of husband…All I can do is pray God will keep us both and make me the husband Salina needs and deserves."

"We could pray together now, if you like," Reverend Yates suggested, and so they did.

☆☆☆☆☆☆☆

June 7, 1863
Washington, D.C.

Major Duncan Grant absently handed his embossed invitation to the dour-faced butler at the grand entrance of the home belonging to a prominent, wealthy Washingtonian. Duncan did not want to be here, but he was ordered by his superior officer to at least put in an appearance. It wasn't that Duncan had anything against people having a good time at social gatherings, but he had more work to do than he could handle at the moment. He had to get it all done before he could even think of requesting a few days' leave to go home to Gettysburg and check on his pregnant wife. Annelise's last letter had mentioned false labor pains, but the doctor had examined her and decreed that the baby was merely making ready for his or her birthday. No harm done, and Annelise was really doing very well.

Duncan ran a finger between his neck and the constricting collar of his dress blue uniform coat. His wife and unborn child were not the only thoughts occupying his mind on this balmy evening. He accepted a crystal cup of punch from a liveried server and sipped the fruity liquid slowly. Duncan had seen only preliminary reports, but on the Mississippi River front the Union's siege of Vicksburg was well underway. Ulysses S. Grant—no relation that Duncan was aware of in spite of their common surname—was bombarding the city twenty-four hours a day. The notion fairly boggled the mind. *How could the Rebels not give in under such adverse conditions?* Reports claimed that the Southerners there had burrowed into the hills and were living in caves, eating rats and whatever else they could find, while Grant and his troops were determined to starve them out of the last Rebel stronghold along the Mississippi.

Other items of note which had crossed his desk at the War Department this afternoon included sketchy details concerning the battle at Franklin's Crossing near Fredericksburg, and an obscure message from his right hand man, Lieutenant Lance Colby. Colby's missive contained a single cryptic line: *Barnes has been spotted in Alexandria.*

Ten months had passed since Duncan was ordered to follow Jeremy Barnes, in hopes that he would lead Duncan to Garrett Hastings and whatever plot he was concocting at the time. Jeremy no longer posed an immediate threat, since he was no longer working for Garrett and that Network of Southern civilian spies. Instead, the young Rebel lieutenant was off riding with Jeb Stuart's trouble-some cavalry. For all intents and purposes, Garrett's Network had folded when Salina and Taylor Sue had been taken into custody in San Francisco, and to date there had been no further mention of any pending Confederate campaigns designed to capture the western territories and California, or to annex the northern states of Mexico in the name of the Rebel Cause. That matter, at least for the time being, lay dormant.

This matter dealing with *John* Barnes, however, was far from settled; it was personal now, and Duncan was on guard for any move his fellow major might make. The man had disappeared for weeks, and had suddenly resurfaced from whatever rock he'd been hiding under.

Duncan would have to be discreet, but he intended to start his inquiries, for even while they wore the same color uniform and both professed to defend the Union, that didn't mean they weren't at odds. Major Barnes had been using the war as a cover for his murderous vendetta against the Hastings of Shadowcreek, and was still bent on the destruction of Jeremy Barnes as well.

"Major Grant, how do you do?" A congressman shook Duncan's hand, much too vigorously. Then another politician joined them, followed by a collection of money-making govern-ment contractors. Without being completely rude, Duncan bided his time, only half-listening to their ongoing advisements. "Gentlemen, if you'll excuse me, I see someone I must speak to across the room. Pleasure seeing all of you again," Duncan politely lied.

Quick strides carried Duncan across the floor. "Lieutenant Colby."

Colby turned to follow Duncan into the foyer for a touch more privacy. "Here you are, Major—I thought you didn't much care for the Washington social scene. You got my message?" Lance Colby asked in hushed tones.

"I don't care for the social scene," Duncan said firmly, "But I'm here, and yes, I got your note. What news?" the major wanted to know.

"Nothing yet," Colby shook his fair blond head. "I'm working on it, though."

"Keep at it, Lieutenant." Duncan asked, "Where is your wife?"

Colby rolled his pale blue eyes. "Powdering her pretty little nose, I believe."

Duncan held his tongue from any caustic remarks. He genuinely felt sorry that Lance Colby had to deal with Lottie Armstrong—*Mrs. Colby*, to be precise—on a daily basis.

Lottie, Salina Hastings' cousin on her mother's side of the family, seemingly had no conscience. She'd done everything in her power to drive Salina and Jeremy apart, including using Colby in the process. Lottie's deceit, however, had backfired, and Colby had found himself a blameworthy participant in a rather hasty wedding. Caleb Armstrong, Lottie's father, had been civil enough to keep the shotgun from plain sight, but anyone who knew the true story knew that Colby had had to marry Lottie to make an honest woman of her. The baby Lottie was carrying was admittedly Colby's, not Jeremy Barnes's as she had originally tried to claim.

Duncan had to give Colby a good portion of credit, for not only had Colby done the honorable thing in marrying Miss Armstrong to atone for their indiscretion, but Colby entered into the marriage with the intention of fulfilling his vows to the best of his ability. Colby meant to make good his word, whether Lottie liked it or not.

As far as Duncan could tell, Lottie Armstrong Colby was content enough—so long as she was allowed to play the socialite at all the uppercrust functions and spend Colby's money on new dresses and bonnets whenever she pleased. Lottie was a shallow creature, yet Colby seemed to see some redeeming quality in her. Duncan was at a loss as to what that might possibly be. He didn't trust the young woman an inch, and he was comforted to know that Colby didn't either. Their work with the War Department could be at risk if they were discovered...

"Have you heard anything else I should know about?" Duncan questioned Colby.

The lieutenant nodded. "Jeb Stuart held another review of the Rebel cavalry out near Brandy Station."

"That's right off the Orange & Alexandria Railroad, not far from Culpeper Court House." Duncan consulted a mental map of Virginia in his head.

"Yes, and the scouts brought back information saying he had ten thousand men out there. If one didn't know any better, one might think such a massed body of cavalry could signify a possible movement, wouldn't you agree, Major?" Colby suggested.

"Perhaps, but where would they go? The Army of Northern Virginia isn't concentrated. They've still got troops entrenched on the hills at Marye's Heights above Fredericksburg, for Pete's sake,"

Duncan shrugged. He'd grown skeptical of the high command during his tenure with the Union Army. President Lincoln could not seem to find a suitable leader who would fight Robert E. Lee without bumbling or somehow throwing away opportunities to crush the Rebels. First it was Irvin McDowell, then George McClellan, John Pope, McClellan again, Ambrose Burnside, and now Joe Hooker. There was talk that if Hooker couldn't do the job, perhaps General John Reynolds would be asked to take over the Army of the Potomac. Reynolds was a Pennsylvania man, as was Duncan, a good soldier with a promising career ahead of him. Who could tell what went on in the minds of the President or the Secretary of War? Duncan had long since ceased trying to second guess any of them. He stuck to his own job, performing it well enough to have established a credible reputation, and he willingly let it go at that.

The war was into its third year, and showed no signs of coming to a conclusion. Losses at the Battle of Chancellorsville in May had been staggering. Casualties were costly, but the North at least had the manpower to send replacements to the front lines. The South did not have such resources, yet being outnumbered was a predicament that rarely seemed to bother Robert E. Lee. His Confederate forces continued to fight ferociously, perhaps because they claimed to have so much more at stake than their Northern counterparts.

"It doesn't matter where the Rebs are going, Major Grant," Colby said purposefully. "I'm requesting permission—respectfully, of course—to put in for a transfer. I'd like to fight with the cavalry for a change, either under Buford or Gregg, if possible."

Duncan presumed that Colby missed their old scouting assignments, for it was obvious that he chafed in the offices at the War Department. "Do you have a death wish, Lieutenant?" Duncan wondered.

"No, nothing like that, just a hankering for some action. Not that Lottie would miss me. She'd probably relish the idea of being a war widow, but she'd be hard pressed to endure a year-long mourning period for me, I reckon." Colby knew his wife well. To seclude herself and wear strictly black mourning clothes would be absolutely abhorrent to Lottie's way of thinking. "It's just that I'd like to see what kind of cavalier I might make. I joined up to ride in the cavalry initially, remember, but found I enjoyed secret service work. Since we've not had any more cases like Garrett Hastings' Western Campaign, I thought now would be as good a time as any to put in for active duty in the field," Colby shrugged.

"I'll fill out the necessary papers first thing in the morning," Duncan assured him. He wouldn't stand in the way of Colby's ambitions. "All I want from you before you leave is all the information you can get me about the sighting of John Barnes in Alexandria. Fair exchange?"

"I'll take that," Colby nodded. "I won't say anything to Lottie just yet, though. She'd hate to think that she couldn't stay in Washington while I'm away." A grin crossed Colby's face: "I could always send her to live with my family in Gettysburg for a spell if she didn't want to go home to Ivywood."

"Please, no," Duncan groaned. "Annelise is in Gettysburg with my family. She doesn't need the kind of trouble Lottie could stir up just now, thank you anyway."

"Any word on when Annelise is going to have that baby of yours?" Colby inquired.

"Two weeks, possibly three," Duncan replied, the pride clearly discernible in his voice. He'd been utterly stunned when Annelise first told him that they'd created a child. He was soon to be forty *and* a new father. Colby had given him a good dose of grief over that. For all the years Duncan had known Annelise Spencer Hastings, he'd respected and loved her because she was Garrett's wife. After Garrett's death, Duncan discovered that John Barnes was trying to have Annelise arrested for having a fabricated part in Garrett's Network. Duncan did the only thing he could in order to protect her: he *married* her, thereby changing her name, and moved her out of Virginia into the safe haven of his family's home in southeast Pennsylvania. Though the news that Annelise was expecting had initially given Duncan quite a jolt, a child of his own was something Duncan considered nothing short of a miracle, one he intended to treasure with all his heart.

"Don't worry, Major, I'll get you that information on John Barnes before the baby's born," Colby said confidently.

"Yours or mine?" Duncan asked, poking fun at their similar circumstances.

Colby took the gibe good-naturedly. "If not by the time yours is born, then certainly by the time mine is."

"The sooner I get that information, the sooner you'll get that transfer," Duncan bargained.

Chapter Five

*R*everend Yates arrived at the Carpenter household early on the morning of June the eighth. He found Salina sitting alone on the porch swing, reading her Bible in quiet solitude.

"Good morning, Miss Salina. What are you reading?" The Reverend set the porch swing into a gentle motion as he joined Salina.

"A pair of rather similar scriptures. My best guess is that the Lord is trying to tell me, once again, to be strong and courageous. Daddy used to tell me that on a regular basis, and Taylor Sue and I encouraged each other with the same sentiments all the way to San Francisco and back. These particular verses, from Psalm Twenty-Seven and Psalm Thirty-One, are almost identical," she said. "Listen:

Wait on the Lord: be of good courage,
and he shall strengthen thine heart:
wait, I say, on the Lord.

> *Be of good courage, and he shall*
> *strengthen your heart,*
> *all ye that hope in the Lord.*

She looked up from the pages of her Bible into the kindly face of the preacher. "He *is* my hope, Reverend. The Lord is my Rock and my Shield. He will never leave me or forsake me—He has promised to always be with me."

"Yes, and His promises can be relied on," Reverend Yates smiled.

Salina nodded. Then as if comforting herself, she added in a serious tone, "The Lord never fails, He keeps His eye on His children, and holds them in the palm of His hand."

The Reverend noted the absence of Salina's usually infectious enthusiasm. "In my estimation, you seem a shade melancholic this morning, Miss Salina. You aren't nervous about the afternoon, are you?"

"No, at least I don't think I am." At last a smile illuminated Salina's face, but in her eyes was an uncustomary somberness. She whispered, "For whatever reason, I just have the feeling that this will not be an average wedding day." Salina rubbed her arms to ward off the gooseflesh that prickled her skin at what seemed a prophetic admission.

"How so?" Reverend Yates asked.

Salina shrugged. She didn't know why she felt the way she did, and she didn't want to attempt an explanation. "Maybe it *is* my nerves, after all." She tried to laugh lightly, but could see by the concerned expression on the Reverend's face that she wasn't very convincing. "Pray for me, Reverend Yates? Pray that I'll be a good wife to Jeremy, that I can make him understand how much I love and care for him. He's not accustomed to it; it's still new to him. Jeremy never experienced what it means to be cherished in all the time he was growing up. I will show him," she said determinedly.

Reverend Yates pondered Salina's keen perception, and in that instant she seemed older than her sixteen years. He placed his hand on Salina's head and asked the Lord to bless her, particularly so on this special day.

"Thank you, Reverend," Salina smiled when they had finished praying. "I do feel better."

"Glad to hear it." The preacher patted her shoulder. "I'll go on in now and see if there's any way I can make myself useful to your aunts. Don't you worry, Miss Salina. All things work together for good."

"I know," Salina nodded.

Not more than five or ten minutes after Reverend Yates went into the house, Ethan and Taylor Sue arrived. Salina couldn't help but watch the poignant picture they made together—she in her flowing dress, he in his smart gray uniform. Ethan did not dismount, but gently lifted Taylor Sue down from the saddle and bent to kiss her good-bye.

"Tell my sister that we'll meet you all over at St. Stephen's later this afternoon," Ethan instructed his wife. "And I'll see you there."

"Good-bye, my darling," Taylor Sue nodded, squeezing his gloved hand. "Don't miss me too much while you're back at camp."

"How can I help it?" Ethan grinned. "Go on now, see if you can do something with Salina between now and four-thirty to help pass the time."

"Don't worry about Salina," Taylor Sue said. "She's only getting married."

Ethan chuckled. "That's the part that's most difficult to get used to. She's grown up, and now she'll rely on Jeremy for protection instead of me."

"She'll have her husband, but she'll still need you, too," Taylor Sue assured him. "You two have always been close—our marriage didn't change that, and neither will hers. Go on now, we'll see you later."

Ethan kissed his wife again, and then rode off in the direction of his Corps headquarters.

"Ethan's not going to the Review?" Salina asked Taylor Sue, seeing that he was not riding toward Brandy Station.

"No, he said he has some other responsibilities to tend to before this afternoon," Taylor Sue answered. She saw a mischievous light in Salina's emerald eyes. "What are you scheming, Salina?"

"I was just thinking that we could go to the Review," Salina delicately suggested.

"Ethan told me this Review is for General Lee's benefit alone. Only General Hood and some of his people were invited to be there." Taylor Sue sighed, "It seems I've missed out on all the parades and gallant revelry."

"Not necessarily." Salina cocked her head to one side. "Come now, Taylor Sue, where is your sense of adventure?"

Taylor Sue shook her head, smiling. "I know you—I can see your mind working. Right about now, you're probably thinking that all we need is access to the proper clothes for such an endeavor. Where do you propose to find the two sets of boys' clothes we'd need, hmmm?"

"In my cousin Brock's room. He's away fighting, he'll never have to know we temporarily appropriated a couple of shirts and pairs of trousers—and maybe a cap or two," Salina winked.

"Salina, think: your wedding is in a few hours' time," Taylor Sue began to protest, but she saw the pleading look on her dear friend's face. She threw up her hands. "Okay. If it's that important to you, count me in."

Salina hugged Taylor Sue. "Oh, thank you! It's just that I want you to see Jeremy in action. He looks so brave and courageous when riding amidst all those cavaliers." Salina's pride in her betrothed was abundantly evident.

"Hurry, then, before we're found out," Taylor Sue urged, adding, "I have the feeling this is going to be another in our long list of escapades. Let's go." Giggling conspiratorially, the two sisters-in-law hastened to make preparations for their ride to the fields near Brandy Station.

☆ ☆ ☆ ☆ ☆ ☆ ☆

"Take a look over there, against the trees."

General Jeb Stuart took a pair of field glasses from the outstretched hand of Major Heros von Borcke. "Where?"

"There, right near that grove," von Borcke indicated, pointing with one hand and resting his other on the hilt of his imposing dragoon sword. "A pair of riders—see them?"

A wide grin stole over Stuart's face. In mock seriousness he asked his Prussian staff officer, "You think they might be spies, Von?"

"Possibly. No?" the foreign major questioned.

"Look again, Von," Stuart chuckled. "The one on the left—I believe I saw you dancing with her the other night at the ball."

"Her?" von Borcke snatched the field glasses and raised them to his incredulous eyes. He studied the pair of riders more closely. "Well, I'll be..." He lowered the glasses and remarked, "Now there's an intrepid little miss..."

Stuart agreed, laughing. "You don't know the half of it."

"Not one of their people, is she? She wouldn't be spying for the Yankees?" von Borcke wanted to know.

"No, no, not for their side," Stuart answered. "She's loyal—extremely so."

"You know this little lady, then?" A questioning look settled on the Prussian's features.

"She is the fiancée of Lieutenant Barnes," Stuart clarified. "I suspect that's why she's sneaking out here dressed in that get-up. She's checking up on him."

"Barnes—he's not back yet. You sent him out very late last night and he has yet to report in," von Borcke informed the General.

Stuart rubbed his bearded chin. Last night he had needed a man for a secretive scouting mission, someone who was reliable and able to keep his mouth shut. Barnes was the man he'd selected, since the young lieutenant excelled in both those traits. Stuart had sent Jeremy out with verbal orders and a newly-drawn map. The General commanded the lieutenant to make notes, take down details, mark anything that might be useful for reconnaissance purposes—especially the location of the Yankee cavalry, if that could be determined.

The orders coming from the high command would be taking the Army of Northern Virginia in a northerly direction on the morrow, and Stuart was determined to obtain as much information as possible concerning the gaps and the mountain passes en route to Maryland and Pennsylvania. Until hearing von Borcke's comment on Barnes's absence, Stuart had merely assumed that the delay meant the reconnaissance had taken longer than originally anticipated. Too much time had elapsed, however, and Stuart thought Jeremy should have been back by now. Evidently, something out there was preventing a direct return. It was conceivable that Barnes might have had to make a detour if he'd run into any trouble.

As an afterthought, the cavalry leader recalled, "Barnes is supposed to be getting married this afternoon. If he doesn't make it back, I have the feeling I'm going to be one very unpopular commander with someone across the way." He nodded toward the place where Salina Hastings and her companion had reined their horses. "On the other hand, the bride claims to understand that in wartime a man's duty is to defend his country's honor, come what may. This is as good a time as any to test her commitment to the idea that duty comes first," Stuart added tersely. "Barnes had his orders from me.

He knows his job, though I expect he'll move heaven and earth if that's what it takes to get back here in time."

Von Borcke continued to observe though his glasses. The cavalry units were all ready and waiting. General Lee and his staff were approaching the little knoll where Stuart had halted for the viewing. Off to one side was General John Bell Hood, who had accepted Stuart's invitation to bring "some of his people" along for the show. Hood brought all ten thousand members of his infantry to watch the cavalry turn out.

General Lee had ordered that the horses should not be over-exerted in the exercises, and the artillery did not fill the air with cannonading as it had three days before. As the review progressed, the only source of amusement proved to be the antics of some of General Hood's men who frequently ran onto the field to snatch up hats which had blown off as the troopers rode past. Between the two branches of the army was a distinct rivalry. Foot soldiers often implied that the cavalry did not match the mettle of the infantry, and of course the cavaliers retorted likewise. In the end, the captured headgear always brought a boisterous cheer, and the teasing phrase *"Whoever saw a dead cavalryman?"* echoed loudly among the ranks of the infantry.

☆ ☆ ☆ ☆ ☆ ☆ ☆

Across the way, Taylor Sue and Salina intently watched the lines of cavalry parade by at a walk. Salina trained her field glasses on the little knoll where General Stuart and his staff officers stood with their mounts at attention. Salina thought that was where Jeremy should have been, as he was during the review on June fifth. A bitter taste filled Salina's mouth, rising from the churning of her stomach. She didn't see Jeremy anywhere.

"Did you spot him yet? Is he out there?" Taylor Sue asked impatiently. "Let me see—let me have a look through the glasses."

Salina obligingly relinquished the field glasses. Taylor Sue looked everywhere, but she too failed to locate Jeremy Barnes. She found Kidd Carney, Boone Hunter and Harrison Claibourne, Curlie Hawkins and Cutter Montgomery, even Jake Landon. But C.J. was missing, as were Weston Bentley and Pepper Markham. Taylor Sue suspected that the absence of those three, plus Jeremy, was not a good sign.

Salina tried to reassure herself as well as Taylor Sue. "Perhaps

General Stuart assigned Jeremy elsewhere this morning because he knows we're getting married this afternoon. Maybe Jeremy had to take a dispatch to General Longstreet's headquarters, or maybe…I don't know. I'm trying to be optimistic."

"Wherever he is, I'm sure Jeremy will be back by four-thirty," Taylor Sue comforted.

Salina bit her lip. Deep down inside, she resigned herself to the very real possibility that she might *not* be her Horse Soldier's bride today. A sense of gloom hovered around her, much as storm clouds obliterate a bright, sunny sky, and she shivered. *Something's gone wrong…*

She tried very hard to shake the feeling of despair. "Come on, we can't stay here all day," Salina said, wheeling her horse. "As you have oft reminded me, I've got a wedding to get ready for!"

A few hours later, having bathed and perfumed herself with fragrant rosewater, Salina stood at attention in the center of the room adorned only in her stockings, pantalets, corset, and chemise. When she was a little girl Jubilee, her mammy, dressed her each morning, as one might dress a doll. Jubilee, however, was with Mamma in Pennsylvania, and presently it was Delia, Clarice, and Taylor Sue who took turns applying her numerous layers of petticoats, hoops, and crinolines, and at last the borrowed blue moiré wedding dress.

Even as the girls fussed and clucked over her, Salina found herself forcing smiles and pretending that everything was going to work out all right in the end. After all, she silently chided herself, where was her faith? Jeremy said he'd be here, and she trusted his word. He wouldn't intentionally let her down; she knew that.

Ruby twisted Salina's ebony tresses into a loose chignon, though a few stubborn tendrils refused to cooperate, escaping their confinement to hang in ringlets in front of Salina's ears. Above her left ear was a solitary red rose which matched those in the bouquet she would carry, their long stems bowed with lengths of red satin ribbon and lace.

Taylor Sue did not allow Salina to check her appearance until all was absolutely ready. She put her hands over Salina's eyes, and Delia and Clarice led her to the full-length cheval mirror. Taylor Sue took her hands away, permitting Salina to see her lovely reflection. "See how pretty you are, Salina?"

Salina stood stock still, her mouth dropping slightly in mild shock. "I look so…"

"Grown up," Clarice nodded affirmatively. "Just wait until your lieutenant sees you!"

"If he recognizes me!" Salina blinked again, still marveling at her mirrored likeness. She did look grown up—maybe even as old as eighteen or nineteen. The off-the-shoulder style displayed her creamy neck and shoulders to perfection, and because she was still so slim from her bout with pneumonia at the end of last year, the corset stays drew in sharply at her narrow waist; it was the petticoats that lent her hips their fullness.

"Jeremy Barnes will declare you the most beautiful belle in all the county," Tessa predicted from the doorway, "If not the whole state of Virginia."

Salina turned and smiled sincerely at her aunt. "I only pray his vision never weakens," she laughed. "I want him to have eyes only for me."

"He's already got those!" Delia insisted with a light-hearted giggle. She handed Salina her gloves.

Salina worked her fingers into the delicately crocheted white lace fingerless gloves, careful to avoid snagging her engagement ring on the tiny loops.

Taylor Sue placed a coin in the bottom of one of the slippers. "That's for good luck," she explained.

"I thought my blue satin garter was for good luck," Salina reminded her sister-in-law.

"Well, so is this," Taylor Sue insisted. "Traditions are meant to be observed."

Clarice held out her hand to Salina. "Come—it's nearly time. We want to get you to the church early so Jeremy won't see you as he approaches."

It was a short drive to St. Stephen's. When they arrived at the church on East Street, Reverend Yates was already there. By half-past four, the scant number of people who'd been invited to witness the ceremony were all seated and quietly listening to the piano as Ruby played selections by Mozart, Bach, and Beethoven.

Ten minutes passed. A clatter of hoofbeats sent Salina's heart racing at a frantic pace, and she took a calming breath. The heat was stifling in the little cloakroom just off the foyer, but she stayed there out of sight while Clarice and Delia took turns fanning her.

Taylor Sue went to see who the riders were, but none of them was Jeremy. Boone Hunter, Harrison Claibourne, Curlie Hawkins, Kidd Carney, Cutter Montgomery, and Jake Landon took their seats in the pews, but Ethan followed his wife back to where his sister anxiously awaited the arrival of her groom.

"Ethan." Salina's bright eyes were wide, her smile timorous.

The sight of his little sister was nearly enough to knock Ethan over with a feather. "Goodness me, Little Sister, but I declare I've never seen you look more beautiful."

Salina flushed at such praise from her older brother. "Thank you," she murmured politely. Then she asked, not a little anxiously, "Where do you suppose he is?"

"I don't know. I thought he would have been here before me. I was delayed by a patient and thought I was late, but not as late as Jeremy. Hang on, Salina, we'll sort this out. I'm sure he'll be here just as soon as he can," Ethan assured her.

Half-past five, quarter to six, and then a quarter past. There was still no sign of Jeremy, C.J., Pepper Markham, or Weston Bentley. Salina moved from the foyer to a back pew to sit and wait. Understandably, the guests, most of them friends of the Carpenters, made their polite excuses and slipped away by twos and threes until the church was practically empty.

Ethan and the other riders also had to take their leave. Each of Jeremy's men brushed Salina's cheek with a wisp of kiss and offered a hasty apology, explaining that obligations required their attention back at camp.

"I'm due back, too, Salina. Colonel Shields expects me," Ethan apologized, shaking his dark head.

"Duty calls," Salina remarked pointedly.

"What are you going to do?" Ethan wanted to know.

"I'm going to wait," she replied stoically, even as the sunset created lengthening shadows and candles had to be lit. "I'll wait here all night if I have to, but I'm not leaving until I know for sure he's not coming. There could be any number of reasons for his tardiness—duty being first on the list."

"If I could wait with you, I would, but I just can't." Ethan squeezed her hand. "Chin up, eh? Next time I see you, you'll probably be a Mrs. and I'll have missed it."

"We'll see about that." Salina surmised that Ethan plainly detected the disappointment in her eyes. Her brother had always been able to read her like a book.

Taylor Sue followed Ethan out to say a private farewell, and then she returned to Salina's side. The candles burned down to the wicks and were replaced with fresh lights. Still Jeremy did not come.

Salina looked at her aunts and cousins and said in soft voice, "You all don't have to stay here with me."

"Let's go back to Tessa's," Ruby suggested gently. "Jeremy will know where to find you."

"No," Salina protested. "I'm staying right here. Quite obviously, something has gone amiss; otherwise he would have been here by now. If he should manage to still show up, I have to be ready—for we won't have much time to be married."

All of them stayed to wait with Salina until nine clock chimes were heard. Tessa insisted that it was long past the time when they all should have eaten. She and Delia went home, followed shortly by Clarice and Ruby.

"I'm not hungry," Salina insisted stubbornly. "Go on and get something for supper," she told Reverend Yates and Taylor Sue. She lit another candle and set it in the window facing the direction from which she thought Jeremy might ride.

"I'll go," Taylor Sue finally agreed. "But I'll be back, and I'll fetch you a sandwich. You could stand a little food, I'm sure."

Reverend Yates nodded, encouraging Taylor Sue to go. "I'll stay with her, just in case he comes."

But as Salina and the Reverend sat on the hard wooden pews on opposite sides of the aisle, they both arrived at the conclusion that there would be no wedding today.

"I *knew* something was going to happen. Those verses I was reading this morning talked about being courageous. A body has got to have courage to go through the trials of life. Courage to stand the testing…" Salina's voice trailed off.

"You know that he would have been here if he could have," Reverend Yates reiterated. "He loves you very much, Miss Salina."

"I know that. I guess that's why I'm so bent on staying. What if he still might show up? I'm not leaving until I know for sure." Salina had her purpose firmly fixed. "You know that story in the Bible, Reverend, the one Jesus told of the five wise virgins and the five foolish virgins?"

The preacher nodded and patiently waited for Salina to make her point.

"There was to be a marriage feast," Salina began. "The five wise virgins brought plenty of oil for their lamps. The five foolish ones didn't, and they ran out. They begged the wise virgins to let them have some of their oil, but there wasn't enough to go around, so the foolish virgins left in search of more oil. While they were gone, the bridegroom came. He took the wise virgins with him into the marriage supper because they had been prepared and were waiting for his arrival. Those foolish virgins, because they were not prepared, were shut out. They were not allowed to attend the feasting, and they were kept apart from the bridegroom. Now, I'm sure it might not be the best comparison, but if Jeremy's truly coming here tonight, then I want to be here, ready and waiting for him." A wistful smile tugged at the corners of Salina's mouth. "Reverend, there's a good chance that my wedding ceremony might be even briefer than the one you performed when you married my Cousin Lottie to that Yankee Lieutenant, Lance Colby."

Reverend Yates grinned. "Yes, that was a quick wedding indeed." He was heartened to note that Salina could see a lighter side to her distress. He was also encouraged to find that she had been paying attention during his teachings in church on Sundays. Those sermons, along with Salina's personal reading of God's word, were making a visible impact on Salina's faith.

The Reverend discerned that Salina was trying to prove not only her faith in God and His word, but also her unwavering faith in Jeremy. If she had the courage to still believe that Jeremy might show up at the church, regardless of how remote the chance might be, then he would not dissuade her. "We'll stay, and we'll wait."

Salina's smile silently expressed her gratitude.

Taylor Sue returned an hour later, alone. "Boone was there," she informed them, "but he had no word. No one knows where Jeremy and the others are. The aunts and your cousins will stay at the house, and if there's any news, Boone will come and fetch us. If anything happens here, Uncle Saul is outside with the carriage and will go back for them. Fair enough?"

Salina nodded tiredly.

Taylor Sue sat down on the wooden pew next to Salina, offering her a sandwich and a jug of water, but when Salina shook her head in refusal, Taylor Sue offered her shoulder instead. "I can't understand why you haven't cried yet, Salina. I'd have been beside myself if something like this had happened to Ethan on the day we got married. Your strength is showing through again."

Salina didn't think it was strength. In fact, she felt she lacked the courage to shed the tears that flooded her heart. She was afraid of not being prepared—if Jeremy were to suddenly, miraculously, appear in the vestibule, she did not want him to see tears staining her cheeks. She wanted to be able to greet him with a loving smile.

She longed to tell him that everything would be all right, that she didn't fault him for circumstances beyond his control. But still Jeremy did not come.

Chapter Six

*I*n the wee hours of the morning Salina fell into a shallow sleep, her head resting against Taylor Sue's shoulder. Just before dawn, the three dozing in their respective church pews were rudely awakened by the thunderous rumble of cannon fire.

Battle! Salina sprang to her feet. Those were the sounds of battle; she recognized them all too well. Somewhere fairly close by the Yankees and the Rebels had found each other, by design or by accident, and they would do their best to destroy one another.

Taylor Sue's eyes were wide. "We should go back to Aunt Tessa's house now, Salina."

Reverend Yates agreed, but it was with a heavy heart that Salina abandoned her position. Jeremy had not come for her, and given the volume of the disturbance, she reluctantly acknowledged that the fighting would keep him away for at least another day.

At her aunt's house, Salina sought solitude as a refuge. She sat alone on the window seat in Delia's room, facing the direction of Brandy Station. Staring down the street in hopes of seeing some sign of Jeremy, the only thing she saw was the smoke and haze of battle soiling the air from some four miles away. *Where is he?* she questioned inwardly. *Dear Lord, I'm sure he's out there in all of that! Please, keep him alive today, and safe. Don't let him die—I love him too much!"*

The fighting raged for hours on end. It was late when the ambulances began to arrive, and orderlies brought the wounded into the house. Salina shrugged off her lethargic disappointment and hurried into action, for she knew her hands were needed. As she descended the wide staircase to the entry hall, she found herself pulled into the flurry of activity. Dozens of injured soldiers lay suffering in the double parlour, the dining room, the study, out on the porch and in the side yard. The ghastly scene before her was not new. Salina's first experience working in a field hospital came after the battle near Chantilly, and in Richmond she'd worked in both a private and a general hospital. Salina knew what to do to be useful. Now was not the time for her to wallow in self-pity, not when others needed her so desperately. She paid no mind when in a matter of minutes the gown that should have been her wedding dress became saturated with blood.

Working tirelessly, Delia, Clarice, Ruby, Tessa, Taylor Sue, and Salina ministered to wounded and dying soldiers, some groaning, others writhing in pain. Salina listened as she rendered what comfort she could; piece by piece she formed an idea of the savage fighting that had transpired around Beverly's Ford, Kelly's Ford, St. John's Church, and the crucial high ground of Fleetwood Hill.

For fourteen hellish hours, the two sides crashed in headlong charges and counter-charges. It was said that the Confederates retained possession of the battlefield, but the Federal horsemen had put up a deadly fight. The Rebels grudgingly had to admit that the Yankee cavalry were much improved over past clashes. The Federals had retreated from the field in the end, but there were those who said, with some bitterness, that they gave it up because they *wanted* to, not because they *had* to. The Yankees had struck hard and with a vengeance, and the harsh lesson learned by the Rebels was one of profound foreboding.

The lone doctor in the house saw to as many of the men as he could, but there were so very many, and not nearly enough medicine to go around.

Salina sat with a man who'd had the bones in one leg shattered and whose arm bore a gaping sabre slash that had nearly taken it off. She offered him a drink of cool water from a canteen, and she hastily wrote a letter for him, promising to send it off to his wife at the first opportunity. Then she attended to a captain who'd been engaged in the fighting near St. John's Church. He knew he had but a short time left to him, and he seemed more concerned about having a report prepared for his superior officer than he was over the wounds he'd incurred.

Salina rapidly wrote the report he dictated to her. Due to the captain's detailed narrative, she could vividly imagine General Stuart spurring his mount, riding hard all over the battlefield, yelling orders, dispatching couriers to crisscross the fields, sending men wherever the threat of the enemy was greatest, maneuvering his troops with speed and skill. According to the captain's conclusions, the Rebels had successfully prevented those people from discovering General Lee's immediate plans for the Army of Northern Virginia, and had sent them back across the Rappahannock River. In a raspy voice the captain implored Salina, "Please, have the report delivered to my colonel at your earliest convenience, if at all possible."

"I'll do what I can," she promised. Next she jotted down the name and address of the captain's family, and offered a gentle, sympathetic smile. "Later on I'll send a note to your mother."

"You've been more than kind, miss. You've been a source of comfort amid the pain, and for that I am most thankful." A weak hand squeezed her arm to emphasize his gratitude; then he breathed his last, and the grip slowly changed from slack to stiff.

Salina knew the captain suffered no more, but death was not easy for her to accept. She plucked the talon-like fingers from her arm, laid his cooling hand across his breast, and drew the sheet over the face of the dead officer. Salina bit her lip, feeling as though a little part of her had died along with him. It was like that each time one of the men she cared for passed out of this life. Her insides twisted with impotent agony over the lives given and lost.

Shivering, Salina sat in silence as orderlies removed the body. Very shortly another wounded man needing attention would be brought to occupy the space. She sighed raggedly, wiping the glistening sheen of sweat from her brow with a swipe of her forearm. When a sudden eerie prickling sensation trickled down the back of her neck, Salina glanced warily over her shoulder to identify the cause, then sucked her breath in sharply. Her cheerless eyes sparked when they collided with a penetrating blue stare. "Jeremy," she whispered hoarsely.

He paused in the doorway of the parlour, one arm drenched with an alarming amount of blood, the other supporting C.J. in an upright stance. Salina's heart lurched before she realized that it was not Jeremy's blood that darkened the sleeve of his jacket, but C.J.'s.

"Come, quickly. You can lay him down over here." She motioned to the vacant bed at her side. Bentley followed directly behind Jeremy, and once C.J. was settled, he took over the care of the semi-conscious rider. "I'll fetch some water from the well," she suggested, her eyes searching in vain for an available pitcher or bucket; but even as she spoke, she felt a weakness in her knees and stayed where she sat.

Jeremy's dusty, blood-spattered boots halted next to her chair. Salina managed to meet his tired, haggard look without flinching. Swiftly he pulled her into his crushing embrace. "Sallie," he breathed in her ear, just holding her.

She was hard-pressed to determine which of them was more relieved by this unexpected reunion; both were trembling. Salina could hear the thump of his heartbeat as her ear rested against his broad chest, her head tucked under his darkly bearded chin. She hugged him tightly, words tumbling rapidly from her lips. "Oh, thank God you're alive! I was terrified that something horrible might've happened to you. Each time they brought in another stretcher I was sick with worry that it might be you—but mercifully it wasn't. You're here at last, whole and unharmed. Yesterday, I conjured all kinds of wild imaginings in my head. I devised a hundred reasons why you never arrived at St. Stephen's..."

He framed her face with his hands and looked her over. He took note of the smeared bloodstains on her clothes, her cheeks, her hands. The rose above her ear had withered for want of water, and the curls escaping from the chignon at the nape of her neck were sticky with perspiration, clinging to her damp skin. "I'm so sorry about yesterday, Sallie," Jeremy apologized with a catch in his voice.

"It's all right—you're not to blame. I had a notion that duty had called you away," she replied quietly. She hesitated adding, *Just as General Stuart predicted it might.* Finally, Salina looked up at him. "What happened to you, Jeremy? To C.J.? To the others? You're not hurt, are you?"

"I'm fine, and most of the others are, too." Jeremy reported a healthy status for Boone, Cutter, Curlie and Kidd Carney. "Remarkably, Bentley's not hurt, even though he did have his horse shot out from under him. Jake took a bullet in the thigh, but it's a minor enough wound that he'll still ride. C.J. wasn't so lucky—he was hit with a chunk of broken canister. Most of the casing fragments were taken out at the dressing station; if the wounds don't succumb to infection, he should live, but there's only a slim chance that he won't lose that arm."

Salina shook her head sadly at the news. She dared to ask, "And what about Pepper?"

"Pepper's dead," Jeremy answered in a low monotone.

"He was killed today, in all that fighting?" She didn't want to believe it.

"No. It was Harrison who died today," Jeremy replied rigidly. "Pepper was killed yesterday while we were skirting an enemy position; we got too close to their picket line. You see, General Stuart came back after our supper the other night. He sent us on a mission that normally should've taken us a few hours at the most, but we tangled with some detached Yanks out on patrol. We were outnumbered, but we skirmished as best we could, playing a deadly game of hide-and-seek with the blue-bellies. It took miles and hours longer than we anticipated to shake those people. Because of that, we had to take the long way back to camp and were just getting there when the Federals attacked Beverly's Ford before dawn."

Salina was much aggrieved to learn of the deaths of Pepper Markham and Harrison Claibourne. Her eyes displayed her sorrow, and the expression was mirrored in Jeremy's blue gaze. "Oh, Jeremy…"

Suddenly it was all he could do to wrench himself from her circling arms. He cleared his throat and said tersely, "I can't stay."

Tenaciously, Salina clung to his hand. "Please, Jeremy, don't go yet. We'll find somewhere we can talk. I'll fetch you something to eat, or…"

"There isn't time, Sallie." He extracted his fingers from her hold. "I had no choice but to bring C.J. here so he could get some help. I gambled that I might have a chance to see you as well, to tell you how sorry I am that yesterday was spoiled for us, but that's all I can do at present. We're moving—the army is heading out." Jeremy once more looked her over from head to toe and back again. He caressed her creamy cheek with his thumb, "I'm sure you were a beautiful bride—or should have been. Someday, Sallie. Someday." He glanced about the parlour-turned-hospital-ward, and his anger at the current state of affairs got the better of him. A harsh grunt rumbled in his throat as he practically shook her: "And for *this* I would marry you, Sallie," he said between clenched teeth, "To have the chance to make you my widow!"

"Don't say that!" Salina snapped, putting her fingers to his lips. "I would marry you regardless, Jeremy Barnes. Don't discount that I am all too familiar with the risks and consequences that might befall you in the line of duty. None of that matters to me. I will wait for you forever, if that's how long it takes, and I will do whatever I must to make you understand how much I love you," she vowed insistently. But her words fell on deaf ears, ignored and unheard.

Jeremy shook his sandy-blond head. He barked, "Just look at you: you're certainly wearing your share of blood spilled for the glory of Virginia!"

"Yes, I reckon I am!" she countered, her own temper flaring. Salina was bewildered by his almost sarcastic fury, but wise enough to judge that it was not actually directed towards her. She'd been shot at before, but she'd never been caught in the heated fray of advancing battle lines as Jeremy had been time and again. She could only imagine what horrors he had endured amid such lethal commotion, and she was almost sure that intense levels of stress and strain were the root of his unexpected irritability.

She looked down at herself. Jeremy was right: Taylor Sue's dress was beyond ruin, caked with the life-blood of the Confederate calvarymen she tended. She was disheveled and must be a forlorn sight to behold. She did not meet his eyes, unable to bear the intense agitation in them.

"You really should go change," Jeremy suggested, his tone a shade more tender.

"Yes, I reckon I should," she agreed, hoping to thaw his temper. She lingered at his side, daring to inquire, "Did we win, Jeremy?"

"We hold the field," he sighed in resignation, working to regain his composure. Jeremy's account was along the same lines as the deceased captain's report: "General Stuart seemed to be everywhere all at once, bellowing orders, rallying the men, riding at the head position with little thought for his own safety. He could have been killed in the thick of it just as easily as any of the rest of us. It was downright brutal—the charges, the hand-to-hand combat, the carnage. The fighting was a grisly nightmare—hot, frenzied, murderous. It's no wonder they sing *When This Cruel War is Over*. If we go north to make this invasion, and can win a convincing battle on *their* soil, maybe then this will be over." A nerve jumped along his taut jaw. "We may be involved in this campaign for the rest of the summer. I don't know when I'll see you again."

Salina reinforced her resolve. "I told you, I'll wait. I'll stay here until you come back for me."

"You don't belong here, you belong at Shadowcreek," he acknowledged gently. "I suppose you'd be as safe there as anywhere. Charlie Graham will be there to watch over you while I can't. Just never let your guard down until we find out for sure about John Barnes. You tell Taylor Sue the same. Pray for us, Sallie, it's going to be a hard fight ahead. I'll come for you when I can." Jeremy kissed her abruptly, then set her away from himself at arm's length. "Good-bye, darlin'. I love you."

He sauntered through the parlour and was out the entry hall before Salina could stop him. She stood staring after Jeremy, her mouth agape, her heart constricting as tightly as the clenched fists she held at her side.

Standing behind her, Bentley squeezed Salina's shoulders in a gesture of reassurance. "If ya'll permit me ta say it, Miss, I reckon our lieutenant hightailed it out of here 'cause he didn't want ya ta see his tears."

Salina pressed her lips into a small, quivering smile. She turned toward Bentley and said, "No, I suppose it wouldn't be considered very manly for that to happen, now would it?"

"Nope," Bentley shook his head. "The Lieutenant—he ain't runnin' from ya, Miss, he's still runnin' from himself a bit. It's dawnin' on him how much ya mean ta him. He needs ya. Days like today serve ta remind men of their own mortality. Aside from that, he's got orders. By tomorrow he'll be long gone from this place."

"But you'll be going with him, won't you, Bentley?" Salina asked anxiously.

"Aye," Bentley nodded with a wink and a wry grin. "And if I leave right now, I just might be able to catch up with him before he's reached the Maryland border!"

"Look after him for me, Bentley," Salina pleaded. "See that he doesn't do anything too reckless."

"There's a tall order," Bentley complained, "But I'll see what I can do." He made it a point to say good-bye to C.J., not knowing if the injured rider could understand his words. "Good-bye ta ya, too, Miss."

"Good-bye, Bentley, and Godspeed." Salina hugged him in farewell.

The doctor arrived to examine C.J.'s deep wounds, and Bentley took that as his cue to leave.

"Bentley!" Salina called, hurrying after him. "Could you do something else for me?"

"And what might that be?" the cavalryman queried.

Salina pulled the dead captain's report from her pocket. "Would you see that this is delivered to the colonel it's addressed to? I believe he's under the command of General Wade Hampton."

"Aye, I'll see ta it," Bentley assured her. "Anythin' else?"

"No," Salina shook her head. "I guess that's all."

"I'll tell the Lieutenant again how much ya love him," Bentley grinned. "That I surely will."

Salina marveled at Bentley's perception. Then C.J. groaned in pain behind her, and Bentley used the distraction as his chance to slip away, leaving Salina to resume her nursing duties.

Chapter Seven

*L*ije Southerland squinted as he strode purposefully from bright sunlight into the dark interior of the saloon. His shrewd sapphire eyes scanned the tables, searching through the thick smoke-blue haze that hovered beneath the low ceiling. "I thought you'd given that up," he said when he arrived at a table near the back with one lone occupant and a bottle of whisky a third gone.

"I did," Drake nodded once, his gravelly voice thick. "I'm not drinking to get stone drunk, Mr. Southerland, I'm just trying to forget." It'd been a long time since he'd touched a drink at all—back in St. Joseph the night of the gunfight, to be exact. Southerland hadn't come right out and said it, but the stern implication was that he didn't cotton to alcohol, or those who depended on it.

In fact, the owner of the South Union spread didn't come right out and say much about women, gambling, or fighting either, but Drake sensed the old man never had to. Many of the ranch hands and cowboys who worked for the SU brand were impressed by the rancher's unspoken, positive influences. Because they didn't want to risk his censure, a good number of them gave second thoughts to their actions out of respect for their employer; Drake was one of those men.

Seating himself in the chair next to Drake's, Lije didn't wait for permission before he picked up the crumpled telegram and read its contents:

> *Fort Laramie*
> *Wyoming Territory*
>
> *Drake—*
> *A letter addressed to you from one Aurora Dallinger of Boston, Mass. has been forwarded to the express office in Memphis. Having read it, I think you should do as Miss Dallinger suggests. Don't look back, Drake. Get on with your life. She's giving you a chance at everything you'll never taste otherwise out here in the desolate West.*
> *As for me, I thought I could wait for you, and would gladly have done so if you'd given me a glimmer of hope. Instead, I've become the wife of Corporal Gilbert Dade, a cavalryman stationed at Fort Laramie, who is not afraid to love me. Good-bye, Drake. It's better this way.*
> *I remain ever your friend if need be,*
> *the former Miss Lacy Whittaker*

"Who is this Lacy Whittaker," Mr. Southerland asked, "aside from someone who obviously cared about you very much?"

"She was a friend of mine," Drake replied coolly. "Her pa ran a way station along my route. She's a darling girl, but I never could quite bring myself to be the man she wanted me to be. Aw heck, her pa wouldn't have let her get tangled up with the likes of me anyhow. I knew that—even though Lacy didn't want to believe it. Old man Whittaker, he'd shoot me first. No, Lacy's right, it's better this way. Eventually the day will come when she'll forget me and she'll give her whole heart to this calvaryman husband of hers." Drake tried, unsuccessfully, not to think of another lovely lady he knew who'd also ended up as the bride of a cavalryman just two days ago...

Out of curiosity, Lije asked, "Have you received Aurora Dallinger's letter?"

Drake reached down to the saddlebag resting on the floor at his feet, propped up next to the table leg. He pulled an envelope from under the leather flap and tossed it carelessly onto the table. "Aurora Dallinger," he whispered the name hoarsely, his turquoise eyes clouding.

The old rancher studied the letter for several long and quiet moments.

Drake mutely watched the piano player as he pounded out one tinny-sounding tune after another. He waited for Southerland to say something, anything, but when he didn't, Drake glanced back and met the older man's knowing expression.

"I'll miss you on the next drive," Lije said sagely. "You're one of the best hands I've ever employed for the trail."

"Who says I'm going to leave you and go to Boston?" Drake raised an eyebrow in question and the scar on his forehead puckered.

"Miss Dallinger makes it sound as though seeing you is your father's dying request." Lije refolded the letter and handed it back into Drake's keeping. "You might regret it down the road if you don't at least make an effort to get there and find out why he wants to see you."

"Maybe," Drake said noncommittally.

"You've never been close to your father, I take it," Mr. Southerland surmised.

"My pa left me to be raised by my mother's brother after she died. I grew up with my Kiowa-Apache people. Pa didn't have enough courage to take me home to his uppercrust family in properly snobbish New England—after all, how would they ever admit that the favorite Dallinger son had *married* an Indian squaw and gotten a child by her? That would have raised too many eyebrows—he'd have been shunned by Bostonian society. I wouldn't have fit into that circumstance then anymore than I would now, if I decide to go."

"How old were you when your father went back east?" asked Mr. Southerland.

"Five, six maybe," Drake answered with a shrug. He only vaguely remembered the tall, black-haired, turquoise-eyed man who was his father. He dimly recalled the happiness and the love of those early years, followed by the more memorable devastation caused by the death of his mother. A harsh feeling of abandonment had haunted him since the day he watched his pa board the east-bound stagecoach. Drake thought he'd gotten over it, but it washed over him anew. "He never looked back." Drake took another swig from the whiskey bottle.

Lije Southerland confiscated the liquor and remarked, "But he still thinks on you. Evidently it would ease his mind to know that you'd grown to be a man. Take my advice, Drake: Find it within yourself to honor his request. Go, if it isn't already too late, and I'm sure you won't regret it."

Drake detected a note of experience in the old man's tone. "How would you know?"

Lije Southerland rested his elbows on the table and leaned forward with a reminiscent sigh. "My oldest son and I had a falling out of sorts just before he left to join the Union forces in Tennessee when the war broke out." Mr. Southerland agonized, "We never made our peace. He was killed at Shiloh and his body shipped back to us in a plain pine box. I never had the chance to tell him how much he meant to me. I suppose I expected him to know it without me saying so, but I was wrong in that, and in the quarrel we were embroiled in—but there's no help for that now. Go see your pa, Drake. Let him tell you what's in his heart."

Drake drummed his fingers on the tabletop. "I reckon I should—but if I do, that'll leave you short-handed when you head back to Texas."

"Not to worry, I'll manage to find another trail boss somehow," Lije said confidently. "Come on, let's get you cashed out. You'll have your wages to take with you. I want you to know you always have a job with me if you ever need it."

"I appreciate that, Mr. Southerland. Honest, I do." Drake shook the old rancher's hand.

Lije and Drake stepped back into the sunlight, crossed the crowded street and walked toward the bank. In his mind, Drake was already making plans. He figured he could be to Washington in roughly a fortnight, maybe less if he pushed it. Perhaps he'd pay a quick call at Shadowcreek…it wouldn't be all that much out of his way. Besides, it would be well worth it to see Little One again. He firmly reminded himself that she would be *Mrs. Jeremy Barnes* by now.

When the banking transactions were complete, Lije inquired, "So, who's this Aurora Dallinger?"

Drake flashed a dubious grin. "Well, I guess she's my sister."

☆☆☆☆☆☆☆

Culpeper Court House, Virginia

As Salina continued to care for the wounded after the battle at Brandy Station, she learned a little more about the fight from the soldiers who survived it. Told by firsthand participants, accounts of the intensity and fierceness gave Salina the chills.

Under the cover of mist early on June the ninth, the cavalry troops of Federal General Alfred Pleasanton, led by brigade commanders Buford, Gregg, and Duffié, had deployed for an attack across the Rappahannock River. Buford attacked the Confederates under "Grumble" Jones at Beverly's Ford and saw action near St. James Church. Gregg and Duffié attacked Robertson's gray-clad pickets at Kelly's Ford, driving them back toward Brandy Station. Fortunately for the Rebels, Duffié's column was delayed. He had gotten himself entangled at Stevensburg, clashing with the 2nd South Carolina and 4th Virginia cavalry units. By the time Duffié's men arrived at Brandy Station, they were too late to participate in the fight there.

Salina's head spun as she tried to sort the multitude of details into some semblance of order. She was dismayed to learn that General Stuart had been driven off Fleetwood Hill, where his headquarters had been established. Over the course of the day, the heights changed hands several times amidst perilous charges and countercharges. At one point, Major Henry B. McClellan of Stuart's staff had single-handedly manned a lone cannon on Fleetwood Hill, and had managed to keep disaster at bay.

Toward dusk, after fourteen long and barbaric hours of fighting, General Lee rode onto the field. He was stunned when he learned not only of the severity of the fight, but also that his son, Brigadier General "Rooney" Lee, had been badly wounded in the leg.

Rebel infantry from Rodes' division of Ewell's Second Corps had been on hand, but the engagement was predominantly a cavalry fight combined with Horse Artillery. When all was said and done, General Stuart had retained possession of Fleetwood Hill, but even he had to agree that he could not pitch his tents on the same ground where he had the previous day. He was compelled to move his headquarters a few miles to the rear due to the gore of dead bodies and the buzzing flies that abounded in the wake of the conflict.

Salina was encouraged in knowing that the Rebels inflicted more damage than they received. Three cannon and five hundred prisoners had been taken, and several battle flags had been captured.

General Stuart was pleased with the mettle of his men, who had pitched into the fracas. They might have been surprised early on, but by day's end they considered themselves the victors.

Yet a disconcerting idea invaded Salina's mind: were the Rebels the only ones watching the two recent cavalry reviews? Surely the Yankees had their own spies...had they been sent to make a count of Stuart's force? Had Pleasanton known for a fact that the Rebel cavalry was near Brandy Station, or had he run into them by mere chance?

One of the men Salina read to said he thought the Yankees were finally wising up and learning how to use their cavalry—they took a page from Stuart's successful drilling and fighting methods, learned from their previous defeats, and turned the results of their training back against the Rebels. The Federals were a much improved and better led cavalry than the Southerners were wont to give them credit for, and from this engagement on, the Yankee cavalry would prove that they were not necessarily the inferior of the two opposing sides. Those people in blue could hold their own in a fight, and their confidence grew by immeasurable bounds.

Salina read about the rumors circulated that some of General Stuart's important papers had been captured, but there was no foundation to such claims. Southern newspapers criticized Stuart strongly, calling the action at Brandy Station a "very unpleasant affair" and a "disastrous fight." Some of Stuart's own staff and fellow commanders thought he had managed his troops poorly that day, and one staff officer purportedly wrote home to his wife:

> *I suppose it is all right that Stuart should get all the blame, for when anything handsome is done he gets all the credit. A bad rule either way. He however retrieved the surprise by whipping them in the end.*

Stuart never read those particular sentiments, but he did read General Lee's report:

> *...The disposition made by you to meet the strong attack of the enemy appear to have been judicious and well planned. The troops were well and skillfully managed...*

The civilian press, however, did not share General Lee's appraisal of General Stuart's actions. In fact, when Salina read the scathing articles in the Richmond papers, she was outraged. Oh, the reporters didn't come right out and blast Stuart's name, but reading between the lines, one could clearly see that they didn't have to.

There was even a letter addressed to President Jefferson Davis from an anonymous woman in Culpeper:

> *...If General Stuart is allowed to remain our commanding general of cavalry we are lost people. I have been eye witness to the maneuvering of General Stuart since he has been in Culpeper...Gen. S. loves the admiration of his class of lady friends too much to be a commanding general. He loves to have his repeated reviews immediately under the Yankees' eyes too much for the benefit and pleasure of his lady friends for the interest of the Confederacy.*

The note, signed by a "Southern Lady," was forwarded to General Stuart from the War Department with the jesting suggestion from his good friend Custis Lee that he either stop such attentions to *specific* ladies, or he should make much ado over *all* the ladies. Stuart failed to share the humor, seeing it as an implication of some assumed immoral act on his part. He replied to a member of his staff, "That person does not live who can say that I ever did anything improper of that description."

Salina smarted from the sting of the unkind remarks leveled against General Stuart, for in a manner of speaking, she herself was one of those ladies who had been a recipient of the General's occasional attention. "Never was there anything in the General's demeanor to suggest impropriety," she told Taylor Sue adamantly. "It sounds as if this *'Southern Lady'* isn't aware that the reviews were at the request of General Lee—General Stuart was following orders."

She read the lines again and stated, "I'm not yet Jeremy's wife, but I'd be furious if someone made such derogatory remarks against him. I've met Mrs. Stuart; she's a charming lady, and it was plain to see how much she and the General mean to one another. I do hope she doesn't believe such nonsense as this article. I'm sure she knows her husband better than the general public ever will. These words, if you ask me, are written out of pure spite and jealousy!"

Taylor Sue was just as indignant. "They paint with their venomous pens only the dark side and not the good. With the exception of this Culpeper woman, how many of the Richmond reporters were really here and saw it for themselves, I wonder?"

Salina shrugged, having no way to know the answer to that question. She would have quit reading the newspapers altogether, but they were the only source of information regarding the movements of the armies.

General Lee ordered the Army of Northern Virginia on a northward march the morning of June tenth; its true destination remained to be seen. This second invasion of the North had all the South's hopes pinned to it. There was, of course, the issue of forage and supplies, and an effort to draw a portion of General U.S. Grant's army away from besieged Vicksburg. The question was renewed as to whether European support might not come to the aid of the Confederacy if a decisive victory in enemy territory could be achieved. *This summer will be crucial in the history of the Confederate States of America*, Salina predicted. Her eyes and the eyes of the entire nation looked anxiously northward.

Chapter Eight

June 16, 1863

*F*or most of the journey from Culpeper Court House to Fairfax Station, Salina was quiet, contemplative, and seemed to be far, far away from where she actually was. She read a little, dozing a bit here and there. She didn't have much to say even when Reverend Yates met them at the depot. It was Taylor Sue who told him how they had cared for the wounded the week after the cavalry battle at Brandy Station. Now that their assistance was no longer a necessity, Taylor Sue, like Salina, longed to be back at Shadowcreek.

Reverend Yates shared with them what information he had gleaned from outside sources and the Remnant. The Army of Northern Virginia had begun the march toward Maryland on the tenth of June. Stuart's cavalry had orders to screen Ewell's corps, staying between the Rebel infantry and the Yankees. The cavalry was responsible for defending the mountain passes at Thoroughfare, Snickers, and Ashby's Gaps. The Rebel infantry had clashed with Federal forces: Rodes was victorious over the Yankees at Berryville, and Ewell won the two-day engagement fought at Winchester.

"Ethan will be putting all his energy into doctoring the wounded," Taylor Sue stated aloud, while silently praying for the safekeeping of her husband. "He refuses to rest as long as there's something he can do to relieve anyone's pain."

"I wonder if he has medicine," Salina murmured absently, knowing there was never enough to go around in the Southern medical corps. She shook her head. "God help them all."

"Amen," Reverend Yates added.

The instant the parson drove the wagon onto Shadowcreek land, Salina tugged on his sleeve. "Please, Reverend, stop here. I want to get out."

Reverend Yates crossed over the bridge that spanned the stream running through Shadowcreek. "Whoa, Esau," he commanded the horse, pulling on the reins to bring the wagon to a standstill.

Salina was quick to shed her shoes and stockings, stuffing them inside her satchel. "I'll meet you at the cabin. I won't be long." She climbed out of the wagon and waved back to the Reverend and her sister-in-law. She headed down the gentle incline, making her way to the creek bed, strolling barefoot along the bank.

Taylor Sue watched her go. "Her spirits have been so low these past few days. I wish there was a way to either put a genuine smile back on her face or trigger a good cry so she can get it over with. I don't know how she does it—she just keeps going on."

Reverend Yates clucked, "Giddy-up," setting Esau into motion again. "Miss Salina," he commented to Taylor Sue, "is a survivor."

At the stream's edge, Salina rolled up her sleeves and hitched up her skirts to prevent them from getting wet as she waded into the cool water. The trees on either side of the shallow waterway formed an arched canopy that cast dancing shadows along the length of the creek. Following the stream, Salina stayed on the winding liquid path until she turned the bend. On the hill above her was where the main house of Shadowcreek had proudly stood. She closed her eyes for an instant, almost able to imagine that the rambling white frame and brick structure still crowned the highest ridge. A hundred happy memories came to mind in a rush. As Salina climbed the slope, however, the memories faded into bleak reality. The house had been burned by Major John Barnes and his subordinate Yankee troops. The Hastings home had been intentionally reduced to piles of rubble and ash.

Salina picked her way carefully through the debris. Only the chimneys and one corner of the parlour still stood, the walls charred and blackened. The lower half of a window remained intact, and Salina rested her forehead against the bubbled and wavy glass pane.

That frantic night had been the first of many times when Salina had to reluctantly place her trust in Duncan Grant. In each instance he proved himself reliable and honored his word to Daddy, and to this day he still saw to the safety and well-being of the remaining Hastings as best he could, for Garrett's sake. Daddy and Duncan had been such good friends. The foundation of their relationship went back to their days together as cadets at West Point. Difference of philosophies had not broken the bond between the Northern man and the Southern man—death alone had achieved that end.

Sighing, Salina left the ruins of the house and ambled toward the iron-fenced cemetery where her Hastings relations were buried. She took a rose from a nearby climbing bush and laid it at the base of the headstone erected in the memory of Garrett Daniel Hastings. It was an empty grave marker, however, for Daddy's body was interred elsewhere.

The sound of a horse and rider met Salina. She was reminded of the cold winter morn when she'd first met General Stuart here, on his way to breakfast at the Sully Plantation, returning from his Christmas Raid at Dumfries.

"Hello, Charlie!" she called, recognizing the rider as her family's long-time friend and neighbor.

"Salina." Charlie Graham tipped his hat. "Taylor Sue sent me to fetch you. She wanted me to warn you."

"Why? What's the matter?" Alarm flared in Salina's eyes.

"Nothing serious," Charlie qualified. "It's just that you and Taylor Sue happened to come home on the day Mary Edith planned a going-away dinner for Randle. He's leaving first thing tomorrow."

"Well, then I'm glad we arrived in time. I would like to see Randle again before he goes back to running the blockade," Salina said earnestly.

Charlie continued his explanation: "Mary Edith's gone and invited Lottie and her Yankee husband to join in the farewell."

"But Randle and Colby are enemies," Salina protested unnecessarily. "They are officers of opposing forces."

"They've agreed to a mutual truce, just for tonight, and I think they're honorable enough to follow through with the effort.

They're brothers-in-law, after all, for better or worse," Charlie added sarcastically, "Come what may."

Salina nodded. The reason Taylor Sue had sent Charlie after her was sinking in: Lottie would already be at the cabin when Salina arrived.

She remembered that their last confrontation had held a trace of civility, but generally speaking, Lottie and Salina were at perpetual odds. It was Lottie, not Salina who had cultivated the differences between them over the years. Lottie was ruthless, conniving, and possessed a mean streak a mile wide. When Salina had returned from her journey to San Francisco and her subsequent stay in Washington, Lottie had concocted lies and arranged situations to drive a wedge of distrust between Salina and Jeremy. Lottie's scheming had nearly worked; she had come close to tasting success with the assistance of the Yankee Lieutenant Lance Colby. Lottie would have done anything to get Jeremy for herself, to take him away from Salina out of pure spite. But her malicious game backfired. Lottie turned up in the family way, and she tried to pin the deed on Jeremy in order to force a marriage between them. Colby, however, the true father of Lottie's baby, had stood up to Caleb Armstrong, admitting his guilt and his love for Armstrong's willful daughter. Lottie had gotten herself a husband by way of a quick marriage ceremony, though the groom was not the man she'd originally intended.

Charlie handed Salina her shoes and stockings. He pulled hair ribbons and a silver brush from his saddlebag, along with a looking glass. He also supplied a washcloth, hand towel, and a cork-stoppered bottle of rosewater. "Taylor Sue thought you might want to freshen up a bit before you have to face Lottie. Go on down to the creek. I'll wait for you here."

Salina nodded, "Yes. Thank you, Charlie, for your help. I won't be but a minute."

In truth, it was at least ten minutes before Charlie lifted Salina onto Starfire's back behind him for the short ride to the whitewashed cabin. In Charlie's opinion, Salina was quite beautiful enough for the coming encounter but he wisely held his tongue. He'd had designs on her once, but he was not the one Salina had chosen, and over time he'd come to live with her decision. It wasn't his place to shower her with compliments, much as he would like to. Her heart belonged to Jeremy Barnes, and that was all there was to it.

"Charlie, the gardens look wonderful," Salina told him as they rode past the productive parcels of land. "You've done wonders with the vegetables and with the flowers."

"I got two acres of oats and one of corn. Not much, but it's better than none. The orchard is doing well, too. There'll be apples galore later on," Charlie predicted.

In the clearing Salina spied Charlie's tent and saw the smoke rising from the cabin's chimney. Mary Edith's lone guard dog paced on the porch, and Salina suddenly missed the dog she'd once had named Duchess.

A neat phaeton was parked alongside the porch. Salina dismounted, then Charlie did the same. He leaned heavily on his crutch, having lost a leg, amputated just above the knee after a bad wound suffered in battle at Stones River, near Murfreesboro, Tennessee.

"Well?" Charlie glanced down at Salina. "Are you ready for this?"

Salina took a deep breath and nodded affirmatively, knowing it was pointless to delay the inevitable. She prayed for the strength to "turn the other cheek" if Lottie chose to be disagreeable, then threw open the front door. "Anybody home?"

"Salina!" Mary Edith embraced her cousin warmly. "Welcome back! We've missed you so since you've been away! You don't mind us having Randle's going-away party here, do you? It was just so much easier than traveling over to Ivywood, what with the twins and all. Bonnie Lee is napping just now, but Annie Laurie's being entertained by her pa. I sure am going to miss his help with the girls!" Mary Edith lamented. "How will I manage without him? I'll miss him something fierce!"

Salina stood beside the rocking chair where Randle Baxter crooned over one of his twin daughters. "Good to see you, Randle. I'm glad we made it back in time to say good-bye before you left."

"Yes, so am I." Randle hefted his daughter to his shoulder. "You're looking as lovely as ever."

"Thank you," Salina smiled appreciatively. "You look quite fit yourself." Her eyes darted about the room until they found Taylor Sue's. Salina's eyes expressed gratitude for Taylor Sue's thoughtfulness in sending Charlie out to find her. The last thing Salina wanted was to come in barefooted and rumpled from the journey home. She knew Lottie well enough to know she would take any opportunity to make Salina feel inferior.

Taylor Sue's nod of understanding was almost imperceptible. She set the table while Mary Edith rapidly stirred the kettle hanging on the low hook of a crane over the fire.

"Allow me to echo Randle's compliment," Lieutenant Lance Colby approached Salina, kissing her hand. "You do look lovely, Salina."

"It's kind of you to say so, Lieutenant." Salina lowered her gaze. His appearance always startled her, for at a glance Lance Colby bore an uncanny resemblance to Jeremy Barnes. After closer inspection, however, one could discern that Colby wasn't quite as tall as Barnes, or as broad of shoulder. Colby's hair was a lighter shade of blond, his eyes a much paler blue. The more careful the examination, the less alike the two lieutenants looked—especially when it came to the color of their uniforms.

Aside from proving his honor by marrying Lottie, Colby's other redeeming quality lay in the fact that he worked for Duncan Grant. To a certain degree Colby could be trusted, as evidenced on the occasions when he relayed messages through the lines between Duncan and Salina. The messages generally pertained to family matters; seldom was anything of a military nature exchanged.

To this day, Colby found it difficult to fathom that the graceful young woman before him had once worked as a spy in her father's Network. Salina, he'd come to belatedly discover, was as intelligent and clever as she was beautiful. He himself had given the order for her arrest in San Francisco, but by then the hatred he initially fostered for her had melted into grudging respect, then lapsed into caring. She'd never hidden her feelings about Jeremy Barnes from him, and Colby had known from the start that Salina would never return his affection. His dealings with Lottie had a distinct role in altering his romantic inclinations toward Salina Hastings, but Colby still admired her for the young lady she was.

"We're beyond such formality as rank, don't you think, Salina? You may call me Lance, if you like, or Colby if you prefer, but I think we know each other well enough by now that we need not stand on military decorum. Randle and I have set all of that aside for the evening. Won't you do the same?"

"All right, Colby," Salina acquiesced, "Just for tonight." She removed her hand from his lingering grasp.

At last Salina faced Mary Edith's twin sister. "Hello, Lottie."

"Salina," Lottie returned coolly. She sat, in all her assumed on airs, at the head of the table, making a dramatic study of her own gold wedding band.

"How are you feeling lately? Is everything well with the baby?" Salina made an attempt at conversation.

"Oh, I'm quite all right," Lottie sighed, and condescendingly reported, "The baby is just fine, or so Dr. Phillips is convinced."

"That's good to hear," Salina remarked. She tucked an errant strand of hair behind her left ear, and in so doing, her engagement ring glittered in the lantern light.

"What have you there, Salina, a new bauble?" Lottie deigned to inquire.

"Jeremy gave it to me while we were in Culpeper." Salina straightened the ring on her left hand's third finger.

"Really?" Lottie asked with feigned innocence. "So that was *prior* to his jilting you?" Lottie intentionally goaded her cousin for a response, "Word has it Jeremy Barnes abandoned you, Salina. They say he left you standing at the altar."

Salina's cheeks flamed in hurt and embarrassment. *Is that what people were really saying about them? That Jeremy had jilted her?* She took a calming breath, understanding that Lottie was being deliberately mean, as was her usual practice. Salina, when she replied, hoped her words sounded sincere, but instead they held a hollow echo of dejection: "He didn't jilt me."

Taylor Sue interjected, "There was reason why their wedding was interrupted. Jeremy was delayed by his orders. He didn't deliberately abandon her, as you are mistakenly insinuating, Lottie. Duty kept him away that day, but never fear, he's already indicated that he'll be back for Salina and they will be wed just as soon as the circumstances will allow."

"Oh, but of course," Lottie demurred, rolling her cornflower-blue eyes, "Whenever *that* might be." She accepted the glass of lemonade her husband practically shoved into her hands. Colby's glance was one of warning, but Lottie willfully disregarded it. Without batting an eye, Lottie added pointedly, "Salina, you simply mustn't listen to the rumors that imply you're not woman enough to pin your man down." Judging by the wounded expression in Salina's eyes, Lottie presumed she'd hit a raw nerve. She maliciously decided to twist the knife just a little. "Knowing Jeremy, I'm sure he would never use the cover of *duty* to cloak a change of heart; he's far too honorable for that—isn't he?"

Salina's eyes flashed fire, and she grit her teeth to prevent a tempestuous rebuttal. Lottie was openly baiting her, and Salina refused to stoop to defend either Jeremy's honor or her own. At the sound of a baby's cry, she excused herself from the table. "I'll check on Bonnie Lee for you, Mary Edith."

Lottie all but gloated. If no one else in the room heard the pleased purring, Colby did, and once again he considered his wife an ill-tempered she-cat. He knew she took delight in having driven Salina from the table, and Colby made sure Lottie felt the press of his elbow against her ribs. He reached across in front of her for the basket of biscuits and whispered meaningfully, "One more scene like that and I'll remove you from this place so quickly it will make your pretty little head spin. Be polite, Mrs. Colby—we're guests here...of your sister's generous hospitality. Taylor Sue is trying to accept us, Salina's as unselfish as ever, even Randle and Charlie are willing to tolerate us. Don't make them regret inviting us," he threatened ominously.

By the time Salina returned to the table with the wide-awake Bonnie Lee, Lottie was carrying on about Washington society and the fashions available in the Northern capital city. "There certainly aren't the shortages there that they say are in Richmond." She went on and on, obviously pleased to hear the sound of her own voice.

It was nearly impossible to contain discussion to neutral topics. Everything, in one way or another, stemmed back to the war. The minute the dessert dishes were cleared away, Colby intentionally brought an early end to the gathering. He declined a cup of coffee, even though it was the genuine article and not some form of creative Southern substitute. Colby didn't want to know where they'd procured the coffee, or the sugar, or the delicious ham. He claimed exhaustion, and declared it would be late as it was before he and Lottie would arrive back at Ivywood. Before he could depart, however, he needed to speak with Duncan's stepdaughter.

"Might I have a word with you, Salina?" Colby inquired cordially. "Outside, perhaps?"

Salina granted his request. She stood on the porch, her back to the glass-paned window, arms folded across her chest.

"My apologies for Lottie's thoughtless remarks," Colby began.

"They weren't thoughtless remarks, Colby." Salina's jaw clenched. "They were calculated to cut deep. I know her underhanded ways. I've just never learned how to keep from reacting, so it's my own fault that I allow her heartlessness to afflict me. You'd think, after growing up together through all these years, that I'd be accustomed to it. I just don't have thick skin where she's concerned," Salina shook her head in resignation. "Lottie knows exactly where to place her barbs to do the most possible damage."

"Pay her no mind," Colby advised. "That will at least annoy her, if only a little."

"Then she strikes out worse at the very next opportunity." Salina knew from experience. "She doesn't think much of me at all."

"On the contrary," argued Colby. "She thinks quite a lot of you, otherwise she wouldn't waste her time trying so hard to get you riled. Tonight it was easy to see through her lies. You're woman enough to get your man, Salina, without a doubt. I know—as do Charlie, Randle, and all the rest of the men out there fighting—that when duty calls, we have no choice but to follow through. You, at least, understand that. Lottie doesn't. If you were my girl, I'd be back— just as I'm sure Jeremy Barnes will be, to make you his own at the earliest opportunity that presents itself."

Having no reply to Colby's observations, Salina mutely stared up into the starry night. She waited patiently for the reason he had drawn her out. It wasn't long in coming.

"Here." Colby handed her a letter from Mamma. "This is for you, and Duncan sends his best."

"Thank you." Salina tucked the envelope into her pocket. "I appreciate your playing the courier, in spite of the risk involved."

"Salina, I told Duncan I'd ask a favor on his behalf." Colby touched her shoulder, turning her to face him. "He's wondering if you might consider going to Gettysburg to be with your mother— at least until the baby is born, maybe a bit longer. He says Annelise is very lonely for you. Just having you there could cheer her tremendously. Will you think on it, Salina? There's no need for a hasty answer. I'll be back in Fairfax in a couple of days. I'll drop by Tabitha Wheeler's boarding house. You can leave word for me with her, as I assume that you'd rather not be seen with me. I understand your Rebel pride," he said leniently.

Salina suppressed a grin. In his mind, Colby still had a hard time reconciling either her Southern upbringing or her devotion to Virginia. She could almost feel his misguided pity because she did not believe in the Union cause. "All right," she agreed to the terms. "I'll think on it, and I'll give Tabitha my answer."

Colby nodded. Softly, he commented, "Again, my apologies for my wife's inappropriate behavior. If it's any consolation, duty notwithstanding, my guess is that it must have pained Barnes greatly to postpone your marriage. If I was him...well, I'm not him." Colby halted abruptly.

"May I ask you something, Colby?" Salina gathered her courage.

"Of course, anything," Colby quickly replied.

"Is it true that you carried a daguerreotype of me in your breast pocket on our return voyage from San Francisco to Washington?" queried Salina.

Colby hesitated, then confessed the truth with a solitary nod.

"Do you still—even since you've married my cousin?" Salina inquired, arching an eyebrow.

His answer was to pluck the photograph in question from the inside pocket of his blue jacket.

"If you don't mind, Colby," Salina held out her hand, "I'd like it back. It belongs to me."

"I beg to differ." Colby reluctantly relinquished the miniature portrait into her palm. "I was with Duncan the day he purchased it from an Irish photographer—he paid twenty dollars for that print."

"Twenty dollars?! He must have thought it worth it at the time. It helped you find me in San Francisco—as I'm sure you showed it to a good number of people between here, St. Joseph, and California, didn't you?" Salina challenged.

"Aye, that I did," Colby admitted.

"Well, since I was captured, it served its purpose. And since you have no further use for it, I would like to send it to Jeremy," Salina stated evenly. "I'm sure Duncan won't mind the expense."

"I suppose you're right." Colby stuffed his hands deep into the pockets of his blue woolen trousers. "I'm sure Barnes will treasure the likeness of you, though I suspect he carries a mental picture of you wherever he goes."

Salina smiled. "He's admitted as much, but I want him to have this just the same."

"Very well." Colby nodded, red-faced and uncomfortable. "And now, I think I'd best collect my wife. We'll be out of your way shortly. Thank you for tolerating us. It seems to have pleased Mary Edith to see Lottie again—it's just too bad everyone else has to be made miserable about it. Those two may be twins on the outside, but I've never seen two people more unalike on the inside," he said, shaking his head. "Take care, Salina. I'll see Tabitha concerning your answer to Duncan's request."

"Good-bye, Colby." Salina slipped the daguerreotype into her pocket with Mamma's letter. It was a distinct relief to know that her photograph was no longer in Colby's possession. It simply wasn't proper—he should carry one of his own wife with him instead. Salina was sure Lottie would insist on having a new gown before she would assent to a sitting at a photographic gallery in the Yankee capital, but Colby didn't seem to be lacking in funds for such items. She almost felt sorry for Colby and wondered if he knew that while Lottie might not love him for himself, she certainly had an affinity for his money and had no qualms whatsoever in spending it at will.

Even after the Colbys made their departure, Salina remained on the porch. Charlie crutched his way over to her, joining her on the swing. "Mind if I smoke?" he asked.

"It's a nasty habit, Charlie," Salina complained, but she didn't deter him.

"There are worse," he countered gruffly, puffing on his pipe. "You all right?" he queried, intending only friendly concern.

"I will be," Salina answered. "Somehow, I've got to shake this lethargic melancholy that threatens to overwhelm me. I've got to get on with my life and quit moping about."

"Amen," Charlie nodded. "If my memory serves me right, I seem to recall how you wouldn't let me wallow in self-pity when you nursed me on the train ride north from Richmond. Remember?"

"I remember," Salina assured him. With a grin she added, "You were a horrible patient."

"Ethan told me the same thing. I wanted to die after I lost my leg, but he wouldn't let me give up hope," Charlie reflected. "I'm glad now that I didn't. You shouldn't give up hope either. You just need to get back to being your sweet, joyful self, and let go of the pain. No easy thing, I know that all too well, and I guarantee it won't happen overnight. But you won't know until you try. So, I dare you."

It was good to hear Salina's melodic giggle again. It rippled forth like waves upon a glassy pond after a stone has been skipped across the surface. "You dare me?" Salina raised an eyebrow in question. "Well, you know I always like a good challenge."

"Yup," Charlie nodded, "I know it well."

Salina sighed, looking up at the bright diamond-like stars. Charlie stopped the swing and left her alone with her thoughts. "G'night, Salina," he said, making his way down the steps and across the yard to his tented residence.

"Good night, Charlie," she called after him. "And thank you."

"Yup," came Charlie's reply, a gray stream of smoke flowing over his shoulder.

*Stars which glitter in deep, inky skies, Cannot truly compare with the sparkle in her eyes...*Salina didn't stay on the porch for much longer. She returned to the cabin to find that everyone had bedded down for the night. Taylor Sue was upstairs in the loft, the babies were quiet, and Randle and Mary Edith lay in the bed behind the quilted partition at the opposite end of the room, whispering sleepily.

Salina lit a tallow candle and touched the spring catch on the side of the hearth. Silently the secret panel slid open. She disappeared into the yawning hole that led down to an underground passageway and the tunnels that ran beneath the cabin. She sat down on the cot, crossing her legs under her, in the little room where Jeremy and his men had been known to seek refuge when in danger. She set the candle on the small desk and then gathered the pillow to her, hugging it tightly while she rocked back and forth.

Jeremy had laid his sandy-blond head on that pillow many a night; just holding it made her somehow feel closer to him. The candle burned low, and when the light snuffed itself out, tears finally found their long overdue release. The salty torrents streamed unchecked down her face in the darkness. Since the afternoon she was to have been married, Salina had managed to keep the storm pent up, but now there was no restraining the violent sobs that wracked her slender form.

After a long, long while, her shoulders quit shaking and the tears were spent. Only whimpering hiccups lingered, and then they, too, subsided. Salina lay down, staring into the darkness until sleep claimed her exhausted mind and body. She drifted into a deep slumber with Jeremy's name on her lips and a prayer in her heart.

☆ ☆ ☆ ☆ ☆ ☆ ☆

Middleburg, Virginia
June 17, 1863

Isabelle Barnes could not have been any more amazed when she answered the insistent knocking at her front door. "Jeremy?" Here was just about the last person she expected to see at her doorstep.

"Aunt Isabelle," Jeremy greeted her with the same title as always. Bending down, he placed a loyal kiss on the woman's cheek. It had been nearly three years since he'd seen her. "Mind if I come in?"

"Why, you could knock me down with a feather!" Isabelle exclaimed, her hand over her heart. "What on earth possessed you to come here?"

"I came to see you," Jeremy answered, tipping his sandy head to one side. In a sense, his coming here was somewhat of a reckoning. His sapphire eyes glittered. "Aren't you happy to see me?"

"Delighted, my boy, delighted," Isabelle hastily assured him. "It's just that you took me by surprise. It weren't you I was expecting, that's for certain sure." She looked up at him, feeling a remote twinge of pride to see that he'd grown into an exceptionally fine young man, aged twenty years by now, if she remembered correctly.

"If not me, then who were you expecting? Is John coming home today?" Jeremy asked outright.

"I hardly think so. He don't come here much since the war began. Don't think I've been complaining about it, neither," Isabelle blurted before she could prevent herself from doing so.

The sentiment behind the remark was not wasted on Jeremy. He studied the woman's lined face. "I fully understand, Aunt Isabelle—in fact, this is the first time I can recall you looking so well. No bruises, no tears staining your cheeks, no broken bones..."

"You hush now!" Isabelle insisted, abashed for speaking so openly of not missing the wretched man who was her husband.

"Well, at least he never used a whip on you, like he did on me," Jeremy tersely reminded her. Isabelle Barnes was one of the few people who knew he bore traces of a long, white scar down the back of one thigh and another low on his back. She knew because she had routinely tended to the injuries inflicted by the heavy hand and foul temper of John Barnes.

"Your Uncle John has a dark side to him," Isabelle said, almost as an excuse. "He gets so very angry sometimes, he just doesn't realize..."

Jeremy cut her off. "He's a mean drunk, worse than any common scoundrel. And he's *not* my uncle."

Isabelle blanched noticeably. She could not deny Jeremy's statement, and she faltered guiltily, "Someone surely must be telling you tales..."

"Tales? I think not." Jeremy shook his head gravely and countered, "You know the truth, don't you?"

Isabelle turned away from the tall, lanky young man towering over her. Clearly agitated, she wiped her hands on the front of her apron. She busied herself with fetching a tin mug for him and offered him something to eat or drink.

Jeremy declined. "Thank you, but no. I didn't come here for refreshment; I came here to get some answers!" He pounded his fist against the table.

Isabelle hesitantly sat across from Jeremy at the tiny kitchen table. She realized that he was old enough to know, but she could not bring herself to volunteer the information he sought. Although she had suffered under the wrath of John Barnes for many years, the man was still her husband, and she felt she owed him allegiance in spite of his cruel treatment. Isabelle asked, "What possessed you to run off to California like you did?"

Jeremy patiently answered, "I was old enough to fend for myself, and I had to get out of here before he beat me to death. He still wants to kill me, you know—he's tried, several times, but I am happy to report that those attempts have been unsuccessful to date."

Isabelle swallowed audibly. "As much as I wanted to, I never could stop him from hurting you. I do think I managed to stand between you and death on at least a handful of occasions," she admitted grimly. "You might have been better off if you'd stayed in California."

"I didn't know it at the time, but my heart was here, not out there in the west," Jeremy returned. "Are you going to tell me what I want to know?"

"If you know that John Barnes ain't your uncle, then you've already learned Campbell Barnes weren't your father. How'd you find this out? Certainly not from your mother," Isabelle deduced.

"Not likely. Actually, Salina Hastings discovered the truth in a coded journal, written in John Barnes's own hand," Jeremy told her. "His mind is twisted with an evil bent, and he's going to die trying to carry out his sinister vendettas against me and the Hastings family."

"The Hastings," Isabelle murmured ruefully, "Always the Hastings. His anger burned toward them long before you came along to add fuel to the fire."

"How could you marry such a man?" Jeremy asked bluntly. "Did you love him?"

Tears stung Isabelle's clouded eyes. "My father arranged for it. I had no dowry, no land, but I was pretty once…It was the best match I could hope for at the time. The Barneses had money, not overmuch, but enough to live comfortable. Cam's fondness for games of chance was inherited from his father before him. Between the two, they squandered the family fortunes by gambling it away. Then to meet a hefty debt, they was forced to put up some of their most prized acreage as collateral. John was furious. Because of the reckless natures of his father and brother, Henry Hastings was owed a great sum of money. Hastings was willing to dismiss the debt if the circuit judge would grant him permission to buy up the mortgaged lands. The judge agreed to the proposal, and the land that should've been John's inheritance was sold instead. Henry Hastings built up the Shadowcreek estate, and the farm was very profitable. Surely you can see where the bitterness took a firm root. I ain't saying John's right, but can you understand the disappointment of losing his birthright?"

"Having no birthright of my own, I don't have anything to draw a comparison with." Jeremy's broad shoulders lifted in a shrug. "The Shadowcreek lands were only part of it, though. I've heard about the duel that cost Irene her first love. Then, some twenty years later, Irene's husband Simon Hollis was killed in a shoot-out—also at the hand of Garrett Hastings. The circumstances were oddly similar—in both instances Garrett was forced to fight in self-defense," Jeremy told his aunt. "Garrett's been dead for the better part of a year, but that hasn't diminished John Barnes's determination to hunt down the surviving members of the Hastings family."

"He always says the circumstances favor them Hastings, no matter what. John won't never believe anything save he's been cheated out of what's rightfully his. Hatred's a deep, cankerous disease coursing through him. He's consumed with envy of them Hastings," Isabelle admitted. "And then there's you. His conviction is that Justine's indiscretion, what resulted in your existence, sullied the name of Barnes permanent. I fear 'tis all this combined that festers and fuels his dark rage, driving him to wipe out all those he holds responsible."

"That's it in a nutshell," Jeremy agreed. So far his aunt hadn't enlightened him concerning anything he didn't already know. He turned the subject, because there was still more he wanted to learn. "I never knew my mother much, only her brief attentions from time to time whenever she suffered compunction and came to see if I was alive. I know I have two sisters somewhere from her first marriage, but I've never met either of them. According to the entry in the journal, which Salina deciphered from code into plain English, Campbell Barnes was not my real father; you have already confirmed that."

"No, Cam weren't your father." Isabelle shook her head, refusing to meet Jeremy's probing blue eyes.

"So, there was a man that my mother had a tryst with somewhere in her scandalous past. Did you know him?" Jeremy asked.

"No," Isabelle said softly. "Justine didn't often confide in me—unless she needed help. Her marriage to Cam happened rather sudden-like. He'd pursued her for months after her first husband passed away, and Justine haughtily rejected his advances. She had a little money left to her, but her extravagant tastes ate the savings rapidly. Your half-sisters were sent to live with their grandparents in Maryland, I think, or maybe Mississippi? I can't remember which now. Justine went away on holiday for a time. When the money ran out, she had to come back. By then, Justine must have figured she was with child, I reckon. It was known to just a few that she'd broken off an engagement with a man from up north somewhere, I don't rightly recall…"

"That man, the one she was engaged to—he was my father," Jeremy concluded.

"Aye," Isabelle nodded, "That man was. Justine had hard labor bringing you into this world. She spoke some awful things, as women are wont to do during their travail. She talked of your father in strictest confidence. I've never told a living soul those condemning things she confessed on the day you were born…"

"What was his name?" Jeremy wasn't aware that he'd pounded the tabletop until he saw Isabelle jump in her chair. He softened his tone. "Did she ever tell you what the man's name was?"

"It was Evan," Isabelle whispered. "You bear the name of your sire within your own."

It was true, Jeremy's middle name was Evan. "But you don't know his surname?"

Isabelle shook her graying head. "Never did hear her make mention of it."

"The initials in the journal were E.S.—Evan fits, if they are indeed one and the same." Jeremy mused. "You never met him?"

Isabelle answered, "Oh, no. He never came round here. He weren't from these parts. Truth be told, I doubt if he ever knowed he fathered a son in Justine. I know once she married Cam she never saw him again. There were others, sure enough, but never again did she lay eyes on her Evan."

"Nor is she likely to," Jeremy said tersely, feeling as if he'd hit a dead end at full gallop. "John Barnes arranged for his own brand of retribution against E.S.—he had Evan killed in an infantry charge during the battle of Shiloh."

"Upon my word," Isabelle breathed, disturbed by the lengths her husband went to in order to mete out his revenge.

"So, my mother pretended I was the son of Campbell Barnes to cover up her sin," Jeremy ground out between clenched teeth. "You know, I worked like a dog in California to earn enough money to pay off the gambling debts Campbell left me as my inheritance, though that was after my mother abandoned me to the guardianship of John Barnes. I was told she fled to a safe haven somewhere in London. She never even said good-bye."

"Justine were real fond of the easy life," Isabelle confirmed. "She didn't bother troubling herself with what she considered matters of insignificance."

"I was just her son," Jeremy spat, "hardly insignificant."

"You must take after him—your coloring, your eyes. I expect that's why she was hard pressed to look at you—you're just a living reminder of potential scandal, my boy. You certainly don't favor your mother, though she's considered a beauty in her own right. This Evan must've been a very fine-looking man to catch and hold Justine's attention. I reckon that's your legacy, my boy. Handsome to look upon, that you are."

"Is that supposed to make up for something?" Jeremy demanded. "Lack of a real father, lack of a mother's love? Is that to make up for the beatings? It's all right because I have a countenance that's pleasant to look at?"

"Nothing can make up for the past, Jeremy." Isabelle covered his hand with her own. It was rough and gnarled from years of hard work, but it was warm and compassionate. "There ain't nothing I can do or say that'll change what's happened to you or alter the circumstances in your past. You're a man now, my boy, and you must make your own way. Forget what's behind—don't look back."

"How can I not look back when I have to constantly watch over my shoulder? John Barnes has tried to shoot me down. He had my real father killed—in battle, no less. He arranged to have Garrett Hastings shot. He tried to have Annelise Hastings arrested on false charges of treason. He kidnapped Salina to bait me. I got Salina away from him, and in the ensuing chase, I honestly thought I'd killed him. But that may not be the case after all. I've no proof whether he's dead or alive, but if he's alive, you can bet he'll find a way to track me down. I still can't decide who he hates the most: me, or the Hastings."

"He hates the Hastings for different reasons than he hates you. John believed Justine tricked Cam, deceived him—which she did," Isabelle clarified. "If your mother hadn't sailed for England after Cam died, she may have been dead herself by now. Cam loved her blind; in truth, he were the only protection she had. When he were gone, she had nothing."

"Well, she won't get anything from me, either," Jeremy said with determination. He pulled a small drawstring pouch from its hiding place between his chest and his soldier's blouse. He slipped the cord over his head and plopped the pouch down in front of Isabelle. "I set this aside for you alone, Aunt Isabelle. I give it to you freely, only if you promise me that John Barnes will never lay a hand on it. Do you give me your word?"

Isabelle stared open-mouthed at the gold coins filling the bag. "Where'd you get such a sum of money?"

"I earned it," Jeremy assured her. "I meant to come by here last August when I first returned to Virginia, but I got involved working with Garrett Hastings, and now I ride with Stuart's cavalry. It is by providential chance that we're here in Middleburg, so I snatched the opportunity to visit. It is my intention to do right by you, Aunt Isabelle. As you said, you were all that stood between me and death at the hand of John Barnes on more than one occasion. This is a mere pittance, a token repayment, for I know that every time you intervened on my behalf, it cost you—a bruise here, a slap there. He always made you pay for treating me with any sense of decency or kindness. I am grateful to you for trying."

"I didn't do hardly enough to warrant such thanks," Isabelle said glumly, "But I, too, wanted to live." She pushed the coins back at him. "It's not right that I should take this from you."

"But I want you to have it," Jeremy insisted. "Go away, don't be here if John comes back. It's enough to get you started and sustained for a good while. He's gone mad, I tell you, and there's no knowing what he might do—to you, or me, or any of the Hastings, for that matter. He's evil, and he's not above killing to satisfy his own sense of vindication. He uses his major's rank and the war as cover." Jeremy's stomach roiled as he became aware that nothing he was saying was news to Isabelle. She knew it all, and had for some time. Until now, she had no recourse, but now perhaps she might choose to follow his suggestion and leave this place while she still could under her own power.

Jeremy pushed his chair away from the table and stood, leaving the money pouch behind. "Thank you for the name of my father. It's not much, but it is something."

"What of you, Jeremy?" Isabelle put a hand on his arm. "If John ain't dead, what'll happen when he catches up to you again?"

Jeremy shrugged his broad shoulders. "God alone knows the answer to that; I certainly don't."

Affectionately, Isabelle patted the arm of the gray-clad cavalryman she would always consider her nephew. "May He keep you in His righteous hand, and safe from the wrath of John Barnes."

Chapter Nine

The Union War Department
Washington, D.C.

You are Lieutenant Alphonse Corbeau?" Major Duncan Grant asked the smartly-pressed, spit-shined man who stood at attention.

"Reporting for duty, sir." Corbeau snapped a brisk salute. "I'm told I'm to assume the responsibilities previously performed by Lieutenant Lance Colby, sir."

"Hmmm." Duncan rubbed his chin, reading the confirming orders. "So you are to be Lieutenant Colby's replacement."

"Yes, sir," Corbeau replied stiffly.

"At ease, Lieutenant." Duncan again studied the parchment pages for a brief instant. "According to your service record, you've seen quite a bit of action thus far. How did you wind up here?"

"Truth be known, sir, I would prefer to be out chasing that devilish Mosby, but a wound inflicted during a raid earlier this spring had me convalescing in a hospital in Alexandria," Corbeau explained. "It was at Miskel's Farm that I was shot, sir. My superior officer was notified that I was almost fully recovered and anxious to return to my unit, but he thought I needed a little more time to heal. He sent me here when he learned of your need for a qualified officer to step in and do the job."

"And you are qualified for this line of work?" Duncan queried. "Your paperwork indicates no previous experience with the Secret Service Bureau."

Corbeau's lips curled into a sardonic smile beneath his neatly trimmed mustache. "The work I did at the time was precisely that, Major—a secret. I've served as both spy and courier. I was to Richmond and back twice between Christmas and mid-March. My superiors have never been disappointed in me yet, sir."

"I don't need to remind you, then, that our work here is strictly confidential," Duncan said politely but firmly. "You will be expected to be a quick study. There is no room or tolerance for error. Do you understand?"

"Yes, sir. What can I do to be of service first?" Corbeau inquired.

Duncan laid aside the documents of introduction and recommendation. He'd never heard of this Alphonse Corbeau before, nor was he familiar with the signature of the colonel whose name appeared on the letters. Out of habit, Duncan exercised his suspicious nature; Corbeau would have to prove his worth.

"First, I want you to go to the telegraph office and see if there's any word on the cavalry, particularly regarding Stuart's whereabouts. Then we'll get you working on some of this filing. Colby wasn't the best organizer I've had the privilege to work with. Perhaps between us we can devise a more successful means of controlling this clutter." Duncan's sweeping gesture encompassed two-thirds of the little office.

"Yes, sir." Corbeau donned his kepi and saluted. "I'll be back shortly, sir."

"Carry on, Lieutenant," Duncan dismissed the officer. As soon as the man was gone, Duncan called in a trusted staff aide. "Check on this, please, Corporal Stanley. See if you can get me verification of the identity and military service record of our new Lieutenant Corbeau. Also, pull these three files: *Elisha Saunders*, *Eric Stenstrom*, and *Elkanah Sorrenson*."

"Right away, Major," the aide replied. Corporal Stanley scurried off to do Major Grant's bidding.

It was well after eight o'clock in the evening when Lieutenant

Lance Colby appeared at Duncan's office. "Where have you been?" Duncan wanted to know.

"Fairfax County—Shadowcreek, more specifically," Colby answered. "I've talked to Salina. I think she's going to agree to go to Gettysburg. Since you're sending me back there with dispatches tomorrow morning, I didn't press her for an immediate answer. She's promised to think it over, and I'm to collect an answer upon my return."

"And your wife?" Duncan questioned. "Will she go peaceably?"

"I haven't told her about the trip yet, but I will. And I didn't tell Salina that the two of them would be traveling companions, but I'm of the opinion that I can keep them from any serious confrontations." Colby shrugged, slightly chagrined. "Salina would never have agreed to consider the proposition if she knew Lottie was going too. But I know how to handle Lottie. I can keep her in check."

Duncan did not want to dwell on Salina's probable reaction to the impending traveling arrangements. It wasn't for certain that she would concede to go, but Colby's report had given him hope. Duncan knew it would mean a great deal to Annelise, and that was the important thing. "All right, if Salina agrees, then I want you to make arrangements to bring her here to Washington first. There are a few things I need to brief her on, and by then I should have another wire from my brother with an updated account of Annelise's condition. You can ride the train with them from here to Baltimore, but then they'll be on their own until they reach Gettysburg. I'll see that Orrin is notified as to what time they'll be arriving. He'll pick them up at the depot."

"I think they'll be all right," Colby said honestly. "Lottie will taunt Salina all the way, I'm sure, but if Salina can disregard Lottie's incessant prattle, she'll be fine."

"There's no other choice," Duncan pointed out. "They'll just have to deal with each other as best they can."

While the major and the lieutenant quietly discussed the logistics of bringing the girls through the lines from Virginia and into Washington, neither was aware that Corbeau hesitated outside the slightly open door, straining to hear to every word.

At a seemingly appropriate moment, Corbeau returned to Duncan's office. The major formally introduced the two lieutenants to each other, and then Corbeau gave his report of what he'd heard in the telegraph office.

"Late this afternoon, Kilpatrick's Cavalry clashed with the Rebel horsemen led by Munford. The Rebels were initially driven through the streets of Aldie and into the fields beyond the town, but they rallied and returned hot skirmishing. Confederate sharpshooters lined the stone walls, and when Kilpatrick's regiments headed back through the narrow roads, heavy fire rained down on them. Our cavalry managed to drive the Rebels back some distance from Aldie, but unfortunately they still hold the gap that's the shortest way through the Bull Run Mountains to the Shenandoah Valley. Casualties were high for both sides.

"In the meantime," Corbeau continued, "Pleasanton ordered Duffié with his 1st Rhode Island regiment to Middleburg. Shortly after 4:00 p.m., the Rhode Islanders surprised and captured Confederate pickets on the outskirts of the town. Duffié called for a charge, and in so doing, reportedly came very close to capturing General Jeb Stuart and a number of his staff. Duffié, knowing that the Rebel cavalry would come back in force, chose to stay and fight instead of withdrawing to Aldie. Duffié's men blockaded the Middleburg roads, and dismounted to make up a line of defense. The Confederates returned, striking from both the west and the south, and overran the Rhode Island defenders. Duffié, with only four officers and twenty-seven troopers left in his 'much-loved regiment,' then set out to join up with Kilpatrick. He had to fight his way through the enemy, who, according to Duffié's account, were 'in front, rear, and both flanks.'"

Duncan slammed his palm on the desktop in exasperation. "Close to capturing Stuart! *Close!* Yet evidently not close enough. That would have been quite the coup!" He paced the floor, agitated, still thinking aloud. "Stuart's a cagey one, and once again he has managed to slip through our fingers. Last summer he was *nearly* taken at Vediersville; then, just as now, the crafty Southern nuisance escaped with his hide intact. Stuart left his famously plumed hat behind in his haste to get away at Vediersville. This time we don't have even a token to show for coming *close* to taking him prisoner!"

Duncan returned to his desk. "God, grant us the manner in which to accept that which we cannot change," he muttered, "and give us the wisdom to do what we can instead!" He sifted through some papers, locating the maps he sought. For the moment, he pushed all thought of Jeb Stuart aside; there was other pressing business at hand. "Lieutenant Corbeau, tomorrow you will accompany

Lieutenant Colby to Fairfax Court House. Colby will introduce you to the necessary contacts at the provost marshal's office and at the outposts. You are to deliver these personally to the commanding officer there. On your return, see if you can glean any information concerning Mosby from the locals. If the man had regular head-quarters, he'd be much easier to pin down."

Duncan's comment was met with a wry grin from each lieutenant. That was one of the main reasons for Mosby's continued successes—he didn't do anything the "regular" way. Mosby and his men did not conduct themselves according to the book of traditional army regulations and rules; hence the designation of "Irregulars" had been applied to Virginia's newly formed 43rd Battalion of Partisan Rangers by both the South and the North.

The citizens of the area where Mosby operated were more apt to shelter the wily partisan leader and the band of "conglomerates" who followed him than to inform the Federals of his last-known whereabouts. It wouldn't be long before it was an established fact that those living in parts of Loudoun, Fauquier, Prince William, and Fairfax Counties—territory becoming known as "Mosby's Confederacy"—were not likely to divulge any *useful* information to the Yankees at all. Somehow, the Federal Army was going to have to put a stop to the man called The Gray Ghost, though Duncan estimated that accomplishing that feat would be just about as easy as capturing Stuart!

☆ ☆ ☆ ☆ ☆ ☆ ☆

Flickering lantern light dimly illuminated the room beneath the whitewashed cabin at Shadowcreek. Salina stirred in her sleep, then rubbed her eyes and slowly opened them. The burned-down tallow candle had been replaced with a more substantial source of light, and alongside the lantern was a plate of food and a brown glass bottle of water. Salina stretched and yawned and found that she was indeed hungry. She sat up, set the tear-stained pillow aside, and took a sip of the cool water before nibbling at a corner of the ham sandwich. She wondered what time it was, how long she'd slept. Taylor Sue was clearly aware that she was down here, but had let Salina rest instead of waking her.

"So, you've finally decided to get up." Taylor Sue peeked from the stairwell leading down from the hearth. "You had me a bit worried."

"Why?" Salina asked, dabbing the corner of her mouth with a fraying linen napkin.

"You've slept the clock around, Salina. You must have been tired," Taylor Sue surmised. She sat down on the three-legged stool next to the desk. "I've come down twice just to see if you had a fever or the chills, but you've been snoring away, rather peacefully, I might add."

"Hmmm." Salina took another bite of sandwich, savoring it. Not all of her dreams had been entirely peaceful, but neither had they been of the nightmarish variety. They had been mostly of Jeremy...Belatedly, Taylor Sue's words registered. "Slept the clock round! What time is it?" she suddenly wanted to know.

"Mary Edith and I just finished the supper dishes," Taylor Sue replied. "Is something wrong?"

"I've slept through one whole day," Salina repeated. "Not two?"

"No, just the one," Taylor Sue assured her.

"All right, then, I still have time," Salina nodded.

"Are you going to let me know what's going through that brain of yours, or will you keep me in suspense?" Taylor Sue prodded.

Salina set the sandwich aside, fishing in her pocket for the letter from Mamma and the daguerreotype print.

Taylor Sue picked up the black and white image of Salina. "How did you come by this?"

"I asked Colby for it. He was reluctant to part with it, but I didn't want him carrying it around with him anymore. That's Jeremy's privilege, not his," Salina answered. "Colby brought me this, though." She held out the letter. "The postmark is two weeks old."

"Well, open it. What does your mamma have to say? Do you suppose she had the baby yet?" inquired Taylor Sue.

"No, not yet, at least Colby said she hadn't." Salina skimmed Annelise's letter.   Reading between the lines, Salina didn't think Mamma hated the little northern farming community as much as she had at first, perhaps because she was settling in with Duncan's family, and more importantly, had her mind on the baby. Mamma plainly stated that she missed Shadowcreek, and she was lonely for Salina's company:

> *Jubilee takes good care of me, fussing and fretting as usual, but I am quite healthy and feel better than I ever have while enduring a pregnancy. Jubilee thinks the baby will come soon, and I am anxious for these bouts of false labor to eventually lead to the delivery of Duncan's child. The closer*

the time comes, the more I find myself weary of the interminable waiting and impatient to hold this child in my arms instead of within. Even Noreen, Duncan's mother, has commented on how long it's been since there was a baby in the house. I think she is looking forward to another grandchild with whole-hearted eagerness.

The heat has been oppressive. News of the recent cavalry battle near Brandy Station makes Pleasanton look like a hero for a change. I don't believe for a minute what they are saying about Stuart being routed. The Southern cavalry and the Confederate population as well are accustomed to victories. If Stuart was uncharacteristically caught off guard, he made up for it in tenacity. According to the reports, the Federals sustained the higher casualties. The Rebel Cavalry are better led, but I fear the Yankees might be learning from their early defeats. If they had such a one as Stuart on their side—well, let's just hope they never find his equal!

Every day I pray for you and Taylor Sue, Jeremy and Ethan, and all of those we know who are caught up in this dreadful war as we are. I miss you terribly. Duncan suggested that I ask you to come for a visit, so that you might see your new brother or sister, but I suspect your heart is too firmly rooted in Virginia soil to make a trek with a northern destination. If you should consider such a request, get word to Duncan. He'll see to your safe conduct. I'd be lying to myself if I didn't admit such a visit would mean a great deal to me.

> I remain affectionately yours,
> Mamma

"What are you going to do, Salina?" Taylor Sue asked when her sister-in-law finished reading the last of the letter aloud.

Salina shrugged. "I'm not sure what I should do. If you were me, would you go?"

"I think I would," Taylor Sue nodded. "While duty may lay claim to our men, we women must tend to the matters concerning our families—regardless of where they may reside in relation to the Mason-Dixon Line."

"But I've just barely come home again..." Salina sighed.

"Jeremy's headed north," Taylor Sue reminded her. "And so is

Ethan. Wouldn't it be something if they made it as far as Pennsylvania, and Ethan could see his new sibling, too?"

"The Lord works in mysterious ways," Salina pondered. "In the morning I'll ride to Fairfax and give Tabitha my answer. Colby said he'd give me two days to make up my mind. I've slept through the first one, so it must be tomorrow."

"I'll go with you," Taylor Sue nodded. "I've a letter to post to my family down in Richmond."

☆ ☆ ☆ ☆ ☆ ☆ ☆

Early in the morning, the two Federal lieutenants set out for Virginia. Neither spoke much, and Colby kept a wary eye on the man who was to replace him. He decided he must be picking up Duncan's suspicious ways. Soon after their arrival at Fairfax Court House, the introductions were made and the maps delivered. Once their orders had been carried out, Colby rode with Corbeau over to the hotel. "They serve a good steak here," Colby commented.

"I suppose this is where we part company, then?" Corbeau inquired.

"Yes, I'll be en route to my new post. Major Grant will be expecting you back at the War Department. Best wishes to you." Colby touched the brim of his cap.

"And to you, Lieutenant," Corbeau returned in like fashion. He got himself a room, but the steak would have to wait. Corbeau had other business to see to while he was here in town.

Colby headed straightaway toward the boarding house, marched up the front steps, and let himself inside. "Mrs. Wheeler?" he called out to the owner of the boarding house.

Tabitha Wheeler was putting away the supper dishes, returning the plates and cups to their appropriate places in the china hutch. "Evenin', Lieutenant," the sprightly old woman nodded, a knowing look in her wise eyes. "Knew you'd be here in time. Got a message for you; I believe it's one you're expectin'." She shuffled over to the large desk at the far end of the dining room and pulled a sealed envelope from one of the drawers.

"Thank you, ma'am." Colby anxiously tore open the envelope and unfolded the single sheet of paper. The message contained in the lines was brief and to the point:

Lieutenant Lance Colby, U.S.A.
Fairfax Court House, Virginia

I'll go. I'll be ready first thing tomorrow morning, and I
will wait for your arrival. If possible, please bring a horse
for me—no need for a proper sidesaddle if one cannot be
acquired. Thank you for your patience.

I remain your friend,
S. R. H. of Shadowcreek

Colby refolded the note and stuffed it into his pocket, grinning. Though he didn't think Salina would ever admit it, she had acted predictably on this account: he had been sure that she would not deny her mamma's request. It was a consolation, hollow at best, to know he'd been right. Rarely was he privy to the vulnerable compassion behind the stoic facade Salina usually allowed him to see. When he'd led a detachment to chase her across the country and when he'd seen her imprisoned at Fortress Alcatraz, she had seemed practically untouchable, unshakable, displaying an amazing level of grit for a young woman. Without a doubt Salina Hastings was an unyielding fighter, a worthy adversary; yet her obstinance, Colby had discovered, was tempered with gentleness and a deep-rooted love for her family. If not for the latter, there was no way she would accede to go North.

"Mrs. Wheeler, it's been a pleasure to see you again." Colby tipped his cap in deference. "I'll follow up on this immediately." Silently he added, *Right after I stop in and check on my wife.*

Tabitha nodded sagely, her keen eyes always observing. "Good-night, Lieutenant."

☆ ☆ ☆ ☆ ☆ ☆ ☆

Lottie seethed with hot indignation. She fumed as she watched her husband mount and ride off in the direction of the Shadowcreek estate. Huffing a heavy sigh, she flung the heavy lace drapery back into its place. Lance must be mad if he thought it remotely possible that she and Salina could be traveling companions! He hadn't even *asked* if she'd like to go meet his Yankee family, he'd made it an *order*—no questions or debate about it.

"Maraiah!" Lottie snapped impatiently, pacing the highly polished floor in her room. "Maraiah, come quick!"

The housekeeper arrived, out of breath from her scramble up the wide staircase. "Yas, Miss Lottie. Ah's here now. What's it ya'd be wantin'?"

"I want you to pack a trunk," Lottie commanded, still stewing. "My husband is taking me with him on a trip North."

"Is ya off ta Washin'ton agin, Miss Lottie?" Maraiah asked.

"No, Pennsylvania," Lottie replied tartly. "I don't know how long I'll end up staying with his family, but I want you to pack the best of everything I own. I'll show those Northerners that we Southrons can hold our own in the line of fashion." She began pulling her favorite frocks from the armoire and tossed them onto the bed, creating a mounting pile of satin, taffeta, moiré, and watered silk.

"What time will Mistah Lance be back ta fetch ya?" Maraiah inquired.

Lottie grumbled, "First thing in the morning! He hasn't even the common courtesy to wait until a decent hour—like noontime! First thing in the morning!" She complained, rolling her corn-flower-blue eyes, "He knows how I hate to get out of bed that early. He's so accustomed to his army ways, getting up at the crack of dawn...and now he expects me to do so as well!"

Maraiah wordlessly packed while Lottie continued to vent her objections. The young matron caught her reflection in the full-length mirror, and she studied her profile with dismay. She was beginning to show, and there was no way to conceal her condition for much longer. Lottie knew she would only grow bigger as the child within developed to term. "I'll be big as house, just like Mary Edith was!" she whispered, horrified.

"Naw, Miss Lottie. Miss Mary Edith done had twins—ya ain't carryin' two babes, ere ya?" Maraiah wondered.

"May the good Lord have mercy, no! I'm not carrying two babes!" Lottie answered vehemently. "One is bad enough!"

"Miss Lottie, ya shouldna be talkin' about da babe in such manner," Maraiah chided. "Ya gots ta give it love, even afore it'd be born. Dat's da way da wee liddle one will know ta love ya back."

"Love me back...?" Lottie trailed off, her thoughts scattering. She put her ringed hand on her abdomen, gently caressing the pro-truding swell. "I'm going to be a mother," she remarked absently, as if only just now realizing the fact for the first time. "And this child *will* love me back."

"Aye, all in good time," Maraiah nodded. The black woman

turned her face away from her mistress. All the servants at Ivywood knew that Lottie Armstrong had married Yankee Lance Colby not out of love, but due to *circumstances*. Maraiah perceived, though, that the Northern man was taken with her. The haughty Southern girl, however, loved no one but her spoiled little self. Oh, Miss Lottie did have a fondness for her twin sister, perhaps even a degree of feeling for her parents—and recently there was a hint of care directed towards her spouse. If that Yankee lieutenant could teach Miss Lottie how to love, he'd have done a life's work in such a good deed. Then maybe she'd be able to pass along some affection to the child they created. It would be remain to be seen, the house-keeper decided, and she wasn't about to hold her breath no how. Maraiah guessed she might suffocate before she'd witness such a thing!

☆ ☆ ☆ ☆ ☆ ☆ ☆

Regretting his decision to keep Salina in the dark about travel-ing with Lottie, Colby silently debated whether or not he should go back to Shadowcreek and explain the situation to Salina more thor-oughly. He reined his horse, almost turned around, but then decided against it. He already had Salina's word that she would go, and it was probably better to just leave it at that, for now. He didn't dare chance giving her an opportunity to back out.

His visit tonight had been for two reasons: first, to discuss the arrangements for the northward journey, and second, to extend a word of caution. While Colby had intentionally withheld the con-dition of traveling with Lottie, he had openly admitted to Salina the sighting of John Barnes in Alexandria. Duncan had made it quite clear that she was to be forewarned.

Salina, however, had not seemed surprised in the least when Colby shared his findings with her. In fact, he'd been a little put out by her calm, unruffled reply. "Jeremy and I had a feeling that he might have survived, but until now we had no proof," she'd said demurely. "I know it's a risk for you, a Yankee officer, to confide such things to me, your Rebel enemy, but at least Jeremy and I know what we're up against, and for that I thank you."

He'd expected fear or rage, but he saw nothing more in Salina's expression than cool-headed composure. Colby arrived at the same conclusion he always did: Salina Hastings was no less than amazing.

Fighting a yawn, Colby nudged his lethargic mount into a bit brisker gait, a pace which was neither walk nor trot. The leaves of the trees overhead did much to block any light given off by the moon, but he was familiar with the path that was a shortcut back to Ivywood. He hoped that by the time he got back Lottie's anger might have spent itself and she would follow his orders without a lot of fuss. He wished he could be there in Gettysburg to see the faces of his family when his Southern Belle arrived at his boyhood home. Duncan had dreaded Colby's decision to send Lottie to live with his family, but the Grants and the Colbys did live on opposite ends of town, so there wouldn't be too much interaction. Duncan couldn't begrudge the fact that Colby wanted his wife in a safe place, and Gettysburg was nothing if not that. Duncan sent a wire warning Annelise, just so she wouldn't be surprised by Lottie's sudden presence in town.

Colby envisioned Lottie ensconced at his family's home, putting on her airs, and he could well imagine that his sisters just might enjoy taking her down a peg or two. Another perspective was precisely what Lottie needed. She might still consider herself the proverbial belle of the ball here in Fairfax County, Virginia, but Adams County, Pennsylvania, would view her with a decidedly different outlook.

If Colby hadn't been so engrossed with thoughts of home and family, and had paid closer attention to the sounds in the night, he might not have been ambushed so thoroughly. It happened so quickly, he never even had time to spur his horse and attempt to escape.

After being knocked off his horse, Colby was held fast by two men while a third punched him in the stomach half a dozen times in rapid succession, then clipped him with a dizzying uppercut to his jaw. Colby's feeble struggle was short-lived. Even before his vision clouded, he did not clearly see the faces of his attackers. Abruptly he was let go, and he crumpled to his knees. He would have fallen on his face if the leader of the assailants hadn't grabbed a handful of hair and yanked his head up violently.

"I haven't...got...any money," he sputtered, coughing and tasting the blood oozing from a gash in his lower lip.

The reply was another swift strike to the side of his already reeling head.

"Hold him steady," a vaguely familiar voice ordered.

Colby's arms were stretched wide and he was dragged to his feet once more. Groping hands rifled his pockets. His wallet, the train tickets, Salina's note, his orders—including his traveling papers—and his watch were stolen from him. "Take his wedding ring, if he's got one, and get his boots, too," the harsh voice commanded. "Wolfe, go get his horse."

"Aye, Lieutenant." One of them released the hold he'd had on Colby's arm.

Colby made an attempt to free his other arm, and was rewarded by another set of bruising blows. Consciousness waned, but before it deserted him, he made out the leering face that wavered in front of him. "Cor-beau…" he wheezed.

"That's right, Lieutenant." A wicked laugh sounded somewhere above Colby's head as he was cast aside like a limp rag doll.

Colby lay sprawled face down on the ground. A heavy boot connected with his ribcage, once, twice. By the third time, Colby managed to raise his arm to guard his side. As the next kick met its target, he heard and felt the bones in his forearm cracking. He groaned in anguish, then awareness eluded him altogether.

"Got a match, Brewster?" Corbeau asked gruffly, stepping over the prone, battered form of his fellow lieutenant.

Brewster struck a match against his holster. "Here." He held the flame in position to illuminate the note.

"*S.R.H. of Shadowcreek*. Salina Rose Hastings," Corbeau deducted the obvious. "First thing in the morning."

"What about Colby's wife?" Wolfe inquired. He held Colby's boots, but he relinquished the gold wedding band to Corbeau.

"Oh, we'll take her, too, just for good measure. To keep up appearances," Corbeau determined. "You two will follow, at a safe distance, and I will escort them in Colby's place." He glanced down at the unconscious Colby. "Get him out of here."

Chapter Ten

$\mathcal{A}$lphonse Corbeau was at Shadowcreek before the first gleaming rays of sunrise changed the eastern sky from gray to gold. He was leading one riderless horse, complete with a side-saddle, and another horse bearing a shrewish blond. He did not envy Colby his wife, no matter how beautiful she was. Her constant complaining was enough to grate on a man's nerves, but Corbeau fought the urge to tell her, in no uncertain terms, to shut up.

He helped Mrs. Colby dismount and held her arm solicitously as they climbed the stairs of the cabin porch.

"Salina Hastings! You'd better be ready to go! I'll just scream if you got to sleep in later than I did!" Lottie banged on the door.

Salina opened the door a mere crack. "Lottie? You're going along?"

"Of course!" Lottie snapped. "What? Didn't Lance tell you he's making me go meet his family?"

"Must have slipped his mind," Salina whispered miserably. She glanced around, spying the man with her cousin. "Where is Colby?"

"Good morning, Miss Hastings, allow me to introduce myself. I am Lieutenant Corbeau," he began, ever so politely.

Lottie cut him off. "He's taking Lance's place working with Duncan Grant at the War Department because Lance is being transferred to field duty. Can you believe he deliberately asked for a transfer? The man is a fool, if you ask me. He could really get himself killed." And in that moment Lottie realized that she certainly did not want to be a widow.

"Lieutenant Corbeau." Salina acknowledged the blue-clad officer with a curt nod. Just because he worked for Duncan did not mean she had to trust him. "But where is Colby?" she repeated her question.

"As Mrs. Colby said, I'm taking his place. He was detained by a matter requiring his immediate attention, so he sent me on ahead. If he doesn't catch up with us later, then he'll probably meet up with you back in Washington. I'm to take you with me now, though. I gather Major Grant is expecting you before sundown."

Salina was still skeptical.

Corbeau withdrew a small piece of paper from his pocket and handed it to her. "Colby said you'd recognize this, and hoped you would trust me to accompany both of you lovely ladies to your destination."

Salina recognized her own note addressed to Colby. After a long, heavy pause, Salina nodded her assent. She didn't like it, but if Colby, detained by some war-related incident, had made other arrangements for them, then she'd have to make the best of it. Salina was slow to admit it, but Lottie's company might actually be welcome in this instance.

"I'll be just a minute." Salina went back inside and kissed Bonnie Lee and Annie Laurie in their cradles without disturbing their sleep. Mary Edith hugged her, Taylor Sue clung to her.

"Be strong and courageous," Taylor Sue encouraged. "Your going is a testimony of your strength. I sense your apprehension—you don't think you can do this. You can, though, Salina—but not without courage."

Salina smiled, "No, not without courage. So here I go, trying to muster the bravery I'll need for this next adventure. I keep reminding myself that I'm not alone—for the Lord is always with me." She quoted a line of the Twenty-Third Psalm, "'Yea, though I walk through the valley of the shadow of death, I will fear no evil.' I know He'll keep me in His hand, and guide me on my way. It's another test of trust and faith. 'Without faith, it is impossible to please Him.'"

"That's right." Taylor Sue squeezed both her sister-in-law's hands. "You'll have our prayers, rest assured. And if you do happen to see Ethan while you're there, give him this letter. Tell him I miss him terribly and love him very much." As an afterthought she added, "You have your gun, don't you?"

Salina nodded gravely. "Of course." Through the window she stole a glance at the Yankee Corbeau. "Never fear, I shall relay your message to Ethan should our paths cross in the North. Pray for me now, Taylor Sue. I wish Colby was here."

"That's a first," Taylor Sue gently teased.

"I suppose it is." Salina's giggle was soft and melodic. "I've got to go—with Lottie, no less," she said firmly, a look of determination settled in her emerald eyes. The sisters-in-law hugged each other in farewell, and then Salina returned to Lottie and Lieutenant Corbeau on the porch.

"You are ready then?" inquired Corbeau, trying to hide his impatience.

"Yes," Salina nodded. She allowed him to take her satchel and secure it behind the side-saddle. She accepted his assistance to mount. He extended the same courtesy to Lottie. Salina's usually keen instincts demanded that she be wary. Corbeau had every outward appearance of chivalry in his manner, but she would not let herself be charmed. He was the enemy, and was to be observed with the utmost caution. Salina had slept well the previous night, and now was alert and on guard. She had told Jeremy to watch his back just in case John Barnes was not dead. At present, she felt compelled to heed her own advice.

Lottie's love of hearing her own voice filled the otherwise monotonous ride with incessant chatter. Salina kept to herself, always watching. When the sun was directly overhead, Corbeau halted, fed the young ladies a lunch of cold roast beef sandwiches washed down with lukewarm cider, and then had them on their way again.

Not long after lunch, Salina felt a distinct prickling start at the nape of her neck and trail down the length of her spine. The three of them, she sensed, were not alone. Someone out there, screened by the thick brush, was covertly surveying them. She kept silent, as there was no need to deliberately frighten Lottie into hysterics without genuine cause. After they'd traveled awhile further, Salina thought she should have felt the sun at her back, but instead it warmed the right side of her face. The landmarks that punctuated the way to Washington were curiously absent, and by her best guess, she figured Corbeau was riding southeast toward Alexandria, not northeast toward the Union capital.

Willing herself to remain collected, she tried to think of something Daddy, Ethan, or Jeremy might do in a similar situation. Salina deliberately slowed her horse until she fell a little distance behind. She listened to the rustles around her, feeling unseen eyes upon her.

"Something wrong, Miss Hastings?" Corbeau called back to her.

"My horse is limping," she made up an excuse. She slid down from the saddle and picked up a hoof of the docile mount, pretending to check for a stone that the mare might have picked up in her shoe.

Corbeau reined his horse alongside Salina's. "I don't see any problem, so what's the trouble?"

"I don't know," Salina answered honestly. "Would you like to check for yourself?"

A displeased sigh accompanied a narrow-eyed glare. "We don't have time to waste, Miss Hastings. The Major is expecting you…" Corbeau dismounted, taking a step towards Salina.

Carefully, while the lieutenant bent to study the hoof in question, Salina edged toward his horse. In an instant, she pulled herself up into the saddle and leveled her pistol at Corbeau.

"What the…?!" An outraged growl tumbled from his lips, followed by a string of oaths.

He was about to reach for his gun, but Salina cocked the hammer of her pearl-handled pistol. "I'll shoot that hand if you so much as graze the holster," she declared with deadly calm.

"Salina!" Lottie was appalled. "Lieutenant Corbeau is our guide. He's taking us to…"

"Alexandria." Salina supplied the name of the Union-occupied town. "Aren't you, Corbeau? You're not taking us to Washington at all. It's John Barnes who's given you orders, not Duncan Grant."

"Honestly, Salina, I think you are obsessed with Jeremy's uncle," Lottie countered. "You're so paranoid…"

"Shut up, Lottie, and get behind me!" Salina ordered firmly. She saw the anger flaring in Corbeau's beady eyes. He never reckoned she'd pull a gun on him, that was evident. The element of surprise had worked in her favor.

Lottie stubbornly didn't move, but Corbeau did. Salina's shot missed his boot by a mere half inch. He jumped, unsettled by her accuracy. He didn't need to be told she'd deliberately missed hitting him. He never took his eyes from her as he maneuvered to get himself behind Lottie's horse.

Lottie had disregarded Salina's instructions, and now Corbeau positioned the blond and the wide-eyed horse into place as a shield. Lottie tried to dismount, but Corbeau grabbed a fistful of her voluminous skirts and held her in her place. Realization dawned: they were in precarious danger.

"Get away from her, Corbeau. But, even if you won't, I'll fire anyway," Salina informed him. "You see, there's no love lost between Lottie and me."

"Salina, please!" Lottie wailed, terrified that her cousin actually meant every word. "I know we've had our differences, and I admit I've been downright mean on occasion..."

"Shut up, Lottie!" Salina shouted.

Corbeau almost believed Salina, so cold were her eyes, her words lacking any emotion. He roughly pulled Lottie down from the horse's back and kept her between his body and Salina's gun. Behind Lottie's wide hoops, he retrieved his own revolver. He raised it into view, aiming to bring down Salina's mount, but she was quicker. She got her shot off first, her target being his hand. The bullet whizzed through the skirt of Lottie's riding habit and the top layer of her petticoats. It hit the mark squarely, causing Corbeau to drop his gun.

Lottie howled in dismay while Corbeau cursed at Salina. He held his wounded hand, swearing in pain while the blood oozed between his gloved fingers. His shifty eyes located the weapon he'd involuntarily dropped.

"Reach for it, and I'll shoot again," Salina warned ominously. "Let go of Lottie, now!"

Corbeau's chortle was laden with evil. "You are a spirited little minx! Too clever for your own good. But you're afraid," he rasped. "You're out here all alone, miles from who knows where, and have no idea who or how many have followed our every step. You can try, Missy, but you'll not get away, I can assure you of that!"

To Salina's consternation, she heard the sounds of multiple guns readied in preparation to fire.

"Throw down the gun, Missy. We got orders to bring you in alive, but that can change if you don't cooperate!" Corbeau hissed.

"I never killed a woman yet, but that don't mean you couldn't be the first." He whistled a shrill, piercing signal. "Wolfe! Brewster!"

A pair of blue riders emerged from the shadowy brush. Corbeau reached for Lottie's horse. Salina aimed and shot it down. Brewster trained his carbine at Salina's heart, but in the next instant, he fell from the saddle, dead before he hit the ground. Salina didn't dare look around to find the source of the accurately-targeted shot. Someone else was out there, and seemingly on her side; she could only pray it truly was a friend.

Lottie shrieked when Brewster fell dead, but sensibly took advantage of Corbeau's slackened grip to make her escape from him.

Corbeau was beyond caring that someone else might be out there. Salina Hastings was his immediate concern. He stooped to pick up his gun with his good hand, and Salina, as promised, shot that one as well. He sunk to one knee, gurgling in pain.

"Stay put, Corbeau! I mean it!" *Thou shalt not kill*, raged in Salina's mind. *But this is war! This is self-defense...Kill or be killed!* She'd been abducted once before, and she swore she would not be taken again without a fight. Here she had to make her stand, for she was not only fighting for her own life, but Lottie's as well.

The second blue rider, the one Corbeau called Wolfe, had Salina in his sights. He pulled the trigger, but she saw it coming and ducked, laying low against the horse's neck. The bullet miraculously missed her. She fired back at him, hitting Wolfe in the shoulder. It was another's shot, however, that again came from behind her, and once again reaped death.

Corbeau was like a wild, enraged animal. Lottie was beyond his reach, huddling in the trees some distance away, crying hysterically. Salina, perched atop his horse, was closer. His maniacal charge spooked the steed into rearing. Salina was almost unseated, yet by sheer will she managed to hang on. Corbeau lunged again, and this time when the horse reared on hind legs she did fall, landing in a heap, barely escaping a clip from the churning hooves. Salina hit the ground with a thud as her pistol launched its last bullet into Corbeau's gut. Her blood-curdling scream equaled Lottie's.

Salina was out of ammunition. She couldn't reload, and Corbeau knew it. He staggered towards her, one injured hand pressed against the gushing bullet wound in his side, the other bloody hand brandishing a glinting hunting knife. "You're...killing...me..." Corbeau raged, waving the sharp point of the blade perilously close. "If

I...go...you're coming...with...me..."

Salina scrambled to gain her feet. Corbeau stomped on the hem of her dress, halting her. She fell flat, still gripping her empty pistol. Corbeau slashed at her sleeve, making a jagged cut through the material. Salina fought to get away from him with all her might.

"You'll...pay...for what...you've...done." Blood and spittle sprayed from his mouth, drooling down his chin, dripping onto Salina's skirt.

Another shot barked, efficiently finding its mark. Corbeau staggered in front of Salina, his knees buckled, then he keeled over face first, landing in her lap. She pushed at the corpse, kicking him away from her. His blood was on her. Hot tears streamed down her face. "Oh, God! Why?!" Her heart-wrenching prayer dissolved into convulsive sobs.

"Little One." A pair of copper hands pulled her up from the ground, sinewy arms securely enfolded her in their embrace. "Little One, hush. It's all right now, you're safe." A tender hand stroked her dark curls.

Salina lifted her head. She was astonished to find herself staring into the vivid turquoise eyes belonging to Drake. Fresh tears welled in her tormented eyes, and she cried, clenching his fringed buckskin jacket in her fists. "I killed that awful man..." She was trembling uncontrollably.

Drake shook his head, his long black hair brushing his broad shoulders. "Sorry, Little One, but I won't let you take credit for my kill. All right, you mortally wounded him, but you didn't kill him. If I hadn't shot him, he might have lingered on for days, and that's a miserable way to die. Better to have it over and done with, quick. You can't take credit for disposing of that life—you're not to blame. Do you hear me?" He sought to comfort her, ease her troubled mind, absolve her from her guilt. He held her close. "Quit crying now, Little One, we've got to get out of here before a Yankee patrol finds us." He used his thumb to wipe away her tears, then landed a brusque kiss on each salt-streaked cheek.

Salina took a deep, steadying breath and disentangled herself from Drake's embrace. She blushed hotly in the wake of clinging to him so desperately. She put a shaky hand to her forehead and found a way to laugh. "Not that I'm not happy to see you, because I am, but what are you doing here?"

"I'll tell you all about it later, Little One," Drake winked, then amended her title: "I mean, Mrs. Barnes."

Salina shook her head ruefully. "I'm not Mrs. Barnes—not yet anyway."

"What? Why not?" Drake asked incredulously. "What's happened now?"

"I'll tell you later," Salina promised. "Where's my cousin?"

"She fainted some time ago." Drake jerked a thumb over his shoulder toward the trees. "She's not made of the same stuff you are, that's for sure."

"Is she all right, though? She's going to have a baby." Salina hurried to Lottie's side. "Lottie?" She smoothed the golden curls back from Lottie's pale face.

Lottie murmured, "Mmmmmmm…" At last she opened her blue eyes. "Salina."

"Are you hurt?" Salina queried.

Lottie's chin quivered. " For a minute, I thought we were going to end up dead."

"We almost did," Salina confirmed, "And we just might have, except for Drake."

Lottie's eyes traveled to where Salina's glance rested on…an *Indian*! Renewed fear swept through her. "Have we gone from the frying pan into the fire?" she asked in a small voice.

Salina laughed. "No, Lottie. Drake is a friend. He'll take us home."

Drake nodded curtly to Lottie. "Pleased to make your acquaintance, ma'am." He collected Salina's satchel, then gave her the option to change into a clean frock if she wanted out of the blood-stained dress she wore, but Salina didn't think they should take the extra time. If there was a Yankee outpost in the vicinity, someone would probably come to investigate the scene. "I just want to go home," she told Drake.

"Come on, then," Drake said in his gravelly voice. "Lottie, can you ride?"

She nodded and hastened to mount up. With much curiosity, Lottie eyed the other two as they conversed. Salina nodded in agreement over something the savage-looking man said to her. Standing so close to one another, they seemed to be quite chummy. For once, Lottie was speechless.

☆ ☆ ☆ ☆ ☆ ☆ ☆

Firelight from the wide brick hearth danced in the serious

turquoise eyes. Drake listened intently to Salina's tale of why she and Jeremy were still unwed. He predicted it was only a matter of time before the marriage would take place. "I know the man well, Little One, and I have no doubt that Lieutenant Barnes will not rest until he sees it through," Drake said knowingly.

"Yes, I know," Salina nodded. "All in good time—all in God's time." The hardest part was accepting that God's timing did not often adhere to the schedule Salina had set in her mind. *His will, His way*, she silently reminded herself. *All things work together for good.*

In turn, Drake shared his letter from Aurora Dallinger with both Taylor Sue and Salina. "Until this came, I didn't even know I had a sister," Drake confessed.

"So you're going to go to Boston? To claim your inheritance?" Taylor Sue asked.

"Inheritance or no, I'm going to see my old man," Drake answered tersely. "But in so doing, I'm having to make choices that aren't particularly easy."

"Such as?" Salina arched an eyebrow.

Drake flashed a wide grin, pulling his long, waist-length hair over one muscular shoulder. "If I go to Boston looking like this they'll never let me in. No. The Dallingers wouldn't take kindly to me showing up as an Indian—half-Indian—or any other fraction of mixed blood."

Salina sat in the rocking chair, rocking slowly. "So, are you going to go as the white man—half white?"

Drake nodded slowly. "Might as well." His elbows rested on the table, and he toyed with a mug of steaming coffee.

"What do you remember about your father?" Taylor Sue asked, sensing that Drake needed to talk but didn't know how to begin.

"I never saw him after he returned to Boston," Drake reflected quietly. He hesitated, obviously having thought about this a lot in the past few days. "My pa did do one thing for me," he began slowly. "He provided for my tuition at a boy's academy in St. Louis. I hated that school. I burned the letter from Pa that told me it had been Ma's dying wish that I learn to read and write, do complex figures, and be tutored in the manners of a true gentleman.

"In spite of myself, I made passing marks, but barely. I was near to graduating when I got expelled for yet another fight. I never troubled myself about going back for my diploma. Instead, I put to practical use the reading, writing and mathematics. The lessons in etiquette suffered from neglect. By now my manners are downright rusty," Drake admitted. "I am socially unacceptable, aren't I?"

The girls' amused giggles indicated their agreement with Drake's leading question. Salina was quick to add, "I'm sure it will take but a little time for you to recall the things you learned in school. I'll wager it'll all come back to you once you make your entry into high society."

Drake's sigh illustrated his resignation. "Perhaps. But I'll need your help."

"What can we do?" Taylor Sue instantly offered. "You've been such a help to us; now it's our privilege to return the favor."

"You've got to cut my hair," Drake stated simply.

Both girls gasped, "Your hair!"

"Yes, my hair," Drake repeated remorsefully. He touched his earlobe and removed the gold hoop, discarding it on the table. "I've thought about this long and hard. If my pa's family is willing to allow me to come and see him before he dies, then I suppose I must play the game by their rules. For years I've lived more as the Indian, but I don't really fit in with my ma's people. I thought I'd try the white man for awhile, and see if I fit in any better on that side of the fence. If I don't like it, I can always let my hair grow…"

Salina returned Drake's reluctant smile. Indeed, he had obviously done a lot of thinking to come to these conclusions. He was taking a great chance, and she admired him for being man enough to try. Once again, Salina thanked the Lord for what He had provided for her. She met Drake's turquoise glance evenly and said, "I still have to go north to Gettysburg to see my mamma."

Drake swirled the last of his coffee in the bottom of the enamel mug, then tipped his head back and drained the contents. He set the mug aside and crossed his arms in front of him. "What's on your mind, Little One?"

"Lottie, if she is well and has suffered no undue effects from this afternoon, is supposed to accompany me. Could you take another detour—to Pennsylvania—before you go on to Boston? I know it's selfish of me to ask, but I would feel much safer traveling with you," Salina told him. "I already owe you my life several times over, why not add another favor to my debt?"

"It'd be no trouble," Drake assured her. One more day would make little difference to his plans. Besides, he was still hesitant about going to Boston. Honoring Salina's request would provide him another day to prepare himself for seeing his father after all these years. He cleared his throat and asked, "Have you got shears here? Which one of you is going to cut my hair?"

Salina couldn't bring herself to do the deed, so Taylor Sue filled the role of barber. The long, heavy black hair whispered a sad note of mourning as it fell with a swish into piles on the floor around the legs of Drake's chair. Salina was witness to an astounding transformation. Admittedly, Drake was an attractive man, but now he was even better looking—if that were possible—in a decidedly different way. Gone was the appearance of the savage, and in its place was a striking, educated man about to discover his fortune.

Taylor Sue lifted his chin and combed his hair to one side, partially covering the jagged scar on his brow. She turned his face from side to side and declared, "I think you'll do—quite nicely."

"Yes," Salina agreed. "I think so, too."

Drake scrutinized his reflection in the looking glass. "It will grow back," was all he would say with regard to his shorn head. Finally he chuckled. "You two are something else!"

Dr. Phillips stopped in at Shadowcreek to check on Salina. He informed them that although Lottie was understandably overwrought, she would be fine. Neither she nor the baby she carried had suffered any physical harm.

"And how is Colby?" Salina asked. Drake had found him, beaten and bloodied, in a ditch not far from the railroad cut. Lottie had been frantic until she was assured that Colby would not make her a widow—not today, anyway.

"He's got broken ribs and a broken arm, and bruises and cuts that will heal in time. His nose was broke, too, so he might have a hump on the bridge when it's healed and mended. His lip took half a dozen stitches. Other than that, he's in better shape than you might think by just looking at him," the doctor replied. When he was satisfied that Salina was all right, Dr. Phillips took his leave.

Salina was making plans. "Drake, could you take us to Washington tomorrow?"

"I don't see why not," Drake nodded.

"Then we'll leave at first light," Salina decided.

☆ ☆ ☆ ☆ ☆ ☆ ☆

Drake offered his arm as Salina alighted from the carriage. Salina turned to him when she heard him fall into step with her. "Where do you think you're going?" she asked.

"With you." Drake had a firm grip on her elbow.

She stared at the huge white columns that held up the portico of the building that housed the Union War Department. Inside, plans were being made even now for a future attack against the Confederacy. Duncan was in there somewhere, and she was determined to find him. Colby was still too out-of-it to be aware of his surroundings, otherwise he could have told Salina precisely where to find her stepfather. She extracted her elbow from Drake's grasp. "Thank you, Drake, but this is something I've got to do alone."

"You don't even know where to begin to look for Major Grant," Drake argued.

Challenge glittered in her green eyes. "I'll find him."

"What if you get caught?" Drake persisted, discerning a touch of doubt in her sparkling eyes.

"I won't!" Salina snapped. Her tone softened, "Please, Drake, just trust me on this one. I can manage."

Drake relented. "All right," he held up his hands in surrender. "But remember, we're here if you need us."

"I appreciate that," Salina nodded gratefully. "I'll be back in a little while."

She mustered her courage like a shield around her, lifted her hoops, and stormed up the front steps, deliberately weaving her way through the people. At the landing, an elegantly dressed man held the door for her. "Thank you, sir," she said, placing careful emphasis on the *r*. She didn't want *sir* to come out sounding like *suh*, as her Southern dialect had a tendency to do.

"My pleasure." He tipped his hat and went his own way.

Once inside, Salina hadn't the foggiest notion of where to begin her search. Her skin crawled with rising goose flesh. She, a former operative and Southern spy, stood inside the Union War Department...Furtively she glanced around. Maybe she should go back and bring Drake with her. She turned toward the door and bumped into a uniformed soldier. "Beg your pardon."

"No harm done. You look a little lost, Miss. Is there something I can help you with?" he asked politely.

"I'm trying to locate Major Duncan Grant," Salina answered, willing her voice not to betray the trepidation she felt.

Her soft drawl, though she tried to mask it, stung the soldier's ears. "What would you be wanting with Major Grant?"

"It's imperative that I speak with him," Salina insisted.

"Is he expecting you?" the soldier pointedly inquired.

"Not exactly, but he'll see me, I'm sure of it," Salina replied confidently. She could see the wary skepticism in the soldier's expression. "I demand you take me to him at once!"

"Demand?" A distorted grin twisted the soldier's mouth. "Well, we'll see about that, now, won't we? Who are you?"

Salina's mind raced, then she smiled, "Tell him that Miss *Sarah Hayes* is here to see him. I've got information that he's been looking for."

"Why don't you just tell me, and I'll be sure the Major gets the message," the soldier suggested.

Salina shook her dark head. "I'm sorry, sir, but that simply won't do. It's privileged information, and must be delivered to Major Grant directly."

The blue-uniformed soldier narrowed his eyes. "We'll just see if the Major is interested in seeing you or not." He pointed to a bench against the wall. "Have a seat, I'll be right back."

In a matter of minutes the soldier returned, and rather grudgingly he said, "Miss Hayes, if you'll be so kind as to follow me, Major Grant will see you now."

Salina smiled triumphantly, but she averted her eyes so he wouldn't see the *I-told-you-so* sentiment reflected there. She was led up the stairs to the second floor, where Duncan worked.

"Wait here," the soldier instructed. He halted at a closed door, rapping his knuckles briskly against the wood.

Duncan emerged from the little office. *"Miss Hayes,"* he greeted, his tone as starchy as his pressed white shirtfront. "How very nice to see you again."

"Major Grant," Salina curtsied politely.

"I'm told you bring information for me." Duncan raised an eyebrow in question. "If you'll follow me, we'll find a private place to chat." Duncan thanked the soldier, then swept Salina along at his side. He unlocked the door of a conference room and closed it quickly once they were inside. "I have been worried sick about you and Lottie. Where have you been, Salina? I expected you here yesterday! And what's all this with the *Miss Sarah Hayes* business, hmmmm? What charade are you up to now?"

"No charades, Duncan, I promise!" Salina returned sharply. "I just didn't feel comfortable giving that soldier my real name. He didn't take much of a fancy to my being a Southerner. I had to hope that you'd recognize the fake name."

"Kind of hard to miss, since that's the name you used the last time you came sneaking into Washington undercover," Duncan replied brusquely. "What's this all about?"

She crossed to the window, which faced the street where the closed carriage was parked. Drake impatiently stood near the front wheel exchanging pleasantries with the driver. He looked quite dapper since exchanging his buckskins for the finely-tailored suit he'd purchased before he left Tennessee. Salina was still adjusting to his transformation. "Do you see the man in the gray frock coat with the burgundy vest and black cravat?"

"Yes." Duncan's voice came from above her head. "Who is he?"

"That man is Mr. Dallinger, a very dear friend of mine. You might remember him better as Drake."

"The stagecoach driver from the express company in San Francisco?" Duncan had to look twice.

"Former stagecoach driver," Salina clarified. "He's come east to take care of some family business."

"Is that so?" Duncan asked. "What's the point, Salina?"

"The point is, Drake was at the right place at the right time, and he saved my life! Inside the carriage are Lieutenant and Mrs. Colby. They, too, owe their lives to him," Salina stated evenly, still looking out the window. "Colby's been hurt, Duncan. Your man Corbeau was not who he pretended to be! He lied to Lottie and to me, and tried to take us away to Alexandria, rather than bring us here. Colby told me that John Barnes has been seen in Alexandria. Now, perhaps you might think I'm jumping to conclusions, but the truth of the matter is that Corbeau was working for Barnes, and only posing to work for you!"

Duncan turned her around to face him. A sick, gut-wrenching feeling twisted his insides. "Where is Corbeau now?"

"He's dead," Salina replied coldly. "Along with the two who were with him—their names were Brewster and Wolfe. They also wore Federal uniforms."

"What has happened to Colby?" Duncan asked. "He at least is still alive."

Salina nodded. "Yes, he is alive. He was ambushed and severely beaten. If there is a doctor nearby, he should be reexamined. His ribs are bandaged, and he's got a concussion and a broken arm. He needed several stitches in his lip and in the gouge above his right eyebrow."

"You tended to him?" questioned Duncan.

"No, actually it was Maraiah, the Armstrongs' housekeeper. She has served as a nurse for their family for years," Salina explained. Looking into Duncan's stormy gray eyes, Salina could plainly see that he was upset. "Once Drake got us back home, Lottie was too distraught to do anything but cry. Dr. Phillips looked in on Colby last night, but couldn't do anything more for him than Maraiah already had."

"And Lottie—is she all right?" Duncan inquired anxiously. "What about the baby?"

Salina answered, "Dr. Phillips said she would be fine. She was just badly scared, like I was."

Duncan gave her a fierce hug. "I'm sorry you had to go through that. I had my misgivings about Corbeau, but I didn't see the connection to John Barnes. I'm very sorry, Salina."

"How could you have known? We were all equally fooled by him," Salina pointed out.

"Come with me," Duncan commanded gruffly, leading her back to his office. "I'll just be a minute."

Salina sat in a chair across from Duncan on the opposite side of his desk. He hastily scribbled some notes, orders probably, and she waited in long, patient silence. Aimlessly her curious gaze strayed around the cluttered little office, noting the piles of paper in every available space. She wondered how Daddy had ever managed to get in here and steal the documents that he had. How had Daddy known which pile contained the materials he sought? Salina supposed the mystery would never be solved.

On Duncan's desk, a handful of report folders caught Salina's attention. The folders, Salina speculated, might contain military service records. She read the names on the folders: *Edward Samuels, Elton Stephenson, Ezra Sprague, Edgar Shipp*, and *Evan*... somebody-or-other. She couldn't make out the surname, except that it also began with an *S*. A fleeting chill caused an involuntary shiver. All of the men had the initials *E.S.*, just like Jeremy's real father, according to the entry in John Barnes's deciphered journal. Her eyes flew to Duncan's face. His thick brows were drawn into a deep scowl; he paused in his writing and his gray eyes collided with hers.

"I don't know what you're thinking, Salina, but I don't think I like it," Duncan admitted. He quickly sealed the documents he'd written. She glanced down at his desk, and he immediately—if not intentionally—set another pile of correspondence atop the folders she'd been peeking at. "You listen to me, young lady," he said purposefully, "Whatever you see in here stays in here, do you understand me? No spying for the other side!"

She nodded quickly, but couldn't help wondering what exactly he was up to. She wanted to ask him, but thought better of it. As Duncan led her back through the corridors and down the stairs, she practically had to run to keep up with his pace. They passed the telegraph office, and she saw President Lincoln inside discussing a matter with Edwin Stanton, the Union's Secretary of War.

"Miss Hayes, if you would be so kind as to follow me." Duncan's request was more of an order. The last thing he needed right now was for the President to look up and see Salina gawking in the hall. Lincoln had graciously pardoned her for her role in the Western Campaign last December, just a few days prior to the Battle of Fredericksburg. At that time Salina had expressed her desire to return to Virginia, which the President had allowed in exchange for her promise to behave herself. For the moment, Duncan wanted to avoid raising any suspicions concerning Salina's sudden change of heart and her inclination to visit the North.

Salina hastened after Duncan, hurried down the stairs, and followed him to the carriage. She rendered the courteous introductions, "Major Duncan Grant, this is Mr. Drake Dallinger. Drake, my stepfather, Major Grant."

The men nodded in acknowledgment and shared a brief handshake. Duncan gave the carriage driver directions, and in a few minutes they reached the boarding house where he resided.

Between Duncan and Drake, they half-carried Colby from the carriage up to Duncan's rented room, with Lottie and Salina bringing up the rear. In shallow, pained breaths, Colby relayed what had happened. "Corbeau...followed me...first to Ivywood...then to Shadowcreek. He attacked...took my orders...He knew...when to collect the girls...and he must have been...rather convincing. He fooled us...all."

"He was to be your replacement," Salina said as a reminder. "I believed what he told me." She added bitterly, "He said you were detained and that he was to fetch us instead. I took the bait—hook, line, and sinker."

"How did you come to the conclusion that something was amiss?" Duncan questioned.

"Instinct at first, I guess. Then I figured out he wasn't leading us toward Washington. He was leading us southward, and I suspect his orders were to take us to Alexandria," Salina replied. "Drake found Colby in a ditch and took him to Ivywood. Then he tracked us down, and if it hadn't been for him, well, I just don't like to think about it. I shouldn't have been as trusting as I was. I forgot that all Yankees aren't like the two of you—it won't happen again!"

"We all...learned a...lesson...the hard...way," Colby breathed.

"I went through Corbeau's pockets after he was dead. Here are Colby's stolen orders," Drake presented the papers to Duncan, "and here are Corbeau's. As you can see, he was indeed working for John Barnes."

Duncan inspected Corbeau's orders which were undeniably authorized by Major Barnes. "This matter will be investigated, I assure you of that!" He met Salina's eyes. Again it was evident that the good Lord had kept Salina safe, and for that he was deeply thankful. Duncan believed beyond the shadow of a doubt that Drake had been divinely led to be in the right place at the right time.

"What do we do now?" Lottie was the one who asked the question.

Colby put in a suggestion. "Send the girls...on to Gettysburg. I'm sure...nothing will...happen there...that will put them...in any danger. You know...as well as I...Major...that there's rarely ever... anything overly exciting...that goes on...at home."

Duncan nodded. "Colby's right, you'll be safe in Gettysburg. In fact, you should go with them, Colby. You're in no shape to report for duty. You need rest and time to recuperate. Mr. Dallinger, might I impose on you to accompany Salina and the Colbys on their journey to Gettysburg? With Major Barnes at large, I'd be much obliged, and feel more at ease, knowing you were with them."

"So would I." Salina implored Drake with her eloquent eyes. "Say you'll come?"

"I'm on my way to Boston—but I suppose another detour won't matter one way or the other," Drake conceded. "I'll go along, Little One, for your sake."

"Then it's settled," Duncan said quickly to forestall any change of mind. "There's a train out of the Baltimore & Ohio Station at six a.m. tomorrow morning, with a transfer in Baltimore and then again at Hanover. It shouldn't take more than six hours. I'll send word to my brother, and he'll meet you at the Gettysburg depot. Tonight, you'll have to stay here." He looked at Salina with a wistful smile. "I realize the accommodations are not equal to those at

Willard's, but they'll have to do."

"They'll do fine, Duncan," Salina nodded, "Just fine."

"Are you sure you're up to another train ride?" Duncan squeezed her shoulder affectionately. "Mosby's been on the loose again, in case you hadn't heard."

The corners of Salina's mouth twitched with a surpressed grin, and she whispered, as though letting Duncan in on a prized secret: "Mosby knows who I am, Duncan. We've met before. I've nothing to fear from him."

Duncan threw his hands up and groaned, "Now why doesn't *that* surprise me?!"

Chapter Eleven

$\mathcal{A}$t Hanover, Drake bid farewell to Salina and the Colbys. "You've less than twenty miles to go. You'll be all right, won't you, Little One?"

Salina lifted her chin bravely. "As you pointed out in Baltimore, the folks up here in the North aren't quite the monsters we Rebels like to imagine them to be. They're people just like us—mostly."

"Just different points of view," Drake reminded her. "Try to see things with an open mind; don't form hasty opinions. You'll get along fine. It's wrong to judge people as a whole for the acts of a few."

"I'll try to remember that," Salina said softly. "It's just that those *few* are usually trying to shoot me, capture me, or invade my home!"

"Well, if these northern newspapers are to be believed, *your people* will be doing the invading soon," Drake affirmed. "I think there's more truth than fiction in reports that the Army of Northern Virginia is heading this way, Little One. People here are bound to be afraid and on edge. You've experienced it for yourself—you can hardly blame them."

"Ha!" Salina retorted. "It's high time for it to be their turn to provide food for the soldiers and forage for the horses. Let's see how graciously *they* like playing host for a grand scale battle!"

Drake cautioned, "Be careful, Little One, or you just might get what you ask for."

"Oh, I've no doubt there'll be conflict here. It's General Lee's intent to fight those people here in their own land. It'll happen, Drake, I'm sure of it," Salina said ominously. "God alone knows when or where, but it's coming."

The sharp blast of the train whistle rent the air. Drake gave Salina a one-armed hug and hastily kissed her brow. "Do take care of yourself. Jeremy probably won't be expecting you on this side of the Mason-Dixon Line. If you do manage to find him, he'll be in for quite a surprise. Give him my best if you do see him."

"I will," Salina assured him. "Drake?"

"Hmmm?" Drake leaned down to pick up his valise.

"May I tell him that you're in Boston?" Salina requested permission. "I'm sure he'll want to know what you're up to these days."

Drake shrugged, "Sure, why not. He'll have a good laugh over it, if nothing else."

"I hope that taking this detour hasn't cost you too much time away from your father," Salina added.

"My old man won't die until he's seen me at least once more," Drake said with conviction. "He usually gets what he wants. If Aurora has told him I'm on the way, I'm sure he'll wait."

"For your sake, I do hope so. Otherwise it will seem like a wasted trip for you." In a mothering manner she smoothed the folded edge of his collar and straightened his tie. "You look very handsome, Drake. I'm sure your father will be proud of you."

"We'll see about that." Drake's lips curled in a crooked grimace. "As for being a wasted effort, this trip could never be considered that. I'm just glad I happened to be on hand when it came time to save your pretty little neck."

"Me, too!" Salina exclaimed. "Go on with you now, or you'll miss your connection."

"I'll miss you," Drake said softly. "But I'll be back down Shadowcreek way one of these days. Count on it."

"I will," Salina nodded. "Good-bye, Mr. Dallinger."

Drake flashed a warm grin. He would have liked to kiss her, but had made a vow to himself that such an occurrence would never happen again. She belonged to Jeremy. "Behave yourself, Little One."

Salina felt a sharp pang of loneliness when she reboarded the Gettysburg-bound train, and seated herself across from Lottie and Colby. Colby was uncomfortable having to sit still for so many hours, but he didn't complain—Lottie took care of that department all by herself.

Through the swollen slits of his eyes, Colby silently watched Salina construct her invisible defenses. The closer they got to Gettysburg, the more distant and withdrawn she became. "That was a difficult good-bye," he commented.

Salina lifted her shoulders in a delicate shrug. "Drake's a reliable friend. I'll miss his company."

Lottie too had witnessed the poignant farewell. "Jeremy Barnes is quite a trusting sort to leave you in the custody of such a one as *him*."

Salina did not deem Lottie's insinuating remark worthy of a reply. She turned and looked out the window, ignoring her cousin's implication. Rolling past were views of lush, tilled fields, well-stocked barns and gardens, the quiet serenity of undulating farmlands. There was no visible sign that a war even existed.

Salina fought back the stinging tears welling in her emerald eyes. Shadowcreek was once just as beautiful and unspoiled a landscape, before the ravages of war and revenge had taken their toll. She had grand hopes that one day the Hastings estate might be restored, yet in her heart cold reason usurped such fantasies. To date the war had permanently altered *everything,* and experience taught Salina that it would continue to do so for as long as the conflict raged. Whatever the outcome, Salina would have to adapt, learn to accept that the only course of action available was to pick up whatever pieces remained and go on. Lamenting what once was would hardly serve to bring it back. Daddy was gone; friends and relatives had been killed or wounded; Mamma had married a Yankee. Each day brought its own set of trials, and Salina prayed earnestly for the courage to endure.

Venturing north into enemy territory was not without risk, and Salina was more than a little apprehensive. Salina felt uncomfortable being the object of Colby's questioning eyes, and she resolved not to let him see how her new circumstance affected her. She almost doubted her own sanity for embarking on this journey, but Mamma needed her. By God's grace she would strive to be strong and courageous.

A short time after crossing the bridge which spanned Rock Creek, the train rolled to a halt at the Western Maryland Railroad Passenger Depot in Gettysburg. The platform was abuzz with activity, people trying to get on the train even before the passengers aboard could get off. Salina witnessed panic on some of the faces. "What's the matter with them?" she asked Colby.

"I don't know. Let's go find out." He spotted Orrin Grant, Duncan's older brother, in the midst of the crowd. "There's Orrin now. He'll know."

Salina, with the aid of one of the porters, assisted Colby as he stiffly descended the stairs to the platform. He was still in a great deal of pain, but he resolutely bore up under the discomfort.

"Lance! My word, man! What's happened to you?" Orrin offered his arm in support, but Colby preferred to stand alone.

"I got into a bit of a scrape down in Virginia. Good to see you, Orrin." Colby tentatively shook the elder Grant's hand. "What's all the fuss about?"

Orrin showed him a copy of *The Compiler*. The printed newspaper headline said *TO ARMS*. Colby read a portion aloud: "In accordance with the presidential proclamation for 50,000 volunteers, troops are pouring into Harrisburg from all quarters..." Colby looked up in question.

"People are leaving town as quickly as possible. The Rebels are said to be headed this way, and rumors have abounded for the past few days. We've not forgotten Jeb Stuart's raid on Chambersburg last October. The good citizens are eager to be out of harm's way, should it come to that. Even the merchants have made preparations and sent their goods east to Philadelphia for safekeeping," Orrin informed Colby. He glanced past Colby to where Lottie and Salina stood a few feet away.

Colby looked over his shoulder, then quickly apologized. "I'm forgetting my manners. Orrin, this is my wife, Lottie, and Salina Hastings, Duncan's stepdaughter."

"Hello, Mr. Grant." Salina bobbed a quick curtsey. Lottie was too busy brushing the layer of dust and cinders from her traveling clothes.

Orrin's features were expressionless as his granite-gray gaze rested wearily on the Southern girls. He nodded in the briefest hint of acknowledgment and muttered to Colby, "You and my brother have spent far too much time down in enemy territory. What have either one of you got against our good Northern womenfolk that you have to go and take Rebel belles to wife?"

Colby wasn't offended by Orrin's insult. He'd expected such a reaction. "We have our reasons."

Orrin grunted, his gray eyes remaining fixed on Salina. "Well, I suppose I can drop you and your wife off at your house, and then I'll take Miss Hastings out to the farm with me. Her mother is beside herself with the anticipation of her arrival."

"You're staying out at the farm now?" Colby inquired. "What about the shop?"

"I've still got my blacksmith shop, but I've been taking up the slack left at the farm by Nathan and Jared's absence. My hotheaded sons, along with your brother Steven, joined up with the 87th Pennsylvania Volunteers and saw action on June twelfth at Winchester. Mercifully, they returned home two days ago—none the worse for the wear. Beth-Anne's afraid that now they've tasted it, they'll want to join up with the regulars and hunt the Johnny Rebs like you do." Orrin again scrutinized Colby's injuries. "And just see how well you've fared!"

"Colby's wounds are not from hunting Johnny Rebs," Salina interjected heatedly. A stern glance from Colby prevented her from stating that the wounds were inflicted by their own Billy Yanks.

"Come on," Colby said. "Let's get the baggage and get away from the press of people here."

Orrin drove south on Carlisle Street through the Diamond, where Carlisle, York, Baltimore, and Chambersburg Streets all met. He made a left at the Court House, and proceeded down East Middle Street, stopping the team and wagon in front of the Colby house.

Lottie swallowed. If Orrin Grant didn't take any pains to hide his staunch disliking of Southerners, how would Colby's family react? She shivered, and cast a glance at Salina.

"I suppose we'll see each other from time to time, Lottie." Salina didn't know why she felt compelled to comfort Lottie, but her cousin seemed to need reassurance. "Do the Grants live near here?"

"They live on the other side of town, beyond Pennsylvania College, in the vicinity of Oak Hill," Colby replied when Orrin did not. "And yes, you'll be seeing one another. Orrin's youngest sister, Dulcie, is engaged to my brother. Perhaps we'll have a joint family picnic on the 4th of July out near Culp's Hill like last summer."

Orrin still made no reply.

"Good-bye, Lottie, Colby," Salina waved from the wagon. The conveyance lurched forward and Salina gripped the seat firmly.

"It's very pretty here," Salina said conversationally. "So green and rich. Shadowcreek used to be like this." Orrin obviously wasn't going to respond to her casual comments, so she asked direct questions instead. "How is my mamma? Is she doing well? What of the baby?"

"Annelise gave birth to a boy early this morning," Orrin finally answered. "Mother and child were doing fine when I last saw them."

"I have a little brother?" She was immensely pleased, but then her smile dimmed. The intent of this trip had been to be with Mamma when the baby was born, and Salina felt a bit deflated to learn that the auspicious event had already passed. "Do you know his name?" she inquired.

"Doesn't have one yet. I sent a wire to my brother before your train arrived to tell him he had a son. Annelise is leaving the naming up to him," Orrin replied.

Orrin Grant was silent for the remainder of the drive. Salina didn't attempt to ask him any more questions. Once they were out of the town proper, they continued along the Mummasburg Road for a piece until they arrived at a comfortable-looking farmhouse. The warmth and welcome of the structure itself was more than Salina had received from her companion.

Jubilee banged through the screened porch door and rushed toward the wagon. Salina was in the loving arms of the tall, big-boned black woman before she could blink twice. "Chile! Ah cain't hardly believe ah's seein' ya fer my own self! Let Jube lookit ya!"

Salina giggled, executing a petite pirouette for Jubilee's inspection. "I'm told I have a little brother, Jubilee. Is he beautiful?"

"Oh, chile, he be dat," Jubilee nodded, flashing a pearly-white grin. She took Salina by the hand. To Duncan's brother she said, "T'ank ya, Mistah Orrin, fer goin' an' fetchin' our Missy Salina. She sure gowin ta be a great comfort ta her mamma."

Orrin nodded curtly. "Tell my wife and mother I'll be back in time for supper. I've business to attend to at the forge."

"Yas, Mistah Orrin," Jubilee replied. "Ah'll tell 'em." She squeezed Salina's hand and led her through the gate, up the cobbled walk toward the house. "Cum on den, ah'll see dat ya meet Miz Noreen and Miz Beth-Anne. Dey's lookin' forward to makin' yer 'quaintance. Miz Annelise, why all she ever does is talk o'ya, an' so dey feel like dey already knows ya."

Noreen Grant, Duncan's mother, and Beth-Anne, Orrin's wife, greeted Salina kindly. "You must come upstairs right away and see your new little brother," Noreen encouraged. Beth-Anne seemed a bit more reserved.

"Thank you, I'd like that," Salina nodded. She followed Jubilee up the stairs to the room where Mamma was resting. A wriggling bundle lay in the crook of her arm. "Mamma?"

Annelise Grant looked up to see her daughter, her vision blurred by a sudden rush of tears. "Oh, my darling! You're truly here with me!"

Salina sat in the chair next to the bed. "He was born before I could get here. I'm sorry about that. I wanted to be with you, but there were things that simply couldn't be helped. May I hold him?"

Mamma handed the baby into Salina's anxious arms. She held him close, gently caressing his ruddy cheek with the backs of her curled fingers. "He's a hefty one."

Jubilee chuckled, "Ah should say so. Ah figure he done weigh nigh unta ten pound, jist like Massah Ethan when he was born. Came kickin' and screamin', dis here boy did. Doc say dere's no doubt da boy got good lungs."

"Orrin sent word to Duncan," Salina told Mamma. "What do you suppose he'll name him?"

"That's up to Duncan," Annelise sighed softly. "It's his right to be able to name his own son."

"Well, until we know for sure, we'll have to find something else to call him." Salina smiled down at her little brother. He had very little hair, deep auburn in color; clear, unblemished skin; and slate-gray eyes, just like his father's. "Duncan will be so proud."

Annelise leaned back into the pillows. "Yes. I hope he gets to see him sometime soon." Her eyes closed. She was exhausted, for the birthing had sapped all her strength, but she was content. "I'm so very tired."

"I can only imagine." Salina squeezed her hand. "You rest now, and we'll talk later." She put her brother back into the crook of Mamma's arm and bent to kiss her brow.

She was almost to the door when Mamma called, "Salina?"

"Yes, Mamma?"

"Sweetheart, I can't tell you what it means to me that you've come. I just want you to know that," Annelise smiled weakly.

"I know, Mamma. I'll see you in a little while." Salina followed Jubilee down the hall to the next bedroom.

"Mistah Chandler done brung up yer satchel, Missy. Ah'll unpack fer ya," Jubilee offered.

From the bedroom window, Salina had a panoramic view of the town of Gettysburg. The buildings of Pennsylvania College were just on the outskirts, and a little ways beyond rose the cupola of the Lutheran Theological Seminary. During the train trip, Colby had told her that Gettysburg, while possessing a population of just under twenty-five hundred, was an important crossroads village. One railroad and twelve country roads and turnpikes led into the farming town like spokes of a wheel. Most of the roads were dirt, but two of them had hard surfaces of stone and gravel. Each took its name from the town or city it led to: Carlisle, Harrisburg, Hunterstown, York, Hanover, Taneytown, Baltimore, Emmitsburg, Hagerstown, Millerstown, Chambersburg, and Mummasburg. In addition to farming, there was the typical collection of skilled professionals, craft and tradesmen, shopkeepers, merchants, and politicians. Gettysburg was the county seat of Adams County, and it boasted two institutions of higher learning: the college and the seminary. Colby explained to Salina that most of the excitement in town was connected with events of the two institutions, especially commencement ceremonies which brought in all kinds of interesting visitors who came to see their sons or brothers graduate.

As she looked out, Salina observed that the Grants' farm, perched between Oak Hill and Oak Ridge, was one of the higher elevations. There was also Seminary Ridge, McPherson's Ridge, Cemetery Ridge, and in the distance Culp's Hill and the Round Tops.

"They say the Army of Northern Virginia is coming this way. If there was to be a battle here, high ground would indeed be a vital key to victory," Salina said, thinking aloud.

"Humph." Jubilee continued to unpack. "Rumors. Ah'll believe dat da Reb Army is comin' when ah kin see da whites o'dere eyes. All dese rumors gots folks runnin' skeered."

"Who's running scared?" Salina questioned.

"Mostly folk like me, Missy. Dere's a good number o' my kind here, but dey be leavin', more an' more each day. Dey don' wanta be captured an' taken South ta be sold back inta slavery. Naw, Missy. Even sum o'da white men skedaddle, too. Dey's got so many menfolk up here, Missy, dey ain't neber gowin ta run outta soldiers if da fightin' keeps a-goin' on an' on. Dey gots more o'ev'rythin' here. Dey hides da horses an' livestock, dey ship food an' goods east ta Phil'delphia fer safety. Miz Noreen an' me, we done stocked up here. Dere's lots of food ta see us through if da Rebs were ta cum here—we won' starve," Jubilee said matter-of-factly.

"Why haven't you gone away, Jubilee? If it isn't safe to be here, then why do you stay?" asked Salina. Mamma had given Jubilee her freedom papers at the same time she had given Peter Tom and Cromwell theirs. The men had eventually left Shadowcreek, but Jubilee had not.

The black-skinned woman still refused. "Chile, ya knows ah could neber leave Miz Annelise. No way, no how. An' Miz Noreen, she say she wouldna let no graybacks take me anyways. She a good lady, Miz Noreen. She help me git my liddle bizness gowin'. She say ah a fine seamstress, an' she got it so ah been takin' in sewin' here an' dere. Ah does fancy work on dresses an' gowns, an' ah does mendin' and fixin' for dem students at da college an' da sem'nary. Dey like da work ah do fer 'em, an' dey pays me a fair wage ta do it," Jubilee told her.

"What about your cooking?" Salina asked, her mouth watering at the very notion. "You could open a restaurant, Jubilee."

"Don' t'ink ah ain't t'ought bout it, but da timin' ain't right. Lord willin', mebee sum day," Jubilee shrugged. "Now, ah's content ta keep on stitchin' and keepin' an eye on Miz Annelise, an' da liddle babe, too."

Salina nodded and let the matter rest. She took her silver-plated brush from her satchel. "Jubilee, would you do me a favor?"

"Anythin' Missy," Jubilee nodded.

"Will you brush out my hair? I've missed that." Salina smiled at the faithful former slave.

Jubilee took the brush. "Ya sit down here on da bed. It'll be like old times at Shadowcreek."

Salina obeyed. It was relaxing to feel the strokes of the brush through her curls. "I'm in need of a bath, what with all the grit and cinders from the train."

"Ah'll fetch da tub an' heat up sum watah fer ya in jist a bit," Jubilee promised.

"Sing for me?" Salina requested. Jubilee's singing was something else that she'd missed.

Jubilee chose not to sing an old spiritual or Negro tune. Instead,

152 / *Not Without Courage*

her rich voice began with a low rendition of *Amazing Grace* followed by the *Battle Hymn of the Republic*. "We's in da North now, Missy. Dey ain't got much use fer Southern anythin' up here—songs or otherwise."

"When in Rome, do as the Romans? Is that what you're saying?" Salina asked, her head nodding with each repetitive stroke of the brush.

"As long as yer here, chile, it's sumthin' ya might want ta consider," Jubilee suggested.

☆ ☆ ☆ ☆ ☆ ☆ ☆

Somewhere in the middle of the night, Salina got up when she heard her little brother's cry. She tiptoed into Mamma's room, finding her sound asleep. Salina quickly picked up the unhappy baby and took him to her room. She had a bottle of cool water, but the little boy didn't seem to be particularly thirsty, just lonely. While Salina rocked him, she caught herself humming *Dixie*. "Well," she whispered, "The best half of you is Rebel, after all. It's that half-Yank side we'll have to watch." Salina smiled as the little boy stared up at her with his wide-open eyes. "Half-Rebel, half-Yank, just like Jeremy said. But you're too young to know the difference—be glad! Rebel, Yank—Yank, Rebel..." Her mind worked, and then she giggled softly, "I'll call you *Yabel*—because you're both." She selected another tune and began humming *Kathleen Mavourneen*. The soothing melody soon had her little brother back to sleep.

☆ ☆ ☆ ☆ ☆ ☆ ☆

Though Salina had been up in the middle of the night with little Yabel, she was up early the next morning. The wonderful aroma of Jubilee's breakfast being served downstairs prompted Salina to dress hastily and make an appearance.

Curious eyes were on her the minute she set foot in the dining room. Noreen smiled, "Please, do join us. You already know Beth-Anne and Orrin. These are their sons—Nathan, Jared, Cody, and Chandler. This is Michael, Duncan's father, and this is our youngest daughter, Dulcie."

"Pleased to meet you all," Salina nodded a bit shyly. She was overly conscious of her drawl this morning, though she shouldn't care what they thought of her.

Nathan wiped his mouth and excused himself rather abruptly. Jared followed suit. "Got work to do, Gram," Nathan made his excuses to his grandmother. "Time's a-wasting."

Orrin kissed his wife and followed his older boys out. "Send a lunch pail out with Chandler this afternoon."

Beth-Anne nodded affirmatively. She wondered if the pretty Southern girl was aware that these Grant men had refused her company deliberately, or if she believed their polite lies.

Michael Grant was the next to depart. He was an English professor at the college and had classes to prepare for. He told Noreen, "I should be home for dinner at noontime."

Jubilee set a plate of fried potatoes, eggs, and bacon strips in front of Salina, and a glass of cold milk.

The stilted silence was broken by Noreen's apology. "I'm sure they don't mean to be rude, Salina."

"I know better, Noreen. No use beating around the bush." Salina thought it better to clear the air. "You can hardly expect the boys to treat me like a long lost family member when they've just returned from fighting against my people."

Noreen nodded. "You're absolutely right, dear. They haven't yet forgiven Duncan for marrying your mother and bringing her here, but perhaps one day we'll all be able to let bygones be bygones."

Salina smiled kindly. The women at the table all knew that day would be a long time coming.

"What are your plans for today, Dulcie?" Beth-Anne asked. "I could use your help with the washing."

"Sorry, Bethie," Dulcie refused blithely. "Steve's taking me on a picnic. We've hardly had any time together since he's come back from...Virginia." She shot a sidelong glance at Salina. "We're going with his brother and his wife. Steve promised Lance that we'd welcome his new bride."

"Perhaps Salina would like to go along and spend some time with the younger set instead of with us older folks," Noreen suggested. "I'll help you with the washing, Beth-Anne."

Dulcie grudgingly extended the invitation for Salina to join them. "If you're up to it, I suppose you're welcome to come along."

"It's nice of you to include me," Salina reluctantly accepted. She didn't want to go anymore than Dulcie wanted her to come, but neither wanted to displease Noreen.

"That's settled," Noreen smiled. She turned to Cody. "If you don't hurry, you'll be late for school, young man."

"Aw, Gram," Cody complained. "I'd just as soon stay home and work the fields with Pa, Nate, and Jared."

"Your Grandpa Mike and I have higher hopes for you than farming," Beth-Anne insisted. "You've got the brains; you just don't apply yourself to your studies."

"If you like book-learning so much, Ma, then why don't you go in my place?" Cody suggested.

"Don't sass me, son, just do what you're told," Beth-Anne said firmly, a smile twitching her lips. "Your Uncle Duncan wants you to go to college too, you know." She knew that mentioning Duncan's name would motivate Cody. The boy admired his uncle a good deal, and would never do anything to let his uncle down.

"I'll let you know later if I hear any good rumors about the Rebs today," Cody said, downing the last of his apple juice. He glanced at Salina, checking to see if she would flinch at his statement.

She didn't. She met the fourteen-year-old's eyes squarely. "I'd like to hear them too," she said. "That way I'll know when my friends will be arriving. Perhaps I'll invite them to supper, if they ever really show up."

Cody grinned. She'd stood up to him, and he liked her for it. "We'll just have to see."

Beth-Anne allowed herself to smile when Cody was gone. "You've disappointed him, Salina. I think he was hoping to scare you. Don't let him—he's a little tease."

Salina smiled in return and continued eating her breakfast.

"We'll be leaving at ten or so. Can you be ready by then?" Dulcie asked Salina.

"Certainly," Salina nodded.

Annelise had no objections to Salina going out with the young people. "You have a good time."

Salina leaned over the cradle. In a low voice she said, "I'll see you later, Yabel."

When Salina went out to the barn, Steve Colby was there, holding the reins of a saddled horse for her. "You do ride, don't you, Miss Hastings?"

"Of course." Salina accepted his assistance. "Thank you."

Steve and Dulcie rode together, and Salina followed just far enough behind to avoid eating the dust kicked up by their horses. Colby and Lottie brought a smart buggy and a big hamper of food. They went beyond town to the picnic grounds near Culp's Hill that

Salina had heard Colby mention yesterday. It was a lovely spot. Salina and Dulcie spread quilts under the shade trees while Steve hefted the hamper out of the buggy. Lottie tended to her husband, who sat propped up against a tree trunk, still recuperating from his four-day-old injuries.

"Set the hamper there," Dulcie instructed. She opened the lid and began distributing the contents. "So tell us, Salina, did you come north to catch a husband like your cousin and your mamma did?"

Colby coughed, nearly choking on a slice of orange. "Salina and a Yankee husband—never!" He winked at her. "Miss Hastings happens to be engaged to a Rebel cavalryman, a first lieutenant attached to General Stuart's staff. There are some who even think that he looks like me."

Salina bit her tongue, holding back a sharp rejoinder. Colby was intentionally teasing her.

"One of Stuart's boys, eh?" Steve asked. "Wonder where he is now."

"Now, I was under the impression that the newspapers up here in the North keep close tabs on General Stuart," Salina replied sweetly. "Even the papers in California were monitoring his whereabouts last fall when he raided Chambersburg."

"Touché!" Dulcie applauded. "She's got a quick wit, Steve. You have to give her that."

"I hear you've a little brother, Salina," Colby changed the topic. "Congratulations."

"Thank you," Salina nodded.

"Which would you prefer, Lottie?" Colby asked his wife. "A daughter or a son?"

"A son, of course," Lottie immediately replied. She knew she would never want to compete for attention with a daughter.

"You're pregnant?" Dulcie questioned, as this was news to her. "Well, Lance, you didn't waste any time starting a family, did you?"

Colby grinned, "I don't like wasting time." He squeezed Lottie's shoulder, silently urging her to play his game with him. He hadn't thought it necessary to tell his family that he'd *had* to marry Lottie to make an honest woman of her.

To her credit, Lottie had the decency to blush at his cue. "Really, Lance. There are more suitable topics for discussion in mixed company. But tell me, when are the two of you to be married?"

Steve and Dulcie glanced at each other. Steve shrugged, and Dulcie answered, "We were supposed to have gotten married on June fourteenth, but Steve was off fighting the Johnny Rebs. We haven't gotten around to setting another date yet. But we will." She caressed her fiancé's cheek.

"Well, you and Salina should be able to sympathize then," Lottie commented pointedly. "Her horse soldier left her standing in the church all alone while he was off fighting the day they were to get married."

"Disappointing, isn't it?" Dulcie asked Salina.

"To say the least," Salina answered coolly, refusing to meet her cousin's taunting eyes.

For the most part, the girls sat and listened to the brothers as they exchanged tales of their recent encounters with the enemy. Salina sensed that Colby was intentionally keeping her and Lottie out of the discussion. He very gallantly said nothing that would cause either of the Southern girls to lose face in front of his brother or Dulcie Grant.

After awhile, Dulcie and Steve went off together to pick berries. Lottie took a brief nap while Colby and Salina chatted amicably. She asked him all kinds of questions about the town and its people.

Colby answered all her inquiries in detail, as he was proud of his little hometown. Then he chuckled, "If I didn't know any better, Salina, I'd almost think you were conducting a reconnaissance mission."

"Hardly; I just want to know," Salina insisted. "Isn't it natural to be curious about someplace you've never been before?"

Colby nodded. She seemed genuinely interested, so he gave her another geography lesson. In the dust he drew a makeshift map, denoting places like Marsh Creek, Willoughby Run, Plum Creek, Wolf's Hill, Evergreen Cemetery, the county prison, and the Almshouse. "The Round Tops are that way," he pointed. "You can see for miles from the crest. Little Round Top looks down into Devil's Den."

"Devil's Den?" Salina arched an eyebrow.

"It's just a big clump of boulders, rocks and stones. Legend says there used to be snakes there—the biggest one was called the Old Devil, after the serpent from the Garden of Eden. The rock formations were supposedly his den." Colby shrugged. "Who can say how such stories get started? They just get passed down from generation to generation. As a prank when we were growing up, my charming brother left me out there in Devil's Den one night. I might have been eight or nine. Told me that if I came home before first light I was a nothing but a yellow-bellied coward."

"And did you stay?" asked Salina.

"You bet I did." Colby chuckled at the memory. "And to this day I get chills when I'm near the place. Silly, isn't it?"

Salina laughed with him. Lottie woke up then, and Steve and Dulcie returned.

"I heard you telling Salina about the night I made you stay in Devil's Den. See what good it did? You're not a coward by any stretch of the imagination, little brother. I made a fine man out of you," Steve boasted, taking all the credit.

Dulcie offered Lottie and Salina some of the sweet berries with cream. Conversation between the two men once again dominated.

"Well, I hate to sound like an old married man," Colby said at length, stretching his stiff limbs, "but Lottie and I are going to go back to town. What do you say, my dear? My ribs are sore, and I could go for another dose of mother's headache powders."

The hamper was repacked in no time. Lottie was ready to leave whenever Colby was, happier to climb back into the buggy than to stay and socialize with Steve and Dulcie. She blithely waved farewell to Salina, feeling no pang of remorse for leaving her cousin alone in the company of those Yankees.

"I suppose we should be going too," Steve said.

Dulcie pouted. "I wish we could stay here all afternoon."

"Maybe another time," Steve promised with a wink. "So, Salina, you want to see that old Devil's Den?"

"I guess so—why not?" She lifted her shoulders in a shrug. She knew better than to allow Steve to catch even a glimpse of her apprehension.

Steve smiled contemptuously. "Come on then, since it's obvious that *you're* no yellow-bellied coward."

Salina followed Steve and Dulcie to the site of the enormous boulders. Strange shadows were cast by the angle of the sun, and Salina knew that this was not a place one would want to be after dark. An overactive imagination might conjure all sorts of nightmarish scenes...She turned to her companions, neither of whom had commented on her reaction to the huge rock piles.

She was alone.

In a small voice she said defiantly, "I am not a yellow-bellied coward!" It would be no use to call for either of the pair, as they were either hiding or long gone—no doubt laughing at her. Salina upbraided herself for falling for such a prank. She should have seen that one coming. Steve meant to frighten her, but she would not allow it.

For a few minutes Salina remained there at Devil's Den, trying to get her bearings. She closed her eyes, trying to recreate a mental picture of the map that Colby had diagrammed in the dirt. She figured she was a good distance from Culp's Hill, and a few miles from the Grants' farmhouse, but there was enough daylight to serve her purpose. She retraced the route they had come, successfully finding her way back to the Taneytown Road. She rode for quite some time before she came upon the red brick gatehouse of Evergreen Cemetery.

Curiosity got the better of Salina. She dismounted and tied up the horse. Nearby, a woman was working amid a row of graves. "Good afternoon, miss. I'm Mrs. Thorne. Is there something I can do for you?"

Salina took a chance and asked, "Would you happen to know where I might find the grave of Garrett Daniel Hastings?"

The woman was the daughter of the cemetery's groundskeeper, and was able to lead Salina straight to the relatively new marker. "That's the one," Mrs. Thorne indicated. "See for yourself."

Salina was left alone in front of the grave marker. The epitaph was carved in sharp relief, not yet worn smooth like the writing on many of the older headstones. Silently, she read the words Duncan had composed in tribute:

> *Courage, Duty, Honor, Pride:*
> *He served his countries well,*
> *loved his family with all his heart,*
> *and trusted the future to God alone.*
>
> *Here lies the best friend*
> *any man could ever know.*
>
> *Garrett Daniel Hastings*
> *b. 31 Dec 1822 d. 21 Sep 1862*

"Oh, Daddy," Salina choked in a dry whisper, caressing the cold, gray marble. In a small vase at the base of the marker was a fading bouquet of flowers, only partially dried and withered. Mamma must have put them there. "Duncan took good care of you—and he's try-ing to take care of us. We Hastings are a trial to him more often than not, I think. Duncan is a good man, and kind, and I can't help but love him—but I reckon you knew that would happen, didn't you? Everything planned out to the last detail…" She sighed, mindless of the salty tears that dripped from her sooty lashes, "Mamma's borne him a son, a fine healthy little boy who has his eyes." She clutched her elbows, hugging them close to her body. "I wonder if you can see him. Duncan hasn't yet, but he will, and he'll be so very proud. I believe Duncan'll make a good father, but he can never take your place in my heart."

The sun dipped lower in the sky and Salina knew she should get going, but still she hesitated, continuing her one-sided conver-sation: "Rumors of an impending Rebel invasion are rife. Perhaps our boys in gray will be here soon; I wish they would come, but part of me wants them to stay away. Something fierce is going to happen here before all is said and done." She shivered even as she spoke.

It was long after dark when Steve and Dulcie returned to the farmhouse on the northern edge of Oak Ridge. They'd searched everywhere they knew to look for the missing Rebel girl, and were properly bewildered to find Salina in the sitting room, calmly play-ing chess with Cody.

"Oh, there you are," Salina said, carelessly glancing up when the couple came in. "I've kept some supper warm for you, as I didn't know what time you planned on coming home."

Steve's eyes glittered with reluctant approval. She had passed the test. It was a mean prank, leaving her alone at the Devil's Den, but it was meant in fun. Dulcie had been upset with him at first, and he'd ended up feeling bad about deserting Salina. But now, to see her serenely acting as if nothing out-of-the-ordinary had happened, he had to admit the Southern girl had spunk. Salina never did men-tion the incident, and from that point on, Steve respectfully left her be.

Chapter Twelve

On Friday, Salina sat at the kitchen table divesting plump red strawberries of their green leaves and stems. Her little brother slept peacefully in the carved wood cradle that she absently rocked with one foot. She continued to call him Yabel, even though Duncan's latest telegram had indicated that the baby boy should be named Garrett Duncan Grant. The other members of the Grant household were beginning to follow Salina's example.

When Salina's bowl was filled with stemless berries, she washed them thoroughly and proceeded to cut them into quarters, making them ready for the next batch of jam.

At the stove, Beth-Anne peeked over Jubilee's shoulder to check the boiling mixture in the speckled blue enamel pot. "How does it look?"

Jubilee lifted the ladle out of the pot for inspection. "It's gettin' thick, an' nearly clear," she reported of the red, sweet-smelling concoction. "Won't be long. Missy Salina kin get da jars prepared."

Since Yabel was fast asleep, peacefully sucking one tightly curled little fist, Salina let the cradle come to a standstill. "I'll fetch the jars, if you tell me where to find them."

Beth-Anne took over the berry-cutting. "Downstairs in the cellar, third shelf along the far wall."

Salina took a candle with her and searched the shelves in the root cellar. She couldn't find the jars anywhere. She closed the cellar door, and even before she reached the kitchen she could smell the rich, sugary-strawberry aroma of jam lingering in the humid air. She informed Beth-Anne, "There aren't any Mason jars in the cellar."

"Dulcie!" Beth-Anne called into the parlour over the sound of piano music. She wiped her hands on her striped apron and marched into the room. "Dulcie!"

"Yes?" Dulcie's fingers halted on the keys.

"Last week I asked you to go into town and pick up some things from Fahnestock's Store. Mason jars were on the list," Beth-Anne mentioned. "Where did you put them?"

Dulcie's guilty eyes betrayed her careless negligence, and she bit her bottom lip. "Oh, Bethie, I think you're about to be very upset with me."

Beth-Anne sighed and pushed an errant strand of sable-colored hair away from her cheek. Frustration was a frequent occurrence when having to deal with her sister-in-law. "Why this time?"

"I forgot to buy the jars," Dulcie confessed, twirling a glossy, nut-brown curl around her finger. "That was the day that Steve came back from Winchester, and it must have just slipped my mind. I was so happy to see him, I just…well, I plumb forgot about the jars."

Beth-Anne left the parlour, but returned in a few minutes with a wad of greenbacks in her hand. She held the money out to Dulcie. "I want you to go into town immediately; we've got to have those jars. The first batch of jam is nearly ready to be poured, and due to your forgetfulness, we have nothing to pour the jam into. Now go, and be quick about it."

"But I can't, Bethie. Steve's on his way over with the preacher—he said they'd be here at half past ten. Don't your remember? Last night at supper Papa said he didn't see any reason why we couldn't be wed tomorrow afternoon. The preacher's coming over with Steve because he wants to talk to us about the ceremony. Most of the details were planned for the original date, so there's little to do, and only a few people to invite. Steve and I just want to be married before something else happens!" Dulcie stated emphatically.

Salina could see the exasperation on Beth-Anne's face when

she returned to the kitchen, hands on her hips. "If you'll tell me how to get to the store, I'll go fetch the jars," Salina volunteered.

Beth-Anne shook her head. "Salina, I appreciate that, but I can't send you into town alone. No offense, but you'd probably need a translator. People here are so on edge with all the rumors of coming Rebels; I'm sure they'd get their back up over your Southern drawl without ever listening to the words you say."

"I could accompany you to town, Beth-Anne, and help carry," Salina rephrased her offer. "Jubilee'll keep an eye on the jam and on the baby while we're gone. Mamma is resting, and Noreen has taken lunch to the boys in the east fields—she'll be back soon."

"All right," Beth-Anne agreed, and untied her apron.

"Jubilee, just tell them we've gone into town right quick, and we'll be back shortly," Salina instructed. As she turned toward the kitchen door, she thought she heard a low rumble. Beth-Anne was right: ever since Salina had come to town, rumors had been flying fast and furious concerning the Rebels' northerly invasion. She wondered if the rumbling was caused by guns and meant a clash somewhere.

"That might be thunder," Beth-Anne suggested. "In which case we should hurry to avoid getting caught out in the rain."

"Or it might be cannon fire," Salina said ominously. "Jubilee, if you sense even a hint of trouble, I want you to take Yabel and skedaddle down to the cellar, you hear?"

"Ah hear ya, Missy," Jubilee nodded. "Tain't no cause fer ya ta worry none bout ol' Jube. Ah'll take care of little Mistah Yabel. Git gowin, now. Da sooner ya go, da sooner ya'll be back."

Beth-Anne and Salina worked together to hitch the team to the buggy. The two women had established a sort of unspoken truce, as Beth-Anne had come to realize that Salina and her mother were actually very nice people. Initially, she hadn't wanted to like them because they were from Virginia. She'd never known anyone from that state before, but if these two ladies were any indication of the population, then Beth-Anne presumed Virginians couldn't all be bad. She supposed the reverse was also true—that Annelise and Salina were growing accustomed to the Grants in spite of their being Pennsylvanians.

"It's good of you to help out the way you do, Salina," Beth-Anne commented on the way into Gettysburg. "Dulcie's nineteen, but I swear you're more responsible in some ways than she is. Oh, she isn't a bad girl, really, just a mite flighty at times. Spoiled is another adjective that comes to mind. Always has been, if you ask me. She is to Noreen and Michael what your little brother is to Duncan and Annelise—a surprise. From Day One Dulcie's been doted on by two older brothers and two older sisters, not to mention her parents."

"Dulcie reminds me of my cousin Lottie in some respects." Salina smiled ruefully in understanding. "Lottie wouldn't know the first thing about canning fruit or making jam—she was more concerned with finishing school accomplishments. Jubilee and Mamma thought it important that I learn how to run a household."

"You'll make a fine wife," Beth-Anne commended. "Dulcie will have to learn on her feet, for she's never taken much instruction from Noreen or her own sisters. She thinks marrying Steve Colby will be the culmination of her romantic, fairy-tale dreams. She's in for a rude awakening, but she'll have to find that out for herself; she won't take advice from any of us old married ladies. But I'll tell you this: Steve will want to be fed, expect his clothes to be cared for, and, in time, require that she bear his children. Dulcie isn't prepared for any of that. I reckon you are, though. It was wise of your mamma to see to the practical side of your education, rather than just polish you off with finishing school."

"I never went to finishing school." Salina did not lament the fact. "I might have, but the war came and spared me. I have to admit, I had more fun with my brother learning how to fish and shoot a gun than practicing the piano. I already know how to crochet and knit and dance—though my sewing and embroidery could use some work."

"I was taught French when I went to finishing school, and I think I learned some Latin, but very little else besides dancing and literature. Doesn't matter much now—I can't remember any of it!" Beth-Anne laughed.

"I can appreciate Dulcie's yearning to get on with her wedding, though. My own wedding was canceled because my fiancé had orders that kept him from getting to the church. I waited and waited—I'm still waiting. One day, we'll get our chance to exchange our vows," Salina said with decided resolve.

"With you as his bride-to-be, your fiancé should consider himself a fortunate man; though I'm sure that's something he doesn't have to be told," Beth-Anne smiled.

"You're kind for saying so." Salina blushed demurely.

Beth-Anne drove the wagon toward the Diamond, and there

they heard the brittle crackle of weaponry fire. It came from the direction of Chambersburg Road. Beth-Anne tied the horses to the hitching post and quickly sought news from someone she recognized on the street.

"Our militia went out not more than an hour ago, headed west," the man informed Beth-Anne. "Sounds to me like they've run into some trouble."

"We should hurry then." Beth-Anne motioned for Salina to follow her into Fahnestock's Store quickly. She told the storekeeper behind the counter what she needed.

"My apologies, Mrs. Grant." Mr. Fahnestock shook his head. "We've only one box of jars left, and no rubber seals to go with them. Everything else has been shipped out," he explained apologetically.

"We don't need the seals if there's any paraffin to be had," Salina reminded Beth-Anne.

"It will have to do. I'll take some paraffin wax instead." Beth-Anne counted out enough bills to cover the cost. "Thank you, Mr. Fahnestock."

"Would you like me to carry that out for you, Mrs. Grant?" the storekeeper offered.

"Yes, please, I would appreciate it," Beth-Anne nodded.

The shopkeeper followed Beth-Anne and Salina and deposited the purchases into the buggy. In the next instant, the three mutely beheld the blue-clad militia pouring back into town, some running, some on horseback, most yelling. Someone was trying to get a rear guard posted. It had been raining off and on for most of the day, and now the horses, wagons, and confused men trampled through the muddy mire. They reported that the Rebels were less than two miles from town.

"If you're heading back up towards Oak Ridge, Mrs. Grant, I'd hurry if I were you," Mr. Fahnestock suggested. Beth-Anne and Salina quickly climbed into the buggy, taking the shopkeeper's advice.

The Diamond was clogged with men, horses, and a vast assortment of conveyances. Beth-Anne made a hasty decision and turned the buggy around, heading in the opposite direction, away from the farm.

"Where are we going?" Salina wanted to know.

"Home—to my home, mine and Orrin's. We're only living at the farm for the summer—we have a house on Baltimore Street," Beth-Anne hurriedly explained. "It's closer than trying to make a run to the farm if the Rebels are really behind our militia, as I fear they must be!"

The two-story brick house on Baltimore Street had been closed up for better than a month and was in need of airing. Beth-Anne and Salina opened the windows facing the street, but kept the shades and shutters drawn. For several hours nothing happened. Salina sat on a chair still shrouded in a dust cover and fanned herself, patiently waiting out the imminent crisis.

The nervous feeling of being trapped, however, was becoming unbearable to Beth-Anne. "That jam must be ruined by now. If Jubilee has gone into hiding, which I pray she has if the Rebels are coming, I can only hope she didn't leave the pot simmering! Dulcie will never think to take care of it, and it'll be a burned, sticky-gooey mess. Annelise might be up and about, and Noreen should have returned by now..." Her voice trailed off. It was foolish to get so worked up over a spoiled batch of jam when there were more pressing matters just outside the front door.

Salina was astute enough to see through Beth-Anne's fussing. Beth-Anne wrung her hands and finally admitted what was really bothering her: "Orrin is bound to worry, and I'm afraid he'll come looking for me. I'd just die if he were captured by the Rebel army and sent to a prison camp in the South."

Salina had no words of comfort for Beth-Anne. What could she say to refute a very possible scenario? She was nervous too, but Salina knew there was nothing to be gained in panic.

By mid-afternoon the town was filled with Rebel Cavalry—Jenkins' Brigade, according to some of the retreating militia. "Jenkins," Salina murmured to herself. She wondered where Stuart was.

A neighbor came over, banging loudly on the side door. "Oh, Mrs. Grant! Mrs. Grant! Can you believe it? Rebels in our town!"

"Come in, Mrs. Albrecht." Beth-Anne opened the door and shut it again quickly. Some of the soldiers in the street wore gray, some butternut, but all of them looked dirty and unkempt. They were shabby and tattered, and many had no shoes to speak of.

"Such a ragtag bunch as you ever wanted to see!" Mrs. Albrecht exclaimed, fanning herself rapidly. "Several of them have asked if I know where the Union army is. How should I know? I wish it was here! Where are our soldiers when we need them?"

Salina left Beth-Anne to the task of calming Mrs. Albrecht. Unwanted tears stung her eyes. For over a week, speculation had the Rebels practically on the threshold of Gettysburg—well, here they were at last! On one hand Salina was proud to know they had made it this far north, but on the other hand she fretted over their presence, her mind throbbing with misgivings.

Beth-Anne looked out between the slats of the drawn shades. She exclaimed indignantly, "They're stealing our horses! And our buggy!" She made a move toward the front door.

Salina saw the gray-uniformed men confiscating the animals and the conveyance. She put a hand on Beth-Anne's arm. "Stay put," she ordered gently, but in a tone that brooked no argument. "Just let it go for now. There's nothing we can do."

"Nothing we can do?" Beth-Anne raged. "Those are *your peo- ple* out there—you talk to them! Tell them to leave our property alone!"

"Beth-Anne." Salina's eyes commanded attention. "Those men outside have their orders—they are the invaders. They have come here for the specific purpose of commandeering supplies. They may plan to occupy the town, and might yet demand its surrender. They are not in the frame of mind to listen to one misplaced Virginian who finds herself on the wrong side of the lines at present!" She marched over to the window and saw dozens of horses being herded through the streets. The Confederates were whooping and hollering; echoes of the Rebel Yell were enough to make spines tingle and skin crawl. "If any of them approach the house, *I* will do the talking—otherwise they'll assume I'm just another Yankee woman. We may all be Americans despite our differences—but a Rebel like me is probably the last thing they'll expect to encounter here in the North. I'm sure they won't harm us, but neither will they take any pains to discover the distinction—and that's what fright- ens me most!"

Beth-Anne reluctantly gave up the notion of retaining her prop- erty; it pained her to let the horses go without a fight. Salina was in a quandary, that was evident, but Beth-Anne was too irritated to have much sympathy for her predicament. "How do you propose we get out of this mess?" she queried sarcastically.

"We wait." Salina's forehead rested against the window frame as she continued to peek through the shutters, watching for...she didn't know what. Absently she murmured, "When the children of Israel were caught between the Red Sea and Pharaoh's army, He made a way for them. He parted the waters, and His children crossed over to safety on dry land. The Lord will come through. He always does." The crush and press of activity outside, however, showed no immediate signs of slowing.

And then Salina thought she saw—*her brother!* She blinked in disbelief, but when she opened her eyes he still didn't disappear. "Ethan!" Salina called out amid the ruckus.

A Rebel captain atop a gray gelding turned toward the row of houses behind him. He swore he'd heard his name called. There it was again: *"Ethan!"*

"Salina?" Ethan maneuvered his horse through the crowded street to the house where his sister stood in the open doorway. "Little Sister!" Ethan dismounted and held the reins in one hand.

She scrambled down the front steps to meet him, flinging her arms around his neck.

Ethan hugged Salina tightly with his free arm. "Salina, what are you doing *here*?!"

"I came to be with Mamma," Salina replied. "She's had the baby, Ethan. We've a little brother. And I've been instructed to tell you, if I chanced to see you while I was here, that your wife loves you. She misses you something fierce. I have a letter for you from her, but it's back at the farm. I never thought I'd run into you today!"

"You mean to tell me you didn't drag Taylor Sue up here with you?" Ethan was disappointed.

"No, she's sitting this adventure out." Salina smiled wistfully. "But she promised to support us through prayer and wants us to always remember that she'll be there waiting when we get home. Now, quick, come inside and tell me what *you* are doing here?"

Ethan grinned broadly as he tied the gray horse to the stair railing, thinking of his russet-haired, brown-eyed wife waiting patiently at Shadowcreek. He could just see the freckles on the bridge of her up-turned nose, and wished he could feel her arms around him. For the present, he forcefully banished her from his mind—such poignant reflections were better left for times of firelit solitude; they were not to be dwelt upon when there was business at hand. He took his sister by the arm. "Come on, let's get you out of this rain. No sense inviting another bout of pneumonia."

Ethan followed Salina into the house, but not too far. He kept the door wide open in order to keep an eye on what was happening in the street. He nodded curtly to both Mrs. Albrecht and Beth-Anne when Salina introduced them, then leaned against the doorjamb and said, "In answer to your question, I'm here because

Colonel Shields sent me ahead in search of medical supplies. I'm told there's a doctor's office nearby—O'Neal is the name. Do you know it?"

Salina turned to Duncan's sister-in-law. "Beth-Anne, will you tell us where Doctor O'Neal lives? Please?"

For a minute Salina thought there would be no reply, but surprisingly Beth-Anne supplied a hesitant answer in spite of Mrs. Albrecht's scowl of disapproval. "On the corner of Baltimore and High Street. If you pass the Presbyterian church, you've gone too far." In addition, Beth-Anne divulged the location of the apothecary's shop.

"Thank you, ma'am, I'm much obliged." Ethan touched the brim of his hat.

"I... I'll expect a favor in return, Captain," Beth-Anne ventured.

"I owe you that much, if it's within my power to do so," Ethan acquiesced.

"Can you get us back to Oak Ridge?" Beth-Anne pleaded. "It's roughly a mile outside of town, to the north. We'll never make it on our own—especially since the horses and buggy have been *confiscated.*"

Ethan thought for moment, then said, "If you all will stay here until I'm free from my duties, I'll arrange to get you back there. I'll come for you just as soon as I can," he promised. "I don't know if there's anything I can do to recover your animals, but I'll look into it. Fair payment?"

"It's a deal," Beth-Anne nodded quickly.

"I may not be back before dark, but I will be back," Ethan assured them.

"We're not going anywhere; we'll wait," Beth-Anne agreed.

"Ethan, what's happening out there?" Salina begged for some news before he left them in frustrating ignorance.

"General Early and some of the other officers are meeting with the town council at the Court House. They've presented their demands, and are waiting to see if they'll be met," Ethan told her somberly. He kissed Salina's forehead. "Stay put until I come back."

Mrs. Albrecht was indignant that Ethan had been allowed right into Beth-Anne's parlour, and she returned disgruntled to her own home not long after the Rebel captain's departure. Left to themselves, Beth-Anne and Salina waited out the interminably slow hours.

"Beth-Anne, look!" Salina grinned triumphantly, pointing to Ethan the minute she spied him on the street. Amazingly, he lead one of the Grant horses behind him.

"He found a way," Beth-Anne breathed incredulously.

Salina lifted her chin proudly. "My brother is a man of his word."

Beth-Anne and Salina eagerly met Ethan at the front walkway. "Captain Hastings," Beth-Anne smiled tentatively, "It seems I owe you an apology."

Ethan merely shrugged, unaffected by her reconciliatory tone. "Regretfully, I was only able to convince the quartermaster to return one of your horses." He put the reins in Beth-Anne's hands. "I hope you understand I did what I could."

Beth-Anne nodded. "I'm surprised you were able to get even one. Please don't think me ungrateful—it seems I misjudged you."

Ethan shook his head. "I'm still your enemy."

They left the house on Baltimore Street, Salina riding behind Ethan while Beth-Anne rode the recovered horse. Beth-Anne led them through alleyways and back streets to avoid the Diamond and Early's men on their way out of town.

Orrin was at the gate the instant he heard them arrive, toting his rifle in hand. He was consumed with relief to find his wife unharmed, but dismayed at the gray-clad captain who dared darken the doorstep of the Grant household with his unwanted presence. Orrin hugged Beth-Anne tightly to him. "We thought the Rebs had carried you off with them!"

While Beth-Anne was quickly telling Orrin what had happened in Gettysburg, their sons came from the house shouting and brandishing their carbines. Nathan and Jared held Ethan at gunpoint.

"No!" Beth-Anne called out, standing firm in Ethan's defense. "This is Annelise's son, and I promised him a chance to see his mother and his little brother. Captain Hastings has been very gracious. He took a great risk bringing us here, and he did manage to return one of our horses. If he hadn't helped us, Salina and I might still be stuck at the house on Baltimore Street. We owe him a debt of gratitude."

"We don't owe this Reb anything, Ma." Nathan leveled the muzzle of his gun at the Rebel's heart.

Orrin didn't cotton to the situation, but he reluctantly surrendered to the pleading look on his wife's face. "Nathan, Jared, put the guns down." He walked to stand directly before Ethan, glaring at him squarely. "You listen to me, Reb, because I'm only going to say this once: you've got fifteen minutes. If you're on the premises when the time expires, I may just shoot you myself. Understand?"

Ethan nodded curtly, his blue eyes ablaze with grudging compliance.

Salina beckoned to her older brother from the porch. "Come on! We don't have much time!"

Deliberately, Ethan shouldered his way past Orrin's sons and went into the house.

Salina tugged on his hand, leading him upstairs. "Mamma isn't going to believe this. You've barely got a few minutes to see her and Yabel. I'll fetch Taylor Sue's letter for you."

"Yabel?" Ethan questioned.

Salina explained in a rush, "Our baby brother has officially been named Garrett Duncan, but I call him Yabel. Half-Yank, half-Rebel."

Ethan shook his head at his sister's absurd logic. "Where did you come up with that?"

"Jeremy inspired it first," Salina laughed lightly. "Mamma's in there—you go to her. I'll be right back with that letter from Taylor Sue."

Once recovered from her initial shock, Annelise cried freely as she held Ethan in her arms. "Praise be to God, for He has surely blessed us with this miracle of being here together." Then she placed her youngest son into the arms of her oldest. "I never would have dreamt it," she whispered reverently.

"Me either, Mamma." Ethan's mouth lifted at the corners to form a faint smile. Though it was still a sore spot with him, he was slowly coming to terms with Mamma's marriage to Duncan Grant. He lightly bounced the baby in the crook of his arm, offering a little finger for the tiny hand to clasp. "Here's another of the Lord's miracles: you providing Salina and me with a little brother. He looks like Duncan, doesn't he?"

"Yes, he favors his father, at least so far—he's barely four days old," Annelise pointed out.

Ethan made the most of his allotted time frame. He could see that Salina was faring well enough, but he wanted to be convinced that Mamma was doing all right here with Duncan's people. He sensed she wasn't necessarily happy, but she was safe and well cared for. With bitter gall he had to admit she was probably better off here than in Virginia for the time being. At home there was still the very real threat that John Barnes might attempt another sinister strike against them.

"Did you get medicine?" Salina wanted to know. She put Taylor Sue's letter into her brother's anxious hand.

"I got some, but it's never enough. The shortages are too great, the demand overwhelming, and there just isn't enough to go around. Thankfully, it's a start." Ethan handed the baby back to Mamma.

"What news of Jeremy?" Salina was curious to learn of her Horse Soldier's whereabouts. "I saw him, you know, after the Battle of Brandy Station. I know why he wasn't able to come to St. Stephen's."

"So you know it wasn't his fault," Ethan gathered, and he saw that Salina nodded affirmatively. "Well, don't give up on him. One of these days, things will work out."

"I know." Salina's smile was a bit lopsided, "All in good time, they say. But please, tell me what you know about the cavalry."

"Have you heard about the fighting at Aldie, Middleburg, and Upperville?" Ethan inquired.

"Not much, really," Salina answered. "The news is so slanted here in the North—although I suppose the same is true in the South. I just haven't been able to find out anything for sure. What do you know?"

"Stuart's troops were at it for five days straight, but the action was strictly defensive. Their objective was to keep the Yanks at bay, defend the gaps and mountain passes, and not let Pleasanton know that Lee's army was moving behind the Blue Ridge. In that respect, they succeeded."

"But I'd heard our cavalry was pushed back, time and again." Salina lamented. "You're telling me that's what they were supposed to be doing?"

Ethan nodded. "You, along with a good many other Southerners, are too used to the flash and derring-do. Cavalry sometimes has responsibilities other than riding circles around the enemy."

"I know, it's just that..." Salina shrugged, then laughed. "You're right, we are used to gallantly fought victories. The Union cavalry has been slow to get organized and put up any decent resistance, but they're learning. Look at Brandy: they weren't running scared there—they pitched in and fought with deadly ferocity."

She was acutely perceptive, and Ethan told Salina as much. He hesitated to tell her the next bit of news, but he knew she would learn of it eventually: "If you hadn't heard much about the fighting around Aldie, Middleburg, and Upperville, then I suppose you haven't heard that Major von Borcke was wounded."

"Von's been hurt?" Salina's eyes grew round. "It can't be so!"

Ethan nodded woefully. "The way I heard it, he and Stuart were out together, and a sharpshooter's bullet got von Borcke in the throat. At first, Stuart's doctor, Talcott Eliason, didn't think that the Prussian was going to make it. Von Borcke rallied, however, and has since been sent south to Richmond to convalesce. Some say the Yankees mistook him for Stuart."

"The Yankees got von Borcke by mistake…" Salina closed her eyes and shuddered at the very thought. "I danced with him at the ball after the Grand Review. He's such a jolly fellow, strutting around with that huge sword of his…Jeremy says he and Stuart are close friends." She wrung her hands in agitation. "So many have been lost on Stuart's staff, including 'The Gallant Pelham,' Channing Price, and now Heros von Borcke. Oh, Ethan, I can't imagine him hurt so seriously. And these cavalry battles—challenge, fall back, strike, then retreat. I don't think I like defensive strategy much."

Ethan lifted his shoulders in a shrug. "My guess is Stuart doesn't either, though sometimes there's no choice. He had his orders to guard the gaps and mountain passes. In fact, he's got new orders now. He'll prove to be more than human if he can carry out all General Lee asks of him."

Salina's eyes lit up with a spark of hope. "Do you think he'll circle Hooker?"

"I don't know," Ethan shook his head in reply. "Word has it Stuart and his troopers are to cause as much trouble as they can in the rear of the Army of the Potomac: disrupt their communications, collect their supplies, screen Ewell's movement, and gather intelligence along the way."

"That's a tall order," Annelise commented.

"It's impossible to accomplish all of that at once," Salina declared.

"Knowing Lee, he probably left it up to Stuart's discretion as to how to get the job done," Ethan surmised. "All I can tell you is that Jeremy is with Stuart. I haven't seen him since we all moved out from Culpeper."

"If you see him in the next few days, will you tell him I'm here?" Salina requested.

"*If* I see him, I'll do that," Ethan assured her with a wink.

There was a loud rapping on the door of Annelise's room. From outside, Beth-Anne whispered frantically, "Time is up and Ethan's got to go! Now!"

Ethan hurriedly kissed Mamma and Salina. "I've stayed longer than I should anyhow—I've got to report back to the commanding officer and get the supplies organized and loaded in the wagons."

Mamma adamantly insisted they pray before Ethan left. Holding hands, the briefly reunited family bowed their heads and thanked God for His blessings and mercy toward them.

Heavy footsteps fell on the stairs, and Ethan was quick to move. He yanked open the door and met Orrin Grant in the hall. As Ethan passed he said evenly, "Thank you. I mean that."

Orrin bristled and did not reply. Through the churning undercurrents came an unspoken message: *Get out of here, Reb.*

Ethan made a swift exit from the Grants' house and returned to headquarters.

☆ ☆ ☆ ☆ ☆ ☆ ☆

Later that night, Salina sat in the open window of her bedroom, facing towards town. On the evening breeze she could hear distant strains of *Dixie*, *The Bonnie Blue Flag*, and other Confederate favorites. A Rebel band must be somewhere in the vicinity of the Diamond, undoubtedly annoying the good citizens of Gettysburg with their secessionist concert. To the east Salina could see a dull red glow, testimony that something was on fire. She didn't know it yet, but General Early had ordered the burning of the railroad bridge across Rock Creek. In accomplishing that, fifteen or twenty railroad cars were destroyed, tracks were torn up, and the main supply line to Gettysburg was effectively cut off.

On the morning of June twenty-seventh, the Rebels prepared to leave Gettysburg. Since the town council had been unable to meet the Confederate demands of sugar, coffee, flour, salt, bacon, onions, whiskey, shoes, hats, and $5,000 in cash, they had arranged instead for the stores to remain open. The Rebels took what merchandise they could find and paid the shopkeepers in worthless Confederate scrip. Thus the Rebels moved out with their confiscated goods, captured horses, and herded prisoners—some of whom were colored people who'd not been fortunate enough to escape the raiders.

It chilled Salina's blood to know that the poor captives would be taken south and returned to slavery. "It's not right, Jubilee!" Salina insisted emphatically.

"Perhaps you could go to Philadelphia," Annelise proposed. "You have your papers, and who can say? You might be able to find your daughter there."

Jubilee folded her arms across her ample chest. "Humph! Ah ain't heerd from her but one time ta tell me she were safe in da North afta she done run away from Shadowcreek. Dat'd be nigh unta ten year ago, an' dere ain't no guarantee she'd be dere now. No, Miz Annelise, ah ain't leavin' ya on account o' no Rebel soljers."

Annelise and Salina both sighed in resignation. It was pointless to argue about Jubilee going farther north to some place safe. The black woman was adamant about staying with Annelise.

"Ah'll not leave ya," Jubilee repeated, firmly standing her ground, "So ya jist betta git used ta da fact Jube is stayin'." To her way of thinking the matter was settled, and she remained at Oak Ridge.

In the wake of Gettysburg's brief occupation, Salina felt somewhat bemused—it was both sorrow and relief for her to see the Southerners gone.

Chapter Thirteen

$\mathcal{D}$ulcie and Steve's reception followed immediately on the heels of the wedding ceremony at the Colby house on East Middle Street. The Grant and Colby families, as well as a few close friends and neighbors, congregated in the festively decorated parlour to eat cake and drink punch. When they weren't busy congratulating the newlyweds, guests swapped impressions and stories of their experiences under enemy occupation.

Beth-Anne gave a detailed account of the ruined strawberry jam to Orrin's sisters, Lydia and Felicia, while Lottie stood in a circle of her own attentive in-laws, telling them about the handful of men from Jenkins' Cavalry to whom she had fed a hasty supper. "I made Lance hide in the attic until I was sure they were gone—otherwise they might have taken him prisoner!" she exclaimed, and received the hoped-for reaction from those around her. She caught Salina's eye, and Salina was quick to look away.

Within a few minutes, Lottie plopped herself down on the horsehair sofa next to her cousin. Salina made no comment, so Lottie tried a different tactic to draw Salina out: "Poor Salina. It seems you're still left without a husband. If this war keeps on, you're likely to wind up the proverbial Old Maid. Honor and duty are such cold comfort, aren't they?" she goaded, her smile sickly sweet.

Salina leveled a cool glance at her cousin. She did not respond to Lottie's antagonistic jab, but replied evenly, "I imagine you must have presented the perfect picture of displaced Southern hospitality to Jenkins' men. Colby must be so very proud that you were able to keep them from searching the house—especially since he was hiding like a fugitive in his own home." Salina saw Lottie squirm, and she added sarcastically, "Did you send the Rebel cavalrymen on their way with your best wishes? Or were you properly dismayed to have them at your table, like a good Yankee wife should be?"

When Lottie opened her mouth to retort, Salina cut her off. "I do pity you, Lottie. You possess neither loyalty nor patriotism, and that's why it's so easy for you to play up to both sides. You bend like a willow in the wind with no stability. At least I know in my heart that I possess the conviction to stand behind my man, come what may. Do you, Lottie? You're married to the enemy, and one day you're going to have to choose between your Confederate family and your Yankee husband in order to survive. You waver on the fence line, and Colby's intelligent enough to figure that out. If I were him, I'd be afraid, knowing you can't commit one way or the other. Even last night—how would Colby know that you wouldn't hand him over to the Rebels, since you were born one yourself?"

Lottie resented the sting of Salina's allegations, and she heartily disliked feeling the tug of war within herself. Lottie pursed her lips together and hissed, "You aren't immune to caring for Yankees yourself, Salina. You're here, aren't you? Your mamma's married to one, and he's the father of your half-brother! If you think I'm going to have to choose sides, what about you?!"

"But I've been aware of that fact for a long time, Lottie," Salina responded. "What you are just now discovering, I settled long ago. I will never go against Virginia." She got up and walked out to the porch. Sitting down on the stone steps, she mulled over what she had said to Lottie about choosing. There simply was no middle ground, and it certainly wasn't safe in no-man's-land, where one was sniped at from either side or both. It was a bit like being lukewarm, she reflected. In the book of Revelation, the Lord instructed believers to be either hot or cold; if they were lukewarm, He would spit them out of his mouth. The passage evoked a powerful picture, and Salina was convinced that it was time to renew her stand, both spiritually and mentally. She bowed her head and prayed, petitioning the Lord for strength and the Holy Spirit for comfort.

For Mamma's sake alone, Salina decided she would stay another week, and then she would return home where she belonged. While she didn't think it was a mistake to have come here to Gettysburg, she wouldn't willingly prolong her absence from Shadowcreek. *My life is in Your hands, Lord Jesus. Lead me in Your path of righteousness; show me where I should go, and where I should stay. Forgive me for my anger towards Lottie. Sometimes I just can't help myself...*

"Mind if I join you?" Colby's voice interrupted Salina's silent prayer as he found her sitting alone on the front steps.

Salina mutely shrugged, leaving the choice to Colby.

Colby sat down beside the dark-haired young woman. "You and Lottie have another tiff?" he asked, already knowing the answer.

"She stirs the trouble," Salina answered curtly. She didn't want to look at him, for tonight was one of those instances when for some reason he reminded her of Jeremy more profoundly than usual, thereby causing her to miss Jeremy more than ever. "Oh, why aren't you inside, mingling with the wedding party?" she snapped miserably. "You're the best man—don't you have a toast to offer the happy couple?"

"All in good time," he assured her. "I did want to speak to you about something else besides the rift between you and my wife— Orrin told me your brother was here in town," Colby ventured, but he gained no reply. "I've heard that your General Early is headed to York or Carlisle, maybe Hanover. Is that what Ethan told you?"

Salina laughed airily. "Do you really think I'd inform against them—to you?"

Colby felt the thorny prick of her mocking laughter. "In truth, I don't care where they go—so long as long as they aren't here!" he stated vehemently. "Frankly, I wish I was out there fighting off the invading graybacks."

"Colby, I know that if you hadn't sustained Corbeau's beating, you'd already be out there in the killing fields," Salina remarked evenly. "Duncan arranged for the transfer you requested. It's your duty as a Federal soldier to defend your Union. How it must chafe you to sit here idle! Unless I miss my guess, you won't sit for much longer. You want to take part in thwarting the 'dreaded' invasion. Galling, isn't it, to have your home occupied by the enemy? To watch them roam and plunder at will?"

"It does leave a bitter taste in one's mouth," Colby grated, his eyes narrow with controlled rage.

"I agree." Salina lifted her chin a fraction, Rebel defiance snapping brightly in her emerald eyes. "It's high time you all got a taste of what we Southerners have been going through since the beginning of the war. We are well acquainted with invasion of our land by you Yankees. It's interesting to see that you don't savor it any more than we do!"

"Interesting? How so?" Colby challenged.

Salina shrugged nonchalantly. "It makes you seem human—to know that it hurts you when the places you hold dear and call home are ravaged by battles and foraging enemy soldiers; that you know fear because we brought the bloody struggle here, and might well best you in your own backyard."

Colby cleared his throat. Salina's appraisal of the situation was agonizingly accurate. Now that he had experienced military violation firsthand, he didn't like it one bit. With determined calm he stated, "Well, as you've already pointed out, I've been idle long enough. I'm going to report to my new commander and see if I can't pitch in for the Union defense—bruises or no."

He wasn't exactly sure how he expected Salina to respond, but her deliberately cool reply stung nonetheless: "Take care, Colby."

It was a dismissal of sorts, he thought to himself. No good-byes, no best wishes—just a bland expression belying the fact that Salina's sympathies were stronger than ever in favor of the rebellious South. She might tolerate the strained friendship between them, but she was reminding him none too subtly that she was still his enemy. Colby offered a stiff, mocking salute, then abruptly left her to study the night sky's bright stars alone while he returned to the party inside.

Barely an hour after Mr. and Mrs. Steven Colby departed for New York for their wedding trip, Lance Colby bade his expectant wife an awkward farewell. Against Lottie's tearful protestations, the Yankee lieutenant departed to find Buford's Cavalry.

☆ ☆ ☆ ☆ ☆ ☆ ☆

Boston, Massachusetts

Aurora Dallinger's fingers skimmed the ebony and ivory keys of the Chickering Parlour Piano with an expert touch. She selected a melancholy piece, for her heart was heavy, and the drawing room was filled with the haunting strains of the tune she played. Upstairs, her father lay dying, and there was nothing she could do to prevent the inevitable.

Drake appeared out of the shadows, just off to one side of the piano. Aurora drew in a sharp breath and exclaimed, "I hate the way you do that!"

"Do what?" Unruffled, Drake leaned a hip against the piano, his copper-brown arms folded across the brass buttons of his tailored waistcoat.

"Appear—disappear—you move through this house with such stealth I never can tell where you'll pop up next!" Aurora declared with mock indignation.

Drake smiled enigmatically, "I like to keep you guessing, Rorie."

Aurora tried to be stern, but she couldn't keep from mirroring his mischievous grin. "You're incorrigible."

"I've been called worse," he remarked indolently.

"I don't doubt it," Aurora attested. "Have you been to see Father?"

Silently Drake nodded.

"No one thought he'd last this long, least of all Grandmamma," Aurora commented softly. "I know how badly he wanted to see you, Drake. You know I wouldn't have sent for you otherwise. It was purely by accident I discovered that you existed at all—but after I'd found out about you and pestered him with a hundred questions or more, he mentioned you often."

"How *did* you find out about me?" Drake was curious. "Certainly not from Grandmamma."

Aurora's blue-green eyes, the only common feature the two Dallinger siblings shared, brightened, and she laughed, "No, not from Grandmamma. I was dusting in Father's study when I found the lacquered box containing the bear claw amulet, the pounded silver medallion, and the broken arrow shaft. They intrigued me. I knew that long before I was born he had spent time in the West, and I started to ask Father about Indians. He got so very angry with me at first. He shut me out and told me time and again to keep my inquisitive little nose out of other people's affairs. I didn't though."

"Hardly a surprise or revelation," Drake murmured, not quite able to disguise the fondness he was starting to feel for his newly-found sister.

"He refused to speak of you for the longest time, but then I think he was relieved to finally have a confidante," Aurora smiled gently.

"I haven't thanked you for taking the risk in doing what you did. If you hadn't sent that telegram—well, we might have remained estranged for the rest of our lives. You made reconciliation possible, Rorie. I owe you a debt of gratitude."

Aurora waved aside her half-brother's appreciation. "My motivation wasn't entirely unselfish, you know—I wanted to see you too."

"So, you've gotten your way. I'm here. He's seen me, you've seen me, and Grandmamma still wishes I'd never been born," Drake replied caustically.

"She'll get over it," Aurora predicted.

"She hasn't for the last twenty-five years," Drake pointed out. "To her stubborn way of thinking I'm still just a red-skinned savage. She will never accept me as a blue-blooded Dallinger; I'm not purebred."

"But you are Father's firstborn, and entitled to a handsome inheritance, I'm sure." Aurora confided conspiratorially, "He's made a will; he didn't want to leave any loose ends…"

Drake sighed, hanging his head. "I know all about the will."

Just this morning, he and his father had discussed the assets that would fall into Drake's possession once the elder Dallinger was dead. "Handsome" was a mild term to describe all that he stood to inherit. Drake was about to become a *very* wealthy man, and he had his misgivings about it. He wasn't sure he was ready to live up to either the expectations or the responsibility that would inevitably land on his broad shoulders.

Aurora looked up, hoping to make her brother smile again. "You know, Drake, I was disappointed the day you first got here. I had visions of war paint and moccasins, a feathered-headdress, and maybe a bow and a quiver of arrows. But when you finally arrived—so handsome, well-dressed, and so obviously educated—all my fanciful imaginings evaporated like steam."

"If it makes you feel any better, Rorie, before I came here I had hair down to my waist and a gold earring and fringed buckskins," Drake divulged with a wink. "I figured I didn't stand a chance if I showed up here looking like that, though. Besides, Pa's in enough physical pain without having to dredge up the past so vividly again."

"He has a beautiful sketch of your mother, Black Swan—wasn't that her name?"

"Yes." Drake's voice faltered perceptibly.

Pretending not to notice, Aurora continued. "I learned of her, and of you, by asking carefully placed questions. Sometimes Father would talk of you and he'd get a far, faraway look in his eyes, forgetting that I was even in the room. He told of how he had to pass the warrior's initiation in order to become a member of the tribe. Horrifying!" She shuddered involuntarily. "He loved Black Swan very, very much. But then she died, and he came back here to Boston utterly heartbroken. Father played the hermit for years before meeting my mother at a church bazaar which Grandmamma forced him into chairing.

"Mother seemed brave to some, foolish to others," Aurora went on to say. "She loved Father as fiercely as he'd loved Black Swan. Mother defiantly took the chance of being socially ostracized for marrying a man who had previously taken a squaw to wife. But Mother didn't care about that, she only cared for him. She did not press for details about the past which he refused to share with anyone. She never held the secret part of his life against him, as his own family did."

"What happened to her?" Drake wondered. "What became of your mother?"

"Some say pneumonia killed her," Aurora answered with a twinge of sorrow, "but I believe it was a broken heart that was her final undoing. I know Father never loved her half as much as she loved him. He didn't believe he could love again; he was sure his heart had gone to the grave with Black Swan. I think that's partially why he left you with your mother's people," Aurora said softly. "It hurt him too much to have you around as a constant reminder after she was gone. He loves you like he loves no other living soul, Drake."

"He loves you, too, though," Drake noted. "Don't sit there and tell me he doesn't."

Aurora's lips lifted in a grin, displaying her dimple, "I know he does. Father claims I was the one who taught him how to love again. That's why the rift between the two of you has plagued him so dreadfully. We're his off-spring, his own flesh and blood, his legacy."

"So?" Drake wondered what she was getting at.

"So, he longed to make things right, but couldn't bring himself to do anything about contacting you. He fears he'll never be able to make it up to you," Aurora stated simply. "I know you've talked with him each day since you've been here, but your conversations are stilted and awkward."

"Eavesdropping, you little sneak?" Drake playfully pulled one of the curls draped over her shoulder.

Aurora nodded, willingly confessing to his accusation. She covered his rough bronzed hand with her own soft white one. "Drake, if you can find it in your heart, please forgive him. Make peace with him and send him to his grave content. He's told me many times that there are things he would do differently if he had a chance to go back, but we all know that isn't possible. Mistakes happen; only forgiveness can soothe the hurt."

The girl was eight years his junior, but she seemed to see things much more clearly than he did. "I'll try." Drake squeezed Aurora's hand reassuringly. "He hasn't much time left, I reckon."

"Make the most of it," Aurora strongly encouraged. A pendulum clock struck the hour of four. "Oh! It's late! I should have left for the Ladies Relief Association meeting by now. Be a dear and accompany me to Mrs. Endicott's house, will you?"

"Sure." Drake was willing to oblige. "What's this, another sewing circle of yours?"

"No, no, the sewing circle is at Mrs. Palmer's. Mrs. Endicott does bandages, and Mrs. Larousse has the knitting." Aurora tried to set him straight on which good deed for soldiers' relief happened at which upstanding matron's home. "All of them have sons in the war, and two have brothers who've gone to fight, too."

"What is it that drives you to be so patriotic, Rorie? You have no brother or father involved in the conflict, so why are you so willing to lend your aid?" Drake wanted to know.

"I just wanted to do something to help," Aurora shrugged, blushing hotly. "Oh, well, if you must know, I have a beau, Drake—but Grandmamma would spit because he doesn't have the pedigree of a titled Bostonian family. Mason's company was sent south before he had the opportunity to speak to Father about his suit for my hand. We've been writing to each other for the past two years. After Father dies, you'll be responsible for household decisions, and then Mason'll have to speak to *you* about courting me."

"We'll see about that," Drake said dryly. "I haven't made a decision yet about sticking around after Pa's gone. Oh, I'll stay for the services and the burial, but I'm not sure how long I'll be in Boston."

Aurora looked crestfallen, but did her best to stifle her disappointment. She knew Drake was born and bred to a whole different life in the West, one much foreign to her way of understanding. It was wrong of her to expect him to abandon his independence, leave all he was familiar with behind and immediately embrace such a tumultuous change as being thrust into the middle of the Dallinger dominion, with all its responsibility and social obligation. Drake was the heir incumbent, though, and he'd have to learn to deal with that in his own time, in his own fashion. She mentally set those matters aside. "Time's wasting. Are you going with me to Mrs. Endicott's or not?"

Drake proffered his arm, smiling indulgently at his younger sister. At times, she reminded him much of Salina Hastings. Determination, an independent streak, and devotion were but a few attributes the two young ladies had in common.

He half-listened to Aurora as she chattered all the way to Mrs. Endicott's regal-looking house. Drake had his mind on other matters, but he did recall promising to return for her in an hour or so, as she requested. An hour would leave her plenty of time to get home, change, and go with Grandmamma to a dinner party hosted by friends of the family whom she called the "Abolitionist Thornehills."

"You're sure you won't come along? The invitation was issued to all of us Dallingers. I could introduce you to some of my friends. I know several who would swoon at the mere sight of your dazzling smile," Aurora teased.

Drake chuckled, "Thanks, Rorie, but no thanks. I appreciate what you're trying to do, but I'm just not fond of society. I won't be shown off as a curiosity for your friends to gossip about. Grandmamma is having a hard enough time dealing with me at home, anyway. Let's give the old lady a break and not subject her to any unpleasantness my presence might evoke. Hmmm?"

"I suppose," Aurora unwillingly relented. The driver stopped the landau in front of the imposing Endicott home. "Don't forget to fetch me in an hour."

"I won't," Drake promised gruffly. He shooed her out of the landau with a backhanded wave. "Go on, have a good time gathering up your bandages."

Aurora rolled her eyes, then quickly kissed him on the cheek. "For all your gruffness, you've a good heart, brother dear. I'll see you later."

Drake had the driver take him to the gentleman's club, where he played a few hands of draw poker and a round of billiards. He listened to snatches of conversations, the most recent news being that President Lincoln had replaced General Joseph Hooker with General George Gordon Meade. The Army of the Potomac was yet again under the command of a new leader.

Drake was certainly not alone in speculating how long this one might last. Several of the men joked, and a few even laid down wagers as to whether or not the new leader of the Army of the Potomac would last until Christmas. Judging by the recent parade of Union generals, odds were not very favorable.

Chapter Fourteen

Gettysburg, Pennsylvania
July 1, 1863

Quick as a wink, Salina scurried from the privy to the back porch. She wiped her bare feet on the doormat, her toes and ankles wet from the moist grass. She had hitched up her robe a bit, but evidently not quite high enough—the hem of both her robe and her night dress were dampened by the early morning's chilled dew. The sky was beginning to lighten and she would have to get up shortly, but even if she could have just fifteen more minutes of sleep she would gladly take it. She'd been up in the night with Yabel again. Her darling baby brother seemed to take comfort only in her arms lately. Mamma said he had a touch of the colic, and insisted that he'd be all right again in no time.

Making a brief pause at the kitchen pump for a drink of cool water, Salina recognized the crackle and bark of firearms in the distance. She pushed the kitchen curtains aside and glanced out the window, eyes hastily scanning the horizon. A shiver of goose bumps crawled along her arms. She swallowed, closing her eyes. A shrill voice in her head screamed, *It's started!*

Salina met up with Cody as he stood at the top of the landing rubbing the sleep from his eyes. "That's a skirmish," he stated mid-yawn. "We're in for another clash."

"I reckon we are," Salina nodded, ascending the staircase. "Hush now. You run along back to bed. No need to wake the house; we'll all find out about it soon enough." Salina followed her own advice and climbed back under the muslin sheet. Distant eruptions from the far-off artillery, however, diminished her craving for extra sleep.

By eight o'clock that morning there was no doubt in anyone's mind that a full-scale attack was well underway. Curiosity got the better of her, and Salina followed Cody and Chandler up to the attic, where they climbed a ladder and slipped through the trap door onto the roof. From this lofty vantage point they beheld a panoramic view of the action. Salina allowed each of the boys a long glance through her field glasses, but then insisted on her own turn. As far as they could tell, the Union pickets had been pressed back for the moment, and a heated conflict had erupted along Herr's Ridge.

Salina couldn't keep still. She abandoned the field glasses to the boys and scrambled back downstairs. In Michael's study, Beth-Anne was just tearing off the June page of the Courier & Ives calendar, revealing that this was Wednesday, the first of July.

"Good morning," Beth-Anne greeted ambiguously.

"For the time being," Salina allowed. "You've heard what's happening out there." She pointed in the direction of the firing.

Beth-Anne nodded, anxiety in her eyes. "I don't imagine either side is going to give up easily this time."

"We'd better get ready," Salina suggested, resolute in spite of her distraction.

Noreen joined them. "Ready for what?" she asked, pouring herself a cup of hot chocolate.

"The wounded," Salina's answer had a portentous ring to it. "Should the fighting spread, which it likely will, and reinforcements be brought up, they'll bring us the injured. The Forneys' farm stands between us and Herr's Ridge, but we're the next closest house," Salina reminded them. She looked askance at the two Northern women. "Neither of you has ever worked in a field hospital?"

"No," the Grant women replied in unison, shaking their heads. "What should we do?" Beth-Anne asked. She and Noreen both looked at Salina expectantly, as if she had all the answers.

Salina promptly found herself responsible for taking charge of the situation. She gave specific instructions for all the necessary preparations. She had Noreen and Beth-Anne, along with Jubilee and Mamma, store as much prepared food as they could in the cellar. When that was accomplished, the women tore sheets into bandages and drew buckets of water, filling the rain barrel, the trough, and the bath tub.

Salina sent Cody and Chandler to gather extra wood and kindling for the woodpile while she collected all the medicinal supplies, kerosene, candles and matches she could locate in the house. At length, the women began making bread, tin after tin after tin. The whole house smelled like a bakery, but the delicious aroma was tainted with burned powder and gun smoke.

Apprehensive, the occupants of the farmhouse on the hill waited as they caught glimpses of fighting from the upper story windows. By ten o'clock, the battle had advanced as near as McPherson's Ridge. Buford's blue cavalry brigades were supported by the arrival of General John Reynolds and the Union First Corps of infantry. The scene became clouded by a blue-gray haze hovering over the fields of firing. With the smoke so thick, Salina was unable to determine to which corps of the Army of Northern Virginia the warring Confederates belonged.

Devin's Yankee cavalry brigade under Buford had a battle line that extended toward the vicinity of the Forney farm. With the fight raging so perilously close, Orrin brusquely ordered the women and children to the cellar. "Stay put," he commanded. "Don't come out until one of us comes to fetch you!"

Salina wanted to protest, but the argument died on her lips as she saw the steely look of animosity in Orrin's granite-colored eyes. Obediently, she went downstairs with the others to wait out the battle.

Pacing the hard-packed earthen floor, Salina was most upset over not being able to know what was happening. The women tried to remain calm, but it was no easy task. The floor and walls vibrated with each round shot by the cannons. Cody and Chandler were troublesome and cross, and little Yabel fussed vigorously.

Hours passed, but seemingly at a rate of three minutes to every one. If Salina didn't know any better, she would've sworn that the longer they stayed downstairs, the closer and closer the cellar walls inched together. On two separate occasions the cellar floor shuddered fiercely when the building was struck by a wayward cannonball. She was sure they would all suffocate before Orrin came back to let them out.

Just after three o'clock p.m., Orrin came to release them from their hiding place. His face was grim, soot-stained. He grudgingly admitted, "Salina was right to be prepared. They're bringing in wounded from both sides. Come quick."

As Salina had predicted, the farmstead had been turned into a makeshift aid station and was currently within the Confederate battle lines. Injured men—the blue-clad from regiments belonging to the Army of the Potomac's Eleventh Corps, the gray and butternut predominantly from Rodes' Division of Ewell's Corps of the Army of Northern Virginia—lay on every available flat space, groaning in pain and crying for water. She hastened to tell Orrin, "We'll need something that can be used as a banner run up on a flagpole. A red quilt would be preferable, or a yellow sheet, if one can be had."

Orrin stared at her with a puzzled expression, failing at first to grasp what she meant.

Salina impatiently explained, "It will signify that we're serving as a hospital. It's no guarantee we won't be hit again if the lines shift," she glanced over her shoulder, noting the extent of the damage suffered by the frame house, "but it will at least let them know what we're doing here."

"I'll fetch a red quilt for you," Orrin complied. The house had already been hit twice—broken glass, strewn bits of brick, and splintered wood was all that remained of the bedchamber belonging to his parents, as well as part of the attic where Salina, Cody, and Chandler had stood just a few hours earlier. Salina shuddered involuntarily. The guest room that she had occupied was also struck.

Jubilee remained secreted in the cellar, where it was undoubtedly safer for her, and she busied herself keeping watch over little Yabel. Mamma, Beth-Anne, and Noreen came up to lend a helping hand. The fresh-baked bread they had prepared that morning vanished almost as quickly as the scanty supply of medicine.

Salina wended her way through the wounded men and located a Confederate doctor. She volunteered to do what she could to best assist him. Caring for wounded men was nothing new to Salina. Here, as at Chantilly and after Brandy Station, she committed herself to bring whatever measure of comfort she could to the men in agony all around her.

The Confederate doctor took stock of the young woman, and the other women standing just behind her. To Salina he said, "You say you've a brother who's a doctor?"

"Yes," Salina nodded. "I've assisted him before; you can rely on me."

The Rebel doctor could see that the little dark-haired maid seemed to possess the most experience, and she did not recoil from the ghastly horrors pressing on all sides. "All right, let's get busy then." The doctor assigned tasks to the other women, but he kept Salina at his side until his orderlies arrived, grateful for her knowledge and her willingness to serve.

After the orderlies asssumed her duties with the doctor, Salina strayed into the yard to snatch a breath of fresh air. The acrid smell of powder and gun smoke was much more pronounced than it had been that morning, and it made Salina's eyes water. She went to the well and hauled up the first of countless buckets of water. Taking the dipper with her, she went from one man to the next, offering a sip of cool liquid, speaking gently, and bestowing tremulous smiles and encouragement. "There's help here. It might take a little time, but eventually you'll get in to see the doctor."

The men talked freely with her, those in gray especially cheered by her drawled words of consolation. At the end of the third row, Orrin confronted Salina. "Don't forget," he remarked tersely, "Those wearing *blue* might need water, too."

Salina's emerald eyes flashed indignantly, annoyed by Orrin's implied accusation: he obviously thought she was favoring the Rebels and ignoring the Yankees. "Each man here is suffering, regardless of the color of his uniform. I'll tend to them all equally!"

"See that you do!" Orrin snarled.

Salina must have walked miles between the rows of wounded men and the well, tirelessly drawing and hauling the buckets back and forth, back and forth.

The fight in the immediate area had gone badly for the Rebels. General Ewell had ordered Oak Hill occupied—which it was, partly by Carter's Battalion of Ewell's Corps, with McIntosh's Battalion from A.P. Hill's Corps in reserve. News came that the Union's General Reynolds had been killed by Confederate sharpshooters, but that did not ease the sting of the failed attack by General Rodes' Division.

Iverson's North Carolina regiments had been virtually ripped to shreds by the Union infantry hiding behind a low stone wall along

Oak Ridge. Daniels' Brigade, also comprised of North Carolinians, was in such confusion that they had been ineffectual in support. In addition, the Rebels were thrown back at Forney's field.

Federal General Abner Doubleday, the successor of Reynolds' command, had managed to stave off what might have been a crushing blow to the poorly coordinated, poorly led, and poorly supported Confederates. There had been little or no cooperation between the gray brigades. Casualties were heavy for both sides, and at present the fight ebbed across the fields and the unfinished railroad cut back to McPherson's Woods.

Michael Grant had left the house early that morning. He'd gone to teach at the college just as he routinely did on any weekday when classes were in session. Classes had been hastily dismissed on this day, however, shortly after the battle broke out. Many of the students left the premises, but Michael had to stay put, unable to pass through the lines to rejoin his family until almost dusk. He was by no means thrilled to find batteries of Rebel cannon—Napoleons, Parrotts, and Whitworths—perched at the edge of his yard where a now-demolished picket fence once stood. Nor was Michael Grant at all pleased to find Jared and Nathan on the roof opposite the broken chimney, assessing the gaping holes and other damage to the house caused by the pair of stray cannon balls.

The industrious labor of Michael's grandsons was not the only evidence of work in progress—somewhere in the gathering darkness breastworks were being constructed. Professor Grant shook his head, much aggrieved. He calculated that this day's battle, though temporarily at a standstill, would very likely bleed into tomorrow's.

☆ ☆ ☆ ☆ ☆ ☆ ☆

The sun was sinking slowly in the western sky; the rain and heat had both slackened. Salina slowed her horse to a walk, cautiously approaching the small collection of tents pitched opposite Mrs. Thompson's house on the Chambersburg Pike. Not even a handful of campfires burned amid the tiny bivouac, and no sign of rank served to identify the occupants other than a Confederate flag flapping in the breeze. She halted altogether as a mustached officer stepped directly into her path and laid hold of the bridle. "Good day, Miss."

"Good day, Major, what's left of it," Salina returned politely.

Glancing about the non-descript scene, she asked for clarification: "Are these the headquarters of General Lee?"

"Yes, Miss, they are," the officer affirmed with a solemn nod. "I reckon you're thinkin' that you want to see the General."

"No, no, that isn't necessary," Salina hastily replied. "General Lee must be very busy planning the next strike. I merely want to leave some things for him, if I may." Salina extended the basket she carried.

The officer searched the contents of the wicker basket. Beneath the red-and-white checked napkin he found fresh bread, buttermilk biscuits and a pint of gravy, apples, a small crock of sweet butter, and a jar of strawberry jam. He unconsciously licked his lips, appreciatively eyeing the fare. "You made this?"

"I did," Salina assured him. She sensed his wary reservation. "I don't expect you find many loyal Virginia ladies riding up here in enemy territory, do you?"

"No, Miss, it's hardly a commonplace occurrence, and that's the truth of it." The Major allowed himself to smile a bit. "What's a nice little Southern lady like you doing in Pennsylvania anyhow?"

"I was on a short holiday to visit relatives here and got caught up in the whirlwind of the battle. I'm a Virginian, born and bred, and I couldn't just sit still knowing you all were out here. I guess I've been homesick, but more importantly, I wanted to do something to help. I've some information that might be of use to General Lee. If I can't speak to him directly, would it be possible to talk with one of his aides, or perhaps his adjutant?"

The Major critically examined the young woman on horseback. Her accent alone was enough to verify that she was not a local citizen. "I'm General Lee's adjutant, Major Walter Taylor, at your service. And you are Miss…"

"Hastings," Salina readily supplied her name. "Salina Hastings of Shadowcreek, near Chantilly. You might have heard of my daddy, the late Captain Garrett Hastings?" She slid down from the horse's back and straightened her skirts. "Please, may I have just a moment of your time, Major? I've got something to show you."

Major Taylor beckoned her forward. He offered her a camp stool near the fire, in front of the largest tent.

"Thank you, Major Taylor." Salina smiled affably at the mustached officer.

"I did have the pleasure of making your father's acquaintance, when he came to report to General Lee once. His death was a great loss," the Major offered sympathetically.

Salina nodded sadly. "Every life is a great loss. Once the skir-mish lines had shifted and the fighting di..." She was about to say *died down* but deemed it a poor choice of words. "Once the fight-ing dissipated," she emended, "they brought scores of wounded to the house where I'm staying. Two of the men I tended had been captured in the unfinished railroad cut west of town, but they man-aged to escape their Yankee captors. Some of the wounded we're caring for belong to the Union General Howard's Eleventh Corps, who had a rough go of it at Barlow's Knoll. Mostly, though, we have Confederates from Iverson's brigade—or what's left of it—and a good many others from O'Neal's brigade. I didn't exactly see the fighting because we stayed holed up in the cellar until it was safe to come out. Is it true that General Reynolds was killed in McPherson's Woods?"

Major Taylor told her that it was true, but he offered no further comment on the day's action at McPherson's Ridge, Oak Ridge, and Seminary Ridge. Salina, however, gently pressed him with her inquiries, and reluctantly he answered her curious questions. "As far as Iverson's brigade is concerned, preliminary reports indicate that casualties are in excess of eight hundred men. If General Early's division hadn't arrived at the scene when they did...well, things might not have turned out so favorably for our side. As it stands now, the Union's First Corps and Eleventh Corps have been routed, pushed back through the town all the way to Cemetery Hill. Our men occupy the streets of Gettysburg."

Salina sighed thankfully and smiled, her heart gladdened by news of the Rebel victory.

The edges of the Major's mustache lifted in a reciprocal smile as he shared her sentiment. He asked curiously, "You said you had some information for General Lee?"

Salina reached down to the top of her boot and withdrew a small folded square of paper. "I realize it's a very rough sketch, as it was rendered rather quickly, but it was done by a local who knows this area extremely well. I thought it might be of some use." She spread the map across her lap, smoothing the crinkles out. Then she straightened her legs, the toes of her boots pointing toward the fire, so that the drawing was clearly illuminated by the flickering orange light.

"This is a map of Gettysburg." Major Taylor instantly recog-nized the depicted area.

Salina nodded her dark head. "And these are the locations of the Union troops." She pointed out the position of the retreated Federal brigades. "I'm staying at a farm near Oak Ridge, here. It's high ground, which most likely is why General Ewell ordered it occupied and fortified. When I left, there was a battery of four guns poised on the edge of the yard."

"Where did you get this map?" Major Taylor wanted to know. "How is it that you know so much about the enemy positions?"

"I've been here a little over a week. I've seen some of the land surrounding the town." Salina explained how she'd eavesdropped on Orrin and Michael Grant after supper. "They've volunteered to aid the Union army. Orrin took some Union scouts out to show them the roads. I don't know if it was Michael himself or someone he teaches with, but I did hear that one of the college professors went up to the cupola of the Seminary and pointed out these very same landmarks to the Union commanders. When I...*happened* to come upon this map...Well, I thought it only fair to offer my aid— little as it might be—to the Confederate command."

Major Taylor contained his grin of admiration. This young woman was not without courage, that was for sure. It was often suggested that the soldiers' proud spirit displayed in the fields was spawned by that of their women at home. He looked closely at the map, studying the sites Salina indicated.

"See here?" She traced a portion of the map with her finger. "Culp's Hill and Cemetery Hill. Both would be key positions, if occupied. There is still a bit of daylight left. Is no one going to take possession of the hills?"

"Our division and brigade commanders have their orders," Major Taylor replied stiffly. "They're to do all they think practicable."

Salina lowered her eyes. "My apologies, Major. I didn't mean to sound impertinent. I'm certainly not a military genius by any stretch of the imagination." Yet inside, a niggling thought plagued Salina. *If Stonewall Jackson were alive today, he would have pressed the enemy...He would have charged the position and taken possession, or died trying.*

In time, that particular point would become a subject of much debate. Stonewall Jackson was dead and gone. On the tenth of May, the Confederacy had been deprived of the incomparable general. A week prior to his death was when Stonewall Jackson had fallen, erroneously shot down by his men during the Battle of Chancellorsville. This Battle of Gettysburg was the first major engagement the Army of Northern Virginia faced without the brilliant leadership of their beloved Stonewall. There was no one like him, no one to fill the shoes of the legendary commander. Salina rubbed her arms to ward off a sudden premonition. When the fury that had been unleashed here at Gettysburg was spent, many would speculate as to the final outcome had Stonewall Jackson lived to fight...

Major Taylor stroked his chin with his thumb and forefinger, inspecting first the lady, then her map. "It is apparent that you are no stranger to the scene of battle, and I must admit, you do know how to pick your landmarks," he noted. "Do go on, Miss Hastings."

"Nothing more than that, really. I'm sure you all have similar maps. In fact, you're probably already aware of everything I've just told you, including that Little Round Top is a choice elevation as well," Salina answered mildly.

"Yes," Major Taylor agreed. "You're sure there's nothing else?"

Salina lifted her eyes from the map to meet the Major's. "Well, if I might be so bold as to ask, I was wondering if you could tell me where I might find General Stuart's headquarters this evening. My fiancé is attached to his staff, and if I could locate General Stuart, I stand a good chance of seeing my intended as well. Do you happen to know where General Stuart is?"

A courtly, gray-bearded man emerged from the tent to join Salina and Major Taylor at the campfire's edge. He quietly stated, "Stuart is at Carlisle. A courier reported his whereabouts shortly before you arrived. Up until that time, we'd had no word from General Stuart for several days, and had no idea as to his position."

No word from General Stuart? Salina's emerald eyes widened in surprise. That seemed rather odd. Stuart's cavalry was frequently described as the "eyes" of the Army of Northern Virginia—and oftentimes the terms "Stuart" and "cavalry" were used interchangeably to refer to either the man himself or the mounted troops under his command. Salina was sure the Rebel cavalry must be on a lengthy reconnaissance, or some other equally serviceable endeavor. *What had Ethan told her just a few days ago? That Stuart would have to be more than human to fulfill all he was ordered to do...*

"Buford is already at here at Gettysburg," Salina commented, "so perhaps General Stuart has run into Kilpatrick or Gregg—they're out there somewhere too. The Federal cavalry is always trying to catch up with Stuart's horsemen...It's possible that he had to take a roundabout detour in order to join you here. He does know where to find you?" Salina didn't realize she'd made it a question until after it was out.

"He does now," came General Lee's tight-lipped reply. The General clasped his hands behind his back, somberly staring beyond the few tents of his humble headquarters and into the darkening night. Winking lights dotting the hills indicated the cooking fires of other encampments.

A wash of chills overran Salina's spine. She suddenly had the awkward feeling of having overstepped her bounds. Hastily she got to her feet. "Forgive me, General Lee, for both the intrusion and for opening my mouth when I would be wise to keep it shut!" She absently abandoned the map and the basket to the care of Major Taylor and rambled on quickly, "I beg your pardon, General, I meant no disrespect. If you'll please excuse me, I'll be well out of your way. I don't know if the map will help at all, but I hope so. Good night, sir. Good night, Major Taylor. God keep you both."

"Miss Hastings." Major Taylor sought to keep her from scurrying off like a frightened rabbit.

Salina halted her steps and swallowed uncomfortably.

"Hastings?" General Lee took a long look at the young woman. "For some reason, you seem familiar to me, Miss, but I can't place the reason why. Have we met before? Richmond, perhaps?"

"You knew her father, General. She's the daughter of Garrett Hastings," Major Taylor reported.

"Hmmm…Captain Hastings, God rest his soul." General Lee's kind eyes crinkled at the corners, deep in thought. "But I've seen you before, I'm sure of it."

Salina remembered the instance the General could not. "Last September, at Ox Hill, a fierce battle raged in the midst of an even fiercer thunderstorm. Stonewall Jackson smashed into part of Pope's army. Two Union generals were killed, and you came to a field hospital near Chantilly to identify the body of General Phil Kearny. You ordered that he be taken through the lines under a flag of truce, to be sent home to his widow, and you posted a guard so that no harm would come to your fallen ex-comrade."

"Chantilly," General Lee recalled, fitting the pieces to the puzzle. "You were working at the field hospital that day."

Salina nodded with a hint of smile. "I backed right into you by accident, just as I have backed myself into deep water here tonight. Not terribly graceful, am I?" she questioned, referring more to her words than her deeds.

"You're just honest, Miss Hastings," General Lee smiled, his kind eyes softening. "Honesty is an admirable trait, and regrettably rare these days, though much preferable to deceit and duplicity. No apologies necessary." He picked up the basket and peeked inside. "Southern-made biscuits—now there's something to remind me of home!"

"I hope you enjoy them." Salina curtsied. "Really, I should be getting back. I've taken up enough of your time, and I've been away from the house as long as I've dared. They need my hands."

"Major Taylor," General Lee directed, "see that Miss Hastings is issued a pass that will allow her to move freely through our picket lines in case she's able to learn anything more that she feels might benefit our intentions. It's the least I can do in repayment for her generous hospitality," he turned to face Salina, "and for the risk you took to bring us your information. You're a courageous young woman."

"Thank you for saying so," Salina smiled prettily.

Major Taylor prepared the pass, then handed it to his commander, who promptly affixed his signature: *R.E. Lee, General.* "If you do hear anything else that you think might be of interest to us, I hope you will not hesitate to pass it along," General Lee encouraged.

"If I do, I will certainly let you know," Salina nodded, tucking the pass into her pocket. "One last question, if I may?"

"Certainly," General Lee replied. "What can we do for you?"

"My brother is an assistant surgeon with General Ewell's corps, I think with either Early's Division or Rodes' Division. Can you tell me where those headquarters might be?" Salina ventured.

General Lee nodded to Major Taylor, who pointed to the map. "That's where you're bound to find your brother."

"Oh, thank you!" Salina whispered.

Major Taylor anticipated what his commander was thinking. He said, "I have dispatches to send along to General Ewell. Shall I detail a courier who can also serve as an escort for Miss Hastings?"

"Yes, that would be suitable, Major. Carry on. A pleasure to meet you again, Miss Hastings." General Lee bowed, then returned to the confines of his tent with Salina's basket and map in tow.

Chapter Fifteen

$\mathcal{L}$ieutenant Amos Brennan was detailed to accompany Salina to town in search of her brother and to deliver the dispatches to General Ewell. As they entered town from the Chambersburg Pike, Salina became witness to the devastation resulting from the day's battle. Errant artillery fire had lobbed cannon balls into a number of buildings, and many were pockmarked with bullet holes. It was the same here as it was out at the Grants, Salina observed, only here barricades had been hastily erected when the rumors came that the Rebels intended to shell the town. And here, too, the citizens were taking in wounded to be fed and cared for. Campfires burned in yards and in the streets, casting eerie black shadows upon building walls.

The Rebel lieutenant stopped here and there to make inquiries on Salina's behalf. As she and Lieutenant Brennan continued on, Confederates along the way tipped their hats to her in polite deference, but no one seemed to know where Captain Ethan Hastings might be found. After a half dozen or more queries, a sergeant finally directed them to where Colonel Shields was distributing his limited inventory of medical supplies. Salina took heart, for she was acquainted with Colonel Shields, and he would surely know where Ethan was likely to be.

The disposition of the troops tarrying in the streets was very high, the Rebels boasting of their hard-fought victory. Salina heard the brisk tattoo of rapping drumsticks, merry fiddles, a tambourine or two, and feisty banjos joined by the boisterous singing of the men:

> *I'll place my knapsack on my back*
> *My rifle on my shoulder*
> *I'll march away to the firing line*
> *And kill that Yankee soldier*
> *I'll kill that Yankee soldier*
> *I'll march away to the firing line*
> *And kill that Yankee soldier...*

> *If I am shot on the battlefield*
> *And I should not recover*
> *Oh, who will protect my wife and child*
> *And care for my aged mother*
> *And care for my aged mother*
> *Oh, who will protect my wife and child*
> *And care for my aged mother...*

> *If I must fight for my home and land*
> *My spirit will not falter*
> *Oh, here's my heart and here's my hand*
> *Upon my country's altar*
> *Upon my country's altar*
> *Oh, here's my heart and here's my hand*
> *Upon my country's altar...*

"Upon my word, if it isn't Miss Salina Hastings!" Colonel Donald Shields greeted Salina and helped her down from her mount. "You're just about the last person I'd expect to find here, of all places!" He took her hands in his own and squeezed them firmly. "I've not seen you since Richmond. How are you?"

Salina smiled warmly. "As well as can be expected, thank you for asking. Today was quite the ordeal."

"Hmmm," Colonel Shields nodded in agreement. "I'm afraid it's going to get worse before it gets better. We've carried the day, but we're paying the price."

"I was looking for my brother. Do you know where he might be?" Salina asked. "Can you tell me which field hospital he's working in?"

"Well, my dear, he volunteered to go to a place called Oak Ridge or Oak Hill—I gather they are near to each other," Colonel Shields replied. "He told me he'd been there just a few days ago and knew folks who own farmland in that area. We saw a hospital flag flying from a house that was within the lines of fire. Ethan seemed to think that you might be there, for he was most certain you had something to do with that flag."

"I did," Salina quickly nodded. "How long ago did he leave here? He didn't go alone, did he?"

"No, not alone. He took three or four orderlies with him. Franklin's here somewhere..." Colonel Shields glanced past Salina's shoulder to look for his nephew. "I need to send him out with more medicine for Ethan. Since you know where this place is, perhaps you could guide Franklin out there."

"But of course," Salina answered without hesitation. She said to Lieutenant Brennan, "Thank you, sir, for your assistance. I'll wait for Captain Shields to arrive, and then we'll ride to Oak Ridge. Give my best to Major Taylor and General Lee when you return to headquarters, would you please?"

"It'd be my pleasure, Miss," Lieutenant Brennan saluted smartly. "I'll be on my way then." Colonel Shields gave Lieutenant Brennan directions to General Ewell's headquarters on the outskirts of town.

Franklin was delighted to see Salina and was ready to go with her to Oak Ridge just as soon as the saddlebags were securely fastened onto his saddle.

"It's about time you got back!" Ethan barked at Salina when she returned. "Franklin, you can set those saddlebags down over here."

Salina washed up, tied on a fresh apron and went to her brother's side. She met his eyes with determination. "What do you want me to do?"

For hours into the night, Salina stayed in the parlour-turned-operating room, serving as Ethan's nurse, assisting through many a gory surgery. She gagged a time or two at the raw carnage facing her, but eventually, she became mercifully numb. She hadn't time to dwell on it. Ethan worked methodically in an effort to save as many of the men as he possibly could. Amputations came as a last measure of recourse, but they were still performed with alarming frequency. Sawed off arms and legs grew in heaps and piles just outside the open windows.

It must have been close to four in the morning when Ethan finally told Salina to go and lie down for a couple of hours. He too could use a rest, but there were too many wounded. He rubbed the back of his tense neck, found a pot of coffee in the kitchen and poured himself a scalding cupful. There he met up with the Federal doctor who had worked at the operating table set up in the dining room.

"Abel Warrick, Boston, Massachusetts." The blue-uniformed doctor proffered his hand to the young assistant surgeon.

"Ethan Hastings," Salina's brother nodded, shaking hands with Warrick. "Fairfax County, Virginia."

"Pretty country down in Virginia," Warrick commented offhandedly, "or at least it used to be."

"Pretty enough here," Ethan returned, straining to remain polite. "All lush and green and, up until yesterday, virtually untouched." Ethan drained his cup, not caring that the coffee burned a trail down his throat. "Better get back to it."

Warrick nodded. "If you need anything, or if I can help you in some way, don't hesitate to ask."

"The same to you," Ethan replied, then headed to the parlour.

☆ ☆ ☆ ☆ ☆ ☆ ☆

The sun was high when Salina came up from the cellar, hurriedly fastening her long, dark, curling tresses into a knot at the nape of her slender neck with a handful of hairpins. "Why didn't you fetch me after two hours?" she quizzed Ethan. "I've slept so long, and you've not had any rest since you arrived."

Ethan glanced across the operating table, noting the refreshed appearance of his little sister. "If it makes you feel any better, Dr. Warrick and I spelled each other and each took an hour's nap."

"Fine, because you'll not do the men any good if you're too tired to keep your eyes open, you know," Salina remarked. "Have you had your breakfast?"

"Not hungry," Ethan declined. "You go on, then come back—I could use your hands again."

"I'm really not hungry either," Salina told him. "Maybe I will be later."

Ethan didn't wait for her to change her mind. He put her to work.

The morning passed in a strangely placid way. Salina couldn't help but wonder if the fighting would renew itself or not. Perhaps she'd slept so long because she half expected to be jolted from her bed by cannonading. For the moment, however, the air was blessedly free of any deadly flying projectiles, which was probably the reason she had slept at all. The Rebel artillery crowning the hill remained in position, ready and waiting, but they were not engaged.

Awhile later, Salina left Mamma tending to the soldiers while Noreen and Beth-Anne baked more and more bread. She took three loaves and another jar of jam, and crossed through the yard. Nathan and Jared had rigged canvas canopies for shelter from the sweltering sun, and Michael and Orrin were occupied in taking away the dead for burial. Cody and Chandler had taken over the chore of carrying water to the injured men.

"Where are you going, Salina?" Cody came into the barn.

"I just have to leave for a little bit." Salina did not disclose her destination. "I'm going to meet someone, and I'll be right back."

"It can't be your horse soldier. I heard tell that Stuart's troops are still on their way from Carlisle," Cody informed her.

Salina's heart quickened. Carlisle was a day's ride away, but if they were already on the move, perhaps they would be here this afternoon, or surely by tonight... "What've you heard about the position of the Union troops?"

"They're still up there on Cemetery Ridge. Good strong position," Cody told Salina. "Too bad. If your General Ewell had pressed the charge, the Johnny Rebs might hold the high ground today."

Salina tipped her head to one side. "You sound disappointed that they didn't take that hill."

Cody shrugged indifferently. "Aren't you disappointed?"

"Whose side are you on, Cody?" something made Salina ask. "If you were old enough, would you have joined the regiment with Nathan and Jared?"

Cody diffidently shook his head. "I'd rather join the Southern army."

"Cody!" Salina was genuinely surprised, but at the same time delighted to have found an ally in the Grant family. "Your father, Uncle Duncan, and your brothers would be beside themselves."

Cody's gray eyes pleaded with her to keep quiet about his feelings and the disclosure of his true loyalties. "I've watched you, and you seem the trustworthy sort. You won't tell them, will you?"

"Hardly. It'll be between you and me," Salina promised him.

"Won't you tell me where you're going?" Cody again asked.

Salina smiled. He probably wouldn't believe her if she told the truth, so she did just that. "I'm going to see General Lee."

Cody's eyes grew round. "You can't do that!"

"Of course I can," Salina laughed. "But that's just our secret too. Understand?" She urged the horse forward, applying pressure with her heels. "I'll be back shortly."

The pass General Lee had signed for Salina proved to be useful in getting through the picket lines. Major Taylor was rather surprised to see the young Virginia woman again. He greeted Salina pleasantly, but would not allow her to approach the General's tent. "My apologies, Miss Hastings. General Lee's left strict orders that he's not to be disturbed."

Salina belatedly noticed the presence of another horse tethered nearby. "Council of war?"

"You might say that." Major Taylor readily accepted the gift of homemade bread and jam.

"There's to be more fighting later on then," Salina surmised.

Major Taylor's mustache twitched slightly. Miss Hastings was indeed perceptive. He cleared his throat and said curtly, "General Stuart has arrived. His columns will be here before dark."

Both Salina's smile and eyes flashed. "That is good news!"

Major Taylor did not voice further comment on the tardy Southern cavalry brigades. Inwardly, he thought about those ranking officers who already made rather embittered remarks concerning the absence of Stuart, some even suggesting that he be court-martialed for his neglect to keep in touch with Lee. The orders given to Stuart were discretionary—just as Lee's orders to Ewell had been about taking possession of that hill *if practicable*, and General Lee had given Stuart free range to carry out those orders the best way he knew how. Stuart was now being accused of having taken advantage of that latitude, and in his supposed attempt to circle the Union army a glorious third time, he had left the main body of the Army of Northern Virginia blind. The confrontation here in Gettysburg had not been by design, but it was far too late to change the fact that the two enemy armies were irrevocably entangled.

Major Taylor abruptly cleared his throat. "I don't mean to be rude, Miss Hastings, but was there anything else you wished to relay to General Lee? Have you any more information today?"

"No, I'm sorry, I don't. We've spent most of the night and all morning tending to the wounded. I'll not stay, I'm sure things here must be very busy, and if I'm gone for too long they'll miss me back at the farm," Salina murmured.

"Many thanks for the bread," Major Taylor added appreciatively.

"You're quite welcome," Salina nodded.

"Hurry home, Miss," Major Taylor admonished. "There are battle plans in the works. I expect action will be employed just as soon as it is prudent for our men to initiate their attack." He saw a last question in Salina's eyes and answered before she could put the inquiry into words: "General Stuart's troops will be on Ewell's left. I'm sure that's where you'll find his headquarters, and your intended, later on tonight."

"Thank you kindly, Major Taylor!" she replied with a wide grin, then bade him farewell.

Salina had just finished unsaddling her horse when the ground beneath her feet trembled. There it was, the commencement of another day's deadly work. For how many hours would they fight, wreaking havoc and destruction in their wake? God alone knew. Thankfully, the fighting was away from the Grant farmstead. They already had enough suffering to deal with.

Chapter Sixteen

*C*ody caught a glimpse of Salina sneaking out of the house in clothes he recognized as his own—his shirt, his britches, and his cap. She might have borrowed his boots as well, but she was clever enough to figure they'd be far too big for her. Cody followed stealthily in the shadows, waiting to confront her in the barn. He burst in on her just as she swung her leg over the saddle. "And just where do you think you're going? Especially dressed like *that*?" the fourteen-year-old demanded.

Salina put her finger to her lips, shushing him. "Hush! Mamma'll have my hide if she finds out—not to mention Ethan! This is my chance, Cody, and I've got to take it. My brother left an hour ago, otherwise I'd not risk it. He'd insist that I'm out of my mind to think I could make it to Stuart's camp alone."

"You're going to Stuart's camp?" Cody asked incredulously. "All by yourself?"

Conspiratorially Salina relented, issuing a challenge, "Unless you want to come with me."

Cody nodded emphatically. "Anybody who's not already sleeping will be shortly. Give me ten minutes. I'll meet you back here."

Salina conceded. "I'll wait."

"Don't leave without me," Cody ordered, turning towards the house.

"I won't," Salina promised, "But hurry."

The dauntless pair escaped the farm without attracting attention to themselves. They moved swiftly but dared not even whisper in the stillness of the night. Emerging from the battered trees lining the Grant property, Salina inadvertently rode through a clingy, invisible spider's web. "Yikes!" She permitted herself a tiny outcry, but Cody warned her to be quiet, and she heeded his command, abruptly wiping her face with her shirt sleeve. If she hadn't tucked her hair up in her cap, the wispy web would no doubt have been threaded all through her curls. "Yuck!" she muttered disgustedly. "I hate spiders!"

"Come on," Cody chuckled softly. "And pay attention." He took back ways, down farm lanes instead of main roads, leading them closer to town. When they'd crossed through a little branch of a creek, he finally indicated to her where they were. "Not far from the Almshouse." Cody pointed on ahead. "You said you thought they were near the Heidlersburg Road?"

Salina nodded and patted her horse's neck. "Is it much farther?"

"No. In fact," Cody sniffed the dark air, "you can smell…campfires—and coffee and bread." He intentionally failed to mention the combined odors of spent powder and death.

Once past the Almshouse, Salina lost sight of the moon as they rode through a small stand of trees. She never saw the two men secluded in the shadows until they leapt out in ambush.

Salina went flying, hurled from her saddle, landing with a bruising thud on the hard ground below. For an instant the wind was knocked out of her, but then she coughed and felt the rush of breath flooding her lungs. Salina struggled fiercely against the man atop her, fighting to extricate herself from the grasp of her assailant, but her puny efforts were futile against his powerful strength. The man straddled her, roughly pinning her wrists above her head, anchoring her securely. As he rose to his knees, she heard the threatening click of a gun hammer.

"Be still, man! I'm not going to hurt you unless I have to!" the voice rasped.

Salina immediately stopped struggling. She had no wish to be shot. Her hair fell free of the dislodged cap and was streaming across her eyes, hindering her view of the man's silhouetted face.

"Sallie?!" The man's voice was incredulous. He let go of her hands as though they burnt him, and refastened the safety lock on his pistol. He scrambled to his feet, and the *girl* before him sat up, sputtering furiously.

Salina pushed the curling strands of hair from her cheeks and focused her wide eyes on Lieutenant Jeremy Barnes. "What are you trying to do, kill me?" she fumed indignantly, but her anger melted into delighted laughter.

By this time Jeremy was laughing, too. He caught Salina in a crushing embrace, kissing the top of her head, the tip of her nose, and finally her smiling lips. "Sallie!" He shook his head in disbelief, his tone only partially scolding.

"Sir?" Boone Hunter disliked having to break up the happy reunion between the lieutenant and his lady. "What about this one?" Boone had a hold of Cody by the scruff of his collar.

"Let the boy go, Boone," Jeremy nodded. "Who is this, Sallie?"

"This is Cody Grant, a nephew of Duncan's. I couldn't have found my way here without his help," Salina intervened. "I promised I'd bring him along to see General Stuart's camp in exchange for letting me borrow this get-up." A wave of her hand encompassed her boyish garb.

"What? Not a dyed-in-the-wool Yankee?" Jeremy taunted Cody mildly.

"No, sir," Cody answered plainly. "If I was to get into this war, I'd run away and join the Southern Cavalry. I saw Jeb Stuart's name in the paper again last week. He's famous up here in the North, you know. The Union hasn't got anybody like him—you Rebs have all the good generals."

Jeremy smiled indulgently. He could tell the boy stories that would curl his toes and destroy his glorious impressions. The past week alone would have opened Cody's eyes to the brutal reality of warfare, that was for sure, but Jeremy didn't have the heart to disillusion him. He remembered, not all that long ago, feeling the very same way the lad did. "Come on, Cody Grant, we'll take you to General Stuart's camp, though the good general himself isn't here right now."

"He's probably still meeting with General Lee," Salina volunteered, dusting herself off.

"And what makes you think that?" Jeremy queried.

"General Stuart was at General Lee's headquarters earlier when I was out there." Salina flashed a grin towards her intended.

"You don't honestly think I've just been sitting idle up here in Pennsylvania, do you?" She did not spare him the chance to reply. "There's work that had to be done, contacts made...information passed along."

"Have you been spying again?" Jeremy challenged, one dark eyebrow raised in a high arch.

"Only a little," Salina admitted, showing him a measurement no more than an inch wide between her thumb and forefinger. "I'm still *behaving*." She turned to the rider accompanying Jeremy. "Boone, how are you?"

"A bit tired, Miss, but otherwise fine. Thank you for asking." Self-consciously, Boone kicked the ground with the toe of one long boot. "By chance, have you heard from Miss Clarice at all?"

"No, not since I left Culpeper," Salina replied. "Have you?" Her cousin was smitten with the young, big-footed cavalier, and it was plain to see the sentiment was reciprocated.

Boone was mistaken in thinking that darkness concealed the rosy flush he felt creeping along his neck and cheeks. "I did get one letter from her before we came North. She's kind to remember me."

"Clarice likes you, Boone," Salina confirmed. "Quite a lot."

"Aw, Miss Salina," Boone hung his head shyly, "how you do go on."

Salina giggled coyly. She looked up at Jeremy and said, "Well, let's not keep Cody in suspense any longer than necessary. Won't you take us to camp?"

"Indeed I will." Jeremy helped Salina mount up, and she and Cody followed the cavalrymen.

Weston Bentley, Kidd Carney, Jake Landon, Curlie Hawkins, Cutter Montgomery, and two men Salina didn't know sat on logs or on the ground in a circle around the glowing fire. Jeremy made the introductions, putting names to the new faces: "These are the Scarborough brothers—Tristan and Archer. They're from Charlotte, North Carolina, but we don't hold that against them." Many Southern men fought specifically to defend their native states, and there was a degree of rivalry between regiments, even within brigades and divisions.

"Tristan, Archer, a pleasure to meet you." Salina's hand was kissed by each of the new calvarymen who'd recently elected to ride with Jeremy.

"Pleasure's most certainly ours, Miss," the North Carolinians answered simultaneously.

Salina sat down next to Jeremy on a log near the dancing campfire. It did her heart good to see them all again. "Anyone heard how C.J.'s doing?" she asked.

"He's in a Richmond hospital by last report," Bentley supplied the update. "He should be healed up soon, and then he'll rejoin us. He's a little put out that he missed all the fun on this side of the Mason-Dixon line."

"I reckon he would be at that," Salina nodded. "So, tell me, where have you all been?"

The accounting of their journey north was woven like an old folk tale. Each man added a part as they went round the circle relaying the latest of their bold capers. They'd fought in a skirmish near Fairfax Station, collected goods from the depot and from the sutlers in Fairfax Court House. "That's where I got these nice new boots," Boone piped up. "They had a lovely pair just my size." The last pair he'd procured had been taken off a dead Yankee after the Battle of Fredericksburg in December of 1862.

The men told Salina the tale of the "Cherry-Pie Breakfast," and of how General Stuart had nearly been captured while feeding "Virginia," his fleet-footed charger. "The blue-bellies chased Stuart until they ran smack into the main body of our column, then turned tail and ran," Jake grinned. "Chalk up another close call for the General."

"Indeed!" Salina exclaimed, shaking her head in wonder. "Ethan told me von Borcke had been shot at Upperville, most likely because some Yankee mistook him to be the General, and now this episode. General Stuart's guardian angels must be working hard to keep up with him!" Then she inquired, "Fairfax Court House. You all were that close to home? Did you see Tabitha or Reverend Yates, or Taylor Sue and Mary Edith?"

"No, Sallie, I'm afraid we didn't have time for social calls on this trip through Fairfax." Jeremy squeezed her shoulders. "The last social call I made was to my Aunt Isabelle, and that was when we were at Middleburg." He saw the curious light in her eyes and quickly added, "I'll tell you about that later."

"We crossed the Potomac at Rowser's Ford." Bentley, picking up on the wordless cue from his lieutenant, resumed the tale. "The river was saddle-high, but there was no better place to ford. General Stuart ordered the caissons unloaded and the ammunition brought across by hand, dry. It took us until three in the morning to get it done, but we did it without losing a man, horse, or shell."

Stuart's troopers had destroyed barges, boats, and a sluice gate at the Chesapeake & Ohio Canal. They took prisoners, combined them with those who had been captured near Fairfax Station, and brought them all along to Rockville, Maryland.

"That's where we picked up the wagon train," Archer added. "One-hundred twenty-five brand spanking new wagons, and teams to go with them. Loads of supplies, all intended for the Army of the Potomac—but we got 'em instead. We came within *ten miles* of the Union capital—oh, they must have been in a panic in Washington!"

"If General Stuart had really wanted to make a name for himself, he could have ridden right into Washington and wreaked a bit of havoc," Cutter remarked candidly. "I wish he would have. We could've captured old Abe Lincoln and sued for peace!"

"But we didn't, and we're still fighting this war." Tristan tossed the remains of his coffee cup into the fire with a disgruntled sigh. "We got a fine reception from the Southern-sympathizing women in Rockville, though. They all turned out to see us—especially the girls from the local female academy."

Salina cast a curious glance at Jeremy. "I'm sure they were very welcoming. Sounds a bit like Urbana all over again. Did General Stuart host a ball there in Rockville, too?"

"Nope," Curlie answered in Jeremy's stead, "but while we were there we did procure some items to help fulfill our wish lists."

"Wish lists?" Salina questioned.

"Lots of the men have lists from their wives or sweethearts," Bentley explained. "While we're up here in the North, we're sometimes lucky to come up with special items and trinkets that can't be found back home. The womenfolk love it when we bring back little things for 'em. I got fifteen yards of plum brocade satin for my missus and a pair of real purty earbobs to match."

Salina nodded in understanding. "But please, do go on with the story-telling." She loved listening to them.

"We burned what wagons we didn't take along with us," Kidd Carney said as he applied his pocket knife to a chunk of wood, whittling away curled shavings. "We were slowed considerably by the ones we did keep. Telegraph wires were cut, putting Washington out of touch with points west. Stuart had a golden opportunity to waltz into the Union capital, for by all reports it was not heavily defended."

But Stuart hadn't gone to Washington. Instead, he followed orders to *"collect all the supplies you can for the use of the army."*

Stuart maneuvered his captured wagon train on to Westminster where a strike was made on the Baltimore & Ohio Railroad, laying waste to railroad tracks and rolling stock near Hood's Mill. Another costly delay was caused by the time taken to parole the four hundred prisoners Stuart's men had taken captive. A skirmish ensued at Westminster, but Jeremy's men sustained no injury, coming through the fight miraculously unscathed.

Jeremy had been with Stuart at Union Mills, where the General and his staff had sampled a tasty breakfast of flapjacks, biscuits, coffee, and buttermilk. "For an hour General Stuart seemed to set aside the war, though it's always in the back of his mind, and went to work singing most enthusiastically around the Shriver family's piano—you know two of his favorites are *Listen to the Mockingbird* and *Jine the Cavalry*. 'If you want to have fun...'" Jeremy quoted a line from the infamous recruiting song. "And General Stuart does like to do that." He continued, "The Shrivers' son, sixteen-year-old Herbert, was our guide on a detour of Littlestown in order to avoid another clash with the Yankees. In return for his service, General Stuart has promised Herbert an education at the Virginia Military Institute, and afterwards a place on his staff. The Shrivers are another divided family—the household we visited supports the Southern Cause while the Shriver relatives living just across the road remain loyal to the Union."

Salina shook her head mournfully. "Brother against brother, friend against friend, fathers against sons..." She listened intently to the recounting of the battle at Hanover, and the skirmishing that continued along the route at Dover. At Carlisle, Stuart thought they would meet up with General Ewell, but belatedly learned that the Second Corps had left the area the previous morning. Stuart's terms for surrender were rejected by Carlisle's citizenry, and so he ordered the town shelled and the post barracks burned to the ground. A courier arrived from the Army of Northern Virginia's headquarters, informing General Stuart that he was to report to General Lee in Gettysburg with all haste. The Rebel Cavalry passed through Heidlersburg, stashed the captured supply wagons in the vicinity of Biglersville, and once past Huntersville, arrived at Gettysburg.

"When did you all sleep?" Salina asked, amazed that they had ridden so long, fought so hard, and were still awake. She took a good long look at the faces round the fire, and saw that each man was hanging onto wakefulness by a mere thread. Any one of them, if they laid their head down for even a second, might drop off immediately into a deep slumber.

"There was work to be done, orders to be followed. Some of us slept in the saddle—we caught winks here and there, wherever we could," Cutter replied with a shrug, then admitted, "In truth, we didn't have time to sleep much at all."

Salina glanced up at Jeremy, whose eyes were also shadowed with fatigue, realizing that he probably maintained his alert composure for her sake. She felt the secure warmth of his arm around her waist and saw the love evident in his eyes as he administered another one-armed hug.

"I should get on back and let you all get some rest. Tomorrow's another day, yet here you are, the gallant cavaliers, struggling to keep your eyes open just to entertain Cody and me," Salina pointed out.

"Your company is well worth it, Miss." Bentley tipped his cap in her direction. "Stay awhile longer," he invited on Jeremy's behalf.

Archer Scarborough took up his fiddle and plied his bow across the strings. The melancholic tune he played was called *Lorena*.

> *Oh the years creep slowly by Lorena*
> *The snow is on the ground again*
> *The sun's low down the sky Lorena*
> *The frost gleams where the flowers have been*
>
> *But the heart beats on as warmly now*
> *As when the summer days were nigh*
> *Oh the sun can never dip so low*
> *To be down in Affection's cloudless sky*

The others joined in on the next verse, but with a decidedly mischievous bent. Rather than singing *Lorena*, they substituted the name of *Salina* instead:

> *A hundred months have passed Salina*
> *Since last I held that hand in mine*
> *And felt the pulse beat fast Salina*
> *Though mine beat faster far than thine*
>
> *A hundred months 'twas flowery May*
> *When up that hilly slope we'd climb*

> *To watch the dying of the day*
> *And hear the distant church bells chime*

Jeremy squirmed, a tad chagrined, as Archer and the others deliberately poked fun at him. Archer and Tristan had heard so much about Miss Salina Rose Hastings that both had felt they already knew her long before they'd been properly introduced. The brothers mutually agreed that Miss Hastings was everything—and more—that the riders had described, but they didn't convey their opinions to Jeremy. It went without saying, just by watching the two of them together, that the Horse Soldier and his lady cared very deeply for one another.

Salina giggled in delight, keenly aware that the men were intentionally testing Jeremy with their melodious jesting. Jeremy usually reacted hotly to their teasing; he was admittedly oversensitive when it came to Salina. In this case, however, he surprised them all by enjoying the prank. He even went so far as to join in with them on the last verse:

> *We loved each other then* Salina
> *Far more than we ever dared to tell*
> *And what we might have been* Salina
> *Had our loving prospered well...*

At that point, Jeremy's resonant voice faltered. The lyrics dwindled away before the song came to its conclusion. Jeremy swallowed hard, thinking on the words of the song. Abruptly he jumped up from the log, startling the men and dislodging Salina from her comfortable place in the cradle of his arms.

Salina's backside landed squarely on the ground, and her emerald eyes looked up at him in askance. Jeremy pulled Salina up by her outstretched hands and continued to hold them as he stared intensely into her firelit face. "Marry me!"

"Yes, Jeremy, when we have the time allotted to us, I do intend to do precisely that." Salina's fingers gingerly caressed his whiskered jaw.

"No," he argued, "not sometime, not down the road in the future—tonight! Now!" Jeremy insisted.

"What?" she blinked in stunned disbelief.

Archer's fiddle halted in a screech as the bow scraped against the taut strings.

"Marry me, Sallie. Tonight," Jeremy persisted. "We'll find the chaplain, and we'll have our wedding."

"You have gone without sleep for far too many days," Salina began, but she saw that he was in earnest. She glanced disparagingly at her attire. "You'd marry me looking like this? I'd rather hoped to be married in a gown, at least... not trousers, for goodness sake!"

"I don't care what you have on—I'm marrying *you*, not your wardrobe, and I'd marry you under water if that's what it would take!" Jeremy's disarming grin was positively infectious.

A slow smile lifted the corners of Salina's mouth and an impish twinkle illuminated her eyes. "You're serious about this."

"Deadly serious." Jeremy's determined tone sent a chill racing down Salina's spine.

"All right," she acquiesced, accepting his forthright challenge. She looked around the fire at the faces of their friends, witnessing their expectant expressions. She turned back to her Horse Soldier, meeting his eyes without wavering. "I'll marry you tonight, Jeremy Barnes, right here, right now. Providing that's acceptable to you all?" She made a conscious effort to include his men.

"Here, here!" the men chanted. "A toast to the bride and groom!" they cheered heartily.

"As for getting married in trousers," Tristan spoke up, "Archer might be able to help remedy that, Miss Salina." He called to his brother, "Archer, where's that blue dress you picked out in Rockville?"

"Why, I'd plumb forgot about that—a nice ready-made dress, it is." Archer scrambled to his feet. "And I'd surely be honored if you'd wear it, Miss."

"She'll be lovely in it," Tristan declared with a whimsical grin.

Salina hesitated briefly. "If you picked up a dress in Rockville, there must have been just cause—a wife, or a sweetheart, perhaps? How will she feel knowing you gave up her dress for my sake?"

"Not a wife or sweetheart, just our pesky baby sister," Archer remarked, but the fondness for the young girl was evident despite his tone.

"We got her lots of other stuff, Miss," Tristan interjected.

"Carrie never knew she was getting the dress, so she'll never miss it," Archer said logically. He went to fetch the frock in question from his saddlebags. He returned carrying a stylish garment beautifully constructed of delicate organdie in the most becoming shade of robin's egg blue, trimmed with royal blue satin ribbon.

"Oh!" Salina sighed ecstatically. "You're sure it's all right for me to borrow this?"

Archer grinned. "Borrow? No. If it fits, you keep it as our wedding gift to you."

Salina held the dress to her, inspecting it joyously, instinctively guessing that it would be a perfect fit. "Married in blue, he'll always be true," she quoted blithely, tossing the gown over her shoulder. She met Jeremy's eyes and said with a bright smile, "You arrange for the chaplain, and I'll be back in a few minutes." Salina disappeared into the tent Bentley pointed out for her use. He stood guard so no one would disrupt the transformation from waif to belle that was occurring inside.

Jeremy dispatched Boone to find the chaplain. While he was gone, Jeremy ransacked his own saddlebags in search of the gold wedding ring he carried with him. It was a plain gold band, one that would nicely complement Salina's garnet-and-diamond engagement ring.

It didn't take long for Boone to return with the exhausted chaplain, Reverend John Landstreet, who rubbed his eyes repeatedly for want of sleep. When Boone had located the cavalry chaplain of the 1st Virginia and explained to him why it was so important for this couple to be married tonight, Landstreet had heartily agreed to perform the marriage service.

Reverend Landstreet reckoned it was worth missing a half hour's sleep to ensure that the couple was properly bound together in wedlock. He downed a cup of coffee and scurried to retrieve his minister's book. Most of the service he'd rendered lately involved comforting and praying with the dying before their souls departed the earth. It was a welcome change for Reverend Landstreet to lend his ministerial authority to this solemn but joyous occasion. Wedding vows contain a promise and hope for the future, and hope was something they all clung to with gritty tenacity.

"This'll be one to tell your grandchildren, Lieutenant," Bentley joshed, clapping a hand on Jeremy's shoulder. "Now you go stand right over there. Your bride'll be out in a minute."

Chapter Seventeen

*S*alina emerged from the tent adorned in the blue organdie gown. It fit, as she had suspected, as though the seamstress had designed it with her in mind. Her ebony curls were knotted in a neat chignon at the nape of her neck, though several stray tendrils stubbornly curled in front of her ears.

Kidd Carney offered to lend her the use of a lacy shawl, which he draped lightly over her head and down her shoulders. Here again, the conditions of the traditional rhyme were met:

> *Something old, Something new*
> *Something borrowed, Something blue...*

She carried no flowers, but twisted her hands nervously behind her back until Bentley offered his arm. Salina kept her eyes averted until she stood opposite the chaplain and Jeremy. When she looked up, it was to seek approval in the eyes of her Horse Soldier, but she witnessed more than mere acceptance in his sapphire scrutiny. Dancing in the depths of Jeremy's eyes was a combination of pride, love, and a hint of anticipation.

Jeremy's mouth went dry, his palms turned clammy. Salina was beautiful, and he couldn't keep from staring longingly at his blushing bride.

"It's all right for you to breathe, you know," Kidd Carney reminded Jeremy.

Jeremy shot a cutting glance at the man standing nearest him.

Reverend Landstreet yawned only slightly before he began the marriage service. He cleared his throat and started by saying, "Dearly beloved: We are gathered together here in the sight of God, and in the face of this company, to join together this Man and this Woman in holy matrimony, which is an honorable estate, and therefore is not by any to be entered into unadvisedly or lightly; but reverently, discreetly, advisedly, and in the fear of God..."

Jeremy's mind drifted momentarily, recalling Reverend Yates' words of counsel. He said that marriage could be successful if both parties were willing to work and sacrifice—it was something to be entered into together, like-minded, and not without courage.

He looked down at his bride. Salina's emerald-green eyes were luminous in the flickering firelight. Her attention was intently focused on what the chaplain was saying; therefore, she missed the sound of a tardy rider's stealthy approach.

"Into this holy estate, these two persons present come now to be joined. If any man can show just cause why they may not be lawfully joined together, let him now speak, or else hereafter forever hold his peace." Reverend Landstreet glanced around, but no one had anything to say. He said to the young lieutenant, "Jeremy, wilt thou have this Woman to thy wedded wife, to live together after God's ordinance, in the holy estate of matrimony? Wilt thou love her, comfort her, honor, and keep her, in sickness and in health; and forsaking all others, keep thee only unto her, so long as ye both shall live?"

"I will," Jeremy replied in a determined tone of voice.

Salina smiled timorously, waiting until Reverend Landstreet asked her the same questions. She, too, answered evenly, resolutely, "I will."

"Who giveth this woman to be married to this man?" the chaplain inquired.

Bentley started to reply, but was rudely interrupted.

"I do," Captain Ethan Hastings declared. "Bentley, if you'll excuse me, you're relieved of this assignment. I'd very much like to be the one to give my little sister to my best friend."

Bentley readily relinquished his position. "Aye, Captain Hastings," he saluted with a grin.

Salina's eyes misted, but she refused the tears. She would not cry this evening, no matter how happy she was—not in this company, not for the sheer joy that welled within her bosom. There would be time for tears after they had all gone back to their duty and the harsh business of war.

"Say it again, Reverend," Ethan requested, grinning down at his beaming little sister.

"Who giveth this woman to be married to this man?" Reverend Landstreet repeated.

Ethan gently patted Salina's right hand, which was securely tucked in the crook of his left arm. "I do."

"Where did you come from? How did you know where to find me?" Salina whispered under her breath.

"Cody was missing, and no one could find you anywhere. I'd heard Stuart's cavalry had arrived, so this was my first guess. Glad I got here when I did." Ethan winked.

"Me, too." Salina returned her brother's generous smile.

"Shall we proceed then?" inquired the chaplain, and they nodded. Reverend Landstreet took Salina's right hand from Ethan's, placing it into Jeremy's. Then he stated Jeremy's part line for line, and waited for Jeremy's echo:

"I, Jeremy, take thee, Salina, to my wedded wife, to have and to hold from this day forward, for better for worse, for richer for poorer, in sickness and in health, to love and to cherish till death do us part, according to God's holy ordinance; and thereto I plight thee my troth."

Salina's vows were identical save for one phrase: "I, Salina, take thee, Jeremy, to my wedded husband, to have and to hold from this day forward, for better for worse, for richer for poorer, in sickness and in health, to love, cherish, *and obey*, till death us do part, according to God's holy ordinance; and thereto I plight thee my troth." She promised to obey, and irreverently wondered if it was the same as promising to *behave*. No matter…Jeremy was holding her left hand, slipping the wedding band onto her ring finger.

Salina had a ring for Jeremy, as well, and she withdrew the gold band from its hiding place in the sash belted around her trim waist. His rough hands were much larger than hers, but she had managed to estimate his ring size accurately. She repeated the same lines Jeremy had spoken when he put his ring on her finger: "As a pledge and in token of the vows between us made, with this ring, I thee wed: In the name of the Father, and of the Son, and of the Holy Ghost. Amen."

Reverend Landstreet had them hold hands again, then he placed his hand over theirs. He bowed his head and prayed for Jeremy and Salina. "Those whom God hath joined together, let no man put asunder," he concluded, and he smiled encouragingly at them. "Forasmuch as Jeremy and Salina have consented together in holy wedlock, and have witnessed the same before God and this company, and thereto have given and pledged their troth, each to the other, and have declared the same by the giving and receiving of rings, and by joining hands; I pronounce that they are Man and Wife, in the name of the Father, and of the Son, and of the Holy Ghost. Amen." The chaplain closed his book, and with a broad smile announced, "You may kiss your bride, sir."

Jeremy slipped the lace shawl from her head to her shoulders. He framed her face with his hands and pressed his lips to hers to seal their vows.

A hearty shout rose up from the men. Bentley commented dryly, *"That's* what you should have done the night we found her at the Richmond Theater."

Jeremy's grin was decidedly lopsided. He brushed Salina's cheek with his thumb. "Lots of water under the bridge since that night, hmmm?"

Salina nodded. "Lots of water."

Reverend Landstreet raised his hands to quiet those present. "Gentlemen, it gives me great pleasure to introduce to you all— Lieutenant and Mrs. Jeremy Barnes."

This announcement was met with another cheer. Salina's heart thumped wildly. She was at long last her Horse Soldier's Bride. *Mrs. Jeremy Barnes...*

During the wedding ceremony Archer had played *Jesu, Joy of Man's Desiring*, a soft, haunting melody composed by Johann Bach, but afterwards he lapsed into rousing renditions of *The Cavalier's Waltz, Nick Malone*, and *La Belle Catherine*. Jeremy swept Salina into his arms, claiming his first dance with his new wife.

As was their custom, the riders took turns cutting in on the newlyweds, each congratulating Salina by placing a chaste kiss on her flushed cheek, and shaking hands with Jeremy to convey their heartfelt well wishes.

When it came time for Archer's turn to dance with Salina, they had only the crackle of the fire for accompaniment until the men began to clap their hands and attempt to make up for the absence of the fiddle with inharmonious *la-la-la's* and *de-de-de's*, which soon dissolved into rollicking chuckles.

"Some of you couldn't carry a tune in a bushel basket!" Archer declared, his hands over his ears. He winked at Salina and groaned sarcastically, "What more can you expect from amateurs such as these?" He hastened to pick up his fiddle, knowing a certain pride and satisfaction that none of them could make music like he could.

While Salina was dancing from one partner to the next, Jeremy took Cody aside and asked him if he knew of a place in the neighboring vicinity that might do as shelter for a few hours' worth of a wedding night. Cody gave him precise directions to an old, unused shed on a farm not too far distant, and Jeremy thanked him.

Jeremy mounted Orion, his big black war-horse, and lifted Salina up behind him. Once the newlyweds were on their way, the remaining riders tickled Cody unmercifully, trying to make him spill the location of the secret rendezvous, but he held his tongue. He was determined to stave off any attempt at a charivari.

At length the men gave up. Bentley decreed sagely, "Aw, let 'em be. Poor young'uns won't have much time together anyhow."

"Besides," Jake Landon added, "From a more realistic standpoint, a noisy charivari might attract Yankee pickets, and the last thing I want to do tonight is pitch into another fracas with the blue-bellies." He yawned. "That'll come soon enough in the morning."

"Let's get some sleep," Cutter agreed. "We'll leave the lovebirds alone—this time—and we'll make it up to them when it's safer for all parties concerned."

The other riders nodded in accord. One by one they spread their bedrolls in a circle around the campfire. With hats pulled low over their eyes or covering their face entirely, each drifted into coveted repose.

☆ ☆ ☆ ☆ ☆ ☆ ☆

"Whoa, boy." Jeremy pulled on Orion's reins, halting outside the unused shed Cody had sent them to. The youngster had been right—it was secluded, no doubt on that point, but that wasn't the only adjective Jeremy could have used to describe the ramshackle site. He cast a furtive glance over his shoulder, half-expecting to find that one or more of his men had followed them.

Salina lifted her cheek from where it rested against one of Jeremy's shoulder blades. Her arms were around his lean middle, and she squeezed him with a reassuring hug. She seemingly read his mind when she said, "Don't worry, Jeremy. Cody will see that the boys stay in camp."

Jeremy dismounted, then reached up to help Salina down from Orion's back. "How do you know that for sure? I can imagine Kidd Carney or Curlie or Tristan *appearing* out of the woods at a most inopportune moment."

Salina giggled softly, for she too could envision such a scene, but she said confidently, "If not Cody, then Bentley or my brother will see to it." She didn't want to remind Jeremy that they were in enemy territory, and that if he or any of his men were captured by a Yankee scouting party, it would only lead to a prison camp...She shook her head, banishing such dark thoughts. She determined to forget the war, even if only for this brief amount of time. They would simply have to make the most of their present situation.

Curious, Salina took a step toward the shed while Jeremy tethered Orion and made short work of sifting through his saddlebags for something. In the pale moonlight, the dilapidated structure appeared to possess a singular air of enchantment. The little building was in a sad state of neglect and disrepair, overgrown with brush, a tangle of ivy, and twisted climbing rose bushes. Salina sighed—then smiled to herself, much relieved to see that the wooden walls still stood and had not collapsed like a fragile house of cards.

"Water?" Jeremy asked, standing directly behind her, offering a canteen.

Salina found that her mouth suddenly became as dry as a bale of cotton. "Yes, please. Thank you," she whispered. She put the canteen to her lips and sipped several cool swallows, then handed the canteen back to him.

Jeremy drank his fill. As he wiped his mouth with a sleeve, his eyes settled on Salina's pretty face. He turned away then, stopping up the canteen with undue deliberation. His usually nimble fingers stiffly unfastened the saddlebags, and he hefted them over one broad shoulder. He untied his bedroll and took his carbine from its leather holster. Then he walked toward Salina, brushing her shoulder with his own. "Stay here a minute," he commanded softly.

Wordlessly, Salina obeyed. She stood near Orion, patting his neck fondly. "He's up to something, you know," she suggested to the horse. "And he's acting just as nervous as I feel!" She hugged her elbows tightly and bit her lip. She knew what was going to happen between them—if the truth be known, she wanted it to—but she was trembling and couldn't seem to stop herself from doing so. It wasn't fear, for Taylor Sue had delicately shared the premise of what a wedding night would entail. If she was a fragile, timid young maid, the prospect might have sounded a wee bit frightening, but instead Salina found herself anxious to fulfill her marital privilege.

"Mrs. Barnes." Jeremy spoke her new name, his warm breath fanning her ear.

"That's me," she nodded, wide-eyed and eager.

Jeremy scooped her up into his strong arms, carrying her over the threshold and into the rustic little shed.

The interior was dimly lit by a stubby tallow candle that threw wavering shadows against the knot-holed walls. A pair of faded patchwork quilts were spread smooth on the floor. A stuffed flour sack served as the solitary pillow, upon which lay a single pink rose Jeremy had plucked from the fragrant bush framing the door.

Salina buried her face in the hollow of Jeremy's neck, hiding her smile. She was touched by his attempt to make their secluded haven a little cheery and cozy. If they ever chanced to take a proper wedding trip one day, no huge four-poster feather bed in the finest of hotels would ever beckon as invitingly as did this makeshift bridal bed.

Jeremy closed the shed's door with a swift booted kick. Gingerly he set Salina down. He licked his lips hesitantly, unsure of what to say, and he swallowed apprehensively.

The uneasy bobbing of Jeremy's Adam's apple did not escape Salina's notice. She wished he would relax—his agitation was tying her stomach in knots. She stood close to him and softly made her request: "Will you kiss me now, please?"

Jeremy's sapphire eyes studied her in earnest. He had difficulty finding words to express himself.

She smiled tentatively, nodding, "It's going to be all right, you know." She stood on tiptoe and lifted her face to meet his.

Jeremy felt her arms steal around his neck, and his responded, binding her to him. Their kiss sparked the now-lawful passion that flared between them. He shrugged out of his jacket; the lace shawl she'd borrowed slipped from her shoulders. One by one, Jeremy plucked the hairpins from Salina's chignon, effectively destroying her hastily arranged coiffure. He combed her thick hair with his fingers, allowing the heavy tresses to fall free to her waist. "I don't want you to be afraid of me," he whispered hoarsely, his concern for her evident.

"I'm not," Salina assured him.

"You know what's going to happen here is what didn't happen between us that night in the barn," Jeremy murmured thickly.

She nodded. "Yes, I know." Salina's smile imparted both her deep affection and a hint of challenge. "We both know God's word teaches that outside of marriage, this isn't right; but now we are married, and entitled, and the Lord will bless our union because we obeyed and we waited until we could come together as man and wife." With charming candor she admitted to her husband, "I've dreamed of this for quite some time."

Her forthright declaration earned a meaningful grin from Jeremy. "So have I," he confessed softly. "I've longed to hold you, Sallie, to have you with me, to take you as my wife..." His kiss was readily accepted and wholly reciprocated. He dropped to his knees, bringing Salina down to recline on the quilts with him.

Unnoticed, the lone candle burned itself out as the Horse Soldier and his bride intimately celebrated their love.

Chapter Eighteen

$\mathcal{Y}$ou asleep?" Jeremy's husky voice penetrated the darkness of the worn-down shed.

"No." Salina nestled close to him, resting her cheek on his bare chest while he absently stroked her head, entwining his fingers in her curls. She could see moonbeams slicing through numerous knotholes in the walls, shedding a dim glow which made up for the lack of candlelight.

Exhausted as he had been after consecutive days in the saddle without sleep, Jeremy no longer felt tired. With Salina in his arms he had no desire to waste time sleeping, knowing that all too soon he would have to leave her.

It pleased Jeremy to find that Salina was no more immune to the powerful crackle of passion between them than he was. Strong, fervent emotions stirred the newly-wedded pair into wakefulness. Jeremy's heart felt buoyant, full of love and wonder at the way his wife loved him with complete abandon. She made him feel cherished, as if he were her own priceless treasure. He savored that feeling, and he silently vowed he would try to make her feel the same. She was precious to him, his love, his life, and while he didn't know exactly how to convey it with honeyed words, he let his actions speak for him.

A good while later, Salina leaned up on her elbow and rested her hand on Jeremy's shoulder. She coaxed him into telling her about his visit with Isabelle Barnes in Middleburg. "I know you went there to ask her about your real father. Did she know anything that might shed some light on his identity?"

"All she knew was that his given name was Evan. No surname," Jeremy answered in monotone. His fingers reached to hold the heart-shaped locket dangling from the chain around her slender neck.

"Of course!" Salina breathed, immediately piecing part of the puzzle together. "It makes sense—Evan's your middle name. Why didn't we see that before?"

He lifted his broad shoulders in a shrug. "Knowing where my own middle name came from doesn't put me any closer to finding out who my father was, or what the rest of his name might be."

"But it might," Salina insisted, then waved her hand as though brushing his concerns aside. "For now, your name is Barnes. I'll share the name with you until we discover what your real name should be. And should you decide to go by that name instead, then so shall I," she vowed, cuddling close to him.

"I love you," Jeremy whispered near her ear, relieved that near-darkness concealed the uncharacteristic tears threatening to spill from his black lashes. He gathered her in his embrace, laying his whiskered cheek against the top of her head. "I covet your strength, Sallie. It's more comfort to me than you might realize."

"The Lord is my strength, my rock, my foundation, my fortress, my shield, my high tower," she noted. "The Lord is my light and my salvation, whom then shall I fear?"

"Whom then shall I fear?" Jeremy repeated absently.

Salina placed a loving kiss on his bearded jaw. "God has given me the desire of my heart," she whispered faintly. "He has given me you."

Jeremy stared at her, moved by the depth of emotion in her words. He found it absolutely amazing that she loved him so much. Playfully, he asked, "There are those who claim we deserve each other. Do you suppose God thinks so too?"

Salina's laugh rippled on the night air. "I imagine He must. It's inevitable that we shall be both trial and blessing to each other. Can you bear with me?"

"Oh, I reckon so—if you can put up with me, then I'll be glad to put up with you," Jeremy assured her. "When the war is over…"

Salina pressed her fingers to his lips. "Ssshhh…No talk of that," she scolded. "Not now. You promised to tell me about the meeting with your aunt, but that's all. Don't even think on…the other…not right now, anyway. I only want you to think about me," she entreated with a mischievous glint in her eye.

Jeremy willingly allowed her to erase all other thoughts from his mind.

☆☆☆☆☆☆☆

The wee hours raced by far too quickly. Salina begrudged the coming of dawn and willed the sun not to rise. Time, however, was most uncooperative. It marched on regardless, seemingly at the double-quick. As the first pale streaks of mauve and apricot pierced the shed's dark interior, she stretched languorously, but then flinched. She was stiff and sore from sleeping on the hard, lumpy ground, and Jeremy was laughing at her.

"It'll pass," Jeremy prophesied. "It can't be so bad that you'd need a rub down with liniment. Trust me."

Salina wrinkled her nose. "Rest assured, I won't need any liniment, thanks just the same."

"It'll be like walking off cramps after riding horseback for too long." His impish wink flustered her.

"Jeremy!" She punched him harmlessly. He chuckled, enfolding her securely in his arms. Again they slumbered.

The carefully fabricated air of tranquillity inside the shed was irrevocably shattered by the sounds that guns make. Salina whimpered slightly when Jeremy eased out of her embrace. He covered her with the quilt and she continued to sleep on, albeit fitfully. He let her rest as he hastily donned his uniform and exited the dilapidated shed.

The absence of Jeremy's warmth at Salina's side disturbed her. She could not ignore the sounds of battle, try as she might, and the next time she opened her eyes it was completely light in the shed. She reached out for Jeremy, but he was indeed gone. Next to her head on the pillow lay only the pink rose.

Scrambling to her feet, Salina resolutely ignored the pain screaming in her stiff muscles. "How soldiers sleep on the ground all the time is beyond me," she muttered to no one. She put aside the sudden wish for a long, hot, lavender-scented bath. She would have to make do with a quick dip in the creek on the way back to the Grants. Snatching up the organdie frock, Salina dressed herself quickly. She hadn't a brush, so a hasty run-through with her fingers had to suffice.

Outside she found Jeremy feeding Orion from a bag of oats. Relief washed through her, ridding Salina of the suspicion that he'd left without saying good-bye.

"You're up," Jeremy commented dryly.

"You have to go, don't you?" Her unnecessary question was laced with melancholy.

"It's time." Jeremy caressed her cheek. "I wish it wasn't, but it is. I've got to get back before Stuart misses me. Besides, it sounds like another fight is already underway." He nodded in the direction of Culp's Hill, where the deep rumblings of cannon and popping of small arms told of the escalating clash. "There's bound to be work to do."

Salty tears stung Salina's eyes. Duty called. She knew it would—he was a soldier—yet the knowing still didn't make it any easier to stomach. "I'll pack up our things and get ready to go."

"I'll take care of it." Jeremy declined her assistance, trying to put some distance between them. Leaving her was going to be painfully difficult...It took him all of two minutes to gather up his belongings, haphazardly stuffing them into a saddlebag. "Go back to the Grants now. Your mamma's bound to be worried."

"She has no cause to fret," objected Salina.

"I've kept you out all night; she might not know we got married," Jeremy pointed out. "That would look like impropriety on our part."

"Ethan or Cody certainly must have told her by now," Salina countered.

Jeremy shrugged. "Perhaps."

"I have the certificate from Reverend Landstreet," Salina reminded him. "And I have your ring."

"Aye," Jeremy murmured. *And your lips bear witness of my kisses*, he observed wordlessly. He stared down at her for a long, solemn moment, intently memorizing her face. In the depths of her emerald eyes shone a determined love. Jeremy expected that Salina's Mamma might at first be shocked at what basically amounted to their elopement, but Annelise would accept the facts. Jeremy was certain that his mother-in-law's sympathetic understanding would prevail.

Salina was slow to notice that next to Orion stood a second horse tethered to the tree. She figured that at some point during the night Cody must have come and left it there to ensure that she had a way to get back. The thought of Cody's presence at the shed made her blush. A knapsack containing the boy's clothes she'd worn last night was hanging from the saddle horn, but Salina speculated that the organdie dress would serve her better in daylight if she should encounter any Yankees on the way back to Oak Ridge.

There simply was not enough time to prolong the inevitable good-byes. Jeremy had to go, no matter how reluctant he was to leave her. Salina had touched a part of his soul he didn't even know existed, and he knew he'd miss her now more than ever. He mentally upbraided himself for entertaining the frightful premonition that he might not ever see her again. That was certainly no way for a cavalier to be thinking. He forced himself to dwell on more positive lines of thought.

In muted tones, Jeremy once more encouraged Salina to return to Virginia and Shadowcreek. "Take what you can get from here and stock up with supplies and food for the coming winter," he admonished in his best husbandly voice, and he promised to come see her whenever he could. "Good-bye, Mrs. Barnes," he said a little gruffly, holding his wife in the strong circle of his arms.

Salina couldn't bring herself to echo his farewell. She clung to him.

"What is it, Sallie? What are you thinking?" he needed to know.

"Come back to me," she held him tightly. "Promise me you'll come back to me."

It was a pledge made with words, but Jeremy knew, just as Salina did, that it was empty of any genuine guarantee. War offered no guarantees—it took lives at will. He could only pray that his own life might be spared so that he could indeed come back to her.

"'Bye, darlin'," Jeremy drawled. He exacted a last kiss in parting, then mounted up and rode away from her.

Jeremy's tall, gallant form disappeared immediately in a blur of hot tears. Salina surmised that he hadn't heard her choked "Godspeed!" for he did not look back. She sank to her knees on the unkempt flagstone walkway in front of the shed. There, she lowered her dark head and wept for her lover.

☆ ☆ ☆ ☆ ☆ ☆ ☆

"Kind of you to join us," Ethan teased, casually resting against the porch railing as Salina approached. He stirred a steaming mug of strong, black coffee. "You look a little fatigued this morning. Didn't get much sleep, did you, *Mrs. Barnes*?"

Salina's head snapped up and she shot a chilling glance at her older brother. "Hush, Ethan!"

Ethan's grin was of the ear-to-ear variety. "In all seriousness, I do want to wish you my heart-felt congratulations." With a wink he added, "It's my understanding you owe Cody for making sure the boys didn't try to give you and Jeremy a charivari last night. He refused to divulge any hint as to where the two of you had gone."

Salina flashed a beguiling smile even as a telltale blush stained her cheeks a becoming shade of pink. "I reckon I do owe him for that."

Ethan's taunting smile faded at the pathetic picture his little sister made: in one hand she held high the hem of her blue organdie dress, thus preventing it from soaking up blood that saturated the ground in puddles where wounded men had lain in the yard a short while ago. With the other hand, Salina shooed away the numerous buzzing flies encircling her head even at this early hour.

He forced himself to regain his teasing tone. "Do tell me," his lips twisted in a wry smile, "how are you this morning?"

Salina lifted her chin imperiously, ignoring Ethan's quizzical look. He had always been able to read her soul through her eyes, and she didn't want that today! Embarrassment had already reddened her cheeks once—it would never do to let Ethan get the better of her. But he knew too much, she decided, and her darling brother was bound to torment her with such knowledge. She answered nonchalantly, "I'm quite all right, thank you for asking."

Ethan chuckled, thoroughly amused by his sister's haughty expression. "Have you eaten?"

"No." She shook her head, belatedly realizing that she hadn't had any sustenance since the previous afternoon. Her stomach grumbled, and she inquired, "Is there anything left to eat?" She surmised that any surplus food would have been given to the wounded soldiers.

"Go on down to the cellar," Ethan suggested in a whisper. "Jubilee will make a little something for you. Then, when you've eaten and changed, I sure could use your help up here."

Salina nodded. "I'll be back in a bit."

Low, murmuring voices halted abruptly when Salina opened

the cellar door and stared down into the cool, earthen room below the farmhouse. "Mamma?" She hurried down the stairs.

Annelise came forward in a rush to hug her daughter. "My darling girl!" She held Salina at arm's length. "It's true then? You were married last night? In this beautiful gown? Where on earth did you get it?"

Salina told Mamma that the dress had been a gift to her from the Scarboroughs, and she told of the spontaneous ceremony conducted by Reverend Landstreet. Proudly Salina displayed her golden wedding band. "You're not upset, are you, Mamma? Please, don't be. It happened so fast. Jeremy and I had to take advantage of the time while it was ours to take."

Annelise stroked Salina's dark curls, resting her forehead against her daughter's. "I was upset at first," she confided, "but when both Ethan and Cody essentially told the same story, completely corroborating each other's alibi, I had to believe what they were telling me. I missed Ethan and Taylor Sue's wedding; I had hoped to be witness to yours. But, alas, evidently it was not meant to be." She hugged Salina. "I'm so very happy for you, sweetheart, and for Jeremy. I know how much you love him. I believe your daddy would have been enormously pleased with the way things have worked out for the two of you. He set great store by that young man of yours."

Salina beamed as though the compliment had been intended for her. She ate the meager breakfast Jubilee set before her—fresh fruit and a biscuit with honey. She drank all of the chilled, frothy milk in her mug. Salina discerned that while Mamma might not be upset with her for running off in the night and getting married, quite obviously Jubilee was. "Are you angry with me?" she asked the freedwoman.

"Humph!" Jubilee snorted. "Ya coulda warned us instead o' sneakin' out lak dat."

Salina smiled fondly at Jubilee. "I'd have told you if I'd known, but I didn't have any warning either. It was rather spur-of-the-moment—Jeremy just jumped up and said he was sure he could convince the chaplain to marry us right then and there. It just happened, and I'm glad it did. Deep down, Jubilee, do you truly object to my being married to Jeremy?"

Jubilee's wide smile revealed her pearly teeth. "Naw, chile," she drawled indulgently. "Dat was bound ta happen—it were bound ta from da day dat boy cum back ta Vi'ginya from Califo'nia. It were plain ta see how it were between ya. Ah done tole ya oncet ta guard yer heart. Seems ta Jube ya was only safe-keepin' it fer dat young man o' yers all along."

"He's a good man, Jubilee," Salina affirmed.

"Aye, an' he'd best take good care o' ya if'n he knows what's good fer him!" Jubilee declared. She, too, hugged Salina tenderly. "Yer a growed up lady now, fer sure an' certain, Missy. All married an' growed. Dat make Jube feel old in her bones, ah tell ya. But den, if'n Jube live long enough, dere jist might be da day when we gowin ta see yer chillen be born, da Good Lord willin'."

Salina's airy laughter held a certain ring of amused disbelief. "That won't be for some time yet, Jubilee. What with the war on, and Jeremy and I apart so much of the time— you'll just have to be patient on that score."

Jubilee rolled her big brown eyes. "Ya was wid him all last night, chile. Now we jist gowin ta hafta wait'n see about bein' patient…"

The implication was not lost on Salina, but she refrained from making further comment on what she considered a ludicrously remote possibility. Certainly she and Jeremy would have children together, at least she hoped they would; but she was sure that such an event would take place farther down the road, providing they both lived through this never-ending War Between the States. The bloody conflict was their major concern at present, not starting a family. Salina duly dismissed her dreams for their future.

After her hastily consumed breakfast, Salina changed from the blue organdie into a serviceable gingham day dress. She rolled the sleeves up to her elbows and tied a starched apron over the skirt. She chatted with Mamma while she held and played with Yabel for a fleeting few minutes, and then she returned upstairs to begin whatever tasks Ethan might assign.

Hours passed, filled with work and the dull sounds of battle. Orrin had heard that the Federals were trying to retake Culp's Hill from the Rebels. It would take them the better part of seven hours, and in the end the Yankees successfully attained that goal.

In the meantime, Salina continued to assist both her brother and the Yankee doctor, Abel Warrick. To the soldiers she routinely distributed bread made by Noreen and Beth-Anne sometime last night. She also brought the men water, either to drink or to dampen cloths for assuaging feverish brows. Both of the Grant women had learned of Salina's impromptu marriage and offered their sincere congratulations.

Throughout the morning Salina had tried to steer clear of one particular wounded man whose unnerving stare followed her every move with open appreciation. The Yankee waited until he was certain both Beth-Anne and Noreen were busy with other patients before he flagged Salina down with a request for water. Unable to ignore the man's petition, she brought a tin mug to him, then quickly turned toward the next bandaged solider in need of aid.

The Yankee, however, was quicker, and prevented Salina's departure by catching her arm with his uninjured hand. "Many thanks for your tender kindness," the dark-haired, dark-eyed, mustached officer smiled, a bit too forwardly. "Miss...?"

"It's *Mrs.*," Salina returned ever so politely. "Mrs. Barnes is my name. Was there something else you needed, sir?"

She saw the look of surprise when she supplied her married title, but it didn't deter the Yankee from his purpose. "I was wondering, *Mrs.* Barnes, if you could find it in your heart to sit here and help me write a letter or two."

"I'd be pleased to be of assistance." Salina tried to sound cordial. She drew a ladder-backed chair up next to the couch where he lay recovering from surgery that had removed shell fragments from his shoulder. She fetched paper, pen and ink, and then sat ready for his dictation.

"You may sign the letters," he said when both had been completed satisfactorily, "from Captain Spencer Hollingsworth, Doubleday's Division, Eleventh Corps, United States Army."

"Very well, Captain." Salina avoided contact with his admiring eyes, mildly wondering if his lengthy designation was supposed to impress her. It didn't. "And the address?"

Hollingsworth recited two postal addresses in New York—one to a brother, and one to his parents. There was no letter addressed to a wife or sweetheart. "You're very kind to do this for me, Mrs. Barnes," he said.

"It's part of my job here, Captain," Salina replied demurely. "I've written countless letters over the past two days, and I'm sure I'll write at least a dozen more before this day's done. I can only hope that if my husband were to need similar assistance, God forbid, that perhaps another woman at some other battlefield might be kind enough to send his letters home to me. I know I'd be worried sick about him, and receiving a letter would at least put my mind at ease." She collected the writing utensils and moved the chair back to its place against the wall.

"Your husband—is he a soldier, then?" Hollingsworth hastened to inquire.

"He's a cavalryman," Salina plainly answered.

"One of my cousins rides with Devin's brigade, and I've a school chum with Gamble's brigade—both of Buford's cavalry. What regiment is your husband with?" Hollingsworth sought more information since making conversation was the only way to keep the intriguing young matron at his side.

Salina flashed an impertinent smile. "My husband is with Stuart's cavalry."

Hollingsworth's eyes narrowed as he continued to survey Salina, but this time with an icy coldness. *"Southerners?!* Then what business have *you* here in Gettysburg?" he demanded sharply.

The interest she'd previously detected in Hollingsworth's eyes flickered out like a spent candle. "Virginians, to be specific, and proud to say so," Salina clarified. "But as to my business here, it is to give what aid and comfort I possibly can to those who are in need. Somebody's going to win this battle eventually; unfortunately, though, there will be hundreds and thousands from both sides who will need all the help they can get just to survive. You ought to consider yourself one of the lucky, Captain, for so far you have survived the onslaught."

Hollingsworth made no reply, nor did he attempt to detain her further.

"If you'll excuse me, I'd best see to the next man who might need my hands." Salina made her retreat from the fawning Yankee captain without further ado. She blindly collided with a blue-uniformed man standing on a wooden crutch to keep him steady. "Oh! I'm so sorry! Are you all right?"

"Would it truly matter if I wasn't?" the Federal lieutenant barked harshly.

Salina's mouth fell agape as she recognized the haggard face of the man with the crutch. It was Malcolm Everett, her cousin Marie's husband. Salina's stomach twisted into a fierce knot: the last time she'd seen him, she'd been locked behind bars at the Presidio in San Francisco. Lieutenant Everett had been instrumental in bringing about her capture by Union authorities, who had urgently sought the valuable documents she and Taylor Sue had translated from code. The fear that gripped Salina stemmed from knowing that Everett had voluntarily betrayed her once, and more than likely would do all in his power to repeat the action if he could.

"Lieutenant Everett," Salina acknowledged him by name. "How is it that you've come to the eastern theater of battle? What brings you here all the way from San Francisco?"

"I felt an overwhelming urge to come east and fight you people," Everett grated. He shook his head and hissed, "Why you didn't hang for treason is certainly a mystery!"

Salina blanched visibly as Everett leveled a hate-filled glare at her, and she felt Hollingsworth's curious glance from across the room as well. Cold reason demanded that she be cautious in dealing with this man who was, unfortunately, distantly related by marriage. Salina shivered involuntarily. Everett's expression was hauntingly reminiscent of the way John Barnes had looked at Salina in the past, and it told her beyond doubt that Everett would indeed betray her again if given half a chance. That thought made her shiver again, almost violently. Knowing that John Barnes was still alive, it occurred to Salina that Marie's husband would be an all-too-fitting candidate for service within the Yankee major's corrupt little band. Salina recalled that Everett was already acquainted with the Widow Hollis from their previous association in San Francisco—who was to say he hadn't cultivated some connection with Major Barnes, her half-brother?

Everett swayed on his feet, and Salina saw that he was about to fall. She propped her shoulder under his arm, lending him support and preventing him from toppling over. "Ethan!" Salina cried out.

Between the two of them, Ethan and Salina managed to get Lieutenant Everett onto an available cot. The Yankee was burning with fever. Ethan methodically probed and examined the leg wound. "You're still carrying a bullet, either a whole piece or a good sized fragment," he reported to Everett. To Salina he said, "I left my instruments in the kitchen near the operating table. Be a good girl and fetch them for me, quick."

"No!" Everett objected vociferously. "I'll not have you cutting on me! I won't let you touch me, you Rebel butcher!"

Ethan's sharp glance was powerful enough to silence Everett in the midst of his tirade. "Dr. Warrick!" Ethan bellowed, wiping his hands on his bloodied smock.

The Yankee doctor approached the bed where Everett lay sweating profusely. "What can I do for you, Dr. Hastings? Is there a problem here?"

Ethan's reply was sour. "He's one of yours, and he doesn't want my help. I'd be just as happy to leave him in your capable hands."

Abel Warrick nodded. "I'll see to him. Thank you, Hastings."

"I didn't do anything but probe the wound," Ethan told Warrick, adding what he knew of the existing bullet or fragment. In the end Ethan merely shrugged.

Warrick's hand squeezed Ethan's shoulder. "Don't take it personal. You took the time and made the effort. I've noticed that going above and beyond the call of duty is a habit of yours."

"I try to do my best," Ethan said somberly.

Malcolm Everett stared at Ethan Hastings with glassy, feverish eyes, then turned on Salina again: "One day you'll pay, Miss Rebel Spy. Yes, you will—you'll pay!"

Salina tried to disregard his threats. She asked, "Does Marie know where you are? Would you like me to write back to San Francisco for you?"

"Of course she doesn't know where I am—she didn't want me to come in the first place!" Everett raged. "She doesn't understand or give two figs for this fighting, but I do…" His voice trailed off as the pain-killer Dr. Warrick had administered took effect. "Tell her…"

"Tell her what? Where is she?" Salina asked.

"She's…at…Ivywood. Tell Marie…not…to worry…about me…" Everett's eyes closed and his head slumped to the side.

"Passed out cold," Dr. Warrick commented. "Good. He'll be easier to work on that way."

Ethan glanced down at his sister. "You're going to go ahead and write to Cousin Marie, aren't you?"

"I'll see to it," Salina nodded, though she could see the disapproval in her brother's eyes. "Ethan, I know Marie would want to learn about the well-being of her own husband."

"I'll leave that decision completely up to you. It's in your hands." Ethan shrugged indifferently. "While you're doing that, I'm going downstairs to take a nap," he yawned wearily. "It's half-past noon. Wake me up in half an hour, would you?"

"All right." Salina double-checked the clock ticking on the fireplace mantle. "One o'clock. You rest—you look as if you could use it."

"Thanks for the compliment," Ethan tried to jest. He tugged on her arm. "Do me a favor, Little Sister: keep to our own from now on. I saw that Captain Hollingsworth pestering you, and now we have Everett to contend with. God alone knows who we'll patch up next, but I'm not going out of my way to help the blue-bellies anymore. We've got enough of our own to look after. I know you want to help anyone that you can, Salina, but some folks won't overlook the fact that we're their enemy even when we're working to save their lives. It's not worth the hassle. Warrick will see to his people, and he's got Noreen and Beth-Anne to help him tend to their kind. If he needs me, he'll find me."

Salina reluctantly nodded. She could understand and would obey her brother's wish. "I'll fetch you in half an hour," she reiterated.

Ethan headed for the cellar door. He encountered Nathan and Jared in the dining room, but was too tired to acknowledge the fuming Unionist brothers. He only wanted some uninterrupted peace and quiet.

Chapter Nineteen

*W*hile the business of tending the wounded was going on inside the Grant farmhouse, military business was going on in the yard outside. The batteries of Rebel artillery which had been posted on July first and second were removed from Oak Hill and redeployed to positions near the unfinished railroad cut and along Seminary Ridge. General Longstreet, at General Lee's instruction, was ordered to organize and carry out plans for attacking those people in blue on the crest of Cemetery Ridge. The fight for Culp's Hill had ended in a Union victory. High hopes were placed on the Confederate attack which was to strike the Union center. Ewell's Corps would again see action in Devil's Den and the Peach Orchard. Stuart had been given orders to move around to the rear of the Federal army and strike through it.

A solitary chime sounded from the clock on the mantle. Salina finished the psalm she'd been reading to a dying Confederate private:

> *...When I cry unto thee, then shall mine*
> *enemies turn back: this I know; for God is for*

236

> *me. In God will I praise his word: in the Lord*
> *will I praise his word. In God have I put my*
> *trust: I will not be afraid what man can do*
> *unto me. Thy vows are upon me, O God: I*
> *will render praises unto thee. For thou hast*
> *delivered my soul from death: wilt not thou*
> *deliver my feet from falling that I may walk*
> *before God in the light of the living?*

The private thanked Salina, and she set the Bible on the marble-topped table next to her. She arched her back to stretch her weary muscles, and she covered a yawn with her palm. The lack of sleep last night was catching up with her. She hoped, as she went to fetch Ethan, that his little bit of a nap would refresh him.

The discharge of a cannon shrieked, exploding with a loud crash that startled the entire Grant household. Salina hadn't meant to scream, but on account of her already frayed nerves she couldn't help it. A second shot erupted. Wide eyes—belonging to patients and inhabitants alike—exchanged anxious glances, searching for reassurance.

The two shots, fired shortly after the hour of one o'clock p.m., narrowly preceded an all-out barrage. Over one hundred and forty Rebel cannon were answered by at least one hundred fifty Federal artillery pieces. The air vibrated with ear-splitting thunder, the ground quaked with violent tremors, windowpanes rattled precariously in their sashes. Prayers went up in a hurry, pale lips moved rapidly, but no one could hear above the horrible din, no one except the Lord Himself.

Cody and Nathan rushed to move wounded men from one of the second story bedrooms down to the first floor, lest an errant missile strike the house again and inflict additional injury. Orrin chanced a visit to the attic, to see whatever he could make out through the smoke hovering like a thick blanket above the fire-belching cannons.

After returning to the relative safety of the house, Orrin wrote a note for the benefit of Dr. Warrick, but Ethan read it over the Yankee's shoulder:

> *Artillery hotly firing from both sides. Must be*
> *close to 300 guns, maybe more—too much*
> *smoke to tell exactly. Rebels overshoot, aim*

too high, render little damage. Federals use
masking fire to conserve ammunition.

The women were once more ordered to take shelter in the cellar, but even there they could not escape the deafening roar. Salina's heart pounded in her chest with each explosion, and her mind reeled with the force. The life of the Confederacy hung in the balance, she could sense that much, and it frightened her.

☆ ☆ ☆ ☆ ☆ ☆ ☆

Much later, long after the massive two-hour bombardment, Salina learned of the brave, ill-fated charge led by General George Pickett's Virginians.

Pickett's Division of Longstreet's First Corps—along with others commanded by Pettigrew and Trimble, both of A.P. Hill's Corps—was selected and given orders to head the attack on the Union center, believed to be a weak spot up on Cemetery Ridge. A line approximately a mile long, comprised of nearly fifteen thousand Confederate troops, assembled behind the screen of trees along Seminary Ridge. Their objective was to converge on a copse of trees roughly three-quarters of a mile to their front, and take the ridge.

General Pickett's rallying cry, "Up men, up and to your posts!" was followed by General Armistead's poignant challenge, "Virginians! Virginians! For your homes! For your lands! For your sweethearts! For your wives! For Virginia!" It was reported that the Rebels stepped off in parade fashion—lines trim, shoulder to shoulder—a grander sight, some said, they had never before witnessed. Shouts echoed through the readied ranks, and then the drums beat out the cadence to which the soldiers marched toward their destiny. The gray-clad infantrymen advanced headlong into a grisly hailstorm of enemy fire. They marched steadily onward, perhaps not without fear, but certainly not without courage.

The approach to the Union-held ridge, however, was uphill over open ground, and the Yankees—far from being weak at that point—were firmly entrenched behind a stone wall used as breastworks. The scene, Salina lamented, was the frightful reverse of the Battle of Fredericksburg: there, up on Marye's Heights, the Rebels had hid behind a similar stone wall, inflicting volley after volley of bullets, shell, and shot into the waves of Union troops. Here at

Gettysburg, it was the Federals who opened fire into the advancing Confederates, blasting gaping holes in the ranks, mowing down hundreds at a time.

The fence along the Emmitsburg Road slowed the Rebel advance, and but a few found themselves following General Lewis Armistead—his black hat raised on the point of his sword—across the last two hundred yards. Those Confederates who succeeded in going over the stone wall at The Angle crashed into the Union guns awaiting them, and they found themselves entrapped in a boiling cauldron of death.

The Grant family was overjoyed with the stunning Yankee victory. Their thrilled celebration was tempered only slightly by whispered threats of counterattack on the morrow. Their General Meade—only six days in command of the Army of the Potomac— had forestalled the Rebel invasion. Their prayers were answered, and they exulted in fervid thanksgiving.

Conversely, Salina wept bitterly when she learned of the terrible slaughter. She cried again when she heard that General Lee had insisted that the failure was his fault, for he had believed his Army of Northern Virginia was invincible.

She cried all the more when word came of the cavalry fight three miles east of Gettysburg township. Stuart had been repulsed, stopped cold by Gregg and Custer. God alone knew where Jeremy was—somewhere out there—in the midst of the murderous struggle.

☆ ☆ ☆ ☆ ☆ ☆ ☆

Boston, Massachusetts
July 3, 1863

Spending the afternoon at the gentlemen's club hadn't been Drake's original intention, but after conducting his business, he'd been interested by reports of the battle raging in southeast Pennsylvania. He only vaguely remembered promising to be back at the house on Beacon Street in time for dinner, and that was two hours ago. Checking his pocket watch, Drake predicted that his sister might be lacking her usual sweet temper by the time he returned.

The time spent had been well worth the risk of Aurora's anger, however, and Drake wagered it was even worth provoking Grandmamma's wrath. He smiled to himself, satisfied that he'd done the right thing. He had wired Lije Southerland two days ago, requesting some advice, and Lije had come through for him. His lawyer-grandson had just met with Drake on matters concerning his father's estate, his vast inheritance, and his responsibilities as a newly-acknowledged member of the prestigious Dallinger family.

Micah Southerland, Lije's grandson, had answered most of Drake's questions concerning the shipping business, both the passenger and freight lines, the mills, the railroad stock, and a side investment in a West Virginia coal mine, as well as various and assorted other details. Drake had pages of notes, lists of items to study. He'd never had much of a head for business, but that was because he'd never needed it. If he was going to play the blueblood, he had to act in a convincing manner, and Micah Southerland stood ready and willing to assist. Drake had much to study, and much on his mind. Rorie would simply have to understand that.

But Aurora Dallinger was so fully occupied that she didn't even recall skipping lunch or discovering her half-brother's absence. She did not hear Drake's arrival downstairs in the foyer, nor did she hear him quietly enter her bedchamber. For several long moments, she went on busily packing a crate, silently observed, until Drake made his tardy presence known.

"What are you doing, Rorie?" Drake asked curiously in his gravelly voice.

Her auburn head jerked up and her hands stilled. Drake saw that she'd been crying, apparently for quite some time, and he demanded to know what had initiated her tears.

"I'm going to Gettysburg," was all Aurora would say. She meticulously packed additional items into the crate—bandages, salves, lint, silk thread, chloroform, laudanum, and quinine.

Drake tugged on her arm. "Don't you know the place is still engulfed in battle? The Rebels destroyed the railroad bridge days ago. No one's going in or coming out. Why the sudden urge to get to Pennsylvania?"

Aurora pulled free of Drake's loose grasp. She pointed to the cherry wood secretary, to a crumpled paper resting on the drop leaf desk. "See for yourself."

Drake picked up a casualty list which couldn't be more than a few hours old, hot off the newspaper printing press. He scanned the names of wounded and dead until his turquoise eyes settled on the one name that mattered: *Mason Lohring*. Aurora's beau was listed as wounded.

"At the club they were talking about Pickett's Charge," Drake murmured. "One of the newspapermen had wired in his account for publication." He'd been so preoccupied since their father's funeral, he had all but forgotten about Salina Hastings. She would be there, in Gettysburg—a formerly obscure farming community enduring pandemonium and terror while a full-scale battle was waged in and around the township limits. He wondered if Little One was all right...

"What can I do to help, Rorie? What do you want me to do?" Drake inquired insistently.

Aurora stopped, momentarily caught off guard by his offer of assistance. She'd been so sure Drake would try to keep her from going. She intended to go, and go she would, whether he fought her on the issue or not. But Drake wasn't fighting her. He was willing to lend her a hand. "I...I guess if you could finish this up for me, I'll throw a few things into a traveling trunk..."

Drake obediently completed the packing of the crate. "There's no guarantee that the railroad can even get into the town, Rorie."

"I'll drive a wagon there myself, if I have to," Aurora said stubbornly. "Oh, Drake..."

Drake went to Aurora's side, putting an arm around his lone sibling. "What, Rorie?"

"I'm so afraid Mason might die before I can get to him," Aurora wailed, drenching Drake's starched shirtfront with her tears.

"Have a little faith, Rorie," Drake encouraged, squeezing her shoulders. Suddenly he laughed at himself. *Have a little faith?* Such a comment could only come from the influence of Little One, Rorie, or maybe even Lije—he wasn't sure which, but it was there nonetheless. Then he read Aurora's thoughts and said, "You leave Grandmamma to me. I'll see that she doesn't interfere."

"I'm so tired of being cooped up in this fastidious, eerie house. I've lived here all my life, Drake, but since Father's gone, it's become so oppressive! Grandmamma cries all the time, the servants won't speak above whispers. If you weren't here, I think I'd go plumb crazy!"

Drake smiled indulgently. "Just remember, we're not going on some nice country outing. This is going to be brutal, Rorie. Don't say I didn't warn you. You're in for quite a shock."

Aurora squared her shoulders determinedly. "If your Salina can handle working in a field hospital, as you've often told me, then I can bear it too."

"She's not my Salina," Drake was quick to clarify. "And we'll just have to wait and see what kind of stuff you're really made of, won't we, Rorie?"

"You'll see," she vowed. "I'll show you I'm not the bit of spoiled fluff you believe me to be. I've been working with the ladies' aid societies. I've contributed to the Sanitary Commission's work. I think I have an idea of what it will be like."

"Good," Drake said flatly. "Then I won't worry about you. What time is the train?"

There was one leaving within the hour, Aurora replied, half-challenging him to stall for more time.

Drake didn't. He turned on his heel with a pair of clipped phrases for explanation: "I'd better get busy then. I'll see you downstairs in twenty minutes."

Aurora nodded. "I'll be ready."

☆ ☆ ☆ ☆ ☆ ☆ ☆

The anticipated renewal of the battle around Gettysburg did not happen on the fourth day of July. Instead, the two armies lay dormant, as if trying to catch their collective breaths, wary and wondering what the other side would do next.

Salina had seen several scouts and couriers from both sides—one or two had even stopped at the well for a drink of water to relieve parched throats from the sultry heat. She had served them willingly, and queried as innocently as she dared in hopes of collecting what information she could.

The rains had started long about noon and showed no sign of relenting. After feeding two dozen men a luncheon of fresh baked bread and chicken rice soup, she paced the wooden kitchen floor in private agony. All she could think of was that Jeremy was out there, and she instinctively knew that he needed her. If this were not the case, he would have found a way to see her by now.

Ethan was far too busy, or Salina would have asked him to help, but instead it was Cody Grant who came to her aid. "Will you go with me to where the cavalry battle was fought?" she implored with threatening tears brimming her luminous eyes. "Please, Cody?"

Cody knew Salina well enough by now to perceive the determined set of her jaw and the proud tilt of her head. "All right, I'll go, since I'm convinced you'd be going with or without me. We'll take the wagon instead of bringing a third horse with us." He didn't want to sound pessimistic, but they should be prepared for the worst.

Salina nodded, agreeing with Cody's suggestion. If Jeremy was hurt, and she prayed he wasn't, he most likely couldn't ride. "You bring the wagon. I'll go on ahead. You'll hurry, won't you?"

"It's pouring down like buckets emptied from heaven," Cody complained. "Wait until it eases up a bit, why don't you?"

She shook her head stubbornly. "I'm going now," she insisted between clenched teeth. "Please, will you follow?"

Cody yielded, squeezing her shoulder gently. "You can count on me, Mrs. Barnes."

The use of her married name brought only the tiniest hint of a smile to Salina's lips. "I'll meet you there."

Salina kept to roads she was familiar with on her way to the York Turnpike, and when she had followed the pike for about three miles outside of town, she found the area where the fighting had occurred. She arrived at the cavalry battlefield with only flashes of lightning and dull rumbles of thunder as her portentous companions.

Salina tied her steed to an abandoned cannon and looked in utter horror at the macabre scene of the battlefield before her. "Dear God!" she breathed, pressing a fist to her mouth to stifle the surge of nausea creeping up in her throat. She should have waited for Cody, she tardily admitted, but he was so slow getting here with the wagon. Her heart was filled with a powerful sense of urgency that required all haste and speed. She mustered what courage she had, and set out beneath the dismal, pouring gray skies. Salina was already soaked to the skin but she cared not a whit about it.

Gingerly, she plodded across the field choked with dead horses and dead bodies, some with arms or legs projecting stiffly upward. The burial details must have started their work earlier in the day, prior to the afternoon's downpour, for in some places there were piles of dead, and others were laid out in neat rows awaiting interment. Her stomach wretched with dry heaves; she willed herself not to dwell on the grotesque, mangled carnage, but only to seek Jeremy. He *was* out here, of that she was sure—somewhere amid the frightful gore.

Rain and teardrops mingled to stream down Salina's face as she resolutely continued in her quest. For the better part of an hour she searched among the broken, muddied, bloodied, rigid corpses. Rain had rinsed the dirt from some of the faces, only to reveal horrific expressions which emblazoned themselves permanently in Salina's mind's eye. Never would she be able to forget the look of tortured countenances frozen with oaths or prayers on their lips; nor would she fail to recollect the haunted, sightless eyes staring at her from all sides. Salina saw hands and arms outstretched, some holding swords, some raised in fists, and some with fingers curled as if clawing the air or grasping for eternity.

The ground, softened by blood and rainwater, was strewn with blankets, knapsacks, sabres, guns, boots, hats, capes, cartridge boxes, canteens, holsters, and every other imaginable debris left in the wake of the ruthlessly fought cavalry battle.

Off a ways stood the house and farm buildings belonging to the Rummels. Lamps flickered in the windows, and Salina reckoned they must have taken in wounded, but she instinctively felt that Jeremy was *here*, lying on this field of battle, in grave need of help. "God, please don't let him be dead," Salina whispered into the suffocating grayness of the low-hanging clouds. What light there was would soon be gone, and she had no desire to be out here alone in the dark. What was keeping Cody?

Salina resumed her search among the deceased. She turned another body over and instantly cried out, for here was the familiar face of Archer Scarborough, the brother of Tristan who'd given her the blue organdie dress to be married in.

Leaning down, Salina closed Archer's wild, unseeing eyes. She then pulled a sopping wet blanket over his head to cover him. No more would he play his lively fiddle in merriment for dancing, she thought mournfully. If Archer is here, she moaned softly, then perhaps she was close to finding where Jeremy might have fallen.

She stood perfectly still, waiting, straining to hear any audible sound or scratch of movement that could signify life. She heard nothing, however, save the splatter of falling rain.

"WHERE ARE YOU?!" she screamed loudly, her anguished frustration reverberating across the darkening battlefield. Her shoulders shook with a fresh wave of sobs when there was no answer to her desperate cry.

Salina turned over two other men who had fallen facedown, and she gagged at the sight of their gruesome death-wounds. Mercifully, her vision blurred with salty tears, and she bit her lip to keep from retching again. She backed away, shaking her head in dazed shock. An unwanted disheartenment descended on her, and iron bands of fear over what she might yet find painfully gripped her heart. She meant to press on, but was compelled to stop abruptly when she felt her skirt catch on something, perhaps a buckle or a scabbard. She jerked at the fabric to free her hem, but it was caught tightly—in a bloodstained fist that clutched the material in a white-knuckled grasp.

"Yeeeeee-aaaahhhhh!" The distraught cry ripped from Salina's throat. Her chest rose and fell unevenly in rapid, terrified gusts, her heart thudding erratically in her bosom. When the initial panic subsided, she took a hard look at the situation. The pinkie finger of the grubby hand clamped unyieldingly on the hem of her skirt wore a gold filigree ring set with a deep green emerald—it was *her* heirloom ring, the one Jeremy habitually wore since the day she'd given it to him in trade for her gold locket.

"Jeremy!" she cried out, finding a wild eye upon her. *"Jere-meeeee!"*

"Sa-li-na?!" her own name echoed out over the dusky field.

"Cody?" she yelled, cupping her hands around her mouth. "Cody! Over here! Come quick! I think I've found him!" But Salina didn't wait for Cody to join her. She was on her knees, laboring to push aside corpses that buried the body attached to Jeremy's extended arm. Once she cleared away the bodies of the dead Yankees, Salina uncovered Jeremy's horse, Orion. "Cody, hurry!" she begged forlornly.

Orion had landed on his side after being shot down. Jeremy was securely pinned under the weight of the great beast. The leg beneath Orion must certainly be broken, but hopefully it wasn't crushed. The men who had fallen to rest on top of Jeremy partially shielded his face from the rain, and now, as the rainwater wet his cheeks, the caked blood liquefied and trickled in reddish-brown rivulets down his neck. His left sapphire-colored eye was open slightly, fixed unwaveringly on Salina's distressed face. His right eye, however, was tightly closed due to the sabre wound that extended from his forehead, just missing the corner of the badly swollen eye, having laid open a good three inches of bearded cheek below the curved arch of his black brow.

Salina knelt beside Jeremy's battered, trapped body, bending over him to prevent the rain from splashing in his upturned face. Her heart-shaped locket dangled from her neck, swinging like a lazy pendulum between them. A strangled sound issued from his pale lips, and she lowered her head closer to hear him better. "What? What are you saying?"

"How...I...prayed...you...would...come..." Jeremy rasped.

"Kiss...me..." his hoarse voice pleaded.

Salina smiled down at him tenderly, her aching heart twisting, and she leaned down to accommodate his poignant appeal. As she pressed her lips to his, the excruciating grip he held on her hand tightened, then went slack. "Jeremy? Jeremy! Don't you *dare* die on me! I've barely been your wife—I don't want to be your widow! Live—do you hear me? *Live!*"

She touched the side of his neck with inquisitive fingers, relieved to feel a faint pulse still surging there.

Cody stood over her at last. "Is he dead?"

Salina started at the sound of Cody's voice, then let out a long, shuddering sigh. "No, he's not dead, he's still alive but hurt pretty bad."

"He's passed out," Cody deducted. "That's good. Maybe he'll not feel the pain so keenly when we move him to the wagon."

Salina glanced up. Cody had been forced to leave the wagon at least a score of yards from where they were kneeling, as there were too many bodies of men and beasts littering the ground to make a closer approach. "You and I will have to carry him," she said simply.

"Sure, but we've got to get this horse off him first," Cody remarked with resolve as he pulled Jeremy's boot from the stirrup. "Cover his face for now, and let's get to work."

Thick, velvet black darkness blanketed the battlefield and all but obliterated the already limited visibility before Cody and Salina loaded Jeremy into the wagon bed. Salina sat cross-legged in the back, cradling Jeremy's head in her lap. She prayed incessantly over his unconscious form while Cody climbed up to the buckboard and drove the wagon at what seemed a snail's pace back to the Grants' house on Oak Ridge.

☆ ☆ ☆ ☆ ☆ ☆ ☆

More soldiers, Lottie fumed as she answered the door of her husband's home on East Middle Street. She didn't even notice the color of the uniforms the men wore anymore—it had ceased to matter since scavengers from both sides had come looking for anything they could find to eat. "I haven't got any more bread!" she bellowed, not bothering to mask her annoyance.

A butternut-clad sergeant tipped his cap in deference. "Much obliged for the offer of food, ma'am, but we're actually looking for any injured you might have here—belonging to the Reb army, of course."

Lottie shook her golden head. "I haven't taken in any wounded. I've been feeding the soldiers what I could, but they've all moved on."

"No Yanks, either?" The Rebel sergeant was suspicious; just because the woman spoke with a Southern accent didn't necessarily mean she was enamored of the Southern Cause.

"No," Lottie reiterated. She rubbed a protective hand over her swollen belly. "There's no one here—no soldiers," she quickly amended. She didn't want to let on that she was all by herself; there was still the family silver and other valuables to be protected.

"Then I beg your pardon, ma'am. We're only trying to collect those who are well enough to travel back to Virginia with us." The butternut soldier touched the brim of his kepi in salute.

"Retreat, you mean," Lottie commented acrimoniously. "The fighting is over and now you're all headed back over the Potomac."

"That'd be a powerful accurate, if not accusing, statement, ma'am," the sergeant bristled. "Again, my apologies for disturbing you."

Lottie closed the door, muttering under her breath about the cursed war. She was angry—and had been since the night Lance had left to rejoin the fight. There had been no word from him, no clue as to his whereabouts, or whether he'd survived the horrific battling of these past three days. She was haunted by a caustic remark he'd tossed at her on their wedding day: *"There's a war on. There's always the chance you could end up a widow."* Lottie shuddered. She did not want to be a widow, that was for sure. Oh, why had Lance put in for a field transfer in the first place? She rested her arms on top of her protruding abdomen in a gesture of protection. If Lance was dead, he'd never know his child. If Lance was dead...

"Dear God," Lottie breathed in the silence of the hallway. "I'm not much for praying, but please, hear me. Could You give me a sign of some sort to let me know that my baby will not grow up fatherless? I need to know, if only for my own peace of mind."

Within the hour, another rapping on the door sounded. This time it was a Yankee sergeant Lottie encountered as she opened the portal. She allowed him to come in out of the rain, and he delivered a note to her. "Lieutenant Colby begged me to stop by and see that this was given into your hand. He wanted to assure you that he was as well as could be expected and unharmed. He hopes that you, too, are getting along, and if you'd like, I can take a reply back to headquarters with me. They'll see that it gets forwarded to him."

Lottie penciled a hasty answer on a sheet of scented stationery, speaking aloud as she wrote. "Tell him that I'm fine...and that I miss him. Tell him, too, that I expect his brother and sister-in-law back within the next few days now that the fighting has ceased, and we will watch after each other until his return."

"Very well, ma'am." The Yankee sergeant tucked the note into his jacket pocket. "Is there anything you need, ma'am? Food, rations, supplies?"

"I'm fine, really," Lottie assured him. "Was there anything else, Sergeant?"

The Yankee soldier rubbed his stubbled jaw with the palm of his hand. "You wouldn't have any Confederates hiding here, would you?"

"No!" Lottie pronounced vehemently. "Those that came have gone already—but you're welcome to search the house if you don't believe me."

"I believe you, ma'am," the blue-clad sergeant nodded. "I'll take your word. Good day, Mrs. Colby."

"Good day," Lottie echoed, a bit less agitated. Again she closed the door, and again she leaned heavily against it. She held Colby's brief message to her bosom. "God?" she whispered, her cornflower blue eyes rolling heavenward, "I reckon this'd most certainly be considered a sign—and I want to thank You, Lord, for keeping Lance alive, because if You hadn't," she paused, "if You hadn't, why, I'd have *killed* him for dying on me!"

Chapter Twenty

*F*ranklin Shields made his way through the crowded, bustling rooms of wall-to-wall wounded until he located Captain Ethan Hastings. His friend the doctor stood before an operating table which faced an open window. Had the day not been so gray, more light might have been gleaned to illuminate the area in which surgery was being conducted on a prostrate soldier. Artificial light was added in the form of lanterns and candles, but the interior of the room still seemed dim and somewhat foreboding. At Ethan's feet were thick pools of congealing blood formed by drops that rained on the floor from the operating table above. After three days of waged battle and the ensuing medical repairs on damaged and broken bodies, the once-glossy wooden floor showed sickening evidence of discoloration and stains.

With a tender touch, Ethan completed his task of sewing up the ragged edges of a deep flesh wound, and with a silent prayer, he beseeched the Lord to bless his patient with a speedy recovery and no infection. Ethan drew his forearm across his brow to wipe away beads of sweat, unknowingly leaving behind a bloody smear on his temple. He nodded to the stewards, who took the recovering soldier from Ethan's table to a vacant cot in the dining room.

"Dr. Hastings," Franklin greeted Ethan when he finally turned toward the center of the room. "What a ghastly mess!"

"Aye," Ethan nodded, wiping his hand on his apron before accepting Franklin's proffered hand in a firm shake. "I'd say ghastly pretty much sums it up." He glanced around, his compassionate eyes scanning the faces of the men he'd been able to help; he didn't like to think about the ones who had died anyway. "It's a difficult job, but somebody has to do it."

"And you do it well," Franklin said in an off-handed compliment. "I should know; I myself have lived to see this day because your doctoring kept me from dying."

A half-smile formed on Ethan's lips. "I told you before: give the glory to God." He clapped a hand on Franklin's shoulder. "What brings you out this way, Captain Shields?"

"Orders," Franklin affirmed. "My uncle—excuse me—Colonel Shields sends his regards. He sent me to tell you that we are indeed pulling out. Whatever wounded cannot be moved at this time will unfortunately be abandoned to the care of the Northerners."

Ethan clamped his jaw tightly, his gut wrenching in impotent ire. He knew the procedure, though he certainly didn't like it. "They'll become prisoners of war," he muttered darkly. "I can't just leave them..."

"If you don't come along, they'll make you a prisoner too," Franklin warned.

"But there are so many. We had over fifty here before the fight yesterday for Cemetery Ridge. Then they brought two ambulance wagons out here to us because they had no place else to go with them. That man I just finished working on," Ethan jerked his thumb over his shoulder, "hopefully will be the last—for awhile. But there's the recovering—cleaning and redressing wounds—who'll tend to them if I don't stay?" he wanted to know.

Franklin Shields replied, "My uncle predicted your reaction almost to the letter. He knows how deeply you care for your patients. That being the case, I've been authorized to allow you to stay forty-eight more hours, but that's all. We cannot guarantee you safe conduct behind enemy lines—you know that. The Colonel does not want you to take any unnecessary chances; he can't afford to lose someone of your caliber. You're to report to his medical headquarters on or about the seventh of July. I've brought rations for you, although you don't seem to be lacking in food here."

"No, but I'm lacking medicine, as usual. Dr. Warrick—he's the Yankee surgeon here—has been very kind. He obtained a supply of morphine and chloroform from the U.S. Sanitary Commission. I guess they already have a depot set up in town and are distributing items to their medical personnel," Ethan explained. "But I can't expect Warrick to supply me with medicine for our men. He's in need of it for his own."

"That's understandable," Franklin agreed, then he repeated, "Forty-eight hours."

"If that's all I can have, then I'll take it," Ethan declared without hesitation. "They need me, and I'll not abandon them into the hands of the enemy until I absolutely have to."

"Very well then, I'll give your answer to the Colonel." Franklin saluted. "He sent with me two ambulance wagons and a handful of orderlies to collect the men you deem well enough to be transported back to Virginia. If you'll point them out to me, I'll have them removed at once."

Sixteen men were loaded into the springless wagons. Two who begged Ethan for clearance to go would probably die before they reached the Maryland state line, just six miles away. It was wrong to give them false hope, but he could see by the looks in their eyes that they would rather die anywhere other than in enemy territory. Ethan indulged their requests for their own peace of mind even while he could do nothing to alleviate their pain.

"Sure you wouldn't prefer to come along with us?" Franklin again put the invitation to Captain Hastings.

"No," Ethan said firmly. "For some reason I feel led to remain. But in forty-eight hours I'll be along directly. My compliments to the Colonel."

"Aye, sir," Franklin nodded, and turned on his heel.

Ethan followed his fellow captain out onto the porch, feeling the ever-watchful, hate-filled eyes of Malcolm Everett piercing the back of his skull. "Godspeed, Franklin."

"And you, Ethan," Franklin said as the two men shook hands. Out of curiosity Franklin queried, "And where is Miss Salina? I thought she would surely be with you."

Ethan's brows bunched together in a frown. He couldn't rightly recall the last time he'd seen his little sister—not since midday, at least. "To be quite honest, I'm not sure where Salina is," he admitted uneasily. "But I think I ought to find out."

"I'll see you in a few days then," Franklin called. He ordered the ambulances to roll forward.

Ethan went to the cellar. "Mamma, have you seen Salina?"

"No, dear." Annelise looked up from feeding little Yabel his bottle. "Why, is she missing again?"

"I don't know for sure. If she is, she can't have gone far." Ethan hadn't meant to worry Mamma, but if she didn't know where Salina was, then something was definitely amiss.

Jubilee stepped forward. "Capt'n Ethan, ah'd venture ta guess Missy Salina done heerd bout da cava'ry fight. Da men, dey was sayin' how fierce 'n awful da fight was. Gen'ral Stuart, he weren't successful in breakin' da rear o'da Union line..."

"How do you know this? You didn't come up the stairs, did you?" Ethan demanded. He had already told Jubilee not to ascend the stairs for any reason. He didn't like making her feel like a prisoner, but he'd rather keep her hidden in the cellar than see her carted off by his countrymen and returned to a life of bondage in the South.

"Naw, suh, Jube didna go up. Ah overheard Mistah Michael and Mistah Jared talkin'," Jubilee clarified. "Dey say 'twas a powerful fierce fight."

Ethan took the cellar stairs two at a time. He found Orrin's wife in the parlour fanning a restlessly sleeping private. "Beth-Anne, have you seen my sister anywhere?"

"No, Ethan." Beth-Anne shook her head, sensing his agitation. "You know, I did see Cody leaving awhile back—he took the wagon and headed east..."

"That figures..." Ethan's dismay was evident. "What was I thinking? I should have seen this one coming, for Pete's sake!" He went back to the porch and stood facing the direction of the area where the Union and Confederate horsemen had reportedly clashed. He wondered how long Salina and Cody had been gone, and wondered if he shouldn't head out there himself. The dark sky was thick with leaden clouds threatening to burst open again at any given moment.

In the space of just a few minutes, Cody and the wagon appeared, turning onto the farm lane from the Mummasburg Road. "Where's Salina?!" Ethan questioned.

"She's with me, in back." Cody jerked his head toward the rear of the conveyance, and halted the wagon just in front of where Ethan stood with his hands balled into fists on his hips. "She was right, you know—he was out there. Thank God we found him." Cody climbed down from the high buckboard seat and moved round toward the back of the wagon. "Give me a hand, would you? He's heavy."

Ethan beheld the prone form of his brother-in-law, whose bloodied head rested in Salina's lap. Ethan's eyes caught Salina's, which were wide and filled with uncertainty.

"Dear God!" Ethan exclaimed. "Why? Why did it have to be him?!"

"Ethan." Salina heard her voice tremble as she spoke. "Ethan, please. He's hurt bad and he needs us. What can we do for him? He can't die, Ethan, he just can't!"

Ethan touched the sleeve of his sister's rain-soaked dress. "I'll get Warrick—he'll help, I'm sure of it."

Salina protested, "But he's a Yankee. Jeremy will be a prisoner of war if they find out about him. I don't trust Everett, Ethan. Please don't say anything to Warrick about who Jeremy is! I wouldn't put anything past Everett—even betraying Jeremy to their authorities."

"All right, Little Sister. It'll be all right." Ethan shared her keen distrust of their cousin's husband. Since Everett had betrayed Salina, what would stop him from betraying Jeremy—or Ethan himself, for that matter? They'd have to be careful. "I'll go get Warrick. If it becomes necessary to tell him anything at all about Jeremy, I'll make him swear his confidence. Agreed?"

Salina sighed and nodded to convey her reluctant consent.

Abel Warrick and Ethan carried Jeremy into the operating room on a stretcher and began a thorough examination of the injuries sustained. Warrick was observant enough to conclude that this particular Rebel was more than merely an acquaintance of Captain Hastings and his sister. "Who is he?" Warrick asked quietly.

"He's one of ours," Ethan replied, sensing Salina's unspoken caution.

"A friend?" Warrick persisted. He noticed the unwarranted attention of Lieutenant Malcolm Everett, lying in his cot just across the hall. Warrick glanced back at Ethan and then Salina, who was going through the pockets of the gray jacket which had been removed from the unconscious Rebel horse soldier.

Salina found a letter and removed a single handwritten page from an envelope with her own name on it. She read the few lines to herself, her heart skittering in her breast:

> *July 3, 1863*
> *Cavalry Hdqts.*
> *Near Gettysburg, PA*
>
> *My darling wife,*
> *I write this quickly as we are about to ride out. Boots and saddles has already been called by the bugler, so please pardon my haste.*
> *I returned to camp this morning, after leaving you at that enchanted little shed, only to find that I've been made a captain. Without my knowledge, General Stuart, put in for my promotion shortly after Brandy Station, and only just received word that approval from the White House in Richmond has been secured. I wanted to share the news with you, Sallie, and I look forward to your help in celebrating this bit of good fortune when next we are together.*
>
> *I am ever your loving husband,*
> *Captain Jeremy Barnes*
> *Stuart's Cavalry, C.S.A*

She managed to stifle the small cry that rose in her throat. *A Captain!* She swallowed and said, "Our friend is..." She looked directly at her brother. "He's a captain..."

"And does this captain have a name?" Warrick asked in a tone hardly above a whisper. He was confused by Salina's reluctance to volunteer any information.

She met the Yankee doctor's eyes squarely, having suddenly devised an alias to ensure her husband's safety. "His name is *Jeremiah Barnett.*"

Ethan said nothing to the contrary, but fell in with his sister's clever little ploy. He winked at her, wordlessly conveying his approval of her scheme and encouraging her to maintain the charade.

Warrick seemed placated. He retrieved his medical kit and some medicine. He ordered one of the stewards to bring hot water, and made his way back to the table where Captain "Jeremiah Barnett" lay. Amid the activity, Warrick skillfully maneuvered a dressing screen between the operating table and the cot where Everett rested, effectively cutting off the Yankee lieutenant's view. "Now, let's get busy, shall we? Captain Barnett desperately needs our ministrations."

Salina nodded as she stood shivering, soaked to the skin in her wet clothing. Ethan told Cody to take Salina downstairs to the cellar where Mamma could get her some dry clothes.

"I won't leave him, Ethan," Salina insisted, still holding Jeremy's cold, unresponsive hand in her own. She worked on kneading warmth back into Jeremy's chilled hands and arms.

"You want to risk another bout with pneumonia?" Ethan asked sharply. "Don't be absurd, Salina. Do what you're told."

Her lower lip trembled. "I can't, Ethan. He needs me. I need to be here with him. Please, I'll be fine."

Ethan leaned to whisper in Salina's ear. "I know you're a good nurse, but honestly, Salina, this is very different. It's nothing like working on strangers—it's harder when it's someone you know."

"I am clever enough to figure that out for myself!" Salina snapped. "But I'm not going! I'll stay here by his side, come what may."

Ethan saw that he was not going to persuade his stubborn little sister to do his bidding. "Cody, get a shawl for her, would you? And some coffee to warm her insides."

"Aye, Captain Hastings." Cody scurried off to obey.

Abel Warrick's curious glance again settled on the two across the table from him. They weren't telling him everything, that was plain, but it was not difficult to guess the identity of the man on the table: the wedding band on the Rebel soldier's scrubbed hand glinted gold in the lantern light, its shiny newness matching the golden band on the ring finger of Salina's left hand. No wonder she was so adamant to stay by his side, the Yankee doctor realized sympathetically. There was no time, however, to commend her bravery or admire her devotion.

Warrick, electing to keep his knowledge of the situation to himself, began a cursory examination, jotting in his case book notes regarding the extent of the Rebel captain's injuries: *Left side— broken leg, three cracked ribs, dislocated shoulder, assorted scratches, lumps, bumps, and bruises*. The hardened knot on the left rear of the Rebel's head caused Warrick more than a little concern. Most likely, the lump had been inflicted by a severe blow to the head with either the butt of a pistol or the clubbed end of a carbine. Head injuries were dangerous and frequently complicated, but Warrick could determine no fractures to the skull. He diagnosed a concussion.

Ethan examined the right side of their patient and found no further wounding beyond the sabre-made gash that was perilously close to the puffy, swollen eye. It took a fair amount of time, but eventually the two doctors, working in tandem, had Jeremy's bones set and splinted or plastered, his ribs wrapped tightly for support, his shoulder back in position and encased in a sling. Jeremy's face was shaved clean of his black-whiskered beard and mustache, and a row of neat, even stitches kept the torn flesh along his cheek from gaping apart.

Salina did precisely as she was told, when she was told—offering instruments, medicine, or bandages when called for. She remained silent and watchful, lips moving in mute prayer. She clung to Jeremy's hand throughout, willing that the warmth of her body might seep into his, to stir his circulation and bring him out of the state of oblivion he had slipped into.

Warrick requested that Cody hold a lantern directly above Jeremy's head. The Yankee doctor wanted to cast a brighter light into his patient's face. He studied the Rebel's blue eyes, then glanced at Ethan. "The pupils are widely dilated. They do not constrict in the light."

Here was another symptom of concussion; Ethan made a mental note as he wracked his brain to remember what he knew of head injuries and cerebral trauma. He was unable to recall much from his medical studies or experience, no doubt because of stress, strain, hardly any food and too much coffee. "What are you suggesting, Warrick?"

"It might be something to watch," Warrick cautioned, carefully selecting his words because of Salina. "I don't have much firsthand experience with eye injuries but before the war I worked with a doctor in Boston who did. I wish he were here. The man's a well-respected expert."

"But he's not here. Captain Barnett, I'm sure, is a determined fighter, but he's suffered a great shock to his system. As you said, we'll have to wait and see," Ethan commented. "Or at least *you* might. After tomorrow, I'm going to have to ride like the dickens to catch up with my army. I've got my orders..."

"I'll be staying in Gettysburg for quite some time—I, too, have orders," Warrick said. "For now, I suggest we bandage his eyes. Give him a few days to heal, and I'll check on him. We'll see then how he responds."

"Will Jere...miah...will he be blind?" Salina asked frankly, a prickly edge to her tone.

The two doctors exchanged a speaking glance, and it was Ethan who tried to sound convincing. "We can't say right now, Little Sister. It's simply too early to tell."

☆ ☆ ☆ ☆ ☆ ☆ ☆

Drake pulled the hired Dearborn up in front of the McClellan House, which stood on the northeast corner facing into the crowded Diamond. Rumor had it that the hotel had taken in some wounded, but that it also kept rooms reserved for the womenfolk who were coming to town in droves, searching for their loved ones. The train had brought Drake and Aurora as far as Hanover Junction, where they'd rented a horse and buggy from the livery and started upon the last leg of the journey. They were both exhausted. It had taken longer than the anticipated fifteen-and-a-half hours such an excursion should have taken under normal circumstances.

But as far as Drake could determine, nothing in Gettysburg was normal. The town and its twenty-five hundred residents had suffered from screaming shells and whizzing bullets and had survived occupation by opposing armies. Observers were beginning to comprehend the backlash of the receding tide of combat. What Drake saw was the aftermath of what must have been a literal hell on earth for three terrifying days.

Once Drake got Aurora settled into a room they'd paid handsomely for, he told her to stay put until he could make some inquiries about the situation. He had his own answers to find, in addition to those concerning Rorie's Mason Lohring, and they included finding the location of the Grant farmstead.

Drake went down to the first floor, and as he neared the front desk he overheard a discussion taking place between the flustered clerk and a black-haired young woman with a sad, trembling voice.

"I'm sorry, miss, but we haven't any rooms available at this point," the clerk explained with a shrug of his shoulders. "I just let my last vacant room to a couple by the name of Dallinger. They came from Boston, ostensibly for the same purpose you have come—to find someone dear to them. First the armies invaded... now sightseers and soldier-seekers are the invaders."

"Would it be too much to hope that you'd allow me to sleep in a chair in the lobby, then?" the young woman suggested. "I have no place else to go!" she cried in desperation.

"Pardon me for interrupting," Drake cut in, bowing his head in deference to the young lady. "My sister, Miss Dallinger, and I seem to be at fault for occupying the last free room. If you've traveled a great distance to find your sweetheart, then please, allow us to share our space with you. Rorie would draw comfort from your companionship, I'm sure, and I certainly won't mind sleeping on the sofa in the adjoining dressing room."

The young woman looked up into Drake's face with the most haunting eyes. They were an arresting shade of deep, velvety purple that only the hue of a pansy petal could match.

"I don't mean to sound forward," he quickly amended. "I assure you that the invitation is issued with no dishonorable intent, merely out of concern for your welfare. I'd just as soon sleep in a chair here in the lobby myself if that's what it will take to get you to accept a place for a good night's rest."

"Mr. Dallinger, I...I don't know what to say," the young woman stammered. "I do have money to reimburse you for the cost of the accommodations." She reached into her reticule.

"Keep your money." Drake dismissed her concern. He picked up her satchel and extended his arm; she slipped her hand through it and curled her gloved fingers around his elbow. "Come with me," he invited. "I'll introduce you to my sister, Rorie. We're here to see if we can locate her beau."

"I'm looking for my father," the young woman volunteered, casting a covert glance up into the striking face of her benefactor.

"Well, then, why not combine our efforts and see if we can't be of some help to each other?" Drake proposed. "What's your name?"

"Elinor Farnham," came the reply.

Farnham. *Farnham*. The name echoed mysteriously in the back of Drake's mind. He'd never met this woman before—he would have remembered if he had—but for some reason he *knew* the name.

Elinor's lips formed a partial smile. "I'm sure I don't know how to begin to thank you for your kindness, Mr. Dallinger."

"You can start by calling me Drake."

☆☆☆☆☆☆☆

Aurora took to Elinor Farnham immediately, and Drake had no reservations about leaving the two Northern women alone together. They'd already shared tears, each able to relate to the other's plight, and he resolved to assist them both—just as soon as he found Little One.

Drake took the rig out past Pennsylvania College to the Mummasburg Road and drove toward Oak Hill. Turkey buzzards soared ominously overhead. Burial details were out in force, hurrying to cover the bloated, blackened corpses, many of which were unidentified and would be interred in mass graves.

As he approached the frame house perched on the hill, Drake could see two men on ladders working to repair structural damage on the outside of the dwelling. Orderlies and stewards were in the process of removing wounded to their respective division hospitals for more extensive treatment. The stench of rotting and decayed flesh—both of human bodies and the carcasses of dead horses—was downright revolting.

Drake was received by Noreen Grant, who cordially offered a glass of tepid lemonade. Their supply of ice, she apologized, had melted quickly in the humid summer heat.

Jubilee passed the entryway, and Noreen called out to her. "Jubilee, this gentleman is in search of your Miss Salina."

"I'm Drake," he said, wondering whether or not the black woman would know him from Salina's shared confidences.

Jubilee did recognize his name, and she led him at once to the place where Salina sat next to a soldier so bound up in bandages that he resembled an Egyptian mummy.

Drake watched Little One work for a moment, her hands occupied with patching a bullet hole in the sleeve of the Union blue jacket on her lap. Drake was fairly certain that she labored so charitably on behalf of the blue-bellies only because the eyes of the sandy-haired man ensconced in the bed next to her could not view her actions.

Salina looked up when she felt him staring at her. "Drake?"

"Little One," he returned fondly.

Salina set the blue jacket down on the foot of Jeremy's bed and ran headlong into Drake's comforting embrace. "Oh, Drake! You've come!"

Drake glanced over Salina's shoulder and encountered the accusing glare of Malcolm Everett. He remembered the meddlesome Federal lieutenant all too well from San Francisco, but it was evident Everett couldn't quite place Drake without his buckskins, golden earring, and waist-length hair. Drake leveled an equally menacing stare back at Everett. The Yankee lieutenant became uncomfortable and rolled over onto his side, facing the opposite wall rather than the well-dressed civilian's cold glare.

The sandy-blond soldier grew restless, a hand coming from under the quilt to claw at the restricting band of linen swathing that encircled his head.

"No, no! No, don't do that, Captain Barnett." Salina was immediately at Jeremy's side. "Dr. Warrick says you must leave the bandages on until the end of the week." She gripped the stiff fingers in her own, and caressed them soothingly until they relaxed. Salina poured water into the basin, moistened a corner of the cloth, and began tenderly wiping the sweat from Jeremy's feverish brow.

He moaned, started to flail, and she lightly crooned something unintelligible to him. Drake didn't hear her words, but they obviously had a calming effect on the man in the bed, and he let the bandages alone. Softly Salina hummed a Southern tune to him, and the potential tantrum evaporated beneath her compassionate touch.

Drake, taken aback at seeing his dear friend so badly incapacitated, stepped quickly out of the way when Dr. Warrick came into the room with an armful of official-looking documents. The Federal inspector was close on the Yankee doctor's heels, ready to issue furloughs or discharges to deserving Union patients in the house.

Everett was one of those to gain his furlough with enough time allotted to heal and recover before he was required to report back to his commanding officer for duty. Spencer Hollingsworth was pronounced well enough to be sent home to his family in New York to recuperate. Of the remaining Confederate wounded, those who could be moved were delivered to a collection point to await transfer to a prison hospital. Only the most severe cases remained.

Jeremy was no worse than some of the other Rebels who'd been removed, yet he was not taken. Drake reasoned that it had to be the blue jacket carelessly laid at the foot of the bed that momentarily saved him from the fate of his fellow Rebels.

Salina held her breath, for she too saw the significance of the blue jacket. She willed the Yankees to go away, and they did. She dared breathe again only after she was certain the Federals had gone.

"That was a close call," Drake muttered, shaking his head. "Clever little Salina."

"That was the Lord." Salina refused to accept credit for the inadvertent act that undoubtedly had spared Jeremy and kept him with her. "Divine intervention, wouldn't you say?"

"I suppose," Drake relented.

"Oh, Drake, I'm so glad you're here." Salina reached a hand toward him.

The glimmer of her wedding ring captured Drake's attention. "So it's done then." He fingered the telltale band paired with her engagement ring. "You went and married the, uh, *Captain* after all."

"Yes," Salina confirmed with a wavering smile. "If he could know you were here, I'm sure he'd take great comfort in it."

"Do I have to call you *Mrs.* Little One, now?" Drake cajoled.

"No." Salina shook her head and found a weak smile. "Plain Little One will do."

Drake skimmed her cheek with a rough thumb. She looked tired and worn to a frazzle. She was quite a lady to endure all she had. "Are you holding up under the strain all right?"

"Me? Of course. I'm just fine." She looked to where Jeremy lay, then met Drake's turquoise eyes with a purpose. "It's Captain Barnett that's got me worried."

"Captain Barnett," Drake repeated, wise enough to comprehend that she was hiding her husband directly under the noses of the unsuspecting Yankees.

Jeremy moved again, uttering a pained groan.

"He's pretty bad off." Drake didn't have to look very hard to figure that much out. "Can't anything be done for him?"

"Dr. Warrick administered some morphine, but I'm not sure how long the effects last from one dose to the next. He wrote instructions for me: a fourth of a grain dissolved in three drops of water, injected with the syringe. Dr. Warrick said to give the Captain enough to make him comfortable, but I'm afraid to do it on my own—I'm not sure how much that would be. Dr. Warrick will be around again shortly, and I'll just let him see to it. Ethan's caution, though, was to make sure he doesn't get too much, or he might become addicted to it."

Drake agreed somberly. "Caution would be prudent when using the drug. If it's anything like peyote you don't want him to grow accustomed to it."

Salina nodded. "I know he hurts. I hurt for him."

"Where does the morphine come from?" Drake inquired.

"Dr. Warrick gets a rationed supply from the U.S. Sanitary Commission—they've come with wagonloads of supplies—not just medicine, but food, clothing, blankets, and all manner of basic necessities and creature comforts. Oh, Drake," Salina sighed in envy, "think if we had such unlimited resources as they have here in the North. How different things might be if..."

"That's not like you, Little One, to indulge in *what-if's*," Drake admonished. "You Southerners generally take pride in standing independently on your own two feet, making do, prevailing against the odds. Don't lose your grasp on that, Little One, or your hope is lost."

"My hope is in the Lord," Salina countered. "If the Captain were to die, God forbid, only his body will be buried. His soul will go to heaven and be in the presence of the Almighty Himself. He'd be with Daddy again."

"And they'd be spying from heaven with no way to relay the information back to you here on earth," Drake teased, trying to puncture Salina's melancholic mood. "I have a question for you," he said suddenly, changing the topic. "Does the name Farnham mean anything to you?"

Salina blanched and her hand strayed to her throat. "Farnham? Yes, I knew a man named Farnham. Why do you ask?"

"How did you know him, Little One?" Drake's interest was piqued. "Who was he?"

"He was a man who rode with Major John Barnes and was involved in kidnapping me, holding me against my will at Carillon."

"They used you as bait to lure Jeremy into what might have been a deathtrap," Drake recalled in a dry whisper.

Salina confirmed his statement with a nod and went on to say, "But Farnham released me, knowing it would cost him his life, and that's how I got free last April. Why do you ask?"

"Hmmm," Drake murmured. "Did he ever mention to you that he had a daughter? About your age?"

"He did," Salina nodded. "Her name was Eileen—no—Elinor. Yes, I'm sure it was Elinor. In fact, I have a package that Farnham gave me before he was killed. He asked me to deliver it to her when the war was over. To explain to her..."

"Explain that you live because her father gave up his life for your freedom?" Drake shook his head. "That's no easy thing to ask of someone."

"Farnham forfeited his life for mine because it was his way of trying to make up for his killing my daddy. Releasing me was his way to atone, you might say." Salina shrugged.

"I see," Drake replied quietly.

"I didn't think of it before, but I wonder if I could find his Elinor. Farnham said she lived near Fairfield with her grandparents. That's not ten miles from here," Salina told Drake. "I have the package he left with me; it's packed in my satchel..."

Drake put a staying hand on Salina's arm. "There's no need to fetch it now. Elinor Farnham won't be difficult to locate."

"How do you know this?" Salina queried, confused. Then she took a guess. "You know her?"

"I met her at the McClellan House in town. She's there with my sister, Aurora," Drake replied.

"Your sister is here with you?" Salina inquired. "You'll bring her round so I can meet her, won't you?"

"In time," Drake replied. "Right now they're planning how to go about finding Elinor's father and Rorie's sweetheart. With what you've told me, we certainly won't have to waste our energies searching for Farnham."

Salina detected an odd catch in his voice, but was too weary to discern its meaning. She dared ask, "Will you tell her for me? Will you let Elinor know how sorry I am?"

Drake pondered. "Let me think on it." He'd barely made Elinor's acquaintance. How on earth was he going to tell her that the man she'd come to Gettysburg to find hadn't lived long enough to be here?

Chapter Twenty-One

*I*f he tried to move, pain gripped his left leg, coiled tightly around his middle, and shot up to his shoulder. He tried instead to lift his head and see what caused the excruciating torment, but his head felt as if it would explode from the heat and the thunderous pounding in his brain. There was only the inscrutable darkness. Darkness and heat and pain.

And then a sweet, gentle voice washed over him. A cool touch stroked his face, caressed his groping hand. He wanted to cry out, but the sounds that tumbled from his lips were nothing more than guttural gibberish. The pressure of her hand squeezing his instilled a vague reassurance. His attempted words held no more meaning for her than hers did to him; nonetheless, he mentally clung to the melodic sound of the phrases she spoke.

Impenetrable darkness and fiery heat and searing pain. *Oh, God, if You're there and can hear me, please rescue me from this awful place!*

☆ ☆ ☆ ☆ ☆ ☆ ☆

Duncan Grant tasted the bile rising in his throat, heedless of the fact that his hands were clenched so tightly into fists that his own short fingernails bit into his palms. It hurt to view his ravaged home in a rose-tinted cast brought on by the gathering twilight.

Prior to the battle, the farm had been a beautiful, tranquil place—a place that had changed little over the course of his life. At present he barely recognized the dwelling before him. The destruction gnawed at Duncan's heart; anger consumed his thoughts. He immediately jumped to the conclusion that the Rebels were at fault for wreaking all the havoc, but then he thought twice and laid the blame where he felt it truly belonged: on the war in general.

In days of old, his family used to come running out onto the porch to welcome him home from wherever his travels might have taken him. Duncan found the farmhouse so filled with strangers that he had to go looking for a familiar face.

"Beth-Anne," Duncan called, poking his head into the kitchen where his sister-in-law was baking bread.

"Duncan!" Beth-Anne greeted her brother-in-law. "Oh, how good it is to know you're well, safe and unharmed! Orrin will be glad—and Annelise will want to see you, that's for sure! Come, let's find her, shall we?"

As they went through the house, Duncan took note of the disorder around him. He didn't have to ask what had happened. It was easy enough to discern that his home had become a field hospital. "You've had to deal with all this while I sat in Washington pushing papers around my desk at the War Department," he grumbled, despising the feeling of helplessness that had descended on him. He had to ask himself, *If I had been here, could I have made a difference?*

"We were fortunate not to get hit any worse than we did," Beth-Anne said optimistically. "Nathan and Jared are almost done repairing the roof and chimney, and soon Noreen and your father will move their things back into their rightful room upstairs. Salina was occupying one of the guest rooms up there, but I think she'll probably settle into the empty room down here once your parents move out of it. Her patient isn't well enough to be moved to the second floor, I reckon."

"Salina." Duncan murmured the name of his stepdaughter.

"She's an amazing girl, that one," Beth-Anne admitted generously. "I don't know what we'd have done without her. She knew what needed to be done to get ready for the wounded they brought to us. She figured they would, and sure enough, she was right."

"Where's my wife?" Duncan wondered.

"I'm taking you to her," Beth-Anne explained. "She's been staying downstairs in the cellar with Yabel and Jubilee, since their room's also been taken over by recovering soldiers."

"Yabel?" inquired Duncan.

Beth-Anne laughed. "You'll have to speak to Salina about that—she started it."

Duncan was puzzled, but did not press the issue as he was sure that whatever it was could be straightened out in time. He found Annelise downstairs in the cellar, right where Beth-Anne said she would be.

"Duncan!" Annelise's eyes lit up. She hesitated only for a minute before she catapulted herself into his strong, waiting arms.

"Well, I am pleased to know that you're happy to see me," Duncan flashed a smile, gratified by her warm reception. "I'm sorry I stayed away so long, but I came just soon as my superior officer would authorize a pass for me. I've a week's leave."

"That should give you ample time to get acquainted," Annelise said mysteriously. She collected her contented child from his cradle and cheerfully handed the two-week-old boy to his father for their first introduction. "Behold your son."

Everything else ceased to matter when Duncan at last held his baby in his arms. All the troubles faded away—only this moment and Annelise were what mattered. His gray glance met the look of anticipation shining in his wife's brown eyes. "He's beautiful, Annelise. Such a handsome lad with a noble name. Our little Garrett Duncan."

Annelise laughed candidly. "Yes, that's what I named him, just as your telegram instructed I should. But actually, we've taken to calling him by the nickname Salina gave him."

"Which is?" Duncan quirked an eyebrow in question.

"Yabel. It's short for half-Yank and half-Rebel," explained Annelise.

"Really?" Duncan was not overly amused with the invented sobriquet, regardless of how appropriate the name was. "So she got here at last—just in time for the battle?"

Annelise nodded. She confided, "And now I'm waiting for her to tell me she wants to go back to Virginia—but that won't be for another six weeks at least."

"How do you figure that?" Duncan inquired. He was listening

to what Annelise was saying, but his line of vision was securely anchored on the round little face of his gray-eyed son.

"That's how long it will be before Jeremy's cast comes off. Dr. Warrick will examine him thoroughly once the broken leg has healed. In the meantime, he'll treat the rest of Jeremy's injuries—but then there's the matter of his eyes..."

Duncan sat down in the rocking chair, holding Yabel on his lap. He was a big, strapping boy, healthy—and his. The pride welling within him eclipsed the bitterness he'd felt upon arriving home. It was good to be back with those whom he loved best. He really ought to tell his wife as much, but he couldn't. The timing wasn't quite right.

Annelise was pleased by the picture Duncan made with his son. She bit her lip, surveying them together. Duncan wasn't the least awkward in dealing with the baby, and he seemed genuinely happy. While their marriage might have been the result of precarious circumstances, as of late she suspected their friendship was deepening into a comfortable love. Those ripening feelings had been the cause of the miraculous child they'd created together, and Annelise believed in her heart that the bond Yabel completed would only strengthen the new level of their relationship.

It took an effort on Duncan's part to tear his adoring eyes away from his son. He asked, "What's this about Jeremy's eyes?"

"He can't see," Annelise reported. "At least, we don't know for sure if he can or not. Dr. Warrick is going to take the bandages off at the end of the week. Jeremy was wounded in the cavalry battle three miles away..."

Duncan had heard of the lethal clash between Stuart's Cavalry and that of Custer and Gregg. He was deeply concerned. "How's Salina handling this?" He knew his stepdaughter cared for that Rebel horse soldier with everything she had in her.

"She's standing by him, like a good wife should," Annelise nodded.

"Wife?" Duncan repeated, raising an eyebrow in surprise. "When did all this come about?" He listened to Annelise recount the details. "Leave it to Salina to get herself married in the middle of a battle!" Duncan slapped his knee. "Go figure!"

Annelise offered to take Yabel, but Duncan wasn't ready to relinquish the child to his mother's arms just yet. "I'll take him for a while, if you don't mind. I want to spend as much time with him as I possibly can. I also want to find my parents, and I'd like to talk to Salina, too."

"I'm sure they're all here somewhere. We do have a full house," Annelise notified him. "We have at least two dozen wounded still with us by last tally. Ethan won't be here for much longer, but Drake and his sister, Aurora, will be here later tonight, and they're bringing a friend with them."

"And where will they stay?" Duncan asked out of curiosity.

"Oh, they're just coming out for supper. They've hired a room at the McClellan House in town," Annelise explained quickly. "All total, I think we had over sixty-five people here at one point, but that was pushing the limits of hospitality, not to mention sanity, to the very brink."

Duncan shook his chestnut head in wonder, still a bit dazed by the shock of it all. "At the War Department, we were on pins and needles, scared to death that Lee would really manage to pull out a victory—he's done it so many times before. Lincoln was beside himself waiting to hear the outcome tapping across the telegraph wires. But in the end it was Meade who won the day, God bless him!" Duncan missed the pained expression that momentarily flickered across Annelise's face, and he continued, "Talk about a memorable Fourth of July! A decisive victory over the Rebels here in Gettysburg, and the fall of Vicksburg in the West. We hold the Mississippi at last. After all those long weeks of siege, U.S. Grant finally defeated the Confederates in their own stronghold. Bully for General Grant—he does our name proud!"

Vicksburg fallen, the men in gray retreating from defeat in Pennsylvania; Annelise's sigh was one of resignation. The only bright spot was that these things might well lead to the beginning of the end of the war. She had the disturbing feeling that the Confederates were likely to be in for a dear and costly struggle until the end indeed arrived. The fight at Gettysburg did not bring the conflict to a conclusion as some had hoped it would, one way or another. She knew that as long as there was even the merest whisper of breath left in them, the Southerners would give battle to the Yankees.

"Come." Annelise pulled on Duncan's hand. "Let's go find your parents."

The first thing Annelise noticed when she got upstairs was not the pungent aroma of death hanging over the area—it was the quiet. Every now and then she thought she could still hear the din of cannon ringing in her ears, but those times were growing more infrequent with each day that passed.

In the quiet she heard a guitar being strummed, and an unfaltering voice began singing a mournful tune:

> *Into the ward of the clean whitewashed halls,*
> *Where the dead slept and the dying lay;*
> *Wounded by bayonets, sabres and balls,*
> *Somebody's darling was borne one day.*
> *Somebody's darling, so young and so brave,*
> *Wearing still on his sweet yet pale face*
> *Soon to be hid in the dust of the grave,*
> *The lingering light of his boyhood's grace*
> *Somebody's darling, Somebody's pride,*
> *Who'll tell his mother where her boy died?*
>
> *Matted and damp are his tresses of gold,*
> *Kissing the snow of that fair young brow;*
> *Pale are the lips of most delicate mould,*
> *Somebody's darling is dying now.*
> *Back from his beautiful, purple-veined brow,*
> *Brush off the wandering waves of gold;*
> *Cross his white hands on his broad bosom now,*
> *Somebody's darling is still and cold.*
> *Somebody's darling, Somebody's pride*
> *Who'll tell his mother where her boy died?*
>
> *Somebody's watching and waiting for him,*
> *Yearning to hold him again to her breast;*
> *Yet, there he lies with his blue eyes so dim,*
> *And purple, child-like lips half apart,*
> *Tenderly bury the fair, unknown dead,*
> *Pausing to drop on his grave a tear;*
> *Carve on the wooden slab over his head,*
> *"Somebody's darling is slumbering here."*
> *Somebody's darling, Somebody's pride*
> *Who'll tell his mother where her boy died?*

Frantic footsteps flew swiftly down the hall. Salina burst into the parlour screaming: "Stop it! Quit singing that song! He's not going to die! *He's not!*" Scalding tears streamed down her blanched cheeks; she quivered with uncontrolled rage, and her chest heaved with a convulsive sob. "I won't let him die," Salina added in a more subdued tone. "I won't." She put a hand to her forehead, realizing what she'd just done, what a little fool she must appear in front of the present company. She looked around beseechingly for a familiar face and all but dissolved into another round of tears when Ethan put his arm around her shaking shoulders and quietly led her away.

Drake hunkered down next to the chair Elinor Farnham was sitting on, the guitar on her lap stilled into silence by Salina's rash outburst. "She didn't mean anything by it," he apologized on Little One's behalf. "She's been under quite a bit of strain these past few days—as we all have been. I think it may have finally affected her. You stay here and keep singing—perhaps something other than that particular ditty, hmmm? I'll go check on her."

Annelise left Yabel in Duncan's capable arms and hurriedly followed Drake down the hall to the bedchamber now designated as Salina's. Ethan was seated on the upholstered mahogany lounge, rocking Salina back and forth in his arms. He looked up at them over the top of Salina's head and spoke reassuringly to Mamma and Drake. "She'll be fine. Just exhausted, that's all." He rubbed her slumped shoulders in a soothing circular motion. "She's just plain tuckered out, right Sis?"

Salina nodded her head slowly, sensing the presence of others in the room. She didn't look up or make any reply. She was dreadfully tired, but there was Jeremy to be considered...

Ethan waited until Mamma and Drake reluctantly retreated to rejoin the others elsewhere in the farmhouse. "Salina, I want you to get some rest, or you won't be any good to Jeremy." He wished he could get Jubilee to make some of her specially brewed tea, knowing it would ensure that Salina slept a whole night through.

Jubilee must have been thinking along the very same lines for in a few minutes she knocked at the door bearing a cupful of her potent herbal tea. "Be good now, chile, an' don' ya fuss none. Dis here's Jube's special brew, an ah want ya ta drain da cup ta da last drop, hear? Go on now, don' argue. Drink up."

Salina wrinkled her nose. She didn't particularly care for tea all that much, specially brewed or otherwise. "There," she said, weakly triumphant, as she returned the empty cup to its saucer. "I'll be all right now. I'll sit with Jeremy for a little while, and then I'll lie down for an hour or two..." A yawn overtook her.

Jubilee and Ethan exchanged a speaking glance; Salina would sleep the clock around, not just an hour or two, but they said nothing. The black woman crooned, "Now, chile, don' fret none bout yer Capt'n. Ah'll fetch dat Drake ta cum sit wid yer young man fer a spell. Ya jist lie down an' take a rest, Missy."

Salina glanced at the recumbent, sandy-haired man in the brass bed. He'd been moved in here just a little while ago, and thankfully he seemed to be resting comfortably. Salina was too tired for any real protestation. She allowed Ethan to help her get situated on the lounge, with a pillow beneath her dark head and a light afghan over her.

Ethan put a finger to his lips to shush Salina. "Jeremy's still sleeping, so now's as good a time as any for you to catch some winks too. Drake will be here shortly, and he'll look after you when I'm gone."

"Gone?" Salina tried to sit up. "You're going to leave while I'm asleep?"

"I've got to go, Salina. I've got my orders, remember?" Ethan smoothed her tear-dampened curls back from her face. "I'm to meet up with Colonel Shields and then go on from there." He tucked an envelope into the pocket of Salina's day dress. "You'll see that Taylor Sue gets that when you go home, won't you?"

"Uh-huh," Salina nodded, succumbing to the quick effects of Jubilee's tea. "Ethan?"

"Yes, Salina?" He leaned close to hear her mumbled words.

"You'll be ever so careful, won't you?" she yawned. "Don't forget…about Everett…Watch your back…for Major Barnes…" Her voice trailed off into a vague whisper and her long eyelashes rested upon her wan cheeks.

"I'll take care, Little Sister." Ethan squeezed her shoulder, not knowing if she could feel his reassurance. He brushed her forehead with a brotherly kiss. "Good-bye, Salina. I'll see you soon, I hope." He also tucked instructions for Jeremy's care into her dress pocket. It wasn't that he didn't trust Warrick, but he wanted to be sure that his brother-in-law was getting the best possible nursing. Salina, he was sure, would see to it.

Ethan bade his mother and his little brother farewell, and shook his stepfather's hand in a restrained but congenial fashion. He nodded to Drake and dutifully kissed the hands of both Aurora and Elinor Farnham. "Please forgive my sister," Ethan said to Elinor. "You see, the dead soldier described in that song you were singing resembles her husband—golden hair, blue eyes. I'm afraid it hit rather close to home. I'm sure you understand."

"I didn't know," Elinor apologized. "I didn't mean to upset her so."

"She'll be fine," Ethan said confidently. "Perhaps you two can meet tomorrow, and then you'll have a chance to talk and laugh about tonight."

"Perhaps," Drake echoed. He couldn't imagine how emotional would be the inevitable meeting between the two of them—especially for Elinor. It remained to be seen how she would react when she discovered the truth of who Salina was.

☆ ☆ ☆ ☆ ☆ ☆ ☆

Blistering trickles of salty sweat meandered down his scorched brow and were absorbed into the linen bandage encircling his head, his damp hair matted against his temples and ears. His dry lips attempted to form the necessary words to request a drink of water, but his stiff and parched tongue refused to cooperate. A groan escaped him, and he couldn't remember ever being so very, very hot...

The voice that murmured over him was not *hers*. He was bemused, for he could not feel the comfort of *her* presence next to him, penetrating the confounded darkness. He wanted to cry, but didn't know how; he wanted to reach out, but he didn't know how to do that either. *Where was she? Why had she abandoned him?* He yearned for her soothing touch, the reassurance that she cared so tenderly for him...Senselessness descended once more, blotting out everything save the oppressive pitch black. If only it might ease the despair he felt clutching tightly at the edges of his reason...

Chapter Twenty-Two

*E*than felt chilled to the bone in spite of the summer night. A steady rain pelted down, and when the breeze picked up, the penetrating cold blew right through him. The discarded navy blue Yankee cape he'd found along the side of the road was as saturated with rainwater as his gray uniform. The sopping wet wool did little to keep him dry, but it did prevent the immediate disclosure of which army he served. It was a miserable night to be out, no question there. He had his orders from Colonel Shields and he had to move on. It was a long, hard ride he had ahead of him to catch up with the Second Corps. Ethan just hoped the wet weather would make the Yankees stay cozy around their campfires and leave him be.

The good-byes said to Mamma and little Yabel had been nothing short of difficult. He had checked in on Salina once more and found that the sedative in Jubilee's tea was producing the desired effect. Salina needed sleep to replenish her strength. She would be refreshed after waking from a night of sound sleep, and then Ethan was sure she'd be able to face each new challenge headlong—one day at a time, never giving up.

The Army of Northern Virginia was in full retreat. Longstreet's First Corps lead the way back to the Potomac River, A.P. Hill's Third Corps followed behind, Ewell's Second Corps brought up the rear. Ethan's heart grieved. After three days of heavy, brutal fighting, the Rebels had been unable to drive the Yankees from their enviable positions on the heights south of Gettysburg.

That third day of battle had been extremely costly in terms of human life. Some of the reports following Pickett's Charge were astonishing: of the thirteen colonels in Pickett's Division, seven were dead and six were wounded. At least three generals—Armistead, Kemper, and Garnett—were presumed dead, mortally wounded, or missing. Casualties among the rank and file numbered into the thousands. *When would it end?*

General Lee had claimed the blame for the failed campaign. He had believed his Army of Northern Virginia to be invincible—but Ethan knew that General Lee was not alone in that. Many Southerners had shared that grandiose view of the seasoned veteran troops. In fact, many of the gray-clad soldiers who lived through the ordeal still possessed a high level of morale and a fighting spirit that was far from broken. Though they were forced to retire for the present time, they knew that another day warfare would undoubtedly rage again between North and South. Ethan, however, harbored a deep-seated belief that there would be no more battles fought on Northern soil. Gettysburg was a lost opportunity for the Confederacy. In time it would come to be known as the "High Water Mark" for the South, and while he was loathe to admit it, Ethan wondered if the tide wasn't indeed shifting to favor the united North.

As he rode on towards Fairfield, Ethan couldn't help but ponder—was anything worth the hundreds upon thousands of wounded and dead that had been left in and around Gettysburg? The Rebels had taken with them as many of the wounded as they possibly could. If the men were well enough to be moved, they'd been loaded into the wagons that Jeb Stuart had captured at Rockville, and transported southward. The wagon train of wounded was reported to stretch nigh unto twenty miles in length.

The dead left behind would be interred by Northern burial details: Ethan believed that the Yankees would see that they were given a Christian burial. Again he shuddered, though not due to the chilling night dampness. *Is what we're doing really the right thing? Merciful God in heaven, were You on the side of the Yankees because we Rebs are determined to fight for what is wrong?* He sighed heavily, tiredly. At this point, Ethan didn't believe there was a clear cut answer to his question. Neither side was wholly right or wholly wrong. The North had its redeeming qualities just as the South had hers, and each had its darker evils. Since he didn't know where to search for answers, Ethan didn't try to find one that would accurately suffice. His duty was to Virginia, and in his position he was charged with the responsibility of caring for the sons of Virginia who fought in the Confederacy. At present, he let it go at that, for he hadn't time to indulge in doubts and misgivings. He decided it was simply better to go on from here and brave the struggle as courageously as possible.

He'd do well to keep alert, he admonished his fatigued mind. He was alone in enemy territory and needed to keep a sharp eye out for any unseen danger.

Ethan spurred his horse onward when he saw the few scattered lights of Fairfield on the horizon before him. He stopped at the Fairfield Inn to warm his hands by the fire and to quickly down a bowl of deliciously warming bean soup. The innkeeper offered him a room for the night, but Ethan declined, knowing he should press on. The little village of Fairfield had seen its share of conflict over the past few days, and he hazarded a guess that if he stayed, he'd get involved in doctoring. He had orders to obey, and didn't dare to risk further delay.

He was barely on the outskirts of town when two scraggly-looking, armed Yankees appeared, greeting him with pistols leveled at his heart. Ethan drew up sharply, reining his horse to a halt. The last thing he'd planned on was being taken prisoner. Would they see past the cape? he wondered. It was dark enough and wet enough for them to confuse dark gray with blue, and he prayed that would be the case. "Good evening, men," he saluted stiffly.

"Sir." Both returned the military gesture.

"What can I do for you?" Ethan asked tentatively.

"You're a doctor," one of the men said matter-of-factly. "We followed you from Gettysburg—you came from that house on Oak Ridge what's been set up as a field hospital. You've been tending the wounded there."

The other piped up, "We're in bad need of a doctor."

"Is one of you hurt?" Ethan queried cautiously, for he could see nothing wrong with the two before him.

"Not us, Doc, it's our Major. The Lieutenant sent us there to get a doctor 'cause he knew there was one—it's where he got himself bandaged up, see? So he sent us out to fetch you to work on our Major."

"He took a couple of minié balls in the leg, and one in the elbow," the first soldier informed Ethan. "He's doin' real poorly. We'll take you to him and you can fix him up right as rain."

Ethan was of the opinion that they believed he was a *Yankee* doctor. Had they been laying in wait for Warrick? Possibly, but they had bagged him instead. Well, at least he knew they didn't want to kill him—not yet, anyway. They needed his skill as a surgeon. When they discovered him to be a Rebel doctor, however, things might take a different turn.

At gunpoint, the two Yankees brought him to a barn where two other men were keeping watch.

"Stebbins! Varney! Where've you been?" the one nearest the door roared.

"Simmer down, Deakins. We got the doctor to see to the Major, just like the Lieutenant said." Stebbins roughly led Ethan by the arm into the barn. He called over his shoulder, "Varney, bring his bag."

"My instruments are in there," Ethan affirmed, "but I'm afraid I haven't got any medicine. If I'm to operate, I haven't anything to deaden the Major's pain."

Deakins replied, "We had some whiskey, and we gave that to the Major. He's beyond drunk, so you get to work before it wears off, hear?" He turned to the fourth man. "Traxler, get those lanterns lit. The Doc's going to need all the light we can provide."

Traxler hustled to obey his orders. Stebbins took the soaked cape from Ethan's broad shoulders, and Deakins looked Ethan over from head to foot. "Well, if you ain't a Johnny Reb..." Deakins lunged for Ethan, but Ethan was more agile, and he sidestepped the charging Yankee in time to watch him crash headlong into the barn wall.

Deakins came up sputtering, blood and spittle spraying from his cut lip. "I'll kill you!"

"It don't matter that he's a Reb right now, Deakins, it only matters that he's a doctor," Varney insisted. He helped Deakins up from the straw-covered floor but held onto him to restrain him from lunging at Ethan a second time. "The Major's bad off. Some help is better than none. We can't do nothing for him. He'll die if we don't let the Reb doctor see to him."

Deakins brushed himself off. He caught Ethan's shirtfront by the collar and ground out between clenched teeth, "If the Major dies, you die. I'll kill you myself, and that's a promise. You hear?"

"I'll do what I can for him, but I can't make any promises," Ethan answered coolly.

"You'd best take care of him the very best way you know how!" Deakins barked. "And maybe instead of gunning you down or hanging you like you deserve, we'll see you safely to the nearest prison camp instead."

Ethan bit his tongue to keep a retort from slipping past his pursed lips. His eyes blazed furiously, but he managed to refrain from rising to the Yankee's bait. He rolled up his sleeves and started giving his own orders. "I'll need water, buckets full. Hot preferably. And horsehair."

"What for?" Traxler asked.

"Just see to it," Varney stepped in. "Get him what he needs; it's for the Major."

"How do you think we're going to get a fire going in this rain?" Stebbins complained.

"Make it in here," Deakins commanded. "The smoke'll just have to go out through the loft windows." He grabbed Ethan's arm and marched him over to a crude operating table. "Get busy. The lieutenant'll be back soon."

Ethan set his medical bag on the top of an upended, three-foot-high-crate. The operating table was nothing more than some warped planks draped with a ground cloth and thrown across two barrels.

Varney brought in a bucket of water, and Ethan washed his hands thoroughly. He laid out his instruments and began his examination of the intoxicated Major's wounds. Obviously the man was in a bit of stupor, but not seriously so, Ethan judged. Perhaps the severity of his pain was gnawing at his consciousness. It would be better if he passed out, Ethan thought. "Can you bring the lanterns closer?" Ethan requested.

Traxler and Deakins obeyed; the lanterns shed enough light to illuminate the patient clearly. Ethan saw the face of the man lying on the table, and he felt like all the air was suddenly and violently drained from his lungs. *Major John Barnes...*

The wounded Major's eyes fluttered open, colliding with Ethan's icy stare. "What the...What are *you* doing here?" he croaked bitterly, but his expression gave away his terror.

When Ethan found his voice, it did not sound like it belonged to him. His calm answer belied the rage churning within him. "I've been brought here—by force—to see to your injuries, Major Barnes." Slowly he lifted a shiny silver instrument from its velvet pocket of the leather case.

"You're going to kill me!" John Barnes panicked at the sight of the sharp-toothed bone saw. He clutched Traxler's arm. "He'll cut me—make me a cripple on purpose! Don't let him near me! Don't let him touch me!"

Traxler, Deakins, Varney and Stebbins inched closer to Ethan. "Who are you?" Stebbins asked.

Deakins took a menacing step forward. "What's your name, Reb?"

"He's Ethan Hastings," Major Barnes grated out in a harsh reply.

Ethan eyed the Major with an indescribable loathing burning in his belly. "Isn't this just rich?" His lips twitched with a sardonic grimace. "You order your men to fetch a doctor, and they bring you the one you'd just as soon kill yourself. Tell me, Major Barnes, why I should bother to lift a finger to save your pathetic hide when I ought to let you die for all the hurt you've maliciously inflicted on my family. If you were to die, Major..."

"If he dies, you die," Deakins growled in reminder.

"But I'd at least have the satisfaction of knowing that my family will no longer suffer at your vindictive hand!" Ethan exclaimed.

Deakins rammed the barrel of his revolver into Ethan's ribs. "I'll tell you once more—if he dies, you're the next corpse!"

Ethan Hastings and John Barnes glared at each other for several drawn out, highly unnerving moments. Part of Ethan's subconscious screamed to let Barnes die, as would be his just reward. But another part—the saner side of him that wanted to live and see his wife again—wrestled with a scripture that leapt to the forefront of his mind: *Avenge not yourselves, but rather give place unto wrath: for it is written, Vengeance is mine; I will repay, saith the Lord...Be not overcome of evil, but overcome evil with good.*

Deliberately, Ethan's fingers curled around his scalpel. The Holy Spirit must have caused him to remember that particular passage, and he knew in his heart he could not murder Barnes, even though the prospect was temptingly within reach. Hoarsely he declared, "One day, Major, God will punish you for your sin, count on that. Until then, I pray He will grant me steady hands to do what

I must to keep you alive." Ethan saw the depth of fear in John Barnes' beady eyes, and he inwardly rejoiced. Let the man squirm, knowing that his life hung in the balance and in Ethan's skilled hands. "Take heart, Major, I'm going to do my best to see that you don't die. I want you to remember for the rest of your days that you owe your life to me. Each day, beginning tomorrow, each breath you draw will serve to remind you of that unrepayable debt. Revenge is your game, not mine, but vengeance will come to you— a vengeance wielded by the righteous hand of the Almighty," Ethan prophetically declared.

"I'll still hunt you down," the Yankee Major wheezed. "You save me tonight, and it won't change the fact that I'll never rest until all you Hastings are done away with."

Ethan made no reply. He went to work tight-lipped, seething. John Barnes writhed uncontrollably as Ethan probed none too gently for the two bullets imbedded deep in his leg. Ethan didn't care that the whiskey consumed by Major Barnes did not sufficiently alleviate his pain. Ethan wanted him to hurt.

Continuing his examination, Ethan discovered that a third bullet had passed clean through Barnes's calf, but the two lodged in the thigh took some time to locate. Methodically Ethan picked out bone fragments and splinters. He boiled horsehairs until they were pliant enough to be used for sutures, and stitched up the bleeding wounds with a nice piece of handiwork.

The elbow was shattered, and required a resection of the damaged joint. Barnes initially thought Ethan was going to amputate the arm, and Deakins and Stebbins objected vociferously until Ethan explained the procedure. "He won't lose the arm, but he won't be able to bend it when I'm finished piecing it back together. It's your choice—what do you want me to do?"

By general consensus the resection was allowed, and Ethan went back to work. His surgery was conducted in disturbing silence. When he was done he wiped his hands on the thighs of his trousers and said, "He's lost a lot of blood, and he's bound to be very weak. There's the possibility that he could slip into a fever," he cautioned, wrapping Barnes's wounds with clean bandages. "He might have a limp, and he'll certainly lose the movement of that elbow, but I think he'll make it."

"You're staying with us until we know for sure he's all right," Deakins reiterated. "You can get used to that idea right now."

Ethan nodded submissively. He would simply bide his time.

There was the remote possibility that a chance to escape might present itself, if he was watchful and ready.

Ideas of escaping, however, disintegrated the moment the lieutenant returned to the barn. He'd clearly been out riding hard and fast, and returned in great haste from wherever it was he'd been. "Lieutenant Everett," Ethan said recognizing the man immediately. "What a surprise to see you here," he lied. Salina had suspected that Malcolm Everett and John Barnes were of the same dishonorable ilk. Here was proof positive.

Everett, however, was genuinely surprised to confront Ethan. "What have you fools done?!" he raged at Stebbins, Varney, Deakins and Traxler. "This is *not* Warrick! I sent you to get the doctor from the Grant house at Oak Ridge, and *this* is who you brought back? Don't let him near the Major. Barnes will have to wait until we can find a real doctor—not some Johnny Reb," Everett spat.

"Too late." Ethan notified Everett smugly. "I already operated on the Major. See for yourself." He stalked out of the barn for a breath of fresh air, knowing without a doubt that either Varney or Traxler was right on his heels holding a gun aimed straight at him.

☆ ☆ ☆ ☆ ☆ ☆ ☆

It had been yet another frightfully long day. Annelise wearily mounted the stairs, more than ready to retire to the sanctuary of her room. Duncan had been closeted with Michael and Orrin for most of the morning, and she did not expect to see him until later in the evening.

To her surprise, she found her husband fast asleep, with his slumbering son laying across his chest. Yabel's little chestnut-colored head was tucked beneath Duncan's stubbled jaw. Both father and son snored softly in unison, and Annelise smiled wistfully. Years ago, she used to come upon Garrett in much the same pose with either Ethan or Salina reclining on his breast. It touched her just as much now to see the father of her new son and the child they shared so content together in their quietude.

Annelise bit her lip, acknowledging that it had been quite some time since she'd thought of her first husband. Life had taken on a decidedly hectic pace since Garrett's death, and there was no looking back now. She was finally adapting to this new way of life, and her new son and new husband were in the center of it. These two Grant men had wormed their way into her heart, stirring emotions she had never thought to feel again.

Duncan moved in his sleep, his unconscious hand resting on Yabel's back to prevent the baby from rolling to one side or the other. His slight shifting created the crunching sound of rumpled paper, and it caught Annelise's attention.

"Your work never ceases, does it?" She whispered the question, not expecting a reply. She removed the pages from beneath his elbow, intending to set them out of the way on the nightstand next to the bed. Duncan was always up to something—that was his job. She glanced fondly at the man lying stretched out across the bed, then curiously at the papers in her hands. Without actually meaning to, Annelise began to read a letter addressed to Duncan. She knew she really had no business doing so, and rightfully shouldn't have, but curiosity got the better of her.

South-Union Ranch, Kansas
18 June 1863

Dear Major Grant:

With all due respect, sir, I am writing in reply to your inquiry dated the 17th instance, in the month of June, in the year of our Lord, 1863.

First, I must inform you that my older brother, Evan, killed at the Battle of Shiloh, is survived by a wife and only two sons who greatly mourn his untimely passing. Personally, I have no knowledge of either the woman Justine Prentiss, whom you made reference to in your letter, nor her alleged offspring, who you claim is some sort of relation, presumably one born on the wrong side of the blankets. The indiscretion that your inquiries hint at is quite intolerable, and I can assure you that no such event has ever tainted our family's good name. It is not likely that this Jeremy Evan Barnes shares anything with my deceased brother other than a similar Christian name. Nothing more.

Second, I trust you will not take offense, sir, when I ask you to please never contact this family again regarding the above mentioned concerns. My mother is occupied with aiding in my recovery due to an injury suffered at the Battle of Jackson of 16 May. She is also deeply distressed over a son currently held in

> *a Southern prison camp, and another son with whom
> she has not corresponded in nigh unto three years.
> She has more than enough on her heart than to be
> troubled with such nonsense as this fabricated tale of
> affront. I have refrained from showing your letter to
> my father, as it would infuriate him to think that any
> son of his was responsible for such misconduct. We
> Southerlands pride ourselves on being an upstanding,
> moral set of people, and I, for one, would appreciate
> your silence and forgetfulness in this matter.*
>
> *Military allegiance aside, please accept my best
> regards, sir, and a measure of success in your endeav-
> ors to track down this unfortunate young man's true
> father. May God help you, and may justice prevail.*
>
> > *Lieutenant Ephraim Southerland*
> > *Staff Assistant and Courier*
> > *Conf. Dept. of Miss. and E. La.*
>
> *Major Duncan Grant*
> *c/o War Department*
> *United States Army*

"My, my!" Annelise was taken aback by the righteous indignation that fairly dripped from the single sheet of parchment. Some of
the animosity conveyed in the lines of the letter might result from
the obvious differences between a Confederate Lieutenant and a
Federal Major, but the stern phrasing made it sound as though this
Southerland family was a premium cut above the rest. She found
herself glad, for Jeremy's sake, that he evidently was not a member
of this blameless family. If Jeremy ever found out who his father
was, then she dearly hoped it was someone whose relations would
welcome him as a prodigal son and love him for himself.

"What are you doing?" Duncan demanded gruffly, whispering
so as not to disturb his napping son.

"I was…" Caught red-handed, Annelise offered the letter to
him. "I've no right to pry. I apologize."

"No matter." Duncan's wary disapproval vanished. He didn't
think any harm would come from Annelise knowing that he had
attempted to locate the name of the man who was Jeremy's father.
"I truly thought this Evan Southerland was the one, but according
to Ephraim Southerland's scathing little epistle, apparently I stand
corrected. It's back to the drawing board once I get back to

Washington." He looked down at Yabel, his gray eyes filled with love for his son. "The passage Salina translated from John Barnes's journal gave only sketchy clues, which indicated that the man was Yankee, his initials are *E.S.*, and he was killed during the Battle of Shiloh. I tried…"

"I'm sure you did, Duncan; you've probably done a remarkable job in your investigation." Annelise knew how thorough and meticulous he was when it came to his projects. "You didn't write to any of the other leads?"

"No." Duncan shook his chestnut head. "None of the others seemed likely out of the score of men that I traced and tracked. The letter I wrote Southerland was discreet—I mean, you don't just disrupt someone's life by telling them they have kin they never knew of. Such knowledge, if not handled properly, has the potential to ruin lives and reputations, let alone trust. I thought I was sure, or I wouldn't have sent the communiqué in the first place." Absently he rubbed Yabel's diapered posterior, and he sighed.

Annelise studied her Yankee husband for a moment. His gray eyes were on her, but he wasn't seeing her—his attention was fixed far, far away. "Duncan?"

"Hmmm?" He shook his head slightly. "Did you say something?"

"I was just curious as to why you've been searching for this man with the initials of E.S. For what purpose? What do you hope to accomplish?" Annelise wondered.

"Aside from providing Jeremy with a clue to his identity, you mean? Well, I suppose I was really doing it for Salina," admitted Duncan.

"But why?" Annelise persisted.

"I suppose I'm just the stepfather trying to win her love by successfully completing a project she cares very much about. I thought it might weigh in my favor, induce her to accept me," Duncan confessed.

"But Duncan," Annelise protested, sitting on the side of the bed and taking his hand in hers, "Salina already accepts you; I know she does. I don't know if she's told you, but I believe that she loves you, in her way."

"I'd like to think she cares," Duncan admitted. "The whole thing sounds foolish, doesn't it?"

Annelise shook her auburn head. "No, not foolish. I'm just surprised you'd go to such lengths to win her affection. I didn't think you cared what people thought of you."

"I usually don't," Duncan affirmed. "But you and your daughter are different. I know there's nothing I can ever do that will convince Ethan my intentions for marrying you were honorable…"

"Ethan will come around eventually," Annelise predicted. "I know him."

Duncan nodded. "I hope you're right; honest, I do."

Annelise ventured to say, "Let me see if I have this straight: You tried to find this mysterious E.S. to give Jeremy an identity and to make Salina happy? And if Salina was happy with the results, she would write to me and mention that you were responsible for that happiness, and she would love you for it—and I would love you for making my daughter content?"

Duncan shrugged uncomfortably, then stated firmly, "It was foolish."

Annelise leaned forward to kiss his cheek. "I think it's touching that you would go through such trouble to please me. I'll let you in on a secret, though."

Duncan raised an eyebrow in wordless question.

"I'm finding that I do love you, Duncan, in spite of myself and your blue uniform. More so every day," Annelise confessed with a warm smile. "Do take care of yourself so our little Yabel will never have to wonder who his daddy was…I want him to grow up knowing you, what kind of man you are. I want him to be like you."

Duncan swallowed audibly and lowered his eyes. His fingers tangled with hers, and then he caught her hand and held it fast. He pressed her fingers to his lips and grinned. "Your powers of perception are as accurate as Salina's."

"Where do you suppose she got them from?" Annelise inquired with a lilt in her voice.

Duncan's gray eyes scanned Annelise's flushed and pretty face. "From the woman I love, I reckon."

Annelise reciprocated his articulate smile.

"Do me a favor?" he requested of his wife.

"Yes?"

"Don't say anything to Salina concerning this. I don't want her to know about the investigation. If I had been successful, it would have been different, but she doesn't need to feel the frustration of running into the last dead end trail. The man she loves is lying downstairs, fighting for his life; that's enough to contend with."

"I'll not say a word to her about it," Annelise assured him. She, too, agreed that this was an instance where some things are better left unsaid.

☆☆☆☆☆☆☆

It was dark when Salina awoke. Her first thoughts were for Jeremy, who was breathing evenly, thank goodness, and she took that to mean that he slept without his usual restlessness.

Elinor Farnham stirred when Salina sat up on the lounge, and she immediately rose from the rocking chair she'd occupied. "I must have fallen asleep. I..." She looked to Jeremy and then back to Salina. "I got the Captain to take a little broth for supper, but not much, I'm sorry to say. Most of it dribbled down his chin and neck—he fought me every spoonful. In truth, I believe he knows I'm not you. He seemed confused, sullen, maybe even a little resentful."

"Thank you for sitting with him just the same," Salina smiled tentatively. "What time is it?"

"Just after eleven," Elinor replied. "If you don't want me here any longer, I can go."

"No, please stay. I'd like to talk to you. I've got something for you." Salina retrieved a small wrapped package from the bottom of her satchel. "Now's as good a time as any to set the record straight between us."

Elinor's furrowed brow betrayed her puzzlement.

Salina handed the small package into Elinor's hand. "I don't know how much Drake has told you, if anything, so I'll try to explain as best I can." She swallowed and began, "My daddy was a Confederate spy. He was captured after the Battle of Sharpsburg—Antietam you'd probably call it, being from up here in the North."

Elinor commented quietly, "I saw some of the pictures Matthew Brady took of the battlefield. They were horribly grue-some." She laughed dully, "And here I've voluntarily stepped right into the very vortex of such grisly and nightmarish scenes..."

Salina remarked, "It takes a good deal of pluck to come here alone in search of a loved one among the dead and dying."

"Sure it does. Drake told me all about how you went out to the cavalry battlefield alone, determined to find him," Elinor dipped her dark head in Jeremy's direction. "You can't do things like that without being brave, not without courage."

"I suppose," Salina conceded. "But love is a big part of it too, mixed in with the courage."

"That's why I came. I guess I was driven by love," Elinor affirmed. "Oh, I know all about what kind of man my father was, and I'm sorry to say he was not of the most sterling character. He fell in with the wrong sort and got himself mixed up in some rather unsavory situations." She swallowed, "I know all of that, but I still love him. He's the only father I have."

Salina hung her head. "I loved my daddy very much, still do. I miss him terribly."

"What happen to him?" Elinor questioned.

"After he was captured, he was imprisoned. He got it into his head to try to escape. Daddy didn't want to hang. He figured if the escape worked, he'd be free. If not, he'd have died at the end of a rope anyway. It didn't work: a Yankee guardsman shot him in the back. The escape was foiled.

"As it turned out, this Yankee guardsman got a transfer not long after my daddy's death," Salina continued. "He was recruited into an independent command led by a major named John Barnes. Barnes, I must tell you, has been holding a grudge against my family for twenty-some-odd years. When he found that this Yankee guardsman had been responsible for killing my daddy, Barnes enlisted his services for another strike against us Hastings. I was the target, and I was kidnapped and held captive by Barnes and his band of men."

"How awful for you!" Elinor exclaimed sympathetically.

"It was rather frightening, more so when I understood that I was being held as bait to lure a man into a trap set by Major Barnes. The man he was after was his nephew, for whom he also carries an unreasonable vendetta." Salina's eyes strayed to Jeremy's still form.

"Your Captain is the Major's nephew," Elinor deduced.

Salina nodded affirmatively. "He came to rescue me from John Barnes at the risk of getting himself killed. The Yankee guardsman, however, had a change of heart about holding me hostage. He didn't like the situation one bit. One day during my capture, he told me he had a daughter about my age. He said he would strike out at anyone who ever tried to lay a hand against her, as Barnes was doing to me. It was obvious to me that the Yankee guardsman loved his daughter very much, though it didn't sound as if he'd seen her in quite some time…"

Elinor's intelligent face paled. "This Yankee guardsman you speak of, did he have a name?"

Salina again nodded. "He knew that in helping me get away from Barnes, he would likely forfeit his life. Barnes would kill him for releasing me—and that's exactly what happened. He said he wanted to help because by doing so he might be able to atone in some way for past mistakes. He gave me this package and asked me to see that his daughter received it. The man's surname was Farnham. I never did hear his given name used."

Tears trickled down Elinor's cheeks unchecked. "It was Garrett."

Chills raced along Salina's spine, sending a tingling, prickling sensation all the way to the tips of her toes. "My daddy's name was Garrett, too. Isn't that bizarre…" she murmured.

Elinor didn't comment. Instead she forced her shaky fingers to unwrap the package, which contained a small New Testament, a cartes de visite photograph of her father, and a letter of explanation addressed to Elinor that verified everything Salina had just told her. Elinor fingered the cartes de visite print. "If he did something good, then perhaps the Lord *did* change his heart. I'd prayed for him for years, and grandma did, too. We thought he turned his back on God years ago—he blamed God for my mother's death—but if he was reading this," she thumbed through the pages of the pocket-sized testament, "then maybe he'd made a clean start." Her sigh was as shaky as her hands. "The Lord took the bad and used it for something good. You're alive, and the Captain here is alive, because of my father. While it might have been your daddy's time to die, surely God must have a reason for sparing you both," Elinor offered softly.

Salina bit her lip. "That's what Jubilee always says, too, and I reckon it must be so. Oh, Elinor, I'm sorry to have to be the one to tell you. And I'm sorry I flew into such a rage when you were singing the other night…"

Elinor hugged Salina. "Don't mention it, it's already forgotten. Ethan explained that part to me. Now, since you're awake, I'll leave you to tend to your Captain, and I think I'll find a quiet place where I can reread this letter. Thank you for being honest with me, Salina. It can't have been easy to have to break such news."

"It wasn't," Salina admitted. "You're taking it rather well at present, but if you want to talk, I'm here."

"Thank you," Elinor whispered, then fled from the room.

"Oh, Lord," Salina sighed, shaking her head. "Give me the strength go on, and Elinor, too." It had been difficult, but it was something she'd had to do. She really hoped that Elinor did understand. "What a tangled mess, Jeremy," she said to him, smoothing the hair along his brow. She rested her palm against his forehead and instantly noticed the absence of his fever—it had broken.

She took his large hand in between her two smaller ones and pressed it to her cheek. "Your fever's gone, Jeremy. Praise You, Jesus!" She bowed her head and murmured prayers of thanksgiving.

All through the night and into the next day Salina sat at Jeremy's bedside. She talked to him, sang to him, read to him, and continuously prayed over him. She administered a sponge bath, washing his arms and chest and the uncasted leg. Just before supper, she stubbornly managed to get some broth into him, and he kept it down. Dr. Warrick came to look in on him, and he told Salina that in the morning, they'd take the bandages from his eyes, at least to change the dressing.

Later, Salina read aloud from a novel by Sir Walter Scott called *Rob Roy*. It was going on midnight when she yawned and said, "I can hardly keep awake, so I think we'll finish this chapter in the morning, all right? I'm going to sit right here beside you, and I'll keep holding your hand. If you need anything, you just squeeze mine and let me know, all right?"

She hadn't expected any response, really; there had been none in all this time. But this time Jeremy *did* reply. It was almost imperceptible, but Salina felt the faint squeeze of his fingers circling her hand. Wide-eyed, she squeezed back in return, and was rewarded with another minute tightening of his fingers around hers.

"You are *not* going to die, Jeremy Barnes! You're coming back to me, I know it!" she breathed.

Chapter Twenty-Three

$\mathcal{D}$r. Warrick drew the window blinds, shutting out as much light as he could and still see what he was doing. He had been surprised at first to see that Salina had propped Jeremy up against pillows in the bed. He wasn't sitting up, but even this slight degree of incline was progress. Judging from his present condition, he was recovering from the shock and concussion. But Warrick had warned Salina that the healing process would be slow and time-consuming.

She was a bundle of nerves, hovering behind Warrick as he made preparations to remove the bandages. "Miss Salina, do me a favor. Sit down, would you? You're making me nervous."

Sheepishly, Salina muttered a hasty apology and returned to her chair at Jeremy's bedside. She took his hand in hers, as was her custom and murmured near his ear, "Dr. Warrick's going to take the bandages off in just a minute. Be still. Everything will be fine."

A firm squeeze on her hand indicated his comprehension.

Dr. Warrick glanced at Salina questioningly.

"He understands," Salina explained with a nod and a bright smile.

"Please proceed, Dr. Warrick. We're both on pins and needles!"

Dr. Warrick, however, did not hurry. He took his time, working methodically until the last bit of bandage encircling Jeremy's head could be unwrapped. Involuntarily, Jeremy's eyelids fluttered, finally free from the pressure of gauze dressings. The reaction that both Salina and the Yankee doctor had hoped for did not occur, and it didn't take Warrick long to discern that the man lying in the bed still had no vision.

"Captain?" Salina said expectantly. She always called him by his rank whenever they weren't alone.

He turned his head slightly in the direction of her voice, but there was no other response. Salina almost cried seeing the angry red wound that marred his forehead and cheek. The puffiness had subsided only somewhat, and dark purple bruises tinted his flesh.

No change in the pupil of the left eye, Dr. Warrick jotted in his case book while conducting his examination. *Right eye still too swollen to notice any sign of change. By all outward appearances, vision is impaired.*

Salina sat in subdued silence. She watched as Warrick applied some salve to the stitched cut, and then the doctor redressed the wound. "Do you have to cover both of his eyes?" she asked forlornly.

"It doesn't appear that he can see out of either one, Miss Salina," Dr. Warrick said gently. "Covering them up will give them equal chance to rest and heal, and we'll take another look at him in a couple of days. The cut is healing quite nicely, though he'll have a scar for a souvenir, that's for sure."

"Quite a beauty," Salina remarked sullenly. "Thank you for coming, Dr. Warrick."

The Yankee doctor patted her shoulder reassuringly. "I'll come back to check on the others tomorrow afternoon. We'll take another look at your Captain the day after tomorrow."

"Day after tomorrow," Salina echoed the doctor's words somberly. How long ago it seemed that Jeremy had come to Aunt Tessa's in Culpeper and told her they could be married "the day after tomorrow..." She kissed the palm of Jeremy's hand, remembering the vows she'd made before Reverend Landstreet and Jeremy's men: *to have and to hold from this day forward, for better for worse, for richer for poorer, in sickness and in health, to love, cherish, and obey, till death us do part...*

Death had not succeeded in parting them, but the first test of their vows was certainly at hand.

☆ ☆ ☆ ☆ ☆ ☆ ☆

Not quite a fortnight after the battle, Beth-Anne spied a tragic note in a days-old edition of the Adams *Sentinel*:

> *But withal, we have been called to part with*
> *some. We have learned only of the follow-*
> *ing:—Killed, Miss Virginia Wade by our own*
> *sharpshooters... The suffering and afflicted*
> *need not be assured that they have the hearty*
> *sympathy of the entire community.*

Michael Grant, who had been to town several times since the end of the battle both to gather news and to replenish the dwindling grocery supply, had more accurate details as to what had happened to the poor young woman known as Jennie Wade.

On the morning of the third day of the battle, while making bread for Union soldiers, Jennie was shot in the back. She had been standing over a dough trough in the kitchen of her sister's home when a stray bullet—reportedly from a Confederate sharpshooter's rifle—pierced a side door and the kitchen door prior to striking Jennie. Jennie's grief-stricken family had had to wait until the fighting ceased before they could bury her. They laid her to rest in a garden near the house during a private funeral beneath the pour-ing skies on the Fourth of July. Jennie was buried in a casket orig-inally intended for a Confederate soldier, some said, and she was the only civilian known to have died in the Battle of Gettysburg.

"The poor girl." Noreen dabbed the tears from her eyes with a lace hankie liberally sprinkled with pennyroyal to mask the terrible odor of the atmosphere surrounding the Grants' house. "Can you imagine? It could have been any one of us, so thick did the bullets fly that first afternoon up here on this hill. Can you just imagine?"

"Jennie Wade might have been the only civilian killed *during* the battle," Jared commented, "but there are at least a dozen or more accounts of people who have died or been seriously wounded from explosions of unspent shells from the fighting. The shells and bullets, if picked up or tampered with, have the potential to be just as lethal now as they were two weeks ago. Farmers around here are going to have to take great care when they start plowing their fields again."

Another story, this one shared by Nathan, told of John Burns, a

Gettysburg resident some seventy years old, who took up his own gun and joined Federal troops in the field to defend his home, his town, and the Union. The old man was wounded three times, but was satisfactorily recovering from the ordeal.

Chandler, not to be outdone by his older brothers, asked if anyone had seen a dog standing guard over some Federal soldiers near what was coming to be called "Iverson's Pits." "The little dog was the mascot of the 11th Pennsylvania Infantry, and answered to the name of Sallie," Chandler said, grinning contritely at Salina. "She was given to the regiment early in the war, when she was just a pup. As she grew, she followed the 11th Pennsylvania everywhere—on the march and in camp. She suffered the same hardships and good times as the men. They say she hated only three things: Rebels, Democrats, and women."

Chuckles and restrained smiles goaded Chandler into proceeding with his tale: "During battles, Sallie would take a position at the end of the battle line, barking and growling as her soldiers fought against the enemy. The 11th retreated through town after being pushed back off Oak Ridge on the first day of the battle, but in the confusion, Sallie got separated from her regiment. She didn't know where to find them, but she knew where they'd been, so she retraced her steps until she found her injured comrades. She stayed with them day and night among the debris, with no food or water. She stubbornly held her position, keeping a silent vigil."

Cody's eyes were dancing and he winked mischievously at Salina. Impudently he queried, "Sounds like a Sallie we all know, doesn't it?"

Salina lowered her gaze and cleared her throat, feeling the blush stain her cheeks. "Tell us, Chandler: What happened to the dog?"

"After the battle a man from the 12th Massachusetts found Sallie and returned her to her regiment," Chandler replied.

"Isn't that something?" Cody shook his head. "Brave, devoted little dog."

"There are scores of amazing stories resulting from all that's happened here," Michael Grant added.

Orrin cast a cool, circumspect glance about the room, his gray eyes settling on Salina. He murmured, "And I expect we'll hear more to come." He still didn't trust the lady Rebel above half.

For days following the end of the battle, the inhabitants of the town gave aid to the wounded and dying left in the wake of the two warring armies, but also kept busy exchanging stories and impressions of their common tribulation, just as Orrin had suggested they would. The Rock Creek railroad bridge destroyed by Confederate troops was soon repaired, and thousands of people—from North and South—flocked to the battlefield.

Duncan's leave expired on the thirteenth of July, and he prepared to journey back to Washington. During the time he'd spent at home, he'd made it a point to visit his sisters, Felicia and Lydia, to see how their families had withstood the turmoil. Duncan also paid his respects to Lottie Colby, and had taken time for a quick supper with Dulcie and Steve. They had been as shocked as he by what they beheld upon returning from their wedding tour to New York. Their little hometown hadn't been prepared; none of the good citizens had ever expected such a terrible battle to occur within the borders and surrounding fields of Gettysburg.

The anonymity of the farming community evaporated much like General Meade's chances for bagging the retreating Southern army under Robert E. Lee. The Army of Northern Virginia had its back to the flooded Potomac River for the better part of a week, and Meade had not followed through with the crushing blow President Lincoln wished for. Meade claimed he was successful in driving the invader from their soil, and Lincoln cried that it must be understood that *all* the territory was *already* their soil. Lincoln did not seek to acknowledge the seceded states and their Confederacy as a separate country, yet neither did he want to cast his victorious general in a bad light.

Lincoln did not send Meade the angry letter he'd composed following the Battle of Gettysburg, instructing him to pursue and attack Lee's retreating forces. Such action might have ended the war. It might have been over and done with had the Army of Northern Virginia been prevented from escaping back over the Potomac River and returning to Virginia to lick its collective wounds. Lincoln relented, however, and his anger with Meade subsided. Under General Meade the Federals had whipped Bobby Lee, and that in itself—combined with the triumphant news of the fall of Vicksburg—was great cause for rejoicing in the land. Lincoln later commented concerning Meade, "Why should we censure a man who has done so much for his country because he did not do a little more?"

☆☆☆☆☆☆☆

Days passed with no sign of either infection or fever in Major John Barnes. The surgery Ethan had performed was considered a success, and Barnes was healing. Stebbins and Traxler procured an abandoned ambulance wagon for the impending journey to Washington. They planned to depart for the Union capital as soon as Ethan declared Barnes to be clearly on his way to a healthy recovery.

"I oughta kill ya, Hastings. Ya deserve nothin' better than to die," Barnes muttered through his tobacco-stained teeth. It was a familiar litany by now, as the Yankee major brought up the same old feud every time his pain became intolerable.

"So you keep telling me," Ethan shrugged, shifting his weight to a different sitting position. The ambulance jostled continuously down the turnpike, hitting bumps and wagon wheel ruts with equal discomfort. He hadn't yet been able to convince his captors to let him get out and walk alongside the rickety conveyance. His legs were cramped with no place to stretch and his arms stiff from being bound by the chafing ropes circling his wrists.

Everett leaned over and said to Barnes, quite loud enough for Ethan to overhear: "How many times do I have to remind you that killing him would be too easy? Let him rot in a prison cell. Let him survive the torture of a living hell."

Ethan's expression did not change; he schooled his features to give away no trace of reaction.

"If ya were Jeremy, I'd not hesitate to put a bullet through yer skull," Barnes spewed vehemently. "I don't have to tell ya Deakins is jist itchin' to pull the trigger himself. But in yer case, Everett's right. Shootin' ya is jist too quick an' easy. I think I like his idea about leavin' ya linger in some overcrowded prison camp."

Ethan said nothing and revealed still less in his expression. John Barnes might be a major, but it seemed he might have over-looked something. Ethan knew there were General Orders estab-lished by both the United States and the Confederate States concerning the treatment of medical officers. It had been duly agreed upon by the Confederacy and the Union that when medical officers were captured on a battlefield, they were to be released immediately and sent back to their own lines under a flag of truce. Scarcity of medical officers warranted this preferential treatment, and if Barnes didn't know that, then Ethan would sit tight until his chance presented itself. He wouldn't be the one to enlighten Barnes, for it would suit him just fine to have the Yankee major assume that he was rotting away in a Federal prison. Ethan fervently hoped the General Orders were still in practice. The prisoner exchange cartel had broken down, but perhaps the fact that he was a doctor would be Ethan's saving grace. He'd heard horrendous stories of inmates in Northern prisons, and he vaguely wondered where they would send him. Johnson's Island in Ohio, or maybe Fort Warren in Boston Harbor? They were but two of the known places where he might end up...

They were headed toward Washington, however, and Ethan concluded that he'd probably be taken to the Old Capitol Prison instead. If that were the case, and Duncan Grant found out about it, then at least there was a chance of smuggling a message through the lines to Taylor Sue to let her know what was going on, and to tell her not to worry about him.

John Barnes stared at Ethan, hostility ablaze in his bloodshot eyes. Salina Hastings had escaped the fate he'd plotted for her, as had that wretched "nephew" of his. He owed Jeremy for leaving him for dead after the explosion at Carillon's Mill and the subsequent chase. If he couldn't get to Jeremy, then he'd just have to see that Ethan paid in his best friend's stead. Barnes shouted at his subordinates, "Varney, Stebbins, hurry it up!"

In an alleyway in Washington, within sight of the unfinished capitol dome, Deakins and Everett took turns delivering heavy punches to Ethan's bound body. After roughing the Rebel doctor up, they stripped his dingy gray uniform of any insignia that would denote his rank of captain. Then they rifled his pockets and found a handful of letters from Taylor Sue, a photograph taken on their wedding day, and a copy of his commission as Assistant Surgeon. They took his wedding band and his pocket watch before they pulled his lolling head up by a fistful of hair and made Ethan watch as they burned his scant few possessions—and certainly anything that would identify him.

Ethan turned away, not wishing to see his keepsakes melt into charred ashes; he offered a token struggle, but his arms were too tightly roped for any effect. He must have passed out, for he didn't remember the ride from the alley to the Old Capitol Prison. One minute he was a crumpled heap outside the gate; the next, he was being escorted under guard into the superintendent's office.

"Hastings, Hastings..." The superintendent scratched his head. "Captain Ethan Hastings. You know, you look rather familiar to me. Have you been here before?"

Ethan merely groaned, so it was difficult to determine if he meant yes or no.

The superintendent searched his files. "Hastings, Hastings..." He found only one such name, belonging to a *Salina Hastings*; other than the woman, only a former prisoner by the name of Gary Hayes was remotely close. "Well, I suppose it doesn't matter one way or another—you'll still be our guest here at the Old Capitol Prison for as long as it takes to find out if you're really who you claim to be. Until then, I hope you'll find your cell not too unpleasant. Good day, sir." To the guards he passed the order, "Take him away."

Ethan licked his cracked, bloody lips before trying to form a response. Then he discarded the idea as taking too much effort. The guards practically dragged him down the corridors and locked him in a cell with a few dozen other Confederate inmates. He sat slumped against the wall, his blackened eyes only half open to observe his surroundings. Daddy had been incarcerated here, so had Salina and even Taylor Sue, for that matter. Ethan's exhalation of breath made his ribs ache. *God, I guess it's my turn to be here. Please, don't leave me or forsake me; You promised to be with me. O Lord, help me find a reason to be thankful for my present circumstance. Your word says in everything give thanks, for this is the will of God, but I'm hard-pressed to think of anything right this minute*, he confessed. Ethan's heavy eyelids fell and the encumbering exhaustion laid claim to his consciousness.

☆ ☆ ☆ ☆ ☆ ☆ ☆

"May I have...some water...please?" The hoarse voice sounded dry and gravelly. It had taken a great effort for Jeremy to force the words past his lips.

Salina abruptly lifted her dark head when she heard the raspy voice. She must have dozed off reading. She marked the place in her Bible that spoke of Joseph being sold into slavery by his brothers, and quickly set the leather bound volume aside.

"You're awake! I heard you—you asked for water. Of course you may have some water." She hastened to pour some from the pitcher and held the glass to his lips.

Jeremy drank a little, then settled back into his pillows. The words came easier: "Thank you, Miss..."

"You're quite welcome, Captain," she said with a teasing hint of laughter. "But really, you needn't be so formal. You may call me by name, you know."

"Which is?"

Salina's smile froze on her parted lips; a horrid chill constricted her heart with icy fingers. Jeremy was not jesting with her. "You don't know my name?" she breathed unsteadily, purely incredulous.

"No, Miss, I don't. If I did, I'd take the liberty of using it to thank you for all the help you've given me. You've been more than kind." Jeremy's voice was ragged from disuse, and for the first time in days he found himself able to speak words aloud and string them into sentences. He might even be able to describe this despondent blackness that still pressed on him from all sides if he tried, but decided instead to ignore it as best he could. He reached out his hand, palm turned up, expectantly waiting for the girl to slip her hand into his. "What is your name?"

A rush of tears welled in Salina's eyes and she stared at him open-mouthed in shock. She placed her hand in his to fill his empty grasp, and took a deep breath before she trusted herself to reply. Somehow, she prevented her voice from wavering. "My name is Salina."

"Salina." He liked the melodic sound of it. "Miss Salina, I do thank you for your tender care and unfailing kindness. I reckon I owe you a debt of gratitude which I'll never be able to repay."

Salina put her free hand over her mouth to stifle a choked sob, and she closed her eyes tightly. Warrick had warned her that a loss of memory could sometimes accompany a concussion. The blow Jeremy had sustained to the back of his head could account for his evident mental lapse. She felt him squeeze her hand tentatively.

She returned the gesture and murmured softly, "There's no need for you to even think of trying to repay me. All I want is for you to get better. You've been hurt badly."

Jeremy groaned. "I can feel that. I ache everywhere, but mostly my shoulder, my leg, my ribs, and this side of my head." He reached up to touch the bandages, gingerly running his fingers along the length of material across his eyes. "No wonder it's so dark…"

This time the cry that escaped Salina's throat was audible.

Jeremy's brow dented in a deep furrow. "Salina?"

"Yes?" She managed, her voice strangled.

"You're crying."

"Yes," she confessed.

He reached up, blindly searching for her face. She took his hand in hers and cupped it to the side of her cheek. He felt the dampness of her watery tears. "Don't cry, Salina," he said softly. "I'd much rather hear your laughter again. It reminds me of ripples, like when a stone is thrown into a pond and the circles grow wide on the surface of still water. Other times it sounds like the wind chime outside the window—merry and tinkling."

He felt her cheek grow round as it lifted in a smile. "There's a start," he said. "Laugh for me?"

She tried, but failed. "I'm sorry, I can't."

"Well, since it seems I'm responsible for the tears, I shall take it upon myself to replace your smile and incite your giggles." His determination was plain.

"When have heard me giggle?" she wondered.

He paused, trying desperately to recall, but came up empty. "A few minutes ago you were almost giggling; but in truth I can't rightly figure." He shook his head. "I know I must have heard you laugh at some time, because I can hear it in my head. Like your voice, low and sweet—that's something I'll never forget. It's what's kept me going. It's what's drawn me out of the depths of darkness in hopes of viewing the lovely face that must accompany such an inspiring voice." He paused. "But for these miserable bandages, I would know your face." He tenderly traced her cheek, her nose, her long-lashed eyes and brow. His thumb settled on her lips and she kissed it. His hand slid down the curve of her jaw to the hollow of her neck and rested lightly on her shoulder.

Salina watched him intently, allowing him the butterfly caresses. It seemed like an age since he'd touched her or held her in his arms. She could sense that he was searching in his mind for a mental picture, some small detail, but he gleaned nothing.

He sighed, trying to dispel the anger caused by his frustrating ignorance. "You call me Captain. That's my rank?"

"Yes," she replied.

He swallowed. "Salina, what is my name?"

Another tear dripped from her lashes, and he felt it land on his forearm. "Tell me," he insisted.

"Your name is Jeremy Barnes, but in order to hide you from the Yankees, I've invented the name Jeremiah Barnett for you," Salina whispered. "Oh, Jeremy!" Overcome, she pulled away and fled from the room.

Jeremy Barnes lay back against the down-filled pillows. A surge of panic welled in his chest. Frantically he clawed and pulled at the bandages around his head until he was free of them. The darkness did not diminish—where he knew he should have seen light, there was none. He raised his hands before his face, opening and closing his fingers into fists, but he *could not see* the action. Slowly, he put his fingertips to his face. He felt the prickle of his whiskers, and as he inched his fingers up, he felt the puffiness of his right eye and the row of stiff silk stitches. He continued his exploration, touching his brow, running his fingers through his hair, touching his ears. Then he felt the hard knot on the back of his head. Any pressure at all made him flinch, so tender was the lump. "Oh, God! *OH, GOD!*" His cry bordered on hysteria, but he didn't know what to pray. Anxious fingers found the bandage binding his ribs, and then moved lower to discover the hard plaster cast encasing his left leg. As he moved, he felt the stiffness in his shoulder.

"Salina?" he called out. "Salina!" There was no answer. "Salina, please! Come back!"

Dr. Warrick answered Jeremy's cry, and was concerned to find that the Rebel captain had thoroughly undone the bandages. "Now, Captain Barnett," he admonished firmly. "You can't be undoing my handiwork—we're trying to make sure that the wound stays clean and infection doesn't set in."

"Who are you?" Jeremy demanded roughly.

"I'm Dr. Abel Warrick. I've been tending to you. I must say that finding you alert is a promising sign after so many days of unconsciousness."

"She had to tell me my name—I didn't even know my own name! And I can't see—even with the bandages off—why? Why can't I see?!" With each question Jeremy's voice raised in pitch.

"You've suffered a nasty concussion," Warrick tried to tell him calmly, "among other injuries. Do you remember?"

"No," Jeremy grated his teeth, choking out the monosyllable. "I can't remember *anything*!"

The desperation in the young captain's voice moved Warrick. He placed a hand on Jeremy's shoulder and told him honestly, "Captain Barnett, these are accompanying symptoms of concussion—loss of sight, loss of memory. They can either be permanent or temporary in duration. I fervently hope, for your sake, that they are the latter, but you must understand that I can make no guarantees."

Jeremy's chest rose and fell with choppy gusts of breath. "I could be like this *permanently*?"

"There is that possibility," Dr. Warrick answered truthfully. "Head injuries can be rather tricky, but your mind has the capability to mend itself just as your body does. It's simply too soon to draw final conclusions. Medical science is not perfect. You'll have to be patient, and wait."

"For how long?" Jeremy wanted to know.

"That, sir, I'm afraid I cannot tell. I don't know the answer to that myself. All I can do is look after you, and hope for the best."

Jeremy was silent. *Hope for the best...*

"If you're agreeable," the doctor suggested, "I might as well take those stitches out now. I was going to do it first thing tomorrow morning, but now's just as good a time."

"Sure," Jeremy replied dully. "I don't care."

Warrick spoke sharply, "You'd better. She's fought for you day and night—don't you dare disappoint her by giving up now."

"Salina?"

"Aye, Miss Salina. She's cared for you like no other—and there have been many here in need of her nursing. She's willed you to survive through surgery and through fever, and she will continue to stand by you through the recovery process, too, if I know anything about her."

"She took off running when she discovered I couldn't remember her name," Jeremy countered bitterly.

"I'm sure that distressed her," Warrick explained, "Much like finding you cannot see distressed you. She'll be back—that I can guarantee."

"You sound so sure. Why? Has she any fondness for me?" Jeremy couldn't prevent himself from asking.

Dr. Warrick grinned. "Oh, I reckon you might say she has at that." He continued to work at removing the stitches from Jeremy's face. "It'll be sore for awhile," Warrick warned Jeremy. "The scabbing will start to form, and then it will itch. Don't rub it. I'm going to put on some salve and wrap your eyes again. If you do as you're told, I'll see if we can leave them off next time I examine the wound." Warrick gave him another dose of morphine to alleviate his pain.

Jeremy nodded. "I'll behave." He heard the door open and he called softly, "Salina?"

"No, friend. It's me, Drake."

Dr. Warrick stood to leave, pausing at the door. "If you need me, Captain, be sure to have Cody or one of the stewards fetch me. Otherwise, I'll be back in a couple of days."

Jeremy's reply was a mere nod. Listening intently, he heard another man sit down beside him. "Drake," Jeremy repeated. "Drake. I'm sorry, but I can't seem to recall who you are."

"That's all right. Little One told me that you've come to, but that you don't seem to know what's going on," Drake confirmed. "Between the two of us, we'll do all we can to help you remedy that."

"Little One?" Jeremy inquired.

"That's just my nickname for Salina. She's much shorter than either you or I, and there've been times when she's needed us to protect her," Drake said by way of explanation. "The name just fit."

"Can I ask you something else?" Jeremy questioned.

"Fire away," Drake readily permitted.

"What name do you call me by?" he asked hesitantly. "Nicknames aside."

Drake caught the meaning: Jeremy was trying to find out if he was friend or foe. "I call you Jeremy, as Salina does, but in respect for her wishes and your safety, we refer to you as Captain Barnett in front of the others. Annelise Grant, that's Salina's mother, and Jubilee, their former mammy, also hide your identity from the rest of the Union-loving folks in this house. We're in Gettysburg, Pennsylvania; it's a long way from your home in Virginia."

"Am I in danger of some kind?" Jeremy asked, a chill running down his spine. He was completely vulnerable, his foggy mind gathered, and at the mercy of those around him.

"You're a Rebel cavalry officer behind enemy lines," Drake told him. "If those people decide you're well enough to be moved, and they find out you wear a gray uniform rather than blue, you could wind up in a prison hospital."

"The war," Jeremy breathed.

"You remember that?" Drake queried. "You remember the fight that landed you here?"

Jeremy shook his head. "No, not really. I thought for a second that I did, but…it faded. Tell me how we know each other. How did you and I come to be friends?"

Drake spent at least two hours telling Jeremy about their meeting in California, the work they did for the Pony Express, and a handful of the pranks they'd pulled together.

"Sounds like we had some good times," Jeremy said ruefully. "I wish I could recall the fun we used to have."

Drake saw that Jeremy looked weary and worn. None of this could be easy for him. "Why don't you rest for a little bit," Drake suggested, "and later on, we'll play a few rounds of Twenty Questions. I'll tell you anything you want to know, providing I know it myself."

"Where are you going now?" Jeremy wondered.

"I'm going to check on Little One," Drake answered. "She needs a friend too, and there's only so much of me to go around," he quipped. "I'll be back, and we'll talk some more."

"Is she beautiful?" Jeremy hazarded.

"Aye," Drake replied without hesitation. "Greenest eyes you ever saw." He couldn't help but tease, "If I don't miss my guess, I'd venture to say she's got her cap set for you."

"But I'm hurt, broken," Jeremy argued.

"So? That won't stop her from caring about you," Drake informed him with a chuckle. "She's stubborn and independent. She lets very little get in the way of what she wants."

Jeremy nodded. "Spirited?"

"Highly." Drake's lips twisted in a grin. "Try flirting with her a bit, see what happens. I dare you."

"I just might do that," Jeremy decided, "if she'll come back to me."

☆ ☆ ☆ ☆ ☆ ☆ ☆

Drake found Salina on the porch swing where he plopped down uninvited next to her, setting the swing in motion. "Are you all right, Little One?"

"Oh, just terrific," she said sarcastically. In her hand she held a lace kerchief doused with peppermint oil, used as a fragrant sachet against the pungent air. Taking a whiff of something pleasant kept her from being overwhelmed by the foul stench emanating from the surrounding battlefield.

Drake took Salina in his arms, offering her his quiet comfort. She was strong for as long as she could bear it, and then the overdue torrent of tears was released.

She stayed in the crook of Drake's arm, resting her dark head on his shoulder, until the sobs subsided. Salina wiped her tears away and sat up stiffly. "I'm fine. I'll be fine, really I will."

Resolution flashed in her emerald eyes as she recited, "'I can do all things through Christ Jesus who strengtheneth me.' I'll get through this, too, for no matter how much it seems like the end of the world, the sun still rises in the east each morning."

"If it helps you any to know, he doesn't quite remember me, either," Drake confessed. "I sense, though, that every now and then something I say registers."

"Like what? How can you tell?" Salina wanted to know.

"He gets real quiet, almost to the point of holding his breath, and his brow puckers like this." He demonstrated by scrunching his own eyebrows together. "To me it looks like he's trying to picture a scene somewhere in the back of his mind that he heard described. When you talk with him, watch his face—you'll see what I mean."

"What were you talking to him about?" Salina asked.

"The Pony Express." Drake chuckled. "He'd asked why he should know me, so I told him. I don't know if the Captain remembers for sure, but at the very least I've given him something to think about."

"And that's all? Just the Pony Express?" She looked up into Drake's turquoise eyes.

"For now—I haven't mentioned anything to him about John Barnes. Not yet." He shook his head.

"Maybe it's better not to tell him right now—he's got enough to worry about without adding that to the confusion," Salina speculated. "I just wish I could get into his brain and help him think..."

Drake squeezed Salina's shoulders in a one-armed hug. "It's going to take time, Little One. No use in overwhelming him by telling him everything he used to know all at once. Some things may forever be a mystery to him."

Salina slowly nodded. Drake didn't like the crestfallen expression that settled over her face when she whispered, "What if he never remembers me?"

"I wish I had an answer that would cure your doubts, Little One, but I don't," Drake shrugged. "He asked me about you, though."

"He did?" She didn't want to get her hopes up too high.

"He says your voice was all he had to keep him anchored to reality. It's what made him fight to return to awareness. The disappointment that he felt when he took the bandages off and still wasn't able to see must have been unspeakable." Drake's voice was reduced to a low whisper. "He asked me what you looked like, so I described you as best I could: hair like a raven's wing, eyes like sparkling emeralds, creamy cheeks, and lips that rival the color of a rose..."

Salina lowered her eyes as she felt her cheeks grow warm. Sometimes, he made her feel uncomfortable, even though she had his promise that he would never kiss her again. "Really, Drake. How you do go on..."

"You are married to the man I consider the dearest friend I've got," Drake said evenly, sensing her discomfort and wanting to reassure her of his friendship. "You know I would do nothing to jeopardize our relationship. You're married to him—for better or for worse, in sickness and in health— right?"

"Yes," Salina answered without hesitation.

"You vowed to love and cherish one another till death do you part. He's injured and will end up scarred, if not blinded. He might not remember everything, but he didn't die," Drake pointed out.

"I wouldn't let him. I refused to allow him to give up," she interjected. "Surely you don't think I'd stop loving him now, do you?"

"A credit to your stubbornness," Drake grinned.

"I need him," Salina admitted. "Stubbornness, selfishness, call it what you will."

"And he needs you, too. I told you before: the two of you deserve each other," Drake reminded her.

"I reckon we do at that," Salina sighed with a wisp of a smile. "Thank you, Drake."

"You're most welcome—what did I do?" He quirked an inquiring eyebrow.

"You just listen and you keep on being our friend. I don't know what Jeremy and I, Taylor Sue, or even Lottie would have done without you these past few months. Your friendship has proven to be invaluable yet again. I'm sure Aurora is pleased as punch to have found she has a brother like you."

"Rorie, yeah, maybe. Grandmamma, now she's definitely another story." Drake picked at one of the brass buttons on his waistcoat, then hooked his thumb on the gold watch fob dangling from his pocket. "I never set much stock in being wealthy—I always made do with whatever I could earn, or I learned to go without until I could save up for whatever it was I thought I had to have. Now I've got money, a respected name, and assets I never dreamed of having. Just looking around this town, I've been thinking of ways to put some of my money to beneficial use. I want to do something good with it."

"That's very kind of you, Drake."

He shrugged, "If it's kind, it must be because you're rubbing off on me. I have changed since I made the choice to leave the West and journey to Boston—not only physically, but inside, too. I don't understand it, and I don't know if I like it."

Salina's remark was tongue-in-cheek: "You're becoming so polished that soon you'll be the perfect gentleman. I don't know if I'll be able to recognize you a bit." But Drake's assessment was accurate: he *had* changed in some of his ways, though not all. Over the months since their initial meeting in St. Joseph, a good portion of Drake's rougher edges had been smoothed down. Salina speculated that his uncertainty stemmed from a typical fear of the unknown. The more familiar Drake became with his new position and responsibilities as a Dallinger, the more self-assured he'd be. He had said before that he'd give it an honest chance and if he truly didn't like the results, he could just as easily let his hair grow back and head west to California.

Drake rolled his turquoise eyes. "The day I become a perfect gentleman will be a very cold day...Not likely, Little One; you forget—I'm half Kiowa-Apache. Indian blood courses through my veins."

"I suppose you're right, I do forget," Salina admitted. "It's not that important. I mean, your heritage is important to you, as mine is to me, but between us it makes no difference. A friend is a friend—regardless of blood or skin color or which side of the Mason-Dixon Line they reside on."

"Strong words," Drake baited her.

Salina raised her chin. "I wouldn't say them if I didn't mean them."

"True. You're a lady of your word, and of your honor," noted Drake.

"And duty," Salina added. "Which means I should get back to caring for my husband."

"Don't be surprised, Little One, if he tries to flirt with you. I took the liberty of telling him you were sweet on him."

Salina beamed. "Thank you." An amused light touched her eyes as she said demurely, "I'll try not to appear too brazen when I flirt back."

Drake chuckled heartily. He would indeed look forward to the spectacle. Drake's vivid turquoise eyes never left Salina as she crossed the porch and reentered the farmhouse. Jeremy Barnes was a man to be envied, Drake thought. He might not look like much, bruised and battered, laid up like he was, but the love of that little lady would see him through. Drake was about to give up the hope that he could ever be as lucky.

"Supper's almost ready," Elinor Farnham called, sticking her head out the door. "You coming in, Drake? Or would you rather me fix you a plate and bring it out here?"

Drake rubbed his jaw, his eyes momentarily studying the dark-haired Northern miss. "If it's not too much trouble, fix two plates and join me," he invited.

Elinor smiled warmly. "I'll just be a minute."

Chapter Twenty-Four

Someone told me once that you were like a bad penny—you always turned up," Salina quipped as Drake sauntered through the vacant parlour and into the kitchen where she was preparing a luncheon tray for her Captain. "Where have you been these past few days?"

"Why? Did you miss me?" Drake quizzed good-naturedly.

"You're incorrigible." Salina rolled her eyes. "Where have you been?"

"Rorie and Elinor volunteered my services at the hospital, and I've been playing teamster—hauling supplies for the Sanitary Commission. I drummed up a little business for my freight line, you might say."

"How enterprising of you." Salina raised an eyebrow. "I thought you were looking for charitable ways to help this community with your vast sums."

"Oh, I am," Drake nodded. "I've already donated to an orphan fund, and another being collected on behalf of the widows. I also paid some hotel bills for people who had to stay here longer than originally anticipated, and ran out of money…And I…"

"There's more?" Salina's tone was teasing now.

"Yes, there's more—and you're involved," Drake grinned, pulling on one of the curls that had escaped the confines of her mesh snood. He wasn't about to confess it, but Drake was partially beginning to enjoy his new social standing and the privileges it afforded. Absently he wondered if he wasn't also beginning to feel a pang of responsibility to look after his half-sister...He had no time for such reflection at the moment however; there were other matters of import that commanded his attention. He pressed a wad of greenbacks into her hand. "I want you to take this, and next time you go into town, buy some material—flannel, corduroy, whatever. I want you to start making shirts. Some of the soldiers out at Camp Letterman are sorely in need of clothing—Rebs, mostly. The Union's supply comes from the Sanitary Commission, but those resources aren't available to your people. Just don't let on that the clothes you make are for the Rebs, hear?"

Salina nodded, agreeing to keep quiet about the endeavor. She asked, "What is Camp Letterman?"

Drake looked askance at Little One. "You've not been out much lately, have you?" he inquired.

"No, not really," replied Salina, her shoulders lifting in a dainty shrug. "I've been rather occupied."

"I reckon so." Drake didn't have to be told that she was speaking of Jeremy. "How is he?"

"About as well as can be expected, I guess. We talk quite a bit. I know he's still in pain, no matter how gallant he tries to be about it. I always feed him before I give him that dose of morphine Dr. Warrick prescribed."

"I hate to say this," Drake ventured, "but in truth, I reckon he's probably better off having been wounded up here than in Virginia. Fewer shortages. Here, at least, you have enough food and medicine."

Salina reluctantly nodded. "I was thinking along those very same lines just before you came in."

"Well, it was just a thought. There's no need to dwell on that. Just you concentrate on getting our favorite patient better." Drake smiled. "Here, these are for you."

Salina took the roll of newspapers he offered and untied the string that held the papers together. Her emerald eyes opened wide. "These are *Southern* newspapers! Drake, how?..."

Drake put a finger to his lips to shush her. "Sometimes it's better not to ask too many questions. I just thought you might enjoy some news from home."

"Thank you, Drake." Salina wisely stifled her curiosity about the source of the papers. "But you still haven't told me of this Camp Letterman. What is it? Where is it?"

"Out at Wolf's Woods. Do you know where that is?" he asked.

"Yes, about a mile outside of town on the York Pike." Salina shivered and softly added, "It's on the way to the cavalry battlefield."

"So it is," Drake confirmed. "At any rate, there near the railroad they've established a general hospital named in honor of the Union Medical Director, Jonathan Letterman. They've collected a vast number of wounded from the division hospitals and the remaining field hospitals and will tend to them there until they are well enough to either return to their regiments or be taken to prison."

"So that's where they took them." Salina nodded toward the empty parlour. "Warrick was here this morning and supervised the removal of the last of the wounded we had here. All but..."

"He let the Captain stay?" Drake was genuinely surprised.

"Yes," Salina whispered, almost conspiratorially. "He gave instructions to the orderlies to gather up all the men in the parlour, the drawing room, and the two upstairs bedrooms. Never once did he even suggest that there might be wounded men in any of the other rooms. No search was made."

Drake whistled softly, a plain indicator of his amazement. "Little One, that, I believe, would be another instance that you can safely attribute to Divine Intervention—isn't that what you called it?"

Salina smiled. "That's precisely it—you hit the mark squarely."

Drake shook his dark head. "Well, anyway—at Camp Letterman there are tents that have been erected to house the wounded, and others for the officers, doctors, and nurses. That's where I've been, especially since Elinor and Rorie have taken up residence out there. Rorie found her sweetheart."

"She did? Oh, I'm glad, for her sake." Salina was relieved. "Is he all right?"

"No," Drake shook his head somberly. "Warrick looked in on him, examined the stump remaining after the amputation. It's his opinion that Mason is merely lingering. Too much infection, too much fever. It's only a matter of time, I'm afraid."

"How's Rorie taking it? Hard, I expect," Salina surmised.

"Uh-huh," Drake murmured in the affirmative. "But she's as stubborn as you—she'll not leave his side. Rorie's trying to fight for his life as you fought for Jeremy's. And who knows?" He shrugged eloquently.

"God alone," Salina replied, "in His infinite wisdom. How often in these past few weeks have I reminded myself that His ways are higher than ours? He knows the end from the beginning, and makes all things work together for good..." her voice trailed off, and she absently hugged the newspapers to her chest. Then she shook her head. "Stay and have lunch with us." Salina suddenly suggested. "Then you can drive me out there to Camp Letterman. Rorie could probably use all the support she can get right about now."

"You'll leave him alone?" Drake asked skeptically.

"Jubilee will watch him for me," Salina said with certainty. "She and Mamma have been after me for days, insisting that I need to take a break as far as Jeremy is concerned. This is as good an excuse as any for a little breathing room, just for a few hours. It'll do us both a world of good."

"You said you've been talking," Drake reiterated. "Any progress?"

"Some, but he still doesn't remember, and then one—or both— of us gets frustrated." Salina shook her head sadly. "Maybe I'm trying too hard, Drake."

Her summation made him laugh out loud. "Last time I checked, I don't recall you doing anything in half-measures, Little One."

Salina sniffed haughtily and informed him, "I'll take that to be a compliment, Mr. Dallinger."

"Of course, Mrs. Barnes," he grinned, his turquoise eyes seeing right though her feigned regality, "and one of the very highest degree, I can assure you."

☆ ☆ ☆ ☆ ☆ ☆ ☆

Jeremy's sullen attitude almost persuaded Salina to change her mind about going to the general hospital with Drake.

Mamma insisted, however, that Salina should indeed pay her respects to Aurora. "She's been a friend to you, sweetheart, and Elinor, too. It's only fitting that you should return the favor. Jeremy will be quite fine here with us, won't you, Captain?"

Annelise received a mere grumble in response to her question. Jubilee echoed Mamma, "It's only fittin'."

Drake triumphantly proffered his arm to Salina. "The sooner we go, Little One, the sooner we'll be back."

Camp Letterman was well situated on eighty acres of high

ground nestled in a stand of trees that provided shade and cover, at a distance of better than one hundred fifty yards from the railroad track. Water was supplied by a good spring, and a helpful breeze provided necessary ventilation. Approximately sixteen hundred wounded, maybe half being of the Confederate persuasion, were housed in tents aligned in double rows and designated alphabetically by ward. Some four hundred doctors, stewards, orderlies and nurses were on hand to give succor and treatment to the men in need. Salina noted that the area was pretty; before the battle, it had been used as a picnic spot by Gettysburg residents, much as Culp's Hill had been.

The embalming tent, dead house, and graveyard served as grim reminders that the grounds were no longer employed for the purpose of tranquil Sunday outings. Smells of ongoing meal preparation filtered out from the cookhouse, and the U.S. Christian Commission as well as the U.S. Sanitary Commission had headquarters within Camp Letterman.

Drake and Salina found Elinor in her tent, which was among those pitched to comprise quarters for the nurses and attendants. Elinor told them where to find Aurora—and her Mason Lohring.

The pitiful private from the 19th Massachusetts lay convulsing with shivers even as rivers of sweat trickled from his feverish brow. Salina's heart went out to Aurora, who only barely acknowledged Salina and Drake. Mason's leg, amputated just above the knee, was covered with a water dressing, but Salina could plainly see splotches of blood on the dampened cloths as well as discoloration from oozing pus.

"Poor Rorie," Salina murmured to Drake as he led her out of the depressing tent and back to the nurses' quarters. "He's not going to make it, I'd wager."

Drake could only concur with Salina's sympathetic remarks.

"Miss Salina!" a Southern voice called out from one of the canvas tents. "Miss Salina! Why, I'll be jiggered! What are you doing here?"

Salina halted abruptly, recognizing the familiar drawl. She looked around for the man who hailed her. "Kidd Carney? There you are!" She hastened to the tent where Jeremy's fellow rider lay casually resting. His left arm was suspended in a sling, but he did not appear to be otherwise afflicted. "How good it is to see you! But what are you doing *here*?" she wanted to know.

Kidd Carney smiled as he ruefully relayed the circumstances of his capture during the cavalry fight on July the third. His retelling of the charges and clashing fury came from haunting, firsthand experience. "I can still hear Custer shouting, *'Come on, you Wolverines!'* Those Michigan boys are ruthless fighters, let me tell you. One of the colonels from the 1st Virginia Cavalry summed it up accurately enough when he said that the fighting was hand to hand, blow for blow, cut for cut, and oath for oath. Three hours may not seem like an eternity, but believe me, it was more than a lifetime!"

Carney went on to say how he'd escaped his captors, but was unfortunate enough to be recaptured west of town and taken to the hospital at the Theological Seminary. "Dr. Ward did a fair job of treating me, and while I was there I met some of the other Rebels being held prisoner—Major Henry Kyd Douglas among them. Douglas was the youngest staff officer serving with Stonewall Jackson's staff before Stonewall died. He's still with the Second Corps, or at least he was until he was captured. Friendly fellow, easy to like. He had a regular stream of visitors and seemed to have a multitude of friends from this area. He shared some of the goodies they brought for him.

"There was a pair of sisters from Gettysburg who took a real shine to him," Carney went on, "and whenever Dr. Ward wasn't around, they'd whisk Douglas into town with them for supper or an evening's stroll. Then he'd come back to the Seminary, none the worse for wear, and Dr. Ward none the wiser. I made an attempt to follow Major Douglas's inspirational lead, and I managed to talk a young Union miss into procuring a set of civilian clothes for me." Carney grinned mischievously. "Unfortunately, though, my plan failed miserably, and I got caught again. So, here I am. But with any luck, another opportunity will present itself. I'll just keep trying."

Salina gave the rider a cursory glance; he wasn't all that much taller than she, though decidedly a bit broader of shoulder. His young, winsome face *possibly* might be considered somewhat comely if only... A slow smile came to Salina's lips. "You never know, Carney, another such opportunity *might* present itself when you least expect it."

Kidd Carney's smile mirrored Salina's. "I'll keep my eyes open," he nodded. "Rest assured."

"You do that," Salina encouraged. "What about the others? Bentley, Boone, Curlie, Jake, Tristan, Cutter? I know that Archer Scarborough is dead." A note of sadness crept into her voice. "And Jeremy..."

Carney sat ramrod straight upon his cot. "He can't be dead, ma'am. I saw his horse get shot out from under him, but I'm sure the Captain must have survived." He tried to make it sound more like a statement than a question.

"Jeremy did survive," Salina informed him, "for the most part." She told Carney of Jeremy's injuries, his blindness, and his lack of memory.

"Hmmm." Carney shook his head. "Difficult to envision Captain Barnes laid low like that. Has the doctor given you any hope?"

"Warrick says that the concussion to his brain has caused these problems, and with time they may prove to be temporary." She lowered her head. "But there's no real guarantee that they won't be permanent."

Kidd Carney pondered, "I'll bet Stuart thinks he's dead."

"I've been wondering about that myself," Salina commented. "I was thinking that perhaps I should write to General Stuart and let him know what's going on—but how would I get such a message to him?"

"If I could, ma'am, I'd deliver such a message to the good General myself, if it was within my power." Kidd Carney met Salina's eyes steadily, his expression suggesting more than the words he was speaking aloud. He knew she was brave and daring, but would she dare take the risk to help him escape?

Salina squeezed Kidd Carney's hand. "Do keep your eyes open, Carney," she whispered furtively. "You never can tell what might happen from one day to the next. Perhaps I'll pay you another call tomorrow? Would that suit you?"

"It would." Kidd Carney exchanged a knowing look with Salina. His eyes told her he would do *anything* to get out of this place.

"Very well," she nodded, "I'll make the effort to visit again, about this same time, I reckon. Are you fond of fresh peach pie?"

Kidd Carney rubbed his stomach. "Aye, ma'am, very fond of it."

"Good." A hint of a smile lifted the corners of her mouth. "Very good indeed. I'll be sure to tell the Captain you've survived. Maybe the mention of your name might trigger a memory, who knows?"

Carney found himself the recipient of one of Salina's dazzling smiles. Captain Barnes, if Carney recalled correctly, had said something once about the way her smile could warm a man's heart and weaken his knees—clearly an indisputable observation on Barnes's part.

☆ ☆ ☆ ☆ ☆ ☆ ☆

The sound of a horse and wagon caught Jeremy's attention. "Someone's coming up the drive," he said. "I can hear them."

Salina pushed aside the curtain to take a better look. "You're right, Jeremy. It might be Elinor, though if it is," she checked the clock on the highboy, "she's early." Elinor was nearly thirty minutes early arriving to drive Salina out to Camp Letterman.

"I don't see...I don't *understand* why you have to go out there again today," Jeremy complained.

"I told you, Kidd Carney is one of your men. He's been riding with you since the Chambersburg Raid last October. He's a good friend, and he's in a precarious situation..." Salina stopped herself from saying, *And I aim to do something about it.* Instead she added, "I didn't spend hours last night making those peach pies for nothing." Salina leaned over and kissed Jeremy's cheek. "I'll only be gone a couple of hours. Behave, hmmm?"

Behave...Salina mentally shrugged. President Lincoln had defined that word for her as not dragging one of his best scouts across the country. Well, she wasn't going to do that, so she still satisfied the requirement he imposed for her pardon. Salina knew she must be crazy as a loon, though, for here she was contemplating the enactment of a plan to spring a Rebel prisoner from a Union military hospital. She didn't hesitate. Carney would have done the same for Jeremy, had the tables been turned, but with Jeremy incapacitated, it was up to her to carry out the rescue.

"So you'll make me wait until you come back before you finish reading the article about the draft riots?" Jeremy sulked, wanting her to stay. She had hardly left his side at all, but he was so lonely whenever she was gone from the room. When she was absent from him, he missed her loquaciousness, and his jumbled thoughts tended to vacillate between shadowy recollections and the dark, unfathomable reaches of his locked mind. Some of the things he dreamed when she wasn't near were nothing short of horrifying.

Salina picked up a July 18 newspaper from Richmond, one of those that Drake had managed to acquire for her. She quickly read out loud to Jeremy the remainder of the article that gave a description of the Draft Riots which began in New York City on the thirteenth of July and lasted for three days before the mob was finally dispersed.

The trouble in New York started when names were drawn and

published by the provost marshal—names of men who were to be drafted into service for the Union army. A menacing mob more than 50,000 strong could not be contained by city authorities and the police force. The wild crowds burned a Negro church and orphanage, made an attack on the offices of the New York *Tribune*, and sacked the home of the provost marshal, delivering destruction while terrorizing the city and generally wreaking havoc. Homes and property belonging to noted abolitionists were targeted by the vandals, although people of color were the primary victims of the mob's rage.

The unruly mob, predominantly made up of Irish working men, continued unhampered in their frightful rampage until Federal troops called in from Gettysburg arrived in New York to quell the rebellion. The rioters' rationale concerned job security: if the blacks were freed from slavery, they would flood the market for unskilled and low-paying jobs. The Irish immigrants did not want the competition, as positions were already scarce enough. They denounced the draft, refusing to fight for an army dedicated to the purpose of emancipation. Order was eventually restored by the troops, but in the wake of the rioting the casualty figures were almost as bad as those of a battle: over one thousand people had been either killed or wounded. Similar instances threatened to arise in Boston and a handful of other Northern cities.

"Craziness," Jeremy shook his head. "Isn't that what all this is—this war—pure, crazy foolishness?"

"We're caught in the middle of it," Salina said solemnly, "for the sake of honor and duty—for Virginia and independence for our country."

"Do you really believe that?" challenged Jeremy.

"We both do." Her reply was heavily tinged with determination, but she was unsure as to whether she was trying to convince Jeremy—or herself. A knock on the bedroom door spared her from delving too deeply into questions she hadn't answers for.

"Salina? It's me, Elinor."

"I'm coming, Elinor," Salina called out. She faced Jeremy again. "I'll be back in a few hours, I promise. Mamma will see to anything you need, or you can call on Jubilee or Beth-Anne."

"Yeah." Jeremy's tone did not belie his displeasure at her departure. He heard a rustling noise, and his frustration rose over not being able to see what caused the sound. "What are you doing?" he asked.

"Nothing for you to worry yourself over," Salina evaded. She adjusted her hoop skirt, making sure that the drawstring bag secured around her waist was completely hidden from view. She slipped a pair of sewing scissors into her pocket along with her gun. She didn't think she'd have to use the pearl-handled revolver, but it was always better to be safe than sorry.

Elinor put on a cheerful enough front when she greeted Annelise and Beth-Anne. She and Salina made short work of collecting the pies Salina had labored in making, along with a half-dozen flannel shirts Salina had completed. Elinor's sprightly countenance didn't fool Salina, however, and as they climbed up into the carriage she said, "Something's wrong; what is it?"

"Mason died last night in Rorie's arms. He revived just long enough to focus on her face, caress her cheek, and expire. Rorie's taking it pretty hard. Drake sent me to fetch you early because they set the funeral for this afternoon. We should just make it back in time." Elinor clucked to the team; the carriage lurched forward.

"Poor Rorie," Salina lamented softly. "Is Drake with her now?"

"Yes," Elinor nodded. "I assured him I'd fetch you just as quickly as I could."

Salina stood on the fringe of the little group gathered at the Camp Letterman graveyard to witness Mason Lohring's burial. Kidd Carney was also counted among the mourners.

As the Union chaplain read the funeral service, Carney inconspicuously made his way to where Salina stood. "Mrs. Barnes," he murmured softly in acknowledgment.

"Private Carney." She casually glanced around, trying to detect if any of the others could hear them. She whispered, "I've explained the plan to Elinor, and she's going to help us, albeit reluctantly. Get yourself to her quarters, and I'll meet you there when this is over."

Carney gave a discreet nod, and quietly slipped away from the assembled company.

Elinor and Salina were both very much aware of the sentries posted around the encampment, and they politely nodded to the one closest to the tent Elinor shared with Aurora. Suprisingly, once inside, Elinor took charge of the situation, orchestrating the final preparations to liberate Kidd Carney from the prison hospital. She pointed to the quilt hanging from a clothesline at the other end of the tent and curtly instructed Carney to divest himself of his attire. Once he was behind the partition, Salina lifted her skirts and used her scissors to snip the drawstrings from around her waist. The smuggled bag contained a merino skirt, garibaldi blouse, and Zouave jacket.

An audible groan came from behind the partition. "Surely you jest," Kidd Carney complained when he emptied the contents of the bag.

Elinor retorted, "It's the best we could come up with on such short notice. The choice is yours—you can take it or leave it."

He didn't stop his grumbling, but in a few minutes Kidd Carney sheepishly stepped out from behind the quilted wall. "You really think this is going to work?"

"Why not?" Salina questioned. "If you play your part, this should be easy enough."

"Easy?" His eyebrows shot up. "Have you forgotten there could be harsh consequences if we're found out?"

"I haven't forgotten," Salina assured him. "I choose to consider it motivation to execute this charade to the last detail."

Carney didn't have time to think up a rejoinder. Elinor took one of her bonnets and tied the ribbons into a big bow beneath his chin. She powdered his face and neck, and dabbed just a faint hint of rouge on his cheekbones. "Bat your eyes," she commanded him. Kidd Carney did, and she giggled outright. "Remember now, pretty is as pretty does," she teased him unmercifully, shaking her finger at him.

Kidd Carney's face flushed beet red, and he scowled at Salina, "If you *ever* tell any of the men about this, I'll flat out deny it!"

Drake knocked before entering the tent, and said, "I just wanted to let you know I'm going to take Rorie out for some supper, get her away from here for a bit. She's had a rough day." He cast a curious glance at the third young lady, and tipped his hat, "Beg your pardon, I didn't realize the two of you had company."

Elinor and Salina exchanged a speaking glance. Salina pulled on Kidd Carney's arm and quickly stammered, "We were just leaving, my friend and I. You have a nice supper with Rorie."

Drake sensed that something was out of place. "And does your friend have a name?"

Salina glanced at Carney, waiting to see if he would truly act out the part she'd set for him.

Drake took the young woman's gloved hand, but he hesitated and didn't kiss it. Instead he made a gallant bow and introduced himself. "The name's Drake. At your service, Miss..."

"Ki— Kitty Carney," Kidd Carney improvised in a high-pitched voice, bobbing a semi-awkward curtsey. "Pleased to make your acquaintance, sir. Salina, bless your heart, if you really wouldn't mind giving me a ride out toward Uncle Bobby's farm, I'd be eternally grateful."

It was all Salina could do to prevent herself from bursting out laughing, especially when she saw Elinor having an equal amount of difficulty containing her own giggles. "We'll go directly." She intentionally put herself between Drake and the disguised rider and quickly ushered Kidd Carney in the direction of the tent door.

"Elinor dear, a pleasure visiting with you all. Such kind hospitality will certainly be remembered," Carney said meaningfully as he passed by the Yankee belle. "Perhaps we'll meet again someday, under less distressing circumstances?"

"Perhaps," Elinor allowed. "Godspeed on your journey to your *uncle's* farm, Miss Carney." She, like Salina, had not missed the connotation of *Uncle Bobby's farm. Uncle Bobby* was Robert E. Lee, and the *farm* implied Virginia soil.

"Drake, I left two peach pies with Elinor for you. I do hope you'll enjoy them," Salina called over her shoulder, practically pushing Kidd Carney out the door. "And please, give my condolences to Aurora. Be sure to bring her with you when you come out and visit me and the Captain next time. And you too, Elinor. Good-bye!"

Drake turned the glittering force of his arresting eyes full on Elinor. "What was all that?"

"All what?" she asked innocently, her violet eyes wide.

"*That's* no lady," Drake remarked sharply, thinking how disturbingly close he'd come to politely kissing "her" hand when introductions were made. Something had made him feel uncomfortable, and now that he realized that "Kitty Carney" was not female, he was thankful he'd made do with the bow. Drake held Elinor's elbow in a firm grip and demanded, "What are the two of you up to?"

Elinor shook her dark head. "You'll not get it out of me, Drake—I'm sworn to secrecy. I'm sorry, but I promised Salina, and I intend to honor my word. I will need your help later, though—tomorrow's fine, actually."

"For what?" Drake raised an incredulous eyebrow, scrutinizing her carefully. "More shenanigans?"

"No, but we'll have to go and fetch the carriage back," Elinor finally laughed. She peeked out the flap of the tent to see that Salina and "Miss Kitty" had safely proceeded past the sentries without being detained. "Amazing," she whispered. "Well, at least that's done now."

Drake pieced the puzzle together and took Elinor by the shoulders, "Tell me that what just happened here isn't what I think it is."

Elinor grinned up at him. "You're an intelligent man, Drake Dallinger. I'm sure you can figure it out for yourself." She went behind the quilted partition, returning with a pathetic-looking, thread-bare, gray and butternut uniform in her arms. She quickly stuffed it into the stove to destroy the evidence.

"Little One..." Drake grated out angrily between tightly clenched teeth, shaking his head. "That girl is always up to something—I should have known!"

"See," Elinor's eyes twinkled merrily, "I knew you were a clever man, Drake. I just knew it."

☆ ☆ ☆ ☆ ☆ ☆ ☆

Putting her hand to the barn door, Salina was startled by the eerie hoot of an owl. "Silly!" she scolded herself. "Frightened of an old bird, for Pete's sake!" She shut the door tight behind her and lit the lantern she carried. "Carney?"

"Miss Salina, ma'am." Kidd Carney stood in his ruffled disguise, holding his bonnet in his hand. "Don't think I'm not grateful for what you've done—because I am—but please, tell me you've brought a change of clothes so I can get out of these confounded trappings."

"I brought two sets of clothes for you," Salina said reassuringly, handing him the bundle.

Carney stepped into one of the stalls and made the quick change, shedding his girlie-finery for regular male civilian clothes. "I feel much better now, thanks just the same." He had already washed his face and tidied his hair with his fingers. "I have to admit, ma'am, that what you pulled off today was no small display of heroics. I am much obliged."

Salina blushed at his praise. "Heroic? I thought you torching the mill at Carillon was heroic. Today was...well, I just did what I could. Besides, you're the one who managed to sweet-talk the guard at the post into letting us pass."

"It seemed necessary at the time," Carney explained, rolling his eyes. "What else have you managed to gather up for me?" He looked askance at the haversack she toted.

"There's a second change of clothes, and I put in food enough to last you for about three days—including a whole peach pie." Her laugh rippled.

"That's most generous of you, Miss Salina." Carney tipped the brim of his non-existent kepi.

Salina noted the gesture, and was pleased to present him with a replacement hat. She explained that it had been left by one of the wounded Confederates who'd later died while at Oak Ridge.

"Seems like you've thought of everything," Kidd Carney complimented, adjusting the hat to suit him. "The very soul of efficiency."

Salina shook her head. "I've no horse for you; you're on your own for that, but I'm sure you'll improvise."

"Aye," Carney nodded. "What about the Captain? Is it safe for me to see him?"

"There are too many people inside," Salina apologized. She wrung her hands and added, "He must have been in a lot of pain today while I was gone because he's evidently had quite a bit of medicine. The morphine has lulled him into a deep sleep, and in all honesty, he probably wouldn't remember you anyway. He can't see you, and your name didn't trigger the recognition I had hoped for when I told him I'd found you at the camp."

Kidd Carney accepted the situation. "Then it's probably time for me to be on my way and subject you to no further risk on my behalf." He swung the haversack over his shoulder and kissed Salina's hand. "As I said, I'm much obliged to you. If you ever need anything, please don't hesitate to call on me."

Salina plucked an envelope from the pocket of her skirt. "You did say that you would deliver a message to General Stuart for me, if it was within your power to do so."

Carney took the letter and tucked it into his breast pocket. "Consider it done."

"Godspeed, Carney!" She hugged him quickly, then scurried back to the farmhouse before she was missed.

Chapter Twenty-Five

Calming Jeremy during his nightmare was no easy task. The bad dreams, Salina had noted recently, came with increasing frequency and duration. His wild flailing and unintelligible mutterings caused Salina great concern, but she finally succeeded in settling him down. She dabbed at his temples with a damp cloth and hummed *The Southern Soldier Boy* in a soothing tone. Jeremy was obviously in a good deal of pain from thrashing about, and she gave him an ample dose of medicine to relieve his torment.

Jeremy's hand found Salina's face in the dark, and he traced her features, memorizing them. "I wish I could see you." His voice was hauntingly melancholic. "I want so much to see your face."

"Hush now," she crooned, as if quieting a small child in the wake of a tantrum. "Go to sleep. It will be morning soon."

As morning dawned, Jeremy was acutely aware of it. Salina was still at his side, holding his hand as usual, but her stirring wasn't what indicated the breaking of day—it was the grayness he saw when he opened his eyes. He bit back a startled cry. He closed his eyes—black. He opened them again—gray. *Gray!*

The grayness lightened, and continued to do so for the next ten days. Jeremy soon detected variances of gray, and shadows caused by movement or items around him. On the morning that he opened his eyes to a *colored* blur, he could hardly contain himself. He wanted to confide in Salina, but reluctantly elected not to. He didn't want to raise and then dash her hopes if the situation wasn't really going to last. He wanted to tell *someone*, but didn't dare.

Light streamed through the bedroom window, falling on Salina, who slumbered a few feet away from him on the lounge opposite his bed. Her hair was dark, inky black, and her face was creamy ivory, but he couldn't make out any crisp detail, merely outline and form. He glanced about the room, seeing shapes and shadows. *Dear God, I don't mean to sound demanding, but please—make my sight whole again! Let me remember the details of my life...*

Dr. Warrick's next visit very nearly gave Jeremy away. The doctor declared that his pupils were reacting as they should, but Jeremy purposely feigned being unable to see anything.

The Yankee doctor offered Jeremy a patch to partly conceal the blatant scar tissue marring his face. "Or I have some tinted spectacles, if you'd care for them. Not that you need them, but it's an option for you."

Jeremy took both with a noncommittal shrug. "If I can't see, what use are they to me?"

"None really," Warrick shrugged. "Just a matter of preference. Some of the men I've worked with are very self-conscious about their appearance. These items are to satisfy one's vanity more than anything else."

Jeremy again contemplated his scar, and wondered if he had been considered handsome before. Salina didn't seem to recoil from his countenance, but was that because she'd grown accustomed to his disfigurement?

"I'll be back again Saturday morning," Dr. Warrick was saying. "We'll get you out of that cast and walking again—with some assistance at first, of course."

"Of course," Jeremy acquiesced lightly.

The Yankee doctor cast a puzzled glance at the Rebel captain. There was something different about him.

☆ ☆ ☆ ☆ ☆ ☆ ☆

As was her habit, Salina brought fresh cut flowers into the room first thing in the morning. She artfully arranged them in a crystal vase that caught the light and threw rainbow patterns on the wall. She opened the window sash wide to allow new air to circulate through the room, the lace curtains fluttering on the early morning breeze. The one thing different about today, however, was the pink rosebud gracing the bouquet of dew-kissed blossoms.

Jeremy watched her through lowered lashes, pretending to be asleep. There was something *significant* about that pink rose, he thought to himself, wasn't there? A vague vision of picking a similar rose from a climbing bush wavered behind his half-closed lids, then disappeared. Where had he plucked the flower from? Why? He remembered placing it on a pillow that rested atop quilts…not a bed exactly, but someplace where dim candlelight flickered…

He shook his head when the image faded, and the action brought Salina to his side. She touched his shoulder. "Good morning," she whispered. "Are you awake?"

"Yeah," came his hoarse reply.

She poured him a glass of water, which he drank greedily. "Are you hungry? Jubilee's making flapjacks and biscuits. Or we've plain toast if you'd rather, as well as eggs and sausage. Whichever you choose."

Jeremy's appetite was the one thing that had not suffered in any way, shape, or form. He requested toast, eggs, fried potatoes, and a helping of the sausage.

Salina came back carrying a wicker tray laden with two place settings, two plates of food, and two glasses of sweet orange juice. She smiled, though he knew she didn't think he could see her, and sat down beside him to share breakfast. She spread a checkered napkin across his chest to catch anything that might get spilled, and picked up the fork, guiding his hand to where the toast sat on his plate. "It's right here. I put apple butter on it, just how you like it."

She reached up to tuck a curling strand of hair behind her ear, and as she did, Jeremy caught the glint of sunlight winking in her diamond ring and on the golden band that encircled the third finger on her left hand.

His heart stopped for a full minute before it resumed with a dull thudding in his chest. *She's a married lady…*No. No, surely he hadn't imagined her encouraging smiles, or the scent of rosewater whenever she sat so invitingly close to his side, or the feel of her lips at his brow.

Jeremy brooded in silence for most of the day. He was not overly gregarious when Drake came by with Aurora and Elinor, nor when Annelise visited with little Yabel for a few minutes.

Salina didn't comment on Jeremy's crabbed attitude; she merely kept up a parade of smiles and tended to his every need. She'd left his side rarely in all these days, and had seemingly recovered from his failure to remember her name. Drake told him she'd been deeply hurt by that, but she never let on in front of him.

Jeremy had recognized, though, that when Salina had returned to the room that night—presumably after accepting the fact that his memory completely evaded him—she did so armed with raw determination and a good supply of summoned strength. Since then, she was bent on helping him remember things. Each day she spent hours telling him about the cavalry battle he'd been wounded in— which was only a small part of the larger action that had taken place on the last day of the Battle of Gettysburg. She'd told him about riding with Mosby and Jeb Stuart. She'd painted word pictures for him of the Grand Review on the plains near Brandy Station, and she told him bits and pieces of what she knew of his family. She reiterated to him that Drake was a close and trusted friend, as was her brother, Ethan.

Frustration was gaining a foothold in Jeremy's mind. He *knew* things, but he couldn't *remember* them. He knew details as a spectator would, but he did not feel that he'd ever been a participant in any of the events Salina told him about. He thought back to that morning—the rose in the vase. That *was* something he remembered. He tried in vain to grasp the hope that if he could remember a pink rose, then perhaps there were other things that would come back to him. By thinking along those lines, he was able to curtail the anger he felt at his situation.

After Salina read another chapter in *Rob Roy*, she offered to shave Jeremy's shadowed jaw. He remained perfectly still as she carefully scraped his face with the sharp edge of the razor blade. When she finished, she bathed his face with a cool washcloth. She did not shy away from his uncovered wounded eye, but tenderly ministered to the puffy area with no marked aversion.

"I'm going to have a peach of a scar, aren't I?" Jeremy commented dryly.

Salina inspected his face for a moment, taking hold of his jaw and turning his head toward the light spilling from the hurricane lamp on the nightstand. "I reckon," she agreed after careful scrutiny.

Then she shrugged. "It certainly won't be any worse than Drake's scar, once the redness fades. You're fortunate that your eye was spared any serious damage. If the tip of that Yankee's sabre had been even a quarter of an inch deeper, well…like I said: you're fortunate." She caressed his cheek lightly.

Jeremy took hold of her fingers, and his thumb brushed first across her wedding band, then the protruding garnet stone of her engagement ring. "Why haven't you told me that you're married?"

"Why?…" Salina was undeniably shocked at his accusing tone. "Why haven't I told you that I'm married? Well, I suppose that's something I've overlooked…I thought you knew…" She checked herself and stated simply, "I'm sorry. I shouldn't have assumed—I mean, you didn't know my name at first, so it would stand to reason that you don't know I'm married."

"Who is he?" Jeremy asked abruptly, hating the taste of hot jealousy rising in his throat.

"My husband, you mean?" Salina had to smile.

Jeremy nodded.

Salina took Jeremy's hand in hers. "He's very near," she said enigmatically. She cupped his palm to the side of her face and deliberately touched the gold band circling the third finger of his own left hand. She restrained the bubble of laughter that threatened to peal, and said, "Do you know that you, too, wear a gold wedding band?"

Jeremy felt the cool metal of the ring he wore. He had not thought about it.

The laughter spilled free when he didn't answer her. "If I didn't know any better," she chided, "I'd almost believe you thought me a shade wanton. Me, a *married* woman, flirting mercilessly with a poor, wounded soldier who just happens to be in my care…"

"Can you deny that?" Jeremy challenged.

Again, she laughed. She leaned forward and kissed his smooth-shaven cheek. "What do you think my husband would do if he found out about you? About us?"

"If you were my wife, and I suspected such impropriety, why I'd…" His voice trailed off. "Who *is* he?" came the repeated demand.

"He's you," Salina answered plainly, rubbing the golden band on his hand. "I put that ring on your finger, just as surely as you put these rings on mine." She guided his fingers to her left hand and the pair of golden rings she wore.

When Jeremy attempted to speak, his voice cracked. "What a fool I must be in your eyes." He shook his sandy-blond head despairingly. "How stupid can I be?"

"Not stupid," Salina argued. "For days on end I've been telling you everything else I thought you'd want to know, yet I completely neglected to fill you in on the part about us. I didn't mean to leave out those details..."

"No wonder you were so determined," he said, somewhat in awe. "Sallie Rose, if you hadn't been so stubborn and yelled at me time and again that I couldn't die...The fight in you brought out the fight in me."

She squeezed his hand so tightly it almost hurt. "Did you hear that?" she asked in a hoarse whisper.

"What?" he asked, listening.

"You called me *Sallie Rose*," she said excitedly. "That's your name for me. You tried to get me to change my name once to protect me from being found by John Barnes. It wasn't an overly subtle tactic, but you've called me by that nickname ever since. Sallie Rose."

Jeremy lay very still. A picnic scene flashed as quick as lightning, then dissolved. "Is there a burned out place where only chimneys stand?"

"The main house at Shadowcreek," Salina replied with a wide smile. "That's where you first talked of changing my name to yours."

"We're married?" he questioned again, agitated that he could not recall a wedding ceremony or any of the other details that would surely follow. "How long?"

"Just over a month." She rested her forehead against his. "We were married on the night of July second, and I love you more now than I did then, if that's possible."

He was weary of the tentative flirting, and now that he knew she belonged to him, he did not hesitate to claim her lips with his own, kissing her thoroughly. Behind his closed eyes disjointed pictures of previously shared kisses flashed in rapid sequence. He pulled back for a minute, his lungs greedy for air, and accidentally knocked his head against the headboard. "Owww!" he muttered, lifting his head swiftly and bringing a hand to his forehead.

"Jeremy? Are you all right? I'm sorry!" She touched his shoulder. "What is it?"

"I don't know..." His head was pounding fiercely. "I haven't had a headache this bad for awhile."

"Here, lie down." She helped him get settled, then put a wet cloth across his eyes and forehead. "Shall I send for Dr. Warrick, do you think?"

"No, it's all right. I just bumped my head, that's all," he murmured. "Is it time for another dose of medicine?" he wanted to know.

"Not quite." Salina bit her thumbnail nervously. It was his head that was the problem—what if bumping it again had done more damage... "You're sure you're all right?"

"Yeah," Jeremy affirmed. "If you don't mind, maybe I'll just drift off to sleep."

"It's past nine," Salina said, glancing at the clock. "Perhaps I'll turn in, too."

"Stay here then," Jeremy entreated. "Sleep with me, not over there across the room."

Salina smiled. "I thought you'd never ask—but if it makes you uncomfortable, or your head hurts, or your leg or shoulder bothers you, then I'll move back to the chaise lounge." Quickly she exchanged her day dress for a cotton nightgown. She carefully climbed into bed next to Jeremy and gently laid her head on his good shoulder.

"Mmmmm," he breathed, his lips tarrying near her temple, one arm settling around her waist. "I wish you'd told me a long time ago we were married."

She placed a light kiss on his neck. "Go to sleep. And if you dream, make sure it's of me."

☆ ☆ ☆ ☆ ☆ ☆ ☆

Salina moved reluctantly. She didn't want to wake up. She hadn't slept so well or woke so contented since the night she'd drunk Jubilee's drugged tea. A yawn escaped her, and she rose up on an elbow to greet the man beside her. "Good morning."

"Morning," he returned, absently stroking her tangled curls.

"How's your head?" she inquired.

"It doesn't throb," he observed. "Suppose you could help me walk again with the crutches today? I think I'd like to sit outside for a bit this morning."

"Certainly," she agreed, delighted by his request. "It must seem stuffy to you, cooped up in here all the time."

"Were you still planning to go into town today?" he inquired nonchalantly.

Salina nodded. "I promised Mamma I'd pay a call on Lottie, my usually disagreeable cousin."

Jeremy's brow furrowed. "She doesn't like me much, does she?"

Salina held her breath. "Not anymore. Not since she tried to pawn a baby off on you, and her plot was foiled by the Yankee lieutenant who ended up marrying her." She gave him brief details, wondering if he would piece together the rest.

"She tried to come between us," Jeremy stated, then waited anxiously for Salina's reply, needing to know if what he'd guessed was correct.

"Yes," Salina nodded. "Jeremy, do you remember that?"

"I'm not sure," he confessed. "But it seems like there was something to do with lies…missing mail…false information…"

Salina hugged him. "Don't try to wrack your brain too hard, but I think you've got it. Be patient, it'll come to you," she said certainly. "Give it time."

Drake came to sit with Jeremy on the porch while Salina was gone to town with Beth-Anne and Annelise. He pelted Drake with every question he could think of concerning Salina and their relationship.

"I don't know all the answers to what has gone on between you," Drake protested. "Why don't you ask her?"

"Oh, I do intend to. Why didn't you tell me I was married to her?! You only told me that she doted on me."

Drake chuckled. "Like Little One, it was something I assumed that you'd remember. I stand corrected, and I do apologize. I'd have told you weeks ago, if I'd thought of it."

A shadow crossed Jeremy's face, and he ducked.

Drake stopped laughing. He turned to look over his shoulder at laundry drying on the clothesline, flapping in the wind. The shadow cast by a worn pair of overalls intermittently crossed his friend's face. Cautiously, he put his hand in front of Jeremy's eyes and waved, but got no response.

"Drake?"

"Yeah," he answered.

"For a moment I thought you'd left, you got so quiet," Jeremy said.

"Just thinking." Drake stared at the Captain curiously. "Just thinking."

☆ ☆ ☆ ☆ ☆ ☆ ☆

Salina and Drake were both present when the cast was removed from Jeremy's mended leg on the fifteenth of August, exactly six weeks from the day the plaster had been put on. The limb was stiff and the muscles sore from such limited movement. "We'll work that out," Salina said confidently. "I broke my arm last year, and it was the same when I got my cast off. The muscles just have to get used to functioning again."

Dr. Warrick smiled at the young woman's accurate assessment. "She's right, you know. Miss Salina, have you ever thought about becoming a nurse full time?"

"But I am," she grinned. "I've a patient to whom I'm loyally devoted. His well-being is my first priority."

Jeremy proudly turned toward his wife's voice. Today, he could see the dark line of eyebrows and the curve of her rose-red lips. He absently fingered the polished wooden cane Drake put into his hands.

"Come on, man," Drake encouraged. "Let's see you try it on your own once."

Jeremy stood, wobbly as a newborn colt, but he shuffled a few steps, intentionally banging into the bed.

"Careful!" Salina rushed to his side. "I've got you."

Drake laughed at that. "If he topples over, Little One, he'll take you down with him for sure."

"He's much bigger than I am, isn't he?" She tipped her head back to look up into Jeremy's face. At this close range, she thought she saw a flicker of recognition in his blue eyes—or was her imagination simply getting the better of her?

"Maybe I'd better sit down," Jeremy said quickly to mask his shock. He'd *seen* her face!—and a pretty one it was indeed. A man could lose himself in the depths of those sparkling green eyes.

Salina stared at Jeremy intently. *Something* was different about him—something she couldn't quite put her finger on. "Are you all right, Captain?"

"Just as well as can be expected," he assured her. She was too perceptive—and in that fleeting moment he remembered that about her. He had to take care that she didn't guess his secret sooner than he was ready to reveal it.

"How do you feel?" Dr. Warrick asked in a concerned tone. "Dizzy? Light-headed?"

"No." Jeremy shook his head. "Just weak."

"That's understandable," the Yankee doctor nodded. "But other than that?"

Jeremy answered with contrived heartiness. "My ribs are free, my sling gone, my stitches out, my leg mended; Salina tells me the bruises have faded and the little cuts have healed. I reckon I'm about as close to being healthy as I've been in some time."

"What about the eyes? The memory?" Dr. Warrick quizzed.

"Sometimes I get flashes of things I used to know," Jeremy hesitantly disclosed, waiting to hear Salina's sharp intake of breath. Odd, he mused to himself, how *sound* had come to play such an important role in these past few weeks. It was something he'd taken for granted when he had his sight before. But without vision, other senses sharpened to perceive the people and things around him.

Salina did breathe in sharply, just as he'd known she would. "Are you smiling, Salina? Does that make you happy?" It was important for him to know.

"Of course," she answered. "It must've been just awful for you to not know who you are. You might not know everything as yet, but there's still the hope that you'll remember."

Hope. Strength. Courage. Salina possessed them all. Jeremy squeezed her hand. "All in good time?"

"As the good Lord wills," she nodded.

"Amen!" Drake and Dr. Warrick added simultaneously.

Chapter Twenty-Six

*T*wo nights later, long after Salina had retired, Jeremy stealthily got out of bed and lit a candle. He sat at the desk, pulled a sheet of paper from the drawer, and uncorked the ink bottle. With a steady hand, he dipped the pen and began to write the words and lines that had besieged him throughout the day:

The Aftermath of a Murderous Cavalry Charge

Her gentle hand caressed with such a loving touch,
Her soft voice penetrated my then sightless realm,
Her sweet lips oft grazed along my hot, fevered brow,
She encouraged when fear threatened to overwhelm.

Her nearness evoked the vague and shadowed memories
Residing in the cobweb-infested confines of my head.
Her lingering scent stirred an ache deep within my
being,
Her determined will kept me from ending up with the
dead.

331

> *She spoke of days I once failed to remember,*
> *She talked with me of things which I simply could not see,*
> *Her unwavering devotion ever-cheered my withered soul,*
> *She cares not that I am scarred and maimed, only that I*
> *am me.*

He nodded, immensely pleased with his work. He sat back in the chair and stared at his reflection in the mirror above the burning candle. The last poem he'd written had been completed by lantern light, he vaguely recalled. He struggled to bring the memory into clearer focus: a tent, at headquarters—where? With General Stuart, he guessed that much. He thought he could actually picture Stuart's distinct, bearded face and intense blue eyes. Then a troubling thought came to Jeremy: would Stuart know where he was? Did he believe Jeremy to be dead? Jeremy knew Salina was hiding him from the Yankees. Warrick seemed to be aware of who he was, but wisely kept his own counsel if he suspected anything out of the ordinary.

He heard a footfall in the hall, just outside the door. "Jeremy?" An urgent rapping accompanied the turn of the doorknob. "Salina?"

Jeremy instantly extinguished the candle and proceeded to knock over his cane with a clatter. The chair scraped noisily on the wooden floor as he stood.

Salina reached out for her husband, but felt him gone. "Jeremy?"

Drake entered the room and quickly shut the door behind him. He faced his friend, and in the moonlight from the window, Drake determined correctly that Jeremy could see him—quite plainly.

Jeremy put a warning finger to his lips, wordlessly demanding that he keep silent about the discovery he'd just stumbled upon. "Drake, is that you?" he said stiffly.

"Aye, friend, it's me." Drake whispered, opting to play along with the charade for the time being.

Salina pulled her wrapper on and belted it tightly around her waist. "What is going on here?" she demanded with a yawn.

"I crashed into something," Jeremy hedged, "and I dropped my cane."

Salina bent to retrieve the wooden walking stick and placed it in Jeremy's searching hand. She pushed her loose curls away from her face. "Drake, what on earth are you doing here at this time of night?"

"I came to warn you both," Drake said without preamble; there was no time to beat around the bush. "Lieutenant Malcolm Everett has been seen in town, and he's been scouring the remaining field hospitals in the vicinity—including Camp Letterman. He's looking for you, Jeremy, and his orders are signed by none other than Major John Barnes. He's also been spouting off about sending your brother to prison, Little One."

"No!" Salina cried, and felt her knees go weak as the blood drained from her face. In the next instant, she fainted dead away.

Jeremy caught Salina before she hit the floor. He eased her seemingly lifeless body onto the bed.

"You *can* see!" Drake hurled the allegation at his friend.

Jeremy fessed up. "The vision in my left eye is almost fully normal—the right one doesn't focus so easily or so well, but I can make do. Promise me you'll say nothing to her yet about it—nothing. Swear it."

"Okay, all right." Drake put his hands up in resignation. "I think it's mean of you to keep it from her."

"That's my affair," Jeremy said coolly. "In the drawer—get the smelling salts."

Drake lit the hurricane lamp and obeyed. He saw the unstoppered ink well, the pen, and the recently penned poem. "Were you planning on cleaning this up, or letting it give you away?"

"I'd have cleaned it up," Jeremy snapped. "Leave it for now. Just help me with her, would you?"

In a matter of minutes Salina was revived, and Drake was holding a cup of water to her lips. She glanced up and offered her thanks without speaking, then her gaze searched for Jeremy. He was sitting sedately in the rocker, holding onto her hand.

She squeezed lightly. "Turnabout's fair play, is that what they say?"

"Aye," Jeremy nodded. "But I'm not nearly the nurse you are. I'm afraid I can't take care of you as well as you've taken care of me. You gave me a fright. Are you okay?"

Salina put a trembling hand to her eyes, squeezing them shut. "I think I am now," she ventured, but her voice belied her words.

Drake apologized for being the bearer of such bad news. "But I had to warn you. Everett came sashaying through camp, just as bold as you please. He didn't see me, and I was careful to ensure that I wasn't followed here."

"What do you suggest we do?" Jeremy asked. "Leave here?"

"There are too many Yankee patrols," Salina protested. "Who's to say one of them won't pick us up as easily as they must have taken Ethan?" Her heart wrenched at the thought of her brother in a Federal prison somewhere.

"*Us?* You're not going anywhere," the two men insisted in the same breath. "It's too dangerous."

"Dangerous, ha!" Salina exploded, but then she backed down without further argument, muttering something unintelligible under her breath about having to *obey*.

Drake formulated ideas aloud: "Everett's bound to come out here looking for Jeremy, but perhaps you can convince him that Jeremy has gone."

"We'll get Cody to hide you somewhere for a few days until this all blows over," Salina proposed.

"What do you think?" Drake consulted Jeremy.

"I suppose we should do what Salina is suggesting." Jeremy had rapidly arrived at the conclusion that evacuation was probably the safest plan. "We'll go with Cody now—if you think he'll take us. We'll still have the cover of darkness for a few hours yet."

Drake nodded. "I think it's our best bet."

"You go with them, Drake, and stay with Jeremy. If Everett remembers you, he'd probably just as soon see you behind bars, too," Salina pointed out.

"But you forget, I'm Drake *Dallinger* now. That carries quite a bit of weight," Drake reminded her.

"It won't make a bit of difference to Everett," she said prophetically.

"And what about you, Sallie? Will you be safe enough from him here?" Jeremy shook his head, remembering imprecisely that Everett had been involved in having Salina arrested for something once before. "Will you be in more danger if we leave you alone?"

"I'll be safe enough," Salina assured him. "Mamma and Jubilee are here, and if need be, Duncan could be counted on." She rose to her feet, and when she felt steady, she went to retrieve her satchel from the armoire. Salina emptied the last of her own possessions and began filling it with things Jeremy would need—a change of civilian clothes, an extra blanket, a toothbrush and comb, the shaving kit, and her Bible. "You'll read to him while you're away, won't you?"

Drake promised her that he would.

"Good. I've marked the place," she noted. She leaned over to retrieve an extra pair of socks she'd seen in the bottom drawer of the bureau, and while she had her back turned, Jeremy slipped a new bottle of laudanum into the satchel.

Drake glanced curiously at his friend. If Jeremy's injuries were all but healed, surely he didn't need the pain-killers any more...Drake shelved his questions for a later time.

Jeremy's eyes were on Salina, and he saw the gold heart-shaped locket dangling from the chain around her neck. It swung gently to and fro, like a pendulum. He groaned as if in pain and swayed on his feet; the last barriers to his lost memory shattered like a broken kaleidoscope. All the missing puzzle pieces fell into place with a deafening rush as his pulse raced furiously in his ears. His mind was washed free of obstructing shadows, and he knew who he was and what he was about.

In vivid detail Jeremy remembered Salina standing over him on a rain-drenched battlefield among the dead. He remembered that locket, swinging just as it did now, and he recalled his last words to her before he'd lost consciousness and slipped into the near-coma and ensuing complications brought on by his concussion.

"Jeremy?" Drake didn't know what to make of the bewildered expression on his friend's face.

Jeremy swiftly turned toward Salina, reaching out for her. "How I prayed you would come," he repeated ominously. "Kiss me."

Salina stared at him, for she too recalled the haunting phrases. She moved into his embrace, still staring in awe at him, but willing to grant his request. Unwanted tears spilled from her wild eyes. "Oh, Jeremy!"

"Hush now." Jeremy held her tightly to him. "Don't you fret, you hear?" He lowered his head to kiss away her tears, but some of the tears that spilled down her cheek came from his own eyes. "Be strong, Sallie Rose. For my sake."

"I will," she vowed. "Go now. I'll get Cody and send him to meet you in the barn." She paused to look back at her husband once more. He reached the bed and with contrived awkwardness moved his hands until they came in contact with the packed satchel.

"Good-bye," she murmured, still shaken and a little confused. "I'll be praying for you."

Within the quarter hour the three men were several miles away from the farmstead on Oak Ridge.

☆ ☆ ☆ ☆ ☆ ☆ ☆

"Now there's a fine friend!" Elinor Farnham breezed into Salina's room, pulling the curtains wide open and allowing yellow-white sunlight to flood the chamber. "If you'd planned to waste the day in bed, why invite us over for a late breakfast in the first place? Come on, rise and shine. Rorie and I are hungry."

Salina groaned in response to Elinor's abrupt entrance. A dull ache throbbed in her temples, and the mention of food made her stomach roil. "I'm sorry, Elinor. I completely forgot what day it was today." Salina pulled the sheet over her head and rolled away from her friend.

"Well, isn't that a fine how-do-you-do?" Elinor complained, hands on her hips. "Well, we'll just see about that!" She tugged the sheet off Salina, and encouraged Aurora to help her tickle Salina out of bed.

"Please, stop!" Salina protested, adding groggily, "I just might throw up again."

Elinor ceased her playful romp immediately. "You really are sick, aren't you? Why didn't you say so?"

"I'm not feeling very well," Salina excused herself. "And if you wouldn't mind, I'd really rather you go away and leave me suffer in peace."

"Nonsense," Aurora declared. "Is there something we can do for you?"

"No," Salina shook her head. "We'll just have to get together for tea or something later on."

"Come on, get up. You'll feel better if you don't think about it," Elinor suggested. "We've got the day off from working at the hospital and we wanted to have a little fun."

Aurora sighed, "Anything to keep our thoughts occupied…" She was determined to follow her older brother's seemingly sound advice, and was trying to put Mason's death behind her. Life would go on, just as Drake said, and she had to go on living too.

"Steve Colby has become a resident tour guide, and he's promised to take us round the battlefield and show us where the hottest fighting happened," Elinor explained. "Don't you want to come? I'll wager you've been no farther than town in weeks."

"All right," Salina relented. "Give me a few minutes, and I'll get dressed. Jubilee will make you something to eat if you're hungry; but I, for one, am not."

"Hurry then," Elinor admonished. "We'll wait for you in the kitchen."

Salina stood with a long exhalation of breath. She had no desire whatsoever to go out and see the battlefield, as so many visitors thronging to town did, but at least it would be something to pass the time while Jeremy was away. Since his hasty departure with Drake and Cody, Salina spent nearly every waking moment missing him, wondering where he was, and praising God for the miracle of his restored memory. She had heard nothing of Everett's whereabouts, and she hoped Jeremy and Drake would soon be able to return.

Salina made her way to the armoire and selected a bright-colored frock. Perhaps something colorful would inspire a better mood. Halfway through her toilette she thought she would vomit again, the nausea was so strong. "Don't think about it," she commanded herself, brushing her hair out with less than gentle strokes. She wove her curling tresses into a loose braid, tying the end securely with a hair ribbon.

Donning her chemise and other undergarments, Salina reached for the skirt of red and yellow plaid. She hadn't been eating all that much lately; how could the fastening bind around her waist so? She angrily tossed the skirt aside and stood before the cheval mirror, studying her figure. Her waist did appear to be a little thicker, she noticed with a degree of alarm. She selected another dress from the armoire, this one a little looser in fit than the first, and put it on.

Aurora appeared at the door again as Salina was fastening her boots. "I'm coming, I'm coming!"

"You're sure you're up to this?" Aurora sounded genuinely concerned.

Salina smiled indulgently. "If you are, Rorie, then so am I. I'll make it."

To Salina's relief, the nausea dissipated as the morning wore on, and by afternoon she ate a little bit of a sandwich Jubilee had packed in the picnic hamper.

Steve narrated every mile of the tour, and he winked conspiratorially at Salina as he told of the hair-raising conflict that had raged in Devil's Den, the Peach Orchard, and the Wheatfield. She shivered, thinking back on what an unnerving place Devil's Den had been *before* the battle. If she thought the odd configuration of stones was disturbing on the day Steve and Dulcie had left her there, it was doubly so now.

They drove by Little Round top, where Joshua Lawrence Chamberlain and the 20th Maine had saved the Union's left flank during the second day of fighting. When his men had run out of ammunition, Chamberlain had ordered a bayonet charge against the oncoming Rebels, and the Maine men had triumphantly prevailed.

"I'll take you up on Cemetery Ridge," Steve said as he helped the three girls back into the barouche one by one. "That'll be the conclusion of the tour—at the Angle, where Pickett's Charge failed."

"From there could we go out to the cavalry battlefield?" Elinor wanted to see where the horsemen had waged their fight, but that's where Salina drew the line. Those memories were too poignant to relive as an outing for pleasure.

Aurora understood and took Salina's part, saying that it was too far to go today. "Salina already didn't feel well this morning. Perhaps we should head back so she can get to bed early for some proper rest. I'd venture that working such long hours for so many weeks has finally taken a toll on her."

Steve mentioned something about Dulcie expecting him home for supper at a certain hour, and so Elinor modified her request. "Maybe we'll have time another day."

Coming down the Taneytown Road, Steve approached Evergreen Cemetery. Salina suddenly put a hand on his shoulder as they passed the brick gatehouse. "Please, can we stop here for just a minute?"

"Sure, for a minute." Steve looked puzzled, but Salina did not offer any explanation for her desire to visit the old cemetery. He assisted Salina in alighting from the carriage. The Thornes, caretakers of Evergreen Cemetery, had worked wonders to restore the burial ground to a semblance of order, he thought, though there was still ample evidence to show where Federal batteries had crowned the ridge with cannon.

Salina darted through the graveyard, finding Daddy's headstone easily. It still stood, she was relieved to see, as tall and proud as the man the marble marker was intended to honor. Knowing that on this ridge the Union forces had anchored their defensive line, Salina almost felt as though she'd slipped behind enemy lines just to be here. Glancing around, she saw that some of the markers had been knocked down by shot and shell, and many bore mute witness to the tempest that had raged furiously in this sacred area. Even Daddy's grave held the marks of several ricochets, and two bullets were still lodged in the stone. "How fitting for you to be behind the lines, Daddy, and proudly displaying the marks of battle. Some things never change, I reckon."

For a few minutes Salina remained in an attitude of prayer, until she felt the presence of Aurora and Elinor behind her. She kissed her fingertips and touched the cool marble in a parting gesture of farewell, for she had the distinct feeling that she would not be coming back to this place before she returned to Virginia. Reverently, with a single tear, she took her leave.

"Thank you for waiting for me," Salina whispered to Aurora Dallinger and Elinor Farnham. The three walked back to the carriage arm in arm, supportive of one another. She settled into her seat between Aurora and Elinor with a deep, cleansing sigh. "I do appreciate your indulgence. It means a lot to me."

Elinor had seen the marker, and correctly guessed that it was where the body of Salina's father was interred. She gave Salina's shoulders a squeeze. "I can imagine."

Aurora nodded. "Me, too." And she also hugged Salina in a gesture of friendship.

The three ladies who had chatted so amiably during the earlier ride were now distant and subdued, Steve noted, not knowing the reason behind their somber dispositions. Their ususal conviviality was missing because each was absorbed in her own thoughts. The grieving daughters were drawn together in their sorrow, each privately mourning the passing of her deceased father.

☆ ☆ ☆ ☆ ☆ ☆ ☆

Mamma was the one who opened the window curtains wide the next morning, and she questioned Salina's new penchant for lying around in bed like a lazy Southern belle. "Come on, sleepyhead. It's long past time to be up and about."

"I really don't feel good, Mamma. Please, just leave me be," Salina mumbled.

Annelise detected a sour odor wafting from the chamber pot. "You've been sick."

"I know, Mamma. I'll see to it in a bit. Right now, I just want to sleep. I'm so very tired," Salina complained.

Mamma exited the room, taking the chamber pot with her to dispose of the smelly contents.

Jubilee was the next intruder, and Salina would have continued to disregard her presence, but the black woman clucked over her, poking her shoulder. "Ah's tole ya, ya ain't gowin ta hafta be all dat patient ta start ya a family, now, didn' ah?"

Salina's head snapped up. "Jubilee, you think I'm…"

Jubilee folded her arms across her ample chest. "Ah do, Missy. Jube done said ya gowin ta bear dat young man o' yers a chile. Didn' ya hear what it was ah was sayin'?"

"I was ignoring you," Salina admitted, again burying her head beneath the pillow. "Just like I'm trying to do now." But then she thought for a moment, tardy in realizing she'd skipped her monthly, and then she thought back to the night Jeremy and Drake left: *I fainted…* An alarming chill crept down the back of her neck and traced the line of her spine. *Mamma used to faint when she was pregnant…* And the nasty was she was feeling certainly had the earmarks of morning sickness… Salina peeked out from under the pillow and met Jubilee's knowing eyes. "Can it be? It was just that one night when we got married…"

Jubilee chuckled. "Dat'd certainly do."

Salina sat up and waited for the room to straighten from its sudden tilt. When the dizziness passed, she lamented, "I wish Jeremy was here. I…" she paused. "But I can't tell him yet. What if it's not for sure? What if it's just a touch of flu or something I ate?"

"Den keep it ta yerself, chile, an' when yer as convinced as Jube is, den ya let dat boy know," Jubilee advised. "Here, eat dis. Ya gots ta keep somethin' down."

Salina reluctantly obeyed. She emptied the small bowl of rice and admittedly felt better for it.

For the second morning in a row, Salina selected a looser-fitting day dress and tied her apron over it. She decided that one had to look very closely to see any noticeable change in her, so she rationalized that she could hide her suspicions for a time. Jubilee could be trusted to keep her secret, even from Mamma.

But she had to tell *somebody*. Salina found her journal, which had suffered neglect for weeks on end. As she wrote the date across the top of the page, she recognized it was her seventeenth birthday, and she laughed softly. She spelled the words out, *August Twentieth, Eighteen Hundred Sixty-Three*, and jotted down a hasty entry:

> *I have my suspicions that I might be with child. There are indications that my "honeymoon" with Jeremy in the enchanted little shed was fruitful. If that be the case, in the spring I shall be a mother…*

Salina bit the end of the pen, missing her husband profoundly and giving in to daydreams of a little boy who would be a miniature version of his father. If she gave birth to a girl, on the other hand, with her coloring and Jeremy's eyes, the tiny little belle would surely create a stir...

"Sweetheart, when you're dressed, come into the parlour," Mamma instructed. "I've a surprise for you."

Salina closed the journal and put the pen and ink away. She slipped the gilt-edged book back into the desk drawer, failing to discover a handwritten page stashed there. Mustering a cheerful disposition, she yanked open the bedroom door. "What kind of surprise, Mamma?"

"Why, sweetheart, it's your birthday, I'll not tell—you'll have to come see for yourself," Annelise giggled. "Here, be a dear and hold your brother for a minute." She went down the hall in front of Salina, pausing at the parlour door, giving a signal to someone inside.

Salina didn't notice, as she was too absorbed in looking over her little sibling. She whispered so that only Yabel could hear, "I just might make you an uncle before your first birthday. Now what do you make of that, hmmm?" She giggled lightly and sighed, "Amazing, if you ask me."

She followed Mamma into the parlour, lightly bouncing Yabel in her arms. "What is it, Mamma? What's my surprise?"

Mamma did not need to answer, for Salina's surprise was evident—Jeremy stood before her, and there was something *decidedly* different about him. "Jeremy!" she exclaimed, her delight mixing with concern. "What are you doing back here?" Salina hastily relinquished her brother to Mamma's waiting arms, and Annelise discreetly left her daughter and son-in-law alone together.

Jeremy watched Salina's curious eyes flit over him from head to foot—whether she was counting limbs or just making sure he was all in one piece, he didn't rightly know, but the depth of the love visible in her glance was unmistakable. He still had his cane and was wearing the dark-tinted glasses Dr. Warrick had given him. He found it easier to focus when the light wasn't so blinding, and the dark spectacles provided him with something to hide behind. "Happy Birthday, Sallie," Jeremy said with a lopsided grin, twirling a long-stemmed pink rose between his thumb and forefinger.

"It is now," she beamed. She started toward him, but he put up a hand, mutely ordering her to stay put.

"I couldn't stay away. I can't just abandon you here—not with Everett at large and roaming about at will. When I leave again, I'm taking you with me." His tone left no room for argument. Without further hesitation, Jeremy walked a straight line to her, all except for sidestepping the tea cart to avoid knocking it over.

Salina all but held her breath as she watched his unwavering approach.

Jeremy took advantage of her speechlessness. He continued on as if nothing were out of the ordinary. "It's not much, I'm afraid," he said, offering her a small package wrapped with brown paper and string. "Open it."

Inside was an elegant, but empty, picture frame. She glanced up at him. "What shall I put in it?" she asked him, trying to see behind the glasses that hid his eyes. She thought for sure she could see his sapphire eyes twinkling with carefully constrained mirth.

"I have an idea for something that just might work." He took her by the hand and led her toward their room, remembering to use one hand along the wall for guidance in case Annelise should suddenly reappear and see them together.

"You can see!" Salina whispered emphatically when they were out of earshot, behind the closed door of their bedroom. "It's obvious to me that you can, so don't you dare try to deny it!"

"Okay, I won't," Jeremy grinned mischievously.

"But Jeremy, how? When? You're not jesting with me?" She still wasn't quite sure.

"Nope—not jesting." He rummaged through the desk drawer until he found the poem he'd composed for her. It fit perfectly in the confines of the frame.

Salina read the poignant lines, written in his own hand, and she knew he *had* to be able to see to write anything down for himself. She was at a loss for words to express how deeply his lines touched her heart.

Jeremy hunkered down next to her as she sat on the edge of the lounge. "Well, don't you have anything to tell me?" he prodded.

"I…" He *couldn't* know about the baby, Salina told herself after hastily jumping to the wrong conclusion. Knowing Jeremy, he was merely fishing for compliments, she was sure. "I love the poem, Jeremy, it's very good."

"Every word is true," he insisted, leaning forward to kiss her. Jeremy stood and lifted her into the comforting haven of his arms, whispering ardently, "How I do love you, Sallie."

Author's Note:

It is my goal to be as accurate as possible when it comes to the historical part of my stories. I have been fortunate to work with various historians, battlefield tourguides, authors, historical society members, descendants, re-enactors, and fellow Civil War buffs to collect reliable information. My own Civil War library has more than three hundred books in it, but there are some books that I find myself turning to time and again for reference. If the readers are interested in digging deeper into the historical aspects, here are some suggestions for further reading:

Books:
* *At Gettysburg, or What a Girl Saw and Heard of the Battle* by Tillie Pierce Alleman
* *The Civil War Dictionary* by Mark M. Boatner, III
* *Culpeper: A Virginia County's History Through 1920* by Eugene M. Scheel
* *Days of Darkness: The Gettysburg Civilians* by William G. Williams
* *Diary of a Southern Refugee During the War* by Judith W. McGuire
* *Everyday Life in the 1800's* by Marc McCutcheon
* *Farewell My General* by Shirley Seifert
* *I Rode With Stonewall* by Henry Kyd Douglas
* *The Letters of Major General James E.B. Stuart*, edited by Adele H. Mitchell
* *A Manual of Military Surgery* by J. Julian Chisolm
* *Jeb Stuart: The Last Cavalier* by Burke Davis
* *Songs of The Civil War*, edited by Irwin Silber
* *A Strange and Blighted Land/Gettysburg: The Aftermath of a Battle* by Gregory A. Coco
* *They Followed the Plume* by Robert J. Trout

Magazines:
America's Civil War
Blue & Gray Magazine
Civil War Times Illustrated

CD's/Tapes (audio/VHS):
A&E's *Civil War Journal*
Gettysburg, Turner Home Entertainment
PBS *Civil War Series* produced by Ken Burns
Songs of the Civil War, produced by Jim Brown, Ken Burns and Don DeVito
Tenting on the Old Campground (Civil War Era Songs Volume 4) by the 97th Regimental String Band

Manuscripts/Letters:
Major General J.E.B. Stuart to Flora Cooke Stuart from the Stuart Family Collection/Virginia Historical Society

Salina smiled up at her husband and deliberately removed the obstructive tinted glasses. She pulled his sandy-blond head down, tenderly kissing his eyes. "My own dear Horse Soldier. You've come back for me!" It was a rare opportunity they were blessed with, and she knew it.

"I love you, Jeremy Barnes," she added, her smile as bright as her eyes. She rested her cheek against his chest and clearly heard the hammering of his heartbeat, which matched the pounding cadence of her own. She sighed wistfully and squeezed him around his middle. Salina had missed Jeremy so very much in the few days he'd been away, especially since she'd grown accustomed to having him nearby all these weeks. Now that the interlude of his healing was over, Salina did not want to think of how difficult it was going to be to once again relinquish him to the inevitable call of duty.

Salina shook off her melancholy. She resolved to make the most of the little bit of time they had been granted. She put aside all thoughts of Major Barnes and Lieutenant Everett, even of her imprisoned brother. She momentarily dismissed her suspicions concerning their baby, and she decided to leave the question of Jeremy's true surname for another day's investigation. The only thing Salina wanted was to be with Jeremy.

Jeremy framed his wife's face with his hands, his sapphire gaze probing her thoughtful expression.

"We'll leave at twilight," she whispered suddenly, already calculating a route of escape for them. "We'll travel by dark to Virginia…"

"Whoa, whoa, whoa—hold on, Sallie Rose," Jeremy chuckled, amused yet pleased at this latest display of Salina's courage. "There's nothing that says we've got to leave here tonight. We'll make some plans, rest assured, but just you be patient." With a lopsided grin he tapped the end of her nose with the tip of his finger and drew her close in a one-armed hug. He murmured against her lips, "We've got time on our side."